I0775580

The Best Part of Breaking Up

HEATHER MCPEAKE

Copyright © 2023 by Heather McPeake

All rights reserved. No part of this book may be used or reproduced in any form whatsoever without written permission except in the case of brief quotations in critical articles or reviews.

This book is a work of fiction. Names, characters, businesses, organizations, places, events, and incidents either are the product of the author's imagination or are used fictitiously. Any resemblance to actual persons, living or dead, events, or locales is entirely coincidental.

Printed in the United States of America.

Cover design by Heather McPeake

ISBN : 979-8-218-27194-7

Echo Books
Memphis, TN

1.

This is easily my least favorite opening line, reminiscent of law school interviews and awkward first dates. The journalist – Jeanine – sits across from me, watching intently as I squeeze three lemon slices and a sprinkle of stevia into my water. I wonder if this is going to end up in the article. I feel like articles love to pepper in little details like this, the kind that are supposed to make you feel like you were really there.

I smile evenly. "After that questionnaire your office sent over, I feel like you may know how to respond to that better than I would."

Jeanine laughs. "That was just a formality. It's more important for me to meet everyone in person. Get a sense of your vibe."

I consider the blush silk blouse, gray pants, and matching blazer I wore here from the office and wonder if I have a vibe. If I do, I hope it doesn't say, *I worked through lunch*, the way my stomach surely does as the waiter sets a basket of chips and bowl of salsa on the colorful patio table between us. I scoop one into my mouth with Jeanine still watching me, hoping to buy myself enough time to respond. Because even though I hate this question, I feel like I have to respond – preferably politely – and not in the least because I've already rescheduled this meeting. Twice.

Tell me about yourself.

Do I offer up my LinkedIn profile: *Graduated Memphis Law at twenty-three; senior associate at Freeman, Maxwell, & Lewis at twenty-eight; community board member of Girls Going Places and volunteer chair of the local legal clinic for four years running?*

Or maybe my Twitter bio: *Millennial yuppie. Perpetually considering a capsule wardrobe. Loves baked goods and vintage sunglasses. Knows way too much about murder.*

Perhaps it'd be easier to send her a playlist (the '90s rap I listen to on my morning run; the indie pop I play in my car; the moody '00s tracks I drag out when I've had a bad day), or even to dig up my dating profile from three years ago, the one I created before I gave up on relationships: *Make me laugh. And no, I don't mean by sending me an unsolicited picture of your *eggplant emoji*.*

"Why don't we talk about why I'm representing Teddy Glass," I offer. "That's really why we're here, right?"

Jeanine laughs. "You don't waste time."

"Time is valuable," I smile. "Yours and mine."

My smartwatch buzzes against my wrist, and I silence it without glancing at the message, instead taking time to snag another chip from the basket. Despite the early heat of summer, this is one of my favorite spots. The salsa is spicy. The tortillas are handmade. The cantina lights give off a festive glow. I remind myself, amidst this sunset-glow ambiance, that I *do* actually want to be here. When I took this case, I knew it would involve a certain level of notoriety. I also know that not all press is good press.

"So it's about money, then?" Jeanine presses.

"I don't care how much money my client has. You already know this, because you've looked into my career."

She smiles knowingly. "I know you've logged an impressive number of pro bono hours at free clinics. I know that from the looks of your resume, you probably haven't had anything remotely resembling 'free time' in a decade. And I also know you have an unprecedented talent for making lose-lose situations feel like a win-win. But my readers don't know that. Yet."

She lets that last word dangle out there the way someone teases a dog with a Frisbee. I don't bite.

"I'm not interested in winning in the court of public opinion," I admit.

"Some would argue that's the only court worth winning in."

"I would argue those people didn't have a very good attorney."

Jeanine smiles, relaxing enough to take a few chips herself.

"You don't care if people like you?" she muses.

"I didn't get where I am by making people like me."

"And yet you're known for your negotiation skills."

I should be, I think smugly. *I've only been mediating petty squabbles between emotionally stunted adults since I was seven.*

My watch buzzes again, and in my attempt to silence it while I demurely scoop a chip into my mouth, I dribble salsa down the front of my blazer. I dab uselessly at the stain with a napkin before shrugging it off and draping it over the back of my chair. I save my apologies for my dry cleaner.

"The truth is," I tell her, "Teddy Glass is just a person, and marriage is just a contract, and I'm just trying to do them both justice."

"Is there really any justice in a divorce?"

"Well, you know what they say," I offer. "Nothing's fair in love and war."

"What about you? Is there anyone special in your life? Do you think there's a happily ever after in the cards for you?"

"I think it's important, especially for women, to remember that there's more than one kind of happy ending. Even when it comes to relationships, sometimes the happy ending is... well... the *ending*."

Another message buzzes against my wrist, and this time I check it. It's from my firm's best and most criminally underrated P.I., Angela. She's my favorite because – irony of ironies – I'm the only one who has seemed to notice how easily women of a certain age tend to stop being noticed. All her message says is, *911*.

I miss Jeanine's next question as another message swoops in, this time with an address. As cryptic as this is, I don't need anything more. I'm already wiping my mouth with a napkin, gathering my bag, and forcing myself away from the promise of warm, savory, cheese-smothered *pollo adobe*. My stomach groans in protest. Jeanine is watching me, dumbfounded.

"I hate to do this," I tell her, taking a final sip of my citrusy-sweet water, "but something's come up. You can call my office to reschedule?"

At this point, she just laughs. "Would it do any good?"

"Hey, we all do what we've gotta do, right?"

***

I push my sunglasses into my hair as I step into the dim ambiance of Maestoso, with my heels clicking purposefully along the black and white art deco tile. It's barely seven o'clock, but a collection of suits is holding down the bar for happy hour, the tables are full with dinner reservations, and a big movie screen near the back plays one of those old films with Fred Astaire and Ginger Rogers. Later, people will crowd the palm-ringed dance floor and laugh as they stumble through choreographed moves from another decade. This early though, only a few couples sway in time to the jazzy tune.

The hostess greets me with an expectant smile. I spot my mark at a corner booth before she can ask if I'm dining in.

"I'm meeting someone," I tell her without slowing down.

After the past couple of weeks, I'd recognize that glossy black hair skimming those slumped, T-shirt clad shoulders anywhere. From across the room, you'd almost think he was right around thirty instead of over fifty. You also might assume he drinks too much whiskey, works part-time at a record store, and resides in his mother's basement like a cardboard box of discarded adolescent dreams.

You'd be right about the whiskey.

Within moments, I'm sliding into the vinyl horseshoe bench seat beside him.

"Teddy," I sigh. "We talked about this."

Music mogul Theodore Glass smiles at me as though I'm a delightful surprise who definitely isn't here to call him on his bullshit. He raises his martini to me in toast, though it only contains a few drunken olives, sloshing about in a thimble-full of booze.

"Heidi!" he says, in his signature husky baritone, grinning like we're old friends. "You want a drink?"

I smile evenly. "I want to know what you're doing here."

Of course, I already know the answer to this. Anyone in this restaurant could easily follow his gaze – the one that keeps darting to a table across the room that is hosting a large family dinner, where everyone's favorite influencer Gigi Russo is holding hands with a clean-cut guy in golf slacks and a polo. The stack of gifts near the end of the table makes this gathering feel like a birthday celebration. There's a white-haired woman sitting at the head who looks like someone's grandmother. For all I know, it's *her* birthday celebration.

I can already imagine the clickbait headlines: *Teddy Glass crashes woman's ninetieth birthday dinner in a drunken rage!*

Thankfully, none of them seem to notice us – yet – but something about the way that Gigi is laughing like she's on camera gives the distinct impression she knows she's got an audience, and the way her hand smooths across the golf pro's thigh means that – even though her socials have over a million followers – the only audience this is intended for is Teddy.

When the divorce filing came across my desk, I could've said no. Maybe, given the precarious swarm of memes and hashtags already surrounding the case, I should've said no. I already have a full caseload, a new team of summer interns I'm trying to bring up to speed, and a commitment to teach my twelve-year-old Girls Going Places mentee Kamille how to swim by August. But then my boss sidled into my modern office and threw out the one word he knew I wouldn't ignore: partnership.

Everyone has that thing that makes them tick, and it is no secret this is mine. I've been working towards this ever since I joined the firm as a tenacious twenty-five-year-old, and seven years later, I still haven't taken my foot off the gas. It's a popular opinion that I don't care who I have to run over to get there; I think most of those people wouldn't care so much if it weren't for the fact there is a woman driving the car.

"Okay, I know this looks bad," Teddy defends. "And I know you're disappointed –"

"I'm not disappointed."

"-- but god. It's just not fair, ya know? She gets *him*. She gets *my studio*. Gets the whole damn city, it feels like. And I get *nothing*."

I peg this mood as sulky. I can do sulky. I settle my designer purse that only contains a laptop and a collection of fancy pens onto the seat beside me and do my best to soften.

"Hey," I soothe. "You don't get *nothing*. I'm on your side, remember? You're literally getting *everything*: the house, the cat, that badass business you've spent every waking hour of the past thirty-some-odd years building up. It's all yours. Assuming that you don't commit felony assault in front of all these people."

"Honestly, assault sounds like the better choice right about now," he says, fingering the stem of his empty martini glass in a way that makes me acutely nervous. I slide it away from him under the guise that I'm going to the bar to grab a refill. I'm not. I've already got plans for procuring the world's largest bottle of water, closing his tab, and threatening the bartender with a lawsuit if he serves him anything else. Where is his damn publicist?

"C'mon, don't be like that," I tell him. "*You've* got your whole amazing life ahead of you. *She's* got genital herpes and a truckload of debt from a sordid affair that will probably haunt her for the rest of her days."

Even as I say it, I'll admit, Gigi Russo doesn't look very haunted. She's beautiful and blonde, with big doe eyes, gratuitous curves, and the effortless kind of glow that looks great in festival wear. She leans her shoulder adoringly into her partner's and tousles her hair like they're sitting on a beach somewhere. I succumb to an inward sigh. This would be so much easier – for me and for Teddy – if he didn't love her. I can't believe the future of my entire career hangs on the heartstrings of a lovesick middle-aged man.

"Ya know, Heidi, I hear you," he says stubbornly, "but my therapist says it's important to feel my feelings."

"I agree. That is important. But can we also agree that a crowded restaurant where your soon-to-be-ex-wife is hanging out with her new boyfriend might not be the ideal place for those feelings? Especially the... stabby, gin-soaked sort?"

He grumbles something inaudible that sounds vaguely like, "It was vodka." Then, "But I mean yeah, fine, I guess."

I smile, taking the win. "Let me call you a ride, or order you some food. Have you had the scampi here? It's life-changing. Trust me. Everything will be better tomorrow."

"That's what you always say."

"Well, it's usually true."

"Hey, it's a party!" Paolo the publicist says, smiling like he isn't in fact half an hour later than he should've been. "We having dinner?"

"Is this an intervention?" Teddy says suspiciously, turning his wary gaze to me. "Do you have one of your guys following me?"

"No," I say. A half-truth, maybe, but to be fair, Angela isn't a guy. "I'm meeting a friend for drinks. This encounter was entirely serendipitous, Teddy. I do have a life outside of work, ya know."

This is also precariously half-true.

Teddy nods, still watching me like I'm about to stab him in the back.

"Sure, all right," he says. "First round's on me. Tell your friend."

On the outside, I'm smiling graciously. On the inside, I'm annoyed. The unspoken "what's the difference between lawyer and liar?" hangs between us.

(In case you haven't heard this faded gem as many times as I have, the answer is "the pronunciation".)

I'm on a mission to preserve my credibility – and admittedly, yes, my shot at partnership – as I head for the bar. It's bustling with conversation and lacking any open seats, but I begin scanning the crowd anyway. This is Memphis: I can't go to Target on a Monday night without running into at least two people I've known since middle school. If I can't find an acquaintance in one of downtown's hottest restaurants, I'm seriously going to begin questioning my networking skills.

After a couple of minutes, I come up short, but a gnawing feeling tugs at my attention. It takes me a few beats to recognize it as hunger. If I can't find a friend, I can at least have dinner. They've got great grilled artichokes here. I also wasn't lying when I told Teddy the scampi is a thing of magic. But honestly, a plate of complimentary bread might taste award-winning to me right now.

I attempt to scrunch in near the bar, hoping to stick my name on a list for one of the high top tables. It's just then that a guy steps up beside me, smiling with a sure sense of recognition that I do not share.

"Hey," he says smoothly, passing me a fizzy cocktail. "I didn't expect to see you here."

Speechless isn't something I've been accused of often (read also: ever), but as I blink wordlessly into a set of hopeful dark blue eyes, I wonder if maybe I'm hungrier than I thought, as if perhaps I dreamed up this mystery guy. It's like 'hangry', but... hotter. (Horngry?)

"You look amazing," he continues. "How've you been? How's... everything?"

He looks like he stepped out of an old school Ambercrombie ad and carried that carefree vibe into his early thirties: beachy dark hair, deep dimples that don't require a smile, a physique primed for tons of incongruous opportunities to take off his shirt. The kind of guy who would look great in grayscale, and probably knows it.

My gaze drops to the spot where exactly two of his fingers are touching my elbow. They slip away, and I'm left contemplating the weight of the highball glass in my hand. It's rimmed with spicy seasoning, garnished with a lime, and looks suspiciously like one of my favorite cocktails. And he's looking at me like he actually thinks I might drink it. I give him an amused, assessing stare.

"You don't know me," I point out.

The way his smile falters tells me I'm correct.

"But you're pretending," I guess, "because you're either a serial killer who knows my go-to drink order, since he's obviously been stalking me and is now trying to *drug* me, or you just ran into... an ex-girlfriend?"

He grimaces, and the tops of his cheeks turn pink. It's a good look for him. He takes a sheepish gulp of his beer.

"New stepmother," he admits.

Now it's my turn to grimace. A laugh escapes me before I can stop myself. "Wow. That sounds remarkably complicated. But I appreciate the plot twist."

He shifts closer to be heard as a group of women in their mid-forties pass behind him. They're all wearing skimpy black dresses, led by a ringleader with a hot pink veil. The high notes of their chatter drift by towards the balcony stairs reserved for private parties. He takes this opportunity to lean in confidentially.

"I hope that means you're down to save me."

The corner of my mouth twitches with the hint of a smile. Maybe it's because I'm currently in the midst of my own complicated situation that I actually consider this.

"Which one is she?"

"The one who looks like she just married a man over sixty for his family fortune," he says.

"Blonde with Botox?"

"Brunette with fake boobs."

I see her now, lurking near the bar and casting us sideways glances with the hungry look of a cat-like predator, waiting for the perfect opportunity to move in. Whatever her motives are, they don't seem to leave this guy with many chances of escape. Hers is the only path between us and the door.

"Ah," I confirm. "She's pretty."

He laughs, feigning familiarity in case she's watching – and she *is* in fact watching. Despite the smile, his eyes are desperate.

"That is a highly irrelevant detail, given my current situation."

"Who am I supposed to be in this rescue scenario?" I ask him, slightly bemused. "Your fake girlfriend?"

"Do people really have fake girlfriends? Would that work?"

I give him another once over. With those dark shipwreck eyes, that boyish smile, and the dimple in his left cheek? No, his girlfriends are probably numerous, and quite real.

"For you? Probably not."

"You don't think I could get a girlfriend?"

I give him a knowing smile. "When's the last time you actually introduced someone as your *girlfriend*?"

"Fair point," he says. "So maybe just... my long lost friend? From college?"

"You mean the one you've been pining for since freshman year?"

He grins, looking at me now as if he's seeing me for the first time. "That's the one."

I tip my head from side to side, mulling this over. "That could work."

"It could," he agrees. "As long as she'll dance with me." He glances nervously over his shoulder. "Soon."

"Ah, but therein lies the problem," I say. "She doesn't dance."

I can almost see his Adam's apple bob as he swallows, a gulp so obvious it had to be his pride going down.

"Please."

The look of the bar tells me it's going to be at least fifteen minutes before I've got a hope of getting a seat. And out of the corner of my eye I notice Teddy and Paolo glancing our way. I gather my nerve and take a single sip of the drink in my hand, confirming my suspicions as the flavors of tequila and Topo

Chico mingle on my tongue.

"How'd you know I like spicy ranch water?" I ask, eyes narrowed.

"You've decided it's not because I'm a creepy stalker?"

"Serial killer," I correct. "And no, that's not off the table. Do you want me to dance with you or not?"

"Guessing people's preferred libation is my useless superpower," he says, sweeping a hand nervously through his hair as his gaze flits across the bar. "And this is the one scenario in which I'm praying it'll actually save my ass."

For a long beat, I let him squirm. After one more swig of spicy seltzer, I snag him by the arm. "This song good?"

His hand finds my mid-back, following close through the crowd.

"Perfect."

The dance floor isn't crowded yet, and I acknowledge it's the perfect place to avoid being accosted by someone you're trying to avoid. I hook my arm around his neck once we're safely in the middle. Up close, this guy smells like stepping outside on an early summer evening and catching the faint aroma of a nearby fire, as if his very essence is woodsy and blooming and warm. It's a scent that begs comfortable conversation. Despite my best efforts, I can't help but indulge.

"So, as your long lost best friend," I say, "aren't you going to tell me what brings you here?"

"I came for the... bachelorette party?" he guesses, glancing up at the group of women now cheering from the balcony. The pop of a champagne bottle echoes off the high ceilings. A few people in the dining room join in with an appreciative woop.

"Nice try," I smirk. "That's a divorce party."

"Wow. Okay. I didn't realize that was a thing people usually celebrated," he says, allowing his gaze to drift upward again, as if hoping to prove me wrong. "How do you even know this?"

It's obvious to me that this guy has no idea how many divorce parties I've been invited to, let alone made possible, and honestly, I'd like to keep it that way. Nothing kills a flirty buzz like guys finding out I've built my career on breakups. Even if they aren't serious about a relationship, I've found that men still like to imagine women as people with soft, delicate feelings. The kind who believe in love, or at least don't make their livelihood picking it apart.

"Didn't you see the banner?" I nod to the one strung up over the door to the stairs that reads: *I do, I did, I'm done!*

"I do now," he laughs. "It's a little weird, though, right? Celebrating the end of something that was supposed to last forever?"

"Nothing lasts forever," I say easily.

"Wow. I never knew you were such a romantic," he teases.

"And you are?"

"I must be," he counters, "given that I've apparently been lusting after you for the past fifteen years."

I laugh. "Well, how could you not? Especially after the time I found you locked out of your dorm. Naked."

"Naked? Why was I naked?" he laughs.

"Because you were drunk, obviously."

"Obviously," he nods.

"Because you were a hopeless frat boy. Also, did I mention this happened at eight o'clock in the morning?"

"Oh god. The only thing worse than a naked drunk frat boy is a naked drunk frat boy in broad daylight," he grimaces. "Am I really that cliche?"

"Yes. But lucky for you, I chastely offered you refuge in my room, where I lent you my fuzziest pink robe and fed you my last tray of tiny pizza bagels."

"Of course, how could I forget? Tiny pizza bagels are very sexy. They scream unrequited love."

"When they're someone's last tray, they obviously do. But unfortunately you were too nervous to make a move. Given that I'd seen your butt and all."

"Hey. I've got a great butt."

"And yet, not enough courage to take a chance and tell me how you really felt," I shrug.

I don't think I imagine the way his steps falter. He recovers with a smile.

"Maybe I was nervous," he counters, "because you always seemed so smart, and confident, and fine being alone."

This shivers through me, that feeling of a stranger edging close to something that's too true. I become more aware now of the warm pressure of his hand on my hip and the way his gaze is dancing across my face. I meet his intrigued stare with one of my own.

"I don't remember your name," I muse.

"Ouch. After all these years?"

"To be fair, in all my memories, I just remember calling you 'hey asshole'. As in, 'Hey asshole, why are you naked in my hallway'?"

"Quentin," he says. "And I assume you go by something other than Pizza Bagel Girl?"

"I dunno, that does have a nice ring to it," I smile. "I'm Heidi."

"Heidi," he nods, seemingly feeling out my name on his tongue. "I'm glad we could reconnect."

"Sir," the hostess interrupts. "Your table is ready."

"Thank you. I'll be right there," he tells her. I catch that hopeful glimmer in his eyes again. "Any chance you want to join an old friend for dinner?"

I give him another once over. There's no denying if I had a type, he'd probably be it. Charming and clever, with an easy smile and the kind of eyes that tug straight through my center.

It's not just my stomach that wants me to say yes; it's also the warm, tingly feeling in a long-neglected, elemental part of my very being.

But it is also inevitably at this moment that I glance across the restaurant to see Paolo ushering Teddy out. Actually, he's not ushering him – he's *following* him. And since the table with the birthday celebration is now half-empty, I am safe to assume that Teddy is trailing Gigi. Alarm bells go off in my brain. I probably don't need to follow them out, but I will.

"I'd love to, but I need to run," I say, slipping out of his arms. "Thanks for the drink."

He follows me for a few steps, laughing. "You're leaving?"

"I haven't seen your stepmom stalker in a good five minutes, so I think I've sufficiently saved you. What more did you want?"

"I feel like this is the part where you're supposed to leave behind a glass slipper," he says. "Or maybe give me your number?"

I give him a look. Paolo and Teddy are arguing in the entryway, the maitre d is opening the front doors to encourage them outside, and I've got exactly two seconds to make a decision.

Oh, what the hell?

I reach into his back pocket and snag his phone, reluctantly adding my number and labeling it as Pizza Bagel Girl. I pass it back to him with finality.

"No dick pics. No booty calls. Don't text me after ten o'clock."

He laughs. "You've got a lot of rules."

I smirk. "If you want to see me again, you'll follow them."

I say this even though I really don't expect to see Quentin again, but it feels good to remember what this feels like. To feel young. To feel wanted. To win.

2.

IN ANOTHER LIFE, maybe I would've responded to Quentin's advances. I would've stayed for dinner, for another dance, until the staff was sweeping up and the bartender signaled last call. I might have even invited him back to my place, reveled in his late-night summertime smell, and given him that perfect opportunity to take off his shirt. I certainly would've done more than roll my eyes when I saw the text from him on my way to spin class Saturday morning.

Q: Morning, PBG. Any chance you're free tonight?

H: Define free.

Q: Adjective. Able to act or do as one wishes. As in, "Heidi is free for dinner."

H: You think you're cute.

Q: I know I'm cute. *emoji of a sassy girl tipping her hand*

H: Well, Merriam-Webster, you should also know that I always act and do as I wish. But I'm not free for dinner. In all honesty, I'm probably not free until September.

Q: Perfect. I'll make us a reservation.

Reservation Confirmation Noreply: The High Limit. 2 guests. Rooftop dining. 7:30pm. September 1st.

H: You do realize this is months away, right?

Q: I've waited fifteen years. What's one summer?

I bit into my smile, but I didn't text back. I did, however, click to confirm the reservation. It uploaded itself to my calendar and settled just at the edge of my brain. I wandered through the weekend with an anticipatory feeling in my veins, like I might run into him at the corner market where I buy my groceries, or at the dive bar where I meet my running group for post-jog pints, or simply on one of the many sidewalks of downtown, where I always seem to be rushing purposefully from place-to-place.

I'm sure many would assume that I'm another stereotypical, over-scheduled, heartless automaton clawing her way to the top. I'm not. I just learned a long time ago that love is an excuse people use to treat each other badly. I don't have time for it, the same way I don't have time for another guy who thinks he's so great in bed he'll change my mind. They all think they can change my mind.

I don't need anyone to change my mind.

Plus, I've got plenty of healthy relationships. One of which faithfully sends me into the espresso-scented bustle of the trendy coffee shop where my best friend works every single weekday morning. Unlike every other weekday morning, though, at the start of this week, Meg greets me with a squeal.

"There she is!" she exclaims.

The three customers waiting at the end of the bar for their to-go orders glance up from their phones expectantly. They look disappointed to find I'm a random woman with a sleek ponytail and an unremarkable pencil skirt, stopping in to fuel up on her way to the office. I shrug.

"You're especially chipper this morning," I tell her.

Meg scampers around the counter with my usual oversized cold brew and a dish boasting a beautiful blackberry tart, like she's been waiting for this very moment. She shoves both into my hands before I can protest and beckons me to sit at one of the modern-industrial tables near the front window.

"Am I dying?" I ask, sinking into one of the brown leather chairs across from hers.

"I'm just so proud of you!" she says.

"I…"

She's nearly bouncing out of her seat with excitement as she shoves her phone at me. I set the tart down and take it. I'm met with a photo of myself, looking especially polished and, dare I say, fierce. My hazel eyes are bright, almost green. My hair is my signature wavy, dark caramel.

"Nice picture," I offer. "My eye makeup is especially on point. Where'd you get this?"

Meg jiggles in her seat, impatient. "Scroll down."

That's when I realize this is an article. *The* article. The one I'd put off interviewing for so many times that it had clearly come up against a deadline. Now, here it is in all its online glory, for the entire internet to read.

Apparently Jeanine had done what she had to do.

The best part of breaking up is calling Heidi Krupp.

"Oh god," I grimace. My stomach does a little flip, and I take a long sip of my iced coffee, as if this will somehow soften whatever comes next.

"My best friend is so famous," Meg giggles. "This makes you sound like a total badass. I mean, you are a total badass, but now people will know about it. You basically have a jingle!"

"Yeah…" I offer, wondering how much other incriminating stuff is in here. I audibly sigh when I get to the tidbit about the lemons and sweetener.

"Everyone will want to date you," Meg gushes. "After reading this, *I* want to date you."

I take a consolation bite of blackberry tart, chewing as I scroll. I'm allowing its buttery, citrusy divinity to fortify me against the certain incoming onslaught. God, how many people have read this? My family? My coworkers? My bosses? I'm going to need another vat of coffee.

"Nobody wants to date me," I tell her. "Hazards of the job."

She gives me a look, but she knows it's true. It's not only that I'm career-oriented and financially independent – which either intimidates guys or makes them think I want to be their meal ticket, with very little in between – but it's also the fact that I know exactly how to "take someone for everything he's worth", as my last serious boyfriend put it. He wasn't talking about money, in that scenario, just his dignity, I guess. But still, the point stands.

"I can't read this," I say finally, putting the phone face down between us. "It feels too much like looking for my name on the bathroom wall."

"What? Like, 'for a good time call'?"

"No, like, grammatically incorrect sharpie slander. Such as, 'Heidi, your a bitch', no apostrophe or E."

"Oh," she laughs, deflating a bit. "Sorry. I thought you'd be excited."

"I am," I offer gently. "I mean, nobody could eat this amazing tribute to seasonal fruit and not feel excited."

"We can always take the day off, you know!" she says brightly. "Hang by your building's pool. Go antiquing. What's the point of having a million vacation days if you never use them?"

I consider this with a sigh. "Maybe after –"

"After you make partner," she drones. "I know, I know. But I'm holding you to it! After it's official we're taking a real vacation – one that requires an Out of Office that doesn't include your cell number and an assurance that you can be reached at any time. You can't keep putting off your actual life, you know."

I raise my eyebrows at her in an expression that says, *Wanna bet*? She gives me a narrowed glare of disapproval.

"A real vacation," I concede, rolling my eyes for emphasis. "It's a deal."

"Good, because I could really use one," she says, propping her chin in her hand in a way that smushes up one side of her face. Her bright eyes are shadowy and tired as she smiles. Her day always starts at three-thirty – *in the morning* –, and by the time I pop through she's almost halfway to quitting time. This workload would maybe be fine if all that precious energy was being poured into her dream of having her *own* place, but at present she's stuck running *this* place – and running every single detail, right down to the number of blackberries in each artfully crafted made-with-love-by-Meg tart, by the overbearing owner.

I know Meg well enough to know that her bake shop would look nothing like this. No exposed brick walls or industrial lighting or metal countertops. No, Meg's place would be vintage and cozy, like settling into your grandmother's 1950s kitchen. It would be mismatched tables and colorful chairs, with yellow walls and the best breakfast pastries you've ever eaten in your entire life. You know she knows how to make biscotti? Who the hell makes biscotti? I want this dream for her almost as much as she wants me to find the love of my life. Both seem a little too much like a pipe dream at present.

"You think it's close?" she yawns. "The partnership, I mean."

I smile, licking blackberry compote off my fingers.

"So close I can taste it."

***

The view from the top floor offices of Freeman, Maxwell, and Lewis is one of my favorite in the entire city. In the early morning, the sky is a bright blue blanket over the muddy expanse of the Mississippi. It's one of the first things I noticed when I became an intern, the way that these offices were sleek and bright and modern, unlike the droves of firms out in the suburbs, still holding onto their dark curtains and plush carpet and heavy mahogany furniture.

This morning, as soon as I get off the elevator, I can sense that there's a palpable buzz. An anxious thrum starts up in my chest, like standing too close to a speaker at a concert. It vibrates through me with bone-shuddering certainty.

They read the article.

I lift my chin with steely determination, cruising past the cluster of cubicles where the interns are chatting over morning coffee. The sound of my heels sends them scattering, as if none of them wants to be the one I spot first. This is also unusual. Interns love me. I'm firm, but I'm not fear-inspiring, unless you're particularly underperforming.

"Yolanda," I say, catching her as she's about to round the corner.

"Heidi," she smiles. "Good morning."

"You ready to talk about those briefings?"

I don't miss it. She looks nervous, flitty. Like she's got a secret.

"Yes but, um," she clears her throat, lowering her voice. "Mr. Lewis wants to see you."

This obviously isn't the secret I expected.

"He's here early," I say, trying to keep all emotion from my tone.

"They're in the boardroom," she nods.

They? That anxious thrum turns into a rush, booming in my chest like heart-stopping bass.

"Who all, exactly?"

"Um, I think it's Mr. Maxwell? And he brought someone with him."

The boom turns to a thunderous roar. Erving Maxwell has not set foot in these offices for at least six months. I'd heard he was close to retirement. His retirement, actually, is the reason the firm is even considering another partner. His being here is either really good news or – given the timing, with that stupid article – really *not* good news.

"Thank you, Yolanda."

She couldn't look more grateful as she turns to go. I take a deep breath and smooth my skirt. I'm so glad I wore my power heels today. They're pointy and black with a bright floral print – like they serve an equal purpose of looking fashionable and also boasting a heel I could use to defend myself against an attacker if necessary – which I found at my Auntie Lena's vintage shop, Nine Lives. I can always count on her to set aside the stuff she thinks I'll love, and these were no exception.

"They look like you," she'd said with a wink. "Pretty and powerful."

They certainly make me feel pretty-powerful, and powerful is exactly what I'll need to be if I am about to face whatever is on the other side of that door. I plaster on my courtroom smile – confident, approachable, but not sweet: all lipstick and no teeth.

"Henry," I say affably before I'm even through the door. "I heard you wanted to..."

My gaze sweeps over Henry Lewis, past Erving Maxwell, and comes to land on a guy in a suit who, with his hair swept back neatly, looks way more like an extra in *The Wolf of Wall Street* than an American mall-brand model. I feel my face slip.

"See me," I finish haltingly.

"Quentin," my boss announces with an oblivious smile, "this is –"

"Heidi," Quentin says, sitting up straighter. To his credit, he has the decency to look surprised. His handsome face has gone slack. A hint of a blush blooms across his chiseled cheeks, like I just slapped him. I certainly want to.

"You two know each other?" Henry asks.

Quentin's gaze dances across my features like he isn't sure how to respond. It's clear from the way everyone is looking on expectantly that one of us has to.

"Yeah," I deadpan. "We go way back."

"Of course you do," Erving laughs, missing the irony. It's a mucousy sound, reminiscent of Sith lords. "You can always count on a Maxwell to be well-connected."

My brain cautiously connects the dots, the way one works to disarm a bomb, but there's only one obvious piece of this puzzle at present: Quentin's a Maxwell.

There are plenty of them in Erving's lineage. His three middle-aged sons are glorified ambulance chasers and shady salesmen always looking for a way into the "family business", and every few years one of them parades through the firm like he's planning to acquire an office. For whatever reason, Erving has never given them much more than complimentary coffee, which has never hurt my feelings. They're arrogant and entitled, the kind of people who have never scraped by on ten-cent packs of ramen noodles, or worn extra layers to avoid a gas bill that would keep them from being able to pay rent all winter, or put exactly two dollars and fifty cents worth of gas in their car and hoped it might get them to work the rest of the week. Silver spoon doesn't begin to describe it.

I have to assume, since Quentin is sitting here, that he's just like the rest of them. Even if he isn't, I have to be careful. If I'm certain of anything, it's that everyone has a motive.

"Heidi, have a seat," Henry insists.

I sit, making sure to choose the ergonomic swivel-chair at the head of the table.

"To what do I owe this pleasure?" I say, attempting to regain my composure.

"Erving has recently become aware that you're working Glass v. Russo," Henry explains. "And he thought you could use some help."

The elderly man at the table beams like he's just done me the most gracious of favors. I do my best to conjure up a polite smile.

"Oh, well, thank you, Mr. Maxwell," I offer. "That's very generous of you, but I've been handling cases on my own for quite some time."

"Of course you have!" he boasts. "You're an impressive associate –"

"Senior associate," I correct.

"-- and you wouldn't be here if you couldn't handle yourself. But this is a high profile case. It makes sense to have all of our best people on this."

The second piece clicks into place: Quentin's an attorney.

"Of course." Slowly, I swivel towards the other night's mystery man. "Quentin, why didn't you mention you were one of 'our people'?"

At the sound of his name, he shifts in his seat again. Against his navy suit, his eyes look darker and bluer than they did the other night. His gaze pleads innocence, though his tone remains conversational. He clears his throat.

"I didn't realize you worked here."

"Small world, isn't it?" I say.

"Quentin's finally back from his self-imposed exile in Austin," Erving chimes in, chuckling at what is clearly an inside joke. "If we're lucky, we might convince him to stay."

Stay.

I take a measured breath before doing the math.

"So you want me to split the case," I say. "And the commission."

"I don't need the commission," Quentin offers.

Of course you don't, I think.

"And this won't affect my consideration for the partnership," I add, eyeing the other two men. It's not so much a question as a statement. A hope. A dare.

Henry and Erving exchange a loaded look.

"Let's not worry about that just yet," Henry breaks in. "We need to get through this case and then –"

"And then?" I prompt.

"It's really up to the board to decide on all that," Henry admits, dropping his gaze to the table.

"It's important that whoever is chosen as senior partner can show that they know how to put aside personal pursuits and do what's in the best interest of the firm," Erving adds. He glances meaningfully at his young protege.

I take another breath, attempting to quell the rage rising within me.

"So, just to be clear, you're going to choose between... *us*?"

An uncomfortable silence settles around the room. That's when the last piece clicks into place: Quentin Maxwell is my worst fucking nightmare.

"Why couldn't you have just been a serial killer?" I mutter.

3.

Relationships end for all kinds of reasons. Given my line of work, I'm intimately familiar with many of them. The couple whose relationship couldn't survive their being on opposite sides of the last presidential election? I settled it. The woman whose husband didn't offer to move out of her way while she was vacuuming? Honestly, not the strangest thing I've negotiated. The man whose wife didn't like *Moana*? Yes, hand to god, an animated family film was actually cited in court documents as the final straw. (But really, who doesn't like *Moana*?)

People always assume that someone cheated, but it's not usually infidelity that breaks people up, it's all the other stuff. The subtle, everyday deceptions. The inability to communicate one's needs. The realization that you actually want or need very, very different things. The problem with me and Quentin Maxwell is that we actually want the very same thing. It's because of this that our relationship is doomed before it can begin.

"How was I supposed to know you were an *attorney*?" he asks, following me to my office with a self-assured stride.

"Where'd you go to law school? They didn't teach you the secret handshake?" I say flatly.

"Okay, I'm getting the impression that you think I planned this, which is kind of flattering, I'll admit, but –"

"Hey, asshole," I interrupt. "You actually expect me to believe that you showed up here unawares after you picked me out of a crowded restaurant and handed me my favorite drink *by chance?*"

"Actually? Yes."

"So not only are you a bad liar, but you're an idiot, too," I say. "I haven't worked my ass off for the past ten years to lose to some patrilineal, nepotistic bullshit. Who are you, anyway? Erving's long lost nephew?"

"Grandson," he admits.

"Awesome."

When we make it to my office, I drop my purse in the armchair in an attempt to deter him from sitting. I sink into place behind my desk and power up my computer.

"I guess you're here to claim your rightful throne, then?" I continue. "Fulfill some sort of prophecy?"

He leans against the doorframe, taking in the minimalist details of my space. The clear surface of my desk. The potted bird of paradise lurking by the window. The black yoga mat I keep in the corner.

"I'm here to win this case," he says. "Same as you."

He's peering at the single framed photo by my monitor when I step into his line of vision. I pass him a binder that weighs roughly fifteen pounds. He flips it open like it might contain a cease and desist. Or a concealed explosive.

"What's this?"

"My notes on the case so far. I trust you can bring yourself up to speed? Assuming you even know family law. If you don't, ask one of the interns. I don't have time to hand-hold you."

"And yet I seem to recall you being perfectly content holding hands with me the other night."

"We weren't holding hands, we were dancing. Under false pretenses. But don't worry, it won't happen again."

The longer he looks at me, the more it seems to dawn on him that I might be serious. Of course it's taken him this long. He's probably not used to women doing anything but falling at his feet.

"Are we really going to be adversaries on this?" he questions.

"What would you prefer we be?"

"Friends," he proposes. "Allies. The kind of coworkers who also happen to have a mature, consensual relationship outside of the office."

I grimace. God, did I actually think he was attractive? With his devil-may-care hair and his I-spend-too-much-time-flexing-in-the-gym-mirror body? I have to stop skipping lunch. That's exactly what's to blame for this. All I feel now when I see his hopefully playful smirk is prickly rage.

Prage.

"Are you planning to pursue the partnership opportunity?" I ask.

His gaze shifts over my features, and I watch his smirk fall. The defined shape of his cheekbones make him look suddenly serious. It's a welcome shift, as if anything personal that could ever have been between us is slowly dissolving, leaving only business.

"I'd be stupid not to," he admits.

I give him a curt nod.

"Then perhaps you should forget that we ever exchanged numbers. You might also want to brush up on the agency's very strict policy against interoffice relationships, while you're at it," I say, swiveling towards my computer.

I'm opening emails and typing at top speed within moments. I can feel him watching me for a few beats. Weighing. Assessing.

"Adversaries," he says, peeling himself out of my doorway and inclining his head. "As you wish."

***

The overcrowded aisles of Nine Lives thrift shop is my safe space. When I was a kid, I ended up here almost every afternoon and all day most summers. I would sink into a beanbag in the corner and speed through my homework so I could slip into the latest paperback thriller from the local library. By high school, I spent much of my time rummaging through the latest haul, hoping to rediscover long-forgotten treasures, the kind of things I could repurpose and – more importantly – afford.

In college, I found my way here when I'd burned myself out on studying, those days when I was in search of a sympathetic ear and a meal that didn't come from the microwave. Picking up shifts here is also how I met Meg, who came in every week for a month to obsess over a set of vintage casserole dishes before she finally pulled the trigger, at which point we'd already exchanged phone numbers, life stories, and an endless string of commentary about our favorite binge-worthy TV shows.

This little midtown shop with the upstairs apartment that smells faintly of lemons and incense has always felt like my second home, a place I can show up exactly as I am.

That is, until we started discussing Quentin Maxwell.

"No," Meg gasps. "The fake dating guy! At your office?!"

The late afternoon sunlight glints off the mannequins in sequined dresses lounging in the front window display. This is usually my favorite kind of afternoon, wandering the winding aisles with Sam Cooke on the record player. We stopped by to peruse cutesy teapots, retro coffee cups, and other one-of-a-kind decor that Meg could incorporate into the cafe – assuming she can ever get the suggestions past her ultra-modern business partner. If I had known she was going to sensationalize my *work* news and turn it into *romantic* news, though, I might have passed.

Auntie Lena pops her head over a rack of platform heels.

"You're fake dating someone?" she asks.

"No," I say, at the same time Meg says, "Yes."

Auntie Lena sweeps around the corner with the posture of someone who is perpetually about to rearrange something: her hands always moving but never quite touching, her warm, dark eyes always scanning.

"You know that fake dating almost always leads to *real* dating, right? It's been thoroughly documented." When I give her an incredulous look, she adds, "There are movies."

"My life is not a movie. I'm not fake dating. I just had a momentary lapse in judgment."

"The sexy kind," Meg clarifies, waggling her eyebrows.

Auntie Lena looks entirely too intrigued. She eyes me like a mother, which I guess is appropriate, since she has long felt like the closest thing I've got.

Don't get me wrong. I in fact have and know my mother, but after my parents' divorce, I ended up in this shop the same way everything else does – forgotten, unwanted, desperate to belong – and Helena Berryhill never questioned it. She let me hang around like one of the stray cats she lovingly feeds in the alleyway. After closing time, she would drop me off at home the evenings my mom couldn't find the time to pick me up, and they would make the emotionally avoidant smalltalk of sisters that had long ago lost touch. It was always so strange to see them together: Lena in her classic, simple style, with a Julia Roberts smile and Audrey Hepburn capris, and my mother in the overdone makeup and feathered hair of every soccer mom in the '90s, a look she adopted when she married my stepdad Eric, moved us into his two-story house in the suburbs, and threw herself headfirst into getting motherhood "right" the next two times around.

I love my aunt in a way that I'll never be able to adequately express. I love that she never tried to change herself for anyone else. I love that she didn't talk shit about my dad every chance she got. I can't say I'm especially thrilled, though, that she can always see right through me.

My expression sours.

"There was no sex," I say flatly.

Both of them seem to deflate a bit at this.

"What's the point of being successful if you're not even going to enjoy it?" Meg says in an accusatory tone.

"I enjoy myself plenty," I defend. "But seriously, he's trying to take everything from me, and all you care about is sex?"

"Wait, I think I'm missing something. What's he taking?" Auntie Lena asks.

Meg fills her in on the details while I pluck a pair of wedges off the rack and go find Kamille, who is trying on sunglasses near the front register, like a girl after my own heart.

"What about these?" I ask her, dangling the shoes from my fingertips.

"Those are cool," she grins, pulling off a pair of cat-eye rims and replacing them carefully.

"They're your size."

I love the look on her face when she takes them from me, plopping into the nearest armchair to try them on. They're seventies wedges: sassy enough to make her look young, but quite literally old enough to make her feel older. She strikes a pose with her gangly limbs, almost matching my five seven height, despite being in middle school.

"What do you think?" she asks.

"Amazing," I say. "Like you could take over the whole world."

"You always say that," she laughs.

"Well," I shrug. "When are you going to start believing it?"

Kamille is the oldest of four siblings and lives with her grandmother. I can't pretend to understand the dynamics of her life, but I get the feeling there hasn't always been a lot leftover for her, and I know that feeling like the back of my hand. Maybe this is why we fit together so well. I could sense it the moment I met her, looking awkward and serious at a Girls Going Places event three years ago, and I knew we were going to click.

No surprise: we didn't immediately click. I earned the first sliver of Kamille's trust when I kept showing up for our sessions even though she told me she was too old for all of this and the whole thing was pointless. I won the next bit when I gave her a journal with sparkly pens and told her that her thoughts and words were important, even if she didn't want to share them with me or anyone else. But the day we really clicked was when I took her to the symphony. She'd never been to the theater before, and her eyes were wide as she listened, and she told me she'd never heard music like that in person before – the kind you can feel.

In the end, it wasn't her awkwardness or seriousness that won me over. It was that familiar, independent, determined spark.

"How much are they?" she asks now.

"I've got it," I say, waving my hand. "We never celebrated that year-end report card, remember?"

This is always the same conversation we have at Nine Lives. I don't want her to think that everything comes easily, but I do want her to understand that those very rare Sometimes when you can get Exactly What You Want really do exist. I need her to know that good things don't only get doled out to everyone else, that they find us all every now and then.

At least, I'm holding out hope that they do.

"Plus, you've got music camp coming up," I add. "You still need an outfit for the end-of-the-week concert, right? I thought I saw it on the packing list."

"Yeah," she offers, glancing away.

"What's that look?"

She shrugs a sharp shoulder. "I don't know if I want to go."

"To camp? You talked about it all year. They only picked the top musicians from every school. You earned this."

"Yeah. I'm not worried about the music part. But... you know I'm not going to get to go on the water slides if I can't swim. And if I can't do the water slides, I'll be stuck in the kiddie pool with the little kids. And you know they pee in there. It's basically a public toilet."

"Hey, you won't be sitting in the public toilet. You'll be able to swim. Didn't we set our goal?"

She nods reluctantly. "Yeah."

"We're going to work on it every week. We've got a plan. But attitude is half the battle," I remind her.

She slides on a pair of ridiculously oversized sunglasses. The round, purple, rhinestone-crusted frames make her look like Hermione Granger trying to impersonate Elton John.

"This kind of attitude?"

I laugh. "Exactly that kind of attitude."

She keeps them on, along with the shoes, as I spin the rack. It's high on my list of guilty pleasures, perusing accessories and artwork for something that pops. Almost all of my favorite pieces were things I fell in love with at estate sales and thrift shops – including the vintage Tiffany lamp in my living room, which is still my proudest find to date – but the truth is I don't fall in love easily, and I inevitably spend a lot more time browsing than buying. This doesn't stop me from trying on a pair of rose pink 70s square sunglasses and assessing myself in the mirror.

"You really think he lied to you?" Auntie Lena says incredulously, slipping into the corner of the reflection so that I can see her staring at me over my shoulder.

"Who lied to you?" Kamille asks.

"No one," I say, removing the glasses so I can give my aunt and best friend a withering stare. With Kamille looking at me expectantly, I amend for the sake of honesty, "A coworker."

"A guy who likes her," Meg offers.

I shoot her a look that says, *Really?* at the same time Kamille says, "Oooooh", like a chorus of little kids during a kiss scene in a movie.

"Yeah, yeah," I mutter. "So what, a guy likes me? Boys don't make the world go 'round."

"I mean, obviously. That's the sun. Gravity. Science."

Meg snorts. "She's definitely your mini-me."

"But I still want to know who he is," Kamille adds, smiling coyly.

"His name is... Quentin." I hate even saying it out loud, as if the syllables themselves might summon him like Beetlejuice. "We work together. But he's being a jerk. And contrary to what some people may tell you, guys aren't mean to girls because they like them. At least, not the kind of guys you want to date."

"Ohmigosh, that's always what my friend Amaya says. She's all like, 'I think Jaxon likes you because he kicked the ball at your face in gym.' And I'm always like, 'Okay, but I don't like him like that.'"

I smile. I never tire of middle school logic. Seriously. Stories that rarely go anywhere? Characters showing up with little to no background or introduction? Sign me up.

"Exactly," I tell her.

Auntie Lena laughs, unconvinced. "Not everyone has a secret evil plan, Heidi. Maybe it *was* a coincidence."

"It doesn't matter. Coincidence or not, I deserve that job. I'm going to get that job. And when I do, Quentin Maxwell will no longer be my problem."

We change the subject. Another half hour passes as we sift through bins of records, periodically selecting one to place on the turntable to serenade us as we chit-chat and consider if the items that catch our interest are passing delights or things we can't live without. On our way out the door, with a set of vintage teacups that would look perfect in Meg's dream bakeshop and Kamille's sandals in tow, Auntie Lena brushes my hair over my shoulder before giving it a squeeze.

"No matter what happens with the job, I'm proud of you, Dee."

I wonder, when she says it, why my smile can't quite reach my eyes, the way that feeling can't quite reach my chest, how those words seem to float on the surface, never quite sinking in. I squeeze her hand in return anyway, giving the side of her face a quick kiss before following Meg and Kamille's laughter into the parking lot. I slide my sunglasses securely into place, settling into my confident stride as I step out the door.

4.

THEY GIVE HIM Erving's corner office. I tell myself I'm not jealous, and I'm not – not of the stocked mini fridge, the great view, or the enviable proximity to the lowest ranking of the pre-law interns who grab afternoon coffee orders – but every time I hear him laughing in the hall with Victor Freeman, I'll admit, I kind of want to punch both of them in the face.

"It's temporary," Henry assures me.

"I can win this case on my own," I say uselessly.

"There's no I in team," he counters.

No, I think, *but there's definitely one in WIN.*

"The last thing we want is for the board to think you can't play well with others," he says. It makes me feel as much like a little kid as the metaphor might suggest. "Take the help."

When he leaves, I hook a headphone into one ear, put on a high-intensity playlist, and attempt to focus on work. Instead, I spend forty-five minutes trying to figure out exactly what type of attorney the new young Maxwell is.

I don't mean his specialty, though it only takes me about five seconds to discover that it is civil, mostly, except for the short period when he dabbled in criminal a few years back. I want to know the kinds of cases he takes. I want to know what people say about him. I want to know, if he wins, *how* he wins.

As hellbent on victory as I may seem, I'm not interested in winning if it means I have to compromise my integrity. There have admittedly been times in this business that that's cost me, but I can live with it. I know how much that other feeling – the one that knots in your stomach, that leaves you waking up in the night with your heart pounding and your skin crawling like you've done something dirty that you can't wash off – can cost. I know it definitely doesn't feel like winning.

Plus, you know what they say, about keeping your enemies closer, and whatnot.

I scan the easy stuff first: a few headshots from corporate sites, his hobbies (he's a gym junkie like I expected: jiu jitsu and krav maga), and then I stumble down the rabbit hole.

Everyone always thinks to be a great attorney you have to be great at arguing; that isn't exactly true, although I do enjoy a heated debate. The truth is nobody gets through law school without formidable research skills, so I find out a lot about Quentin in that short amount of time.

I discover that he dropped out of Ole Miss sophomore year and eventually made his way to Texas, where he finished his undergrad and trudged through a law degree that took him five years to complete. I expected to find a lot of big name firms in his background, and I did. He interned with the best of the best. Then he did something very unexpected: he went to work for a low budget, non-profit organization that specialized in domestic violence. This either means he had already burned all his bridges at those big name firms and they didn't want him as an associate, or... he chose to turn them down.

That isn't unheard of, exactly, but it isn't common either.

Who the hell is this guy?

By the time I get on the elevator, I'm still wondering. The deserted, early evening scenery of the office has almost disappeared behind the sliding, mirrored surface when I hear, "Hold the door."

I scowl as a forearm with a tailored shirt sleeve rolled halfway to the elbow juts into the sensor. The doors slide back open, revealing Quentin. Of course it's Quentin. With the way this week is going, it couldn't have been anyone else. He clears his throat as he steps inside.

"I thought you left at five," he says, by way of awkward apology.

"With all the slackers? Not usually."

It's mostly a joke. He doesn't laugh. We attempt to avoid looking at each other, as well as at our reflections, which leaves us both seemingly staring at our shoes. I feel like a jerk.

"How's it coming with those notes?" I ask.

"Fine," he says.

"Good," I nod.

Even without looking at him, his presence seems to envelop me. I can sense that he's wearing that same, guarded expression that he slipped into that first day in my office. Maybe it sounds ridiculous, but it almost makes me miss the smirky cocktail savant who weaves compelling backstories and schedules romantic dinner dates.

The guy I'm not sure was anything more than an elaborate fabrication.

The guy I need to forget ever attempted to charm me with an interesting excuse for a dance and a drink.

I feel like I don't breathe again until the elevator doors open on the ground floor. He motions for me to exit first, and I do. I realize with him behind me that it feels impossible to walk normally in this situation. I'm definitely doing an angry, sexy walk, but not on purpose. It's like my brain only knows how to do regular walking when it's not being pressured to. Especially not when some jerkoff might be looking at my ass. But if he's looking... well, I'd like to think I look good.

On the sidewalk, I slide out of my jacket and into my sunglasses, letting the warm breeze carry me along my usual route. I'm at least a block away from the office when I glance over my shoulder, finding Quentin a few paces back. The day has tousled his hair loose from its swept back precision, and he's got his jacket slung over his shoulder like a frickin' GQ cover model. He looks away quickly when he sees that I've spotted him.

"Are you following me?" I ask loudly.

A few passersby turn to stare at us. I wave them on. They continue to watch Quentin warily as they go, and he stands there with the nothing-to-hide posture of someone being unfairly strip searched. Exasperation clouds his features.

"No, I'm not following you," he says. "I'm going home."

"Mmkay," I say, continuing my trek.

Another block goes by, but before I check, I know he's still somewhere behind me. It's like a sixth sense, the kind that tickles the back of your neck like a whisper, telling you to turn around. When I do, he throws up his hands.

"Maybe we take the same route," he calls down the sidewalk.

I stop so that all he can do is approach me now. He does so tentatively, like I might hit him with pepper spray, and honestly, I still might.

"Where do you live exactly?" I ask.

He scoffs. "I'm not going to tell you where I live."

"Why not?"

"Because you're my mortal enemy, remember?"

"Ah. Yes," I nod. "Your point?"

"What point?"

"I'm not going to let you follow me home."

"I'm not going to let *you* follow *me* home," he counters.

"So we're just going to stand here?"

He sweeps a casual hand through his hair, like this option is fine with him. I fold my arms across my chest, ready to wait it out. Eventually, I roll my eyes and start walking again. This is definitely my angry walk. My heels clack across the sidewalk with measured annoyance, until I'm finally opening the door to my building. As I do this, I see Quentin a few paces behind, staring at me, slack jawed. The realization hits me before he says anything.

"Oh come on," I exclaim. "You can't actually live here!"

I firmly plant myself on the sidewalk and let the apartment building door close behind me, just in case. If he is actually trying to follow me home and may be planning to kill me, I won't make his entering my building easy.

He holds up a flat, gray key fob with the basic outline of a cotton flower on it. I recognize it as the same one I have on my keyring. When he taps it against the reader, the light turns green and the lock clicks open. Something inside me – something that feels a lot like one of the existential threads holding me together – threatens to snap. Maybe in a moment I'll simply collapse to the sidewalk like a spent marionette, unable to continue playing my part in whatever star-crossed script this is.

"Am I supposed to believe this is another amazing coincidence?" I ask bitterly.

"Bernadette set it up," he says.

I eye him, but it checks out. Bernadette is our rock star executive assistant, the same one who recommended this place to me a few years back, once my taste for commuting had soured, because she saw it highlighted in a local article and thought it "looked like me". I remember now that she may have stopped me on my way past her desk a few weeks ago and asked if I still loved it enough to recommend. She just hadn't mentioned for whom.

"I don't really know the area anymore," he says, continuing his defense. "And I definitely didn't know you lived here – or even existed – when I moved in. But you're free to believe whatever you want."

He adds this last bit with finality before retreating inside. Since I spent the past five minutes stalking my way here, it seems silly for me to do anything but follow.

The air conditioning of the small lobby welcomes us. The Exchange is one of those live-work communities with a row of convenient little shops on the first floor and condo-style living up above. Normally, I'm not impressed by the concept, but this one is different. It lives in a remodeled section of the city's historic district, and thanks to some passionate citizens who petitioned the council, they'd kept a lot of the building's character during the renovation. We're surrounded by old marble floors and high ceilings, the kind that make me lower my voice to avoid an echo, though there's no one else nearby.

"I think we need to talk about this," I say. "Establish some… rules of engagement."

"Rules of engagement?" His gaze slides over to mine, equal parts annoyance and intrigue. "Are you planning to take me by force?"

I ignore his innuendo as the elevator descends into view. It's one of the old school ones that boasts copper cage doors that open and close like an accordion. I checked with the city permits on file before I moved in to make sure it has all of the modern safety features, and once armed with that reassurance, I have grown to love it. I slide it open and allow us inside.

"This is – for better or worse – a partnership," I reply. "And the most successful partnerships require that all parties agree to what is and isn't acceptable before things have a chance to get... complicated."

"You think working with me is going to get complicated?"

I allow the fact that we're both standing in this elevator to answer his question. We're surrounded by every indication that things are already spiraling in the unmistakable direction of *complicated.*

He seems to be considering this. In the meantime, neither of us selects a floor. The elevator lingers, unsure of where to go.

"What do you propose?" he says.

"I can draft something. Give you an opportunity to review before we sign off."

"A written contract," he observes.

"A simple agreement," I counter.

Amusement has crept into his features, quirking his mouth enough to hint at a dimple.

"Is this the price every guy pays when he buys you a drink?"

I meet his stare without wavering, though I feel a bit called out. I have in fact been known to establish written guidelines in serious – and casual – relationships, back when I was actually dating. Most guys were skeptical at first. One even tried to turn it into an odd roleplay sort of thing. ("I'll sign your affidavit, but I can't pay my court fees. Surely we can work something out?" *Wink, wink.*) I was game until he tried to get clever with a cringe-worthy pun involving his erection and *pro bono*, at which point I knew written guidelines weren't enough to save us. The point is, anyone who can't appreciate boundaries isn't the one – or the one-night-stand – for me. It makes me feel weirdly transparent, though, to think that Quentin suspects this about me.

"When he shows up to my office and my apartment building all within the same week?" I challenge. "Yes. Yes, I do. You're probably lucky it isn't a restraining order."

He exhales a mirthless laugh. "I can't say much about this has felt lucky."

"What do you mean? You waltzed into town and found yourself in a corner office, already vying for a fancy promotion. Sounds pretty lucky to me."

"I've barely been here a week, and I'm already dodging awkward family situations at a bar and meeting an amazingly smart, sexy woman who I hoped wanted to date me but turned out to be my colleague and now thinks I'm a conniving sleazebag."

"Sleazebag?" I grimace. I can tell he was hoping I might hang on a few other key words in that sentence.

"You know what I mean."

I chew the inside of my lip, considering. "You really didn't know?"

He gives me a desperate look that lets me know he's done answering this question if I'm not going to believe him.

"I'm a good guy, Heidi. A good attorney. Let me prove it to you. We can go back to the office right now and hammer out the details of this agreement if that's what you want."

I don't know why I'm so tempted. I've been looking forward to lounging braless on my couch with a glass of wine, some case notes, and new episodes of my latest guilty pleasure TV show all day. Why am I entertaining walking all the way back to the office in this heat, in these heels, with this guy?

Somehow, I can imagine us settling comfortably into the conference room. Laughing as we make revisions over each others' shoulders. Ordering in dinner. Putting enough of our expectations on paper that we can turn everything between us into something mutually beneficial. Something straightforward. Something that won't eventually split us in two.

I swallow past the feeling and swipe my key fob before pressing the button for the seventh floor. I'm relieved when he does the same and makes his selection for ten. At least I can feel satisfied with the knowledge that there are three whole floors between us. The lift begins to rise.

"I'll have a draft on your desk first thing tomorrow," I tell him.

"Fair enough," he says. "Just don't try to write me off the case, okay? No hidden clauses. No rolling concessions. No bribery. I still want the partnership. There's no scenario in which you're changing my mind about this."

I'm rightfully offended.

"As much as I would love for you to be off this case, that's not how I do things."

"Maybe you could tell me how you do things over dinner? Purely professional, of course."

I get off at my floor and slide the cage door closed behind me with Quentin watching me. His head is tilted slightly to the side, pieces of his hair are falling free, and I wonder if he is thinking some version of the same thing I am: how easy it would have been to continue texting, flirting, imagining that we were the kind of people who could actually keep that rooftop dinner date.

"Not free until September, remember?" I smile.

"Can't fault me for trying."

I laugh, calling over my shoulder just before he begins to disappear. "After tomorrow I might."

5.

Avid Records is tucked into the outskirts of downtown, where the modern touches of gentrification mingle with the squatty, rundown window-front buildings of the 1970s. Basic block lettering stretches across a paneled awning, identifying this as the well-known recording studio and not just another random chicken wing joint or pawn shop, though the place has the same curb appeal.

Looking at it from the outside, it might be hard to imagine that a consumer-driven twenty-something like Gigi Russo would be fighting for half of it. The attorney's fees alone might seem as though they would amount to more than the entire plot is worth. The reality is that she knows what many in the music industry know, which is that Avid is a hidden gem, one of Memphis's claims to music fame. These wood-paneled hallways are lined with photos of low-key legends smoking in the live room and behind-the-scenes greats grinning as they lounge around the ancient, Frankenstein's monster of a soundboard. There's a reverence to it, and you don't have to have a well-researched musical opinion to know it. You can sense it in a single conversation with Teddy Glass.

Quentin is waiting for me when I arrive, leaning against the hood of a new BMW with a stack of papers in hand. I park my SUV in what I assume is a designated space, though the painted lines have long since faded into the cracked concrete. I arm myself with the oversized cold brew from my cup holder before climbing out.

"You ready?" I say, already moving past him for the door.

"*Quentin Maxwell and Heidi Krupp, herein referred to as 'the partners', agree to conduct themselves at all times with the utmost integrity and to maintain a relationship that is solely professional, not personal, in nature.*"

He reads this to me as if I didn't in fact write it. I watch him for a moment, wondering if he expects me to give him a gold star for telling me something I already know.

"Yes. That is what it says," I confirm.

"*The partners will not plan, threaten, or engage in acts of* sabotage. *The partners agree to maintain clear professional boundaries and avoid physical contact, with the exception of business-related handshakes, high fives, or fist bumps, when appropriate,*" Quentin reads. "Really?"

"Is there some part of this you have an issue with?" I ask.

"Fist bumps?!" he exclaims.

"We can remove that part, if you're adamantly averse to that particular hand gesture."

His pointed gaze returns to the page. "*The partners will not share meals. The partners will refrain from gratuitous compliments. If the partners encounter each other outside of a professional setting, they will limit interactions to polite smalltalk totaling five minutes or less.*"

There's more, of course, but he doesn't bother to continue.

"This is pretty standard verbiage," I say. "I don't know why you're freaking out."

"You make it sound like I have no idea how to conduct myself. It's insulting. Also, some of this is circumstantial."

"Such as?"

He points to the part about physical contact. "If you're choking and need the heimlich."

"We won't be eating together, so I'm not sure why I'd be choking."

He drags a finger further down the page. "'Five minutes or less' is also troublingly specific. Are you going to carry a stopwatch?"

"I thought you were on board with this. Ready to work as a 'team'," I say, using air quotes. "We can just as easily go back to being adversaries. In which case, you should head back to the office, since this is my meeting."

"I just don't understand why any of this needs to be put in writing."

"Then you clearly haven't been in this business long enough," I smile.

He sighs before pulling a pen from his jacket pocket and scrawling some addendums near the bottom of the page. I sip my coffee while I wait, annoyed. It's not just that he thinks he's in the position to make demands that irritates me, but also that it's hot out here. The sun is attempting to scorch us like the barren, weedy lot across the street, and it fills me with impatience. I've almost broken a sweat by the time he passes me the amended document.

The partners will be forthcoming about all details related to the Glass v Russo case.

The partners will work all aspects of the case together, as a team, sans quotation marks both literal and figurative.

The partners will not keep secrets.

I scan his revisions with a critical eye. I remind myself that this is for the best. Working this case with Quentin is like speeding down a winding canyon road; the agreement adds some much-needed guardrails. Plus, as much as I don't need his help to prove my worth to the board, I don't need him working against me. This is a win-win.

I pass the document back to him with a resigned sigh.

"Fine."

We add our signatures to the bottom of the page against the warm metal hood of his car. Satisfied, we each take a photo copy to keep in our phones, and I tuck the original into my purse.

"What do you say, Pizza Bagel Girl?" Quentin says, lifting his hand in the air with a half-cocked smile. "Partners?"

God, this was a mistake.

The begrudging, half-hearted high five I give him makes him grin in a way that fills me with regret over most everything we agreed upon. Mostly because I've already got that gut feeling I wasn't thorough enough.

"Hey asshole," I offer. "The use of cutesy nicknames is definitely personal, not professional."

Quentin is not ruffled by this. He beams with a new confidence as he opens the glass front door for me and we head inside.

***

We find Teddy in his office, lying across a worn velvet sofa the color of dried mustard. He has an arm crooked above his head, hand fisted in his black hair. His legs are hooked over one armrest, letting his Vans dangle hopelessly towards the floor. The neck of what is probably a very expensive guitar hangs precariously from his free hand. He looks like he hasn't shaved in a few days, but as far as I can tell he's showered much more recently, which is a plus.

Quentin's gaze drifts to mine with a hint of apprehension. *Is this normal?*

"Hey, Teddy," I offer.

From day one, he's insisted that I call him that. Not Mr. Glass ("that rat bastard who kicked me out at sixteen") or Theodore ("sends me straight back to Catholic school, sweetheart"), just Teddy ("like the bear").

"Why are we doing this, Heidi?" he groans. "She said she'd love me forever. Forever. Why'd she change her mind?"

I could tell him that nothing lasts forever. I could also tell him that people change their minds all the time, but not usually because you want them to. I might go as far to explain that girls like Gigi have a ten-second attention span, and their five-year relationship was probably an actual eternity in her mind. I acknowledge that none of this would be helpful.

"Unfortunately I'm an attorney, Teddy, not a marriage counselor."

Teddy's head falls toward us now, and his gaze settles on Quentin.

"You brought a friend?"

"Colleague," I correct. I make the necessary introductions. To my relief, this encourages Teddy to tip himself upright. Quentin immediately wins him over by jumping into an in-depth discussion I can't follow about some bands I've never heard of and albums I don't remember. I make a mental note to call him out later for being a total fangirl.

"Yeah, I saw you two together the other night," Teddy remembers. "Maestoso."

I wonder, considering the amount of booze Teddy consumed, how he remembers anything about that night at all. I feel my face heat as he points between the two of us, like he's drawing an imaginary line that is irreparably tethering us together, with a grin blossoming on his face.

Quentin gives me the slightest sideways glance, which I do my best to avoid.

"I didn't realize you were there," he tells Teddy amiably. "I would've said hello."

"It's cool, man. Until I saw you two dancing, I was convinced Heidi was spying on me," he laughs. "I didn't realize she had a little office romance going on."

I almost trip on the plush carpet, as if this statement is literally the rug being pulled from under me. I right myself, wiping coffee off my wrist.

"No romance," I say.

It comes out as an unconvincing cough. I can't decide if Teddy's believing this is better or worse than his determining I do in fact have a tail on him, so I don't offer anything more. He rubs his salt-and-pepper scruff in amusement.

"Ohhh, right. Okay." He says this theatrically, as if he's doing this for the sake of a studio audience. Then he stage whispers, "Don't worry. Your secret's safe with me."

I look to Quentin like he's going to help me out here. He doesn't.

"So Teddy," he says, as if they're old friends, "what are the chances of us getting the two of you in a room together for mediation? None of this needs to go to court."

"I've tried, man. I've tried. She won't listen."

I'm trying to give Quentin the look that explains, *She's an influencer who loves an audience. She* wants *to go to court. She'll never take your meeting.* He's too busy admiring the framed gold and platinum records to notice.

I wonder if he's also been too busy to delve into the pages upon pages of case notes that detail Gigi's recent social media campaign, which has pivoted from a fashion-forward guide for all the best music festivals to social justice, particularly centered around women living with emotionally abusive partners. She has avoided mentioning Teddy by name, but she didn't have to. Every post about emotional hijacking, questioning one's self-worth, and how to recover after a relationship with a narcissist has nodded to her soon-to-be ex-husband. The few celebs who have come out in support of Teddy were quickly attacked by a tidal wave of commenters, ready to share their stories and shame those who defend "people like him". The viral hashtag #Glasslighting is also Gigi's handiwork, and its associated content has been particularly damning.

"You know she cropped me out of all of her pictures?" Teddy laments. "Every single one. It's like I never existed. God, I feel embarrassed telling you this. I'm a grown man. I sound like a fucking kid."

Maybe you're wondering in this scenario who I believe, how I could defend someone who potentially wrecked a young woman's sense of self and made her question her own reality. I've learned over time that it's not really about who I believe. The truth is a slippery thing. It shifts and warps and rearranges itself based on who's holding it. Someone could spend a lifetime fishing for it, getting swept up into a cycle in which they realize each catch is yet another of the infinite versions of it, each distinctly different from the last, and yet all shockingly real.

No, I'm not in the business of arguing what's true or who's right. I'm only defending, under the law, what's fair. Based on the facts of the case so far, it only seems fair that we try to salvage what's left of Teddy's life, however much of it remains.

Teddy drags a hand over his face, as if on cue. "I need a drink. You guys want a drink?"

Let the record show it's ten o'clock in the morning. This doesn't stop my counterpart from saying, "You read my mind."

Teddy leads us out of the office, wandering through the maze of wood-paneled hallways that connect recording spaces to control rooms, supply closets to mechanical storage, until we end up in a kitchen with pea green cabinets, cluttered formica countertops, and floral wallpaper that's so outdated it could almost be considered cool. He pulls a bottle of whiskey out of the nearest cabinet and rummages around until he produces two rocks glasses. He plops them on the counter with a clink.

"It's important that we stay focused on what you really want out of all this," I remind him. "The studio. The house. Farkas."

"I mean yeah, of course, the studio. The house is whatever. I don't care about the house. *This* place is home. I've been here since I was seventeen. John Qualls left it to me when he died. You know I was behind the board when The Dead Canaries recorded *Beyond Buffalo*?"

"No shit," Quentin muses. "What was that? Ninety one?"

"Eighty nine," Teddy grins. "This place? I don't know myself without this place. And Farkas. Geej always hated Farkas anyway, unless she was taking pictures with him for her Insta thing. Farkas doesn't give two shits about the Insta thing."

Quentin glances between us as Teddy pours them each three fingers of whiskey, no ice.

"Farkas?" he asks.

I nod to where the scraggy, half-naked, salt-and-pepper cat with giant yellow eyes is watching us from the edge of the counter. He looks more like an unkempt goblin than a housepet. Like Teddy, Farkas has practically lived his whole life here at Avid. I assume he must know how to walk, but each time I've been here he seems to pop up in random places, sitting perfectly still, eyeing me like he's plotting my death. I'm convinced he may know how to teleport. Because of all this, I've kept a respectful distance. Quentin, apparently, has no such self-preservation instincts.

"Hey, Farkas," he says, scratching the top of the goblin's head. Farkas curls his lip, revealing one long canine tooth. I'm sure this means he's about to take Quentin's hand off, but instead, he makes a noise that vaguely resembles a purr.

Teddy laughs. "Dude. He *likes* you."

"I've got a way with animals."

I refrain from rolling my eyes. Of course I'm working with the fucking cat whisperer. At least Teddy seems enthused about it.

"Dude. So did the drummer from EZ Rocks," he says. "When they recorded here a few years back, their drummer was obsessed with Farkas, kept trying to make me an offer on him. Cats like him have some sort of genetic mutation that gives them that chupacabra look, and apparently they're kind of rare, ya know? Anyway they pack up their tour bus, get ready to pull out, and me and my crew are like, 'Hold up, where's the cat?' We run out to the parking lot and find the EZ Rocks bus already pulling onto the street, but then all the sudden it stops, the door opens, and Fred Hare is holding Farkas."

"Oh shit," Quentin laughs.

"Right? Thankfully after a minute they let him go, this guy comes running towards me, and all fucking Fred can do is wink at me. Farkas came back with an EZ Rocks keychain on his collar. It was wild, dude. Worst practical joke ever. I thought he was gone!"

"That's crazy as hell," Quentin chortles appreciatively. "Scout's honor, I won't try to kidnap your cat."

"Good," Teddy says, pointing at him around the grip of his rocks glass. "We can still get along."

"I hope we'll all still be getting along after the next few weeks," I offer, attempting to draw them back to the real reason we're here. "Given that Gigi's attorneys have made it clear they don't intend to settle, we're entering the discovery phase of the trial."

"What does that mean, discovery?" Teddy asks.

"It means we're now in the process of substantiating the claims we outlined in our countersuit. This is all pretty standard stuff, but I want you to know what to expect. We'll have our financial team in here over the next couple of weeks to review your business assets, but we expect her lawyers to bring in their own experts as well. We've also begun preparing our interrogatories – those are the written questions that have to be answered under oath – based on our previous conversations and the information you've provided thus far. After that, we'll move into depositions."

"Hold on, I don't want a bunch of people running in and out of here. This is a place of business." (Teddy says, as he enjoys a glass of whiskey for breakfast.)

"We'll do our best to keep the disruptions to a minimum," I assure him.

As I'm saying this, an older woman wearing a dark tank top and skinny jeans wanders into the kitchen. She's short and stocky, with a sleeve of faded tattoos on one arm and a wild mess of curls sprigging out in every direction.

"What's with the suits?" she asks, as if we aren't standing here.

"Stuff with Gigi," Teddy says. "Guys, this is Zelda. She's my left-hand man. She'll help you with the financial stuff. Documents. Whatever you need."

She raises an expertly penciled eyebrow at him before opening the fridge.

"Will I?" she says, her voice husky and unamused. "At what point do I get to tell them how glad I am that I never have to see that little two-timing twat running around here with her smartphone tripod, posing in my recording booth, ever again?"

Teddy takes a swig of whiskey, sucking his teeth.

"I think you just did," he retorts. His response gives me the impression that he's heard this spiel a time or two.

I give her an even smile. "Not a fan?"

Zelda retrieves a yogurt cup from the fridge. "Of the girl whose musical opinion cites Tommy Gun Taylor as the greatest rap artist of our time? Not quite."

"C'mon, Zel," Teddy says. "She's young."

"Too young for you."

"Don't give me that. She's an old soul."

"That's just something she tells people because she hates that she missed an opportunity to be photographed in a crochet bikini at the first Woodstock."

Zelda turns to us now, giving us another once over, the way a mother does when she realizes her kids have brought home a puppy that's probably going to piss all over the place but is inevitably going to stay. She's a bit softer, regardless.

"Anyway, yeah," she says. "I can help. Just let me know what you need."

"I'd love for us to set up a time to discuss a few things about the studio," I tell her. "Or if you've got some time now?"

"Now's good," she nods.

I begin to follow, but not before remembering I need to deal with Teddy. Then, I see Quentin standing there, rocks glass in hand. He seems to be waiting for this very moment, anticipating the questioning raise of my eyebrows. He gives me a quick, affirmative nod that agrees that we can divide and conquer.

The realization hits me unexpectedly: I'm grateful to have him here. Someone to help me wrangle Teddy. Someone who's on my team, sans air quotes. Someone who seemingly understands the innate value of nonverbal communication. Maybe I underestimated how much of an asset he could be, in the grand scheme of things.

Zelda sweeps by and snags the rocks glass out of Teddy's hand on her way past.

"And it's too early for you to be drinking," she tells him.

She tips the glass to her mouth on her way out the door.

***

"So," Quentin says as we step out into the heat of early afternoon. "When were you going to tell me that you were using me?"

I blink at him in confusion. "What?"

"That night at the restaurant. Maestoso." As he continues to talk, my stomach begins to sink. "Because I thought you were just there for a casual happy hour, but Teddy seemed to think you were there meeting *me*."

I meet his amused expression with a defiant stare. His dark blue eyes bear into mine, as if this is a middle school contest. I've never backed down from a challenge before, and I don't stop now.

"So?" I say, matching his intensity.

"So," he smirks. "You got caught spying on your client. And I saved your ass."

I narrow my gaze. "Do you always start drinking before noon, or was this a special occasion?"

"I was being sociable. Breaking the ice. And you'd be surprised how long you can walk around with a drink before anyone realizes you aren't actually drinking it. The point is to make them feel like they're not drinking alone."

"How magnanimous of you."

"You were using me," he continues. "And that was a shameless red herring. Admit it."

He's right, of course. I just don't want him to be right. Not about the drink or the dancing or my failed attempt at a logical fallacy.

"You were using me first," I say. "And, moreover, you didn't even attempt to refute his idea that we've got a clandestine office romance going on. So you're clearly guiltier than I am."

Nothing about this defense would hold up in court. It's so childish, in fact, that I actually wince, an action that leaves me losing whatever ridiculous staring contest we were waging.

Quentin leans against the side of his car, entirely too smug. "Moreover?"

"Objection, your honor. The defendant is non-responsive."

"Yes, there were some ulterior motives," he says now. "But I, at least, was up front about it. Never at any point did you say, 'Thanks so much for sweeping me off my feet and helping me fool my client'."

I throw my purse into the passenger seat, slamming the door for emphasis.

"You did *not* sweep me off my feet."

"I still didn't hear a 'thank you' in there."

"Hey asshole," I say, more forcefully than I intend. "Thanks for showing up when I needed you."

This comes out all wrong. I mean it to sound sarcastic. Instead, it lands like some sort of inconvenient truth.

Quentin's playful smile falters for a moment, and in that breath his eyes are dancing across my face in a way that makes my stomach flip. I slide my sunglasses on, hoping he can't see it, whatever *it* is. A moment of weakness. A moment of desperation. Another instance in which I'm potentially falling victim to horngry-ness.

The moment passes.

He recovers his crooked smile and gives me a resolute nod, climbing into his car.

"Anytime, PBG. Anytime."

6.

THE FOLLOWER COUNT on my social media accounts is climbing at an alarming rate, the same way the heat index does as the South slips further into June. It's impossible to ignore. Those little red notification dots greet me every time I pick up my phone, to the point that I eventually remove the apps from my homescreen, but not before I spend way too much time scrolling through posts that give me the growing feeling that I don't know myself. Or at least, that I don't know the Heidi Krupp that the internet now associates with that sing-songy tagline.

The best part of breaking up is calling Heidi Krupp.

I feel like a reality TV villain, the kind of girl who will never "have it all" and is portrayed by some as the bitter, fairy-tale witch who prefers to curse those who do.

Meanwhile, others compare me to that best friend who helps you nurse a broken heart, the no-nonsense one who sticks with you at your lowest point, simultaneously feeding you tequila and ice cream while she dyes your hair a sassy shade of pink, helps you secure a great new apartment, and books movers.

The one who shows you all the ways in which you're going to be okay.

I prefer that second version, but even she is hard to recognize. It's as if my online persona has taken on a life of her own, and I'm left lying in bed, scrolling through my phone, simultaneously wishing I could be that cool and also wishing that I was nothing like her at all.

I wasn't always like this.

I think once, like most people, I believed I could pull off the hat trick. I was so sure I could have the place that feels like home, the well-paying career, *and* the guy who makes you laugh and pushes you to be better and somehow just *gets* you, all at the same time. Then life happened. Or rather, my parents' divorce happened. I realized then what so many of us do eventually: that sometimes "having it all" means knowing that nobody has the power to take any of it away from you. Even if, sure, sometimes that also means you don't have a special someone to share it with.

In the cool quiet of my luxurious bed, in my comfortably classy apartment, with a designer purse of case notes by the coffee table, I feel like my seven-year-old self would be proud to know where we ended up. I'm the divorce attorney I wish my parents had had, the one who doesn't hang on billable hours and win records and doing whatever dirty, underhanded things it takes. The one who never, *ever*, puts kids on the stand or uses them as bargaining chips. The one who's always pushing for compromise, for what's right, regardless if it's a pain in my ass. My thirty-two-year-old self, though? I'm not sure how she feels.

The backlight of my phone washes over me as my finger swipes up.

Practicality meets poise. We need more boss babes like Heidi Krupp!

I can't believe a woman would represent scum like that. #Glasslighting

Why is everyone hating on her? If you don't want a divorce don't get one. The rest of us deserve to know our options.

What a shark. Smells blood and swoops in. It's all about the $$$.

Why can the world never handle a strong woman? I'm team Heidi all the way!

This bitch needs to get laid.

Do your marriage a favor and get yourself Krupp 'nup. That's a prenuptial agreement for those who don't know. This girl had our backs, not because she expected our marriage to fail but because she never wants anyone to stay together just because they're scared of the fallout. We're not together because it's too inconvenient to get out of it. We're together because we CHOOSE it everyday. And you know what? She sent us a great wedding gift. So much respect for HK. The best way to avoid disaster is to have a PLAN and hope you never have to use it.

Divorce is eroding the fabric of our country. People used to marry for life! It's a shame you can make a career out of broken homes.

I always lonely until this guru told me how to meet the man of my dreams. I did not believe but now I share the good news! Let me tell you how!

I scroll until my outdated contact lenses feel like sandpaper and my right shoulder aches from the awkward positioning. I think about posting an indignant manifesto. I think about going to work trolling all the trolls. I think about deleting myself from the realm of social media altogether. In the end, I attempt to carry on with my week like usual while the comments swarm in the back of my brain like displaced bees.

Saw your article, my dad texts obliviously. *I know who I'm calling for my next divorce!*

He includes a laughing emoji like the statement is both a compliment and a clever joke. It honestly feels like neither. With my dad, though, you really never know. He has a particularly volatile relationship with my stepmom Amy, but I doubt they'll ever get divorced. And if they do? God help whoever negotiates that one. I wouldn't touch it with a ten foot pole. They should be required to wear those t-shirts like firefighters do: keep back 200 feet.

My dad married Amy only a couple of years after my mom moved me to the suburbs with Eric, and they had two kids, the same as my mom and Eric, as if the whole thing was a continuation of the tit-for-tat argument they started when I was four. Everything was a competition with them.

Who's going to pay for Heidi's braces? (Let's both refuse in an attempt to harass the other into doing it.)

Who's going to help Heidi afford college? (I've got kids in middle school. Can't your dad/mom do it? He/she really hasn't contributed enough.)

Who's going to invite Heidi to Thanksgiving? (Both of us. At the same time. So she ends up hanging alone in an attempt to avoid having to choose.)

Actually, that's not really true. I'm not alone. In recent years Auntie Lena and I usually spend holidays at Meg's house, where she cooks enough delicious food for thirty people, even though there are only about fifteen of us there to celebrate. Our little hodgepodge group gathers to drink too much wine and play board games, and it's way better than hanging out at either of my parents' houses. Eventually they stopped inviting me, except for the occasional passive aggressive mention of their meals with the guilt-ridden "but I'm sure you have plans" tacked onto the end.

But I digress.

The point is that, despite my lack of in-person commentary, Jeanine did a great job with the article. Great enough that the presence of it is now looming in every corner of my life. So basically, it was too great. Way too great. And I'm having a hard time living up to it. Especially when family members are texting me about it, and friends are mentioning it enthusiastically when I run into them, and occasionally when I'm walking through the office I swear I can hear the faint sound of someone humming that familiar tune…

"You're not paying attention," Kamille says, wading into the shallow end of my building's rooftop pool. "What if I drown?"

"We are working on the basics of water safety," I remind her. "You're knowledgeable. You're capable. And I'm right here. You won't drown."

She scrunches up her face. "Do you know CPR?"

"My certification has lapsed, but yes, I mostly know CPR."

"That's not very convincing."

"Let's just focus on what we learned last time."

The days have been mercilessly hot lately, and the water is on the refreshing side of lukewarm. Not so cold that it takes your breath when you jump in, but not so hot that you wonder why you got in at all. Aside from a couple of college girls chatting under the umbrella at one of the patio tables, we've got the place to ourselves. This time of year, we're also lucky enough to have about two more hours of daylight. I adjust my longline bikini top and take my position in the middle of the shallow end, holding a small foam board.

"You ready?"

"Ready," she says, securing her goggles.

Realistically, I know she doesn't need goggles for the exercises we're doing, but it makes her feel better to have them on, so I don't see the harm. She places a hand on either side of the board and sucks in a deep breath, which she holds, though her face never goes into the water. Then, she kicks. The smooth plane of blue around us begins to slosh wildly with her movements. After about thirty seconds, we take a quick break and begin again. And again. I move slowly, guiding her across and back with the board.

Our training continues for the better part of fifteen minutes when I hear a familiar voice at the edge of the pool.

"She's not breathing."

I turn to find Quentin perched on the side of the deep end, shirtless, with his hands braced beside him and his calves swishing through the water. For a second, his presence seems like a glitch in the Matrix. My entire brain stutters, leaving me blinking idiotically before finally registering him: Quentin, the coworker, not the cocktail savant. They're like Siamese twins my mind has to surgically separate.

"Excuse me?" I say indignantly.

"She's holding her breath while she kicks. The key to swimming is breathing, believe it or not."

"What are you doing here?" I question.

This is useless, of course. He lives here. This was bound to happen sooner or later. Apparently sooner won out.

Kamille stops splashing and removes her goggles, leaving faint suction-cup imprints around her eyes. They're now shifting between me and Quentin curiously.

"Do you know him?" she asks me.

"We work together," I reply.

"That's Quentin?" she says. I can tell she's trying to whisper, but her voice carries easily across the water.

At the mention of his name, Quentin smirks, flashing those obnoxiously handsome dimples. I notice his dark blue trunks match his eyes.

"She's been talking about me?"

"Yeah," Kamille says, addressing him now. "She said you were a liar who was being mean to her on purpose, but not because you like her, because you want her job."

My eyes slowly roll to the cloudless early evening sky above us, as if I'm praying for deliverance from the heavens. I can't even chastise her. I mean, she's not wrong. The part of me that's not borderline embarrassed is fighting a proud smile.

"Wow," he says, his gaze shifting back to me. "That's... quite the glowing review."

"Is there something you want?" I ask him.

"Just here to swim," he says innocently. "There's no point having a building with a pool if I'm not going to use it. Especially when it's a hundred degrees and humid."

In an instant, he has slipped off the edge and dipped beneath the surface of the water. He comes back up wet and glistening, slinging his hair back like a supermodel. My suspicions that first day were entirely correct: he does look *really* good shirtless.

I drag my attention back to the foam board, willing myself to forget he exists. The girls under the umbrella definitely haven't forgotten, though. They're eyeing him when he emerges, smiling as they peel out of their Memphis College of Nursing tank tops and giving him coy little waves. I'm sure any moment now he'll saunter over and begin to seduce one of them. Or both of them. It's not like his go-to party trick is that difficult in this situation. These are basically the poster girls for a koozie-clad White Claw and gratuitous shots of cinnamon whiskey.

"What did you mean about breathing?" Kamille asks him, oblivious. "You can't breathe when you're underwater. I thought the whole point was to hold your breath."

He turns to us, treading water easily. "We have to breathe to survive. Knowing when and how to breathe in the water is what keeps you safe."

I can tell the gears in Kamille's mind are turning, inspecting this tidbit of information from every angle and holding it up against what she already knows.

I'll be honest, what he's saying makes sense. I haven't focused at all on breathing. We've been working solely on the mechanics: kicking, floating, how to move your arms and legs together. Kamille is strong enough to be a swimmer, but she's not confident enough yet.

"Can you teach me how?" she calls over to him.

"Maybe," he says.

For a moment, I think he's trying to dodge her question, which infuriates me, not in the least because he's the one who struck up a conversation. I'm ready to tell him to stop wasting our time and go flirt with the nursing students, but then I catch the spark of a question in his eyes. It takes me a full beat to realize he's asking my permission.

I stifle a sigh as I give him a tiny nod of approval.

"We can do it, but we'll have to be quick. How long do we have, Heidi? Three and a half minutes?"

"Please don't make this weirder than it has to be," I mutter.

He swims over until he's standing with us in the shallow end, scantily-clad college girls quickly forgotten. Rivulets of water stream down his chest, following the trail of dark hair that draws a tantalizing line down his toned stomach, below his belly button, into the top of his shorts. He's fit in a way that looks effortless. Is it possible for abs to look so approachable?

I drag my gaze up. I suppose it's a credit to find he's not checking me out. Although, I'm currently wearing sunscreen-smudged makeup with my hair in a lopsided knot and a top that more closely resembles an unremarkable sports bra than beachwear, so there's really not much about me to check out. Not that I want him to be checking me out.

"All right," he says. "First, you have to trust yourself. Not me. Not anyone else. Just you. You have to know that you can do this."

Kamille nods once, determined. "Okay."

"Okay," he says. He instructs her to hold the side of the pool, take a deep breath, then dip her face into the water and blow bubbles out through her nose and mouth.

"I need my goggles," she protests.

"You don't," he insists. "There's nothing to see. And you can go as slow as you want. It's your breath. Trust yourself."

She looks at him for a moment like I think she might tell

him off. I almost want her to. Then, she gulps in a giant breath, squeezes her eyes closed, and splashes her face into the water. She comes back up a few seconds later, gasping, but to my surprise she goes down again. The bubbles confirm she's exhaling, exactly like he instructed. She works on this for a few rounds, slow and determined.

"Like that?" she sputters.

"Exactly like that," he nods. "Now, instead of pulling your face up and out of the water to take the next breath, keep your head down and just turn your face to the side. Take a full breath, then turn your face back down and blow out before going to the other side."

This time there are no protests. She does as he says, falling into a rhythm much more quickly than I expect. Deep breath, swivel to submerge, second side, swivel to submerge. The cadence of it continues for what feels like a full minute. She straightens up, wiping her face.

"That's it," he smiles. "You've got it. Now you just have to practice. The more you do it, the easier it'll be."

"Okay," she says, wiping the water out of her eyes, "but that's not swimming. I'm not going anywhere."

"Once you know how to breathe, you can hold the board and practice this while you kick. Eventually, you can keep adding on, until you're like a dolphin."

"A dolphin? Like, balancing a ball on my nose?"

He gives me a look like she's been spending way too much time around me.

"Like swimming, without gills," he offers.

"Okay," she says. "But how?"

"You've got a good teacher. She knows what she's doing. She can help you."

I am filled with appreciation for a moment that Quentin has not entirely negated my presence here. It reinforces the idea that

we're on the same team – a successful team. And it feels…
surprisingly good.

I give him a grateful, albeit begrudging, close-lipped smile.
Over the top of Kamille's head, he returns it with a wink. A
fluttery feeling spreads through my ribcage before I can stop it.

The partners will refrain from shirtless winking. Definitely
something I should have put in the agreement.

When Kamille glances over, I quickly collect myself. I wade
from where I've been lingering a few feet away, armed with
encouragement.

"He's right," I tell her. "You know how to do this. All we have
to do is keep working on it, and I'm here with you every step of
the way."

She gathers her mouth up into one corner, puckering it in
thought.

"Did you used to be a lifeguard?" she asks Quentin
suspiciously.

"No, but I did a lot of white-water rafting. And it's important
to be up on your water safety for stuff like that."

"That sounds cool," she says.

"It was cool," he nods. "What about you? Planning to do any
white water rafting?"

She shrugs, acting way too nonchalant. "Water slides. At
music camp."

"Awesome," he smiles. "Water slides are my favorite. What
instrument do you play?"

"The violin," she says. "I want to play in an orchestra one day.
Maybe."

"That's great," he nods. "It's important to have goals.
Especially ones you care about."

She accepts this with satisfaction, cocking her head to the
side like a curious puppy.

"You know, you don't really seem like a jerk," she says.

"Kamille," I warn softly.

Quentin laughs. "Thanks. I appreciate that."

He wades towards the stairs now, shaking his head like a wet dog as he climbs out.

"Wait, where are you going?" she asks.

"I think my time's up."

I know he's referring to the agreement. I'm simultaneously impressed and disappointed that he's holding himself to it.

"We're going for pizza after this," she says. "If you want to come."

This kid will be the death of me, I think.

To his credit, he replies before I have a need to launch a formal protest.

"Unfortunately I can't do dinner."

Again, part of me is pleased. But there's that annoying little sliver that agrees that his inability to join us for pizza *is* unfortunate.

Siamese Quentins, I remind myself. *Surgical separation.*

As soon as this case is over, we're parting ways, in all likelihood not on the best terms. Nothing good would come from having pizza with him. Especially getting Kamille involved? She deserves better. *We* deserve better. That's why my more rational self drafted that agreement to begin with. For moments like this. Guardrails.

When Kamille gives me an imploring look, I shake my head.

"It's about time for us to pack up, anyway," I tell her. "Go get changed?"

She climbs out in search of her towel and bag without argument. Before she heads towards the changing rooms, she tosses Quentin one final piece of advice by way of goodbye.

"Home Slice has the best pizza. And we always go on Wednesdays. In case you were wondering."

"Good to know," he smiles. "Thanks."

When she skips off, I wade toward the stairs.

"You were surprisingly decent at that," I say.

"Was that a compliment?" he smirks. "Because I seem to recall that those are expressly prohibited."

"Just an observation."

He nods, accepting this. "Water safety is admittedly one of my more useful skills."

"More useful than sliding into my real-life DMs with a well-chosen drink?"

"Debatable," he says.

His grin sends that fluttery feeling spreading through me again. I guess some people call that butterflies. I call it a major inconvenience. He's beginning the process of toweling off when I climb the stairs.

"You should stay," I offer. "We're heading out anyway."

Now that I'm standing here, dripping wet, I realize he's definitely checking me out. After a beat, he realizes it too. Suddenly he's studying clouds on the horizon like they're going to reveal the solution to world hunger.

"I didn't mean to run you off," he says.

"Please do not fool yourself into thinking you have that power," I laugh. "I've gotta get her home soon."

"She's sharp," he says. "Your kid?"

I have to walk right past him to retrieve my towel. There's no way around it. I do my best to do it at a normal pace, though the concrete is scorching my feet.

"I'm not her mom, if that's what you're asking. But yeah, a few days a week she's my kid."

"That sounds... surprisingly complicated."

"Not quite. It's a youth mentorship program. Pretty straightforward."

"Ah. Right. I guess I should've known, since you don't do 'complicated'," he says, using finger quotes for emphasis. "Tell me, Heidi. Do all of your relationships come with contracts?"

Most days, I might wear this teasing accusation like a badge of pride, but it stings when he says it, like trying to adjust an honorary pin and getting pricked, right over the heart. I've never thought of Kamille in those terms.

"Only the good ones," I retort. I turn my back to him so he can't see whatever my face might be trying to give away. I attempt to gather myself along with my belongings. "By the way, ogling my ass? Not exactly professional."

He chokes out a laugh, running a hand up the back of his hair self-consciously. It somehow makes him look even sexier and beachier, and it annoys the fuck out of me.

"I wasn't... ogling. I was observing. Accidentally."

I sling my bag over my shoulder and strut past him. There's enough room that we don't have to make contact, but I pass close enough that our shoulders touch. In one strategic movement, I shift my weight into him. I don't care if it's juvenile; the moment he begins to fall, I feel delightfully avenged. In a slow-motion, arms-flailing instant, Quentin gracelessly crashes into the water.

The wake from his near-belly flop splashes up over the sides of the pool, soaking the concrete with a satisfying sizzle. He resurfaces with a sputtering gasp.

"What the hell was that?" he asks, swiping water from his bewildered expression.

I give him the world's smirkiest shrug – (shirk?) – and head for the changing room.

"Sorry," I call over my shoulder. "Accident."

7.

"I THINK HE LIKES YOU," Kamille says around a mouthful of bacon-pineapple pizza.

I squeeze lemon slices into my water until they're nothing but spent, yellow husks and discard them on the tiny corner of unused space on our sticky table. I rattle the stevia packet against my palm before tearing it open.

This is why I stopped dating.

Not *this* in particular – sitting at a booth by the window in a little garlic-scented cafe downtown – but this feeling. I'm not sure how to describe it. Inconvenience, maybe? Or possibly encroachment. Something that's infiltrating every aspect of my life.

My last serious boyfriend, Callum, would tell you I'm an emotionally unavailable control freak who's only happy when I'm convincing people that my truth is the whole truth, and nothing but. The truth is that Callum and I were good for almost two years.

We met at a charity fundraiser, during one of those ill-advised relay races where each team member has to periodically stop and chug a red solo cup full of lukewarm beer. We were paired against each other, and in our mutual determination to make it to our next assigned station, we ran smack into each other. Like, hard. Callum was briefly knocked unconscious. He woke up lying flat in the grass with me cradling his head between my knees, and he promptly gave me a grin and mumbled a ridiculous line about how he hadn't realized I was such a knockout. It was one of our favorite stories. He got knocked out, and I fell.

Albeit, my falling happened much more slowly than his being temporarily relieved of consciousness. But still. Over the next few weeks, our lives started to overlap, until we were a venn diagram that had more things in the middle than not. We both worked long hours, both had our favorite date-night restaurants, both enjoyed the same binge-worthy reality TV shows. He was one of the cofounders of a start-up micro-brewery (the one that had supplied the booze for the charity event where we collided), and he would drop by my place smelling of hops and enthusiastically pouring me "test beers" while I caught up on case notes. We had fallen into a comfortable routine. He stayed over three nights a week, joined my running group, even talked with Meg about the possibility of pairing some of their most popular brews with complementary baked goods. They were brainstorming pairings for the holidays. We were planning to visit his parents for Christmas in North Carolina. Things were good.

Then I found the little velvet box hiding in the top drawer of my dresser.

It was his drawer, technically, the one designated for those of his clothes that had made their way to my place. I was adding a clean t-shirt that had gotten mixed in with my laundry when I saw it. I flipped it open without hesitation, and a large diamond ring stared up at me. I wasn't sure what else I thought would be inside, but I was hopeful that I was wrong.

I wasn't.

It was a serious diamond, the kind that could really do some damage if you were wearing it when you happened to punch someone in the face. Do most women think about punching people in the face when they discover their significant other is planning an engagement?

Probably not.

I sank onto the end of the bed, staring at it for a few shapeless minutes until I heard his keys in the door. He called out hello, and I could hear him going through his usual routine: dropping his things on the coffee table, opening the fridge to deposit a six-pack of beer, pulling a pint glass out of the freezer. I made my way to the kitchen with the numb movements of someone in shock.

"What's this?" I asked, sliding the ring box across the bar that separates the living room from the kitchen.

It might as well have been some other woman's underwear, given the amount of accusation in my tone. His eyes went wide with surprise, then anguish, before melting into a sheepish laugh.

"Um," he stammered, readjusting his glasses. "Fuck. Okay. I guess I should've picked a better hiding place?"

I swallowed past the way my mouth felt all dry and clumsy, like I'd just been to the dentist.

"Are you trying to *marry* me?" I asked.

He laughed, pink-cheeked and apologetic.

"I mean, obviously."

"No," I said. It came out automatically, and the force of it seemed to leave him without air.

"... no?"

"We talked about this."

"Okay, this isn't how I wanted it to go," he said in an

apologetic rush. "We were going to discuss it. At Avion. Because I know how much you love the elk tenderloin."

"This has nothing to do with elk tenderloin."

"There was going to be ambiance," he continued in exasperation. "It was going to go... well, not like this."

I stared at him, wondering how he thought ambiance would change my mind. Did he know me at all? I studied his features as if the landscape of his face was foreign to me. His brows knit together in the middle as he sighed.

"Let me try to be clearer," I offered, as calmly as possible. "This wasn't – isn't – part of our plan."

He blinked at me long enough to realize I was serious.

"Is this about the stuff we agreed on? *Two* years ago?"

"Um, yes."

What else would it have been about? People make agreements for a reason. So that they continue to agree.

To be fair, there wasn't anything in the document about marriage specifically. However, it did state that the outlined terms of our relationship were not to be reconsidered for a period of five years. I felt like that made it clear that a surprise proposal was completely off the table.

At the time we first reviewed everything together, Callum had read it and laughed. *"Five years? You've got a lot of faith in us, huh?"* He thought it was romantic, an indication that I thought whatever was between us was enduring. Two years later, though, his gaze dropped to the place where he had braced his palms against the marble countertop. He let out a bitter laugh.

"Wow," he muttered.

In the deafening silence that stretched between us, he picked up the ring box and slid it into his pocket, before beginning the choreography of someone gathering their things to leave. He found his wallet. He located his keys. They jingled with a loud, ominous sense of urgency as he wandered around, as if retracing his steps would help him remember what exactly he was looking for.

"So, what? That's it?" I demanded. "You're *leaving*?"

He held up a hand. "I really can't do this right now, Heidi."

I remember the way the heat crept up my neck, lapping at my face like uncontrolled flames. I imagined any moment my skin might peel away like scorched wallpaper.

"*You* can't do this? *You* decided to break all the rules and now you're upset about it? What did you think was going to happen?"

"I thought you were going to say yes!" he yelled.

I followed him into the bedroom, where he was collecting his socks, underwear, and gym shorts into a canvas grocery bag.

"Why on earth would you think that?" I demanded.

"Because I'm fucking moron, I guess."

"We talked about this in the beginning, Cal. We literally put it all down in black and white. I never led you on."

"No, but you never let me in, either," he spat. "I really thought things had changed, Heidi."

"So you're just leaving?" I demanded. "Because you're mad I didn't change?"

"I'm leaving because you're breaking my fucking heart, and you don't even care," he said, stalking through the living room to locate his shoes. "Do you have any idea how much I've changed for you? We eat at *your* restaurants. We hang with *your* friends. We watch *your* stupid fucking TV shows. *Everything* is about you. And the saddest part is that I loved everything being about you, but only when I felt like you loved me, too."

My eyes were brimming with tears. Hot, angry tears. I was trembling, as if the anger was coursing through me, aching to break out.

"I thought we were on the same page!" I screeched.

"Yours is the only page!"

He seemed to realize that we were yelling and took a deep

breath, the kind that filled him up and left him looking totally deflated on the exhale, as if all the fight had drained out of him. I remember the way his shoulders slumped and how he couldn't stop looking at the floor.

No, we could salvage this.

"Callum..." I began.

I opened my mouth, but somehow didn't say anything else. I really didn't know what more there was to say. There was no way I was going to marry him. My thoughts were racing – forwards and backwards – trying to map exactly how we got here, and exactly where we were headed, to find the combination that would bring us to a comfortably-ever-after. The lines crossed and tangled into a million possibilities, and I was left stranded between them, unsure of which thread would be the one to keep us from unraveling.

"I won't call you," he said, with some finality. "That's what it says, right? What we agreed? A clean break?"

Tears rolled down my face and dripped off my chin as I stood stone still, staring him down. So that was it, then. The ultimatum I hadn't seen coming. And no matter how much I cared about him – and I really *did* care about him – I couldn't bend so we wouldn't break.

"Yeah," I rasped, my throat tight and burning. I licked my lips and could taste the salt on them. "Clean break."

And then he left. And true to his word, he didn't call.

He removed me from his social media, as we had agreed. I didn't show up at his brewery. He didn't show up at the dive bar on the corner for my running group's post-jog pints. There were no late-night texts to say "I miss you", no flimsy guise of returning possessions we ran across, no aftershocks of breakup sex, with each wave less significant than the last. We split with surgical precision, but it wasn't entirely clean. I found myself crying over the grapefruit IPA he left in my fridge, and angrily sobbing over the stubbly beard hair he left on my bar of soap. I always hated when he used my soap. And now I hated him for ruining everything. For being gone.

Sometimes I used to wonder what would have happened if I had just said yes. Maybe we could have had a long engagement. Like, the kind that's so long your friends start joking about how you're never really going to get married (are you?) and then eventually they stop bringing it up at all. Maybe I even could have gone along for a little while and talked him out of it later. Or maybe, in some sliver of a parallel universe, I would've come around eventually. Maybe one day I would have woken up and wanted nothing more than to be Callum's wife. But I didn't. When I followed these scenarios all the way through, they all ended the same way: me, married or almost-married, with that unsteady feeling in my gut like I had betrayed myself to the point that I would never trust myself again.

I didn't stop dating because of Callum. I dated after him, for close to six months, in a casual string of hookups and dinner dates, but it all felt disingenuous. Eventually, I knew all of them would want more than I was willing to give. And eventually, the whole endeavor lacked passion.

What's the point of anything if there's no beating-heart passion?

So yeah, I quit wasting my time and energy on lackluster guys and poured myself into the things that made me feel excited to wake up each morning. You can say I'm obsessed with my work, but at least it keeps my blood pumping. Everybody needs something like that.

Of course, I can't explain any of this to Kamille. Instead, I shake an excessive amount of chili pepper flakes onto my slice of pizza and take a hot, sweet-and-savory bite.

"We're doing our best to get along," I tell her. "It's what people do in polite society."

"I thought he was nice," she reasons.

"Well, we have an – um – agreement," I say, ignoring that lingering sting. "This case is really important to us."

"What do you like about your job? It's just about winning?"

"No." I smile through a pensive pause. "It's mostly about helping people. Fighting for them, when they need someone on their side. Standing up for what's fair. Those things matter."

She nods. "I want to help people, too. Do you think I could, like, play in an orchestra that helps people? My friend Tasha says she's going to cure cancer. I don't know that playing in an orchestra is as important as, ya know, curing cancer or anything."

"Well, fortunately the world needs music and medicine. It's all important," I tell her. "As long as you do it for the right reasons."

"What are the right reasons?"

"Because it.... sets your soul on fire," I shrug. "Because it lets you shine some light into the world. Makes everything feel a little brighter."

"Whoa," she says, slurping down soda from a giant plastic cup with wide-eyed intensity. "That was deep."

I laugh, tucking a lock of hair behind my ear self-consciously. "We all have our moments."

"So you think Quentin's the same as you? Like, that he wants to win the case because that's his way of making the world better?"

I have to admit that it's a possibility, one I hadn't fully considered up until this point, but Quentin's intentions still feel murky to me. Maybe, like so many people, he wants the prestige of partnership. Maybe he is chasing some sort of manifest destiny. Maybe he's simply fulfilling a future that was set up for him before he was born. The truth is, I don't need to know. The less I know about Quentin's personal motivations, the better. They won't change the fact that I want to be the one standing in his way.

"Could be," I say.

"You didn't ask him?"

"No."

"Maybe you should," she says.

"Maybe I will," I offer. A half-truth, at best, but when Kamille smiles, I actually consider it.

We let the conversation settle into the silence of two people sharing a good meal. I glance out the window, where everything is bathed in the soft, luminous glow of the golden hour, and try to allow this feeling to fade like the sun, slowly, the way people stroll past and the trolley rattles down the middle of Main Street. It sticks with me anyway, like the warm doughy smell of the cafe, that lingers even after all our food is gone, leaving me with the vague sense of somehow wanting more.

8.

"YOU WERE SUPPOSED TO BRING A DATE."

I know the voice without turning around, so I don't bother with the effort.

"Good to see you, too, Henry," I say, giving my mentor an even smile as he joins me in line at the bar.

The outdoor venue is already a sea of sundresses and bright, summery polo shirts. Across the lake, the sky is the color of an orange creamsicle. I can't help thinking that an orange creamsicle would take about two point five seconds to melt on an evening like this. I hope it'll be cooler once the sun goes down.

Despite the heat, the week has ended with a sigh of palpable relief. I've never been one to worship the weekend – maybe that's a side effect of creating a barely-there delineation between my *work* life and *life* life – but I know as I stand here in a romper and strappy wedges that I'm grateful to be anywhere that isn't within a hundred yards of Quentin Maxwell.

All week I've had the feeling of looking over my shoulder, trying to carefully plot and stay three steps ahead. I have to admit plotting is exhausting. And possibly unnecessary. At one point this week, Quentin offered me his own notes on the Glass v. Russo case thus far. He got some surprising insight from Teddy that I hadn't to this point, as well as some thoughtful connections to a similar case recently tried in Nashville. He's clearly trying to hold up his end of the bargain, which is admirable, I suppose.

Either way, I don't trust him.

As I order a ranch water with a chili lime rim, I feel Henry's inquiring presence, still awaiting my response. He traded the suit he wore to the office and is now sporting khakis and boat shoes, as if we are about to set sail on a yacht rather than pile into canoes for the sake of publicity. It gives him the vibe of a good-natured father rather than a disappointed boss, but he is in fact disappointed.

In truth, we had discussed that I should bring someone. I always hated that word, 'should', but I know his intentions aren't entirely as misogynistic as they sound. Those canoes bobbing in the water along the edge of the boardwalk are intended for more than one person.

I was going to bring Meg, but she had a baking emergency. Someone hit an electrical pole, so her neighborhood experienced an unexpected power outage while she was at work, and the wedding cake she'd been working on all week melted. Like, actually melted. One side of it was drooping precariously, like it had suffered a stroke. She was in absolute damage-control mode when I left her place.

I offered to stay and help – though what help I could have offered, I'm not sure. Moral support. A power playlist. Emergency cocktails. Meg sent my well-meaning, culinary-challenged self away with the fully stocked picnic basket she had pre-made for this outing and the promise that she would be fine. Fortunately, the former contains food items that were intended to remain edible despite the heat.

"Don't they have any kayaks?" I ask. "I'm really more of a kayak kind of girl."

"The event is called Cocktails and *Canoes*," Henry says with disapproving amusement. "No kayaks."

"Well," I say over the rim of the drink I've just procured. "I've at least got the cocktail part covered. And there are plenty of people here. I'm sure they can find someone to stick me with. Speaking of which, this is a great turnout."

I scan the crowd in appreciation, not missing that Henry's wife, Carolyn – who is looking as demure as ever in linen pants and effortless pearls – is laughing with one of the city councilwomen we've been trying to win over like they're old pals. I try not to buy into the politics when I can help it, but I have to admit it's impressive. Henry and Carolyn Lewis have always been my favorite power couple: thoroughly individual and yet immaculately aligned, always seeming to be on the same page, working towards the same goals. A winning team.

I'm wondering if maybe I could convince Carolyn to join and help me paddle to victory, when I'm intercepted by yet another familiar voice, which settles uneasily around my shoulders.

"Ah, here she is. The woman of the hour!"

Henry and Erving Maxwell are already shaking hands.

I force a smile. "Here I am."

"I didn't expect to see you here, Erving," Henry says in a ribbing tone. "What's the occasion?"

"Just making a few connections," he smiles. "Isn't that what these events are for?"

I don't like the sound of this. I can tell from the brief sideways glance that Henry gives me that he doesn't either, because it can only mean one thing: Quentin is here. I know before I do another scan of the crowd that he is somewhere close by. I can sense it, the way the air before a storm feels full and ominous and electric.

"I saw the article," Erving says to me now. "It was well done.

How much is that kind of publicity costing us these days?"

Only my dignity, I think.

"Actually," I say, trying to match the teasing tone in his voice, "if you count dinner, they paid us."

"Free. Really."

"Entirely gratis," I smirk. "They wanted the story. I think it's worked out pretty well for them. And for us. You should know I tend to make it a habit of bringing in much more money than I spend."

He nods, but the way his mouth is pressed into a frown keeps him from saying anything more about it. Erving has never been my biggest fan, nor I his. He has always regarded the women in our office as little girls playing dress up as attorneys. Bernadette warned me my first week not to waste time trying to win him over. I've made plenty of strong connections without him, and I've always let my work speak for itself. It's never felt like a liability before now.

"Well, I hope your paddling skills are as formidable as your ability to charm journalists," Erving says with a twinkly-eyed smile. "Tonight comes with a surprise competition, of sorts."

"Oh, Mr. Maxwell," I say. "Don't tell me you're betting on races, again?"

Henry gives me a warning look. I take a smug sip of my drink. If I'm meant to be a mindless little girl, I can certainly play the part. I know from office gossip that Erving lost a small fortune on a derby horse last year, and I know he's still bitter about it. Anyway, if he thinks that the competition aspect of this event is a surprise, he's forgotten how long I've been coming to these things.

"What's the prize this year?" Henry asks without missing a beat.

It's the same as it always is, I assume. A chunk of prize money that you're intended to donate to charity. The winner gets to direct funds to their organization of choice and has their picture splashed all over social media. I've only won twice – once at ax-throwing, and another at an inflatable obstacle course – and both times I gladly handed over the funds to Girls Going Places. I'm still damn proud of those wins. And I know how much they could use the money. I'm considering how I'd love to add another when I realize I haven't been paying attention to the conversation.

"Heidi has a great track record," I hear Henry saying. "Perhaps you'd like to join her on this one, Erving? She's recruiting someone for tonight's winning team."

If I weren't wearing sunglasses, Henry could see how my eyes to turn slits. He has absolutely lost his mind if he thinks I'm getting into a canoe with this elderly Sith Lord. The man could break a hip! Or, perhaps more likely, pull a Tonya Harding and knock me out with the paddle to make way for Quentin to secure the promotion.

I'm about to protest when I see Quentin, and my brain does that stuttering thing it seems to every time I encounter him out in the wild. He's wearing a tailored button-down with his sleeves rolled up, fitted dark khakis, and a pair of leather flip flops. He looks annoyingly good. Smoothly confident. And surprisingly... alone.

"Quentin," Erving beams. "Perfect timing. We were just talking about how Heidi desperately needs a partner for the race."

My hackles rise at the use of the word *desperately*. Erving Maxwell would love to imagine I'm desperate.

"That's very kind of you, Mr. Maxwell," I offer. "But I'm actually planning to sit this one out. Give someone else a chance to win this year."

Henry gives me the look he always does when I pitch a flimsy defense or grasp for a poor attempt at precedent, the one that says he's going to give me a few moments to come to my own realization why this is simply not going to work. And, as always, I do.

I'm vying for partnership, and I'm going to show up at an event we're sponsoring and not participate? No. That's a surefire way to screw myself out of something I want. Events like this are a valuable part of the marketing strategy for the firm. They help us generate fresh leads and keep our name connected with the community. If I don't get this opportunity, I don't want to wonder in the back of my mind if it was because I didn't spend an hour of my Friday night cruising around the lake in a boat-built-for-two. Plus, I actually *want* to win this.

"Don't let her fool you," Henry interjects, bolstering me with a nervous laugh. "You're looking at the ax-throwing champion of twenty-twenty-two. She's got competition in her veins."

"Ax throwing. Really," Quentin says. His amused gaze dances over my face in a way that makes me very aware of the air against my skin.

I throw an invisible ax, straight at his chest. "Yup. It's those killer instincts."

"You'd be lucky to have him, Heidi," Erving presses on. "Did you know he spent a summer during college as a white water rafting instructor?"

"I may have heard something about that, yes," I offer tightly.

"Class five rapids," Erving boasts, as if he's the one who barreled down a raging river.

"A real thrill seeker, I take it?" Henry says, flashing Quentin a grin that's fully loaded.

I see an imperceptible twitch in Quentin's chiseled jaw. His smile doesn't reach his eyes. "Not for many years now. We all live and learn, right?"

"I certainly hope so," Henry chuckles. Quentin shifts.

Oh-kay, I think. There's a definite vibe. I don't know what this is, nor do I want to. Men swinging their swords around is the least of my concerns, especially when I have more important matters at hand – like figuring out how I'm going to get into a boat with anyone whose last name isn't Maxwell.

"Canoes sound like an insult to your obvious level of talent," I tell Quentin now. I give the group a smile. "Plus, we wouldn't want Quentin to abandon his date."

I know it's a low blow, but I need to point out that I'm not the only one who showed up without someone on my arm this evening.

"I can't say I've had much luck on the dating front since I moved back. The last girl I asked out told me she's not free until September," Quentin says. Henry and Erving laugh at what they believe is a self-deprecating joke. I narrow my eyes as Quentin meets my gaze. "If you need a partner, I'm at your service."

Erving claps a hand on each of our shoulders, giving an enthusiastic squeeze.

"I love a good show of solidarity," Erving grins, as if it's already settled. "That's what Freeman Maxwell Lewis is all about! I'll find Ramona now and put you both on the list. It'll be fun."

***

As we shuffle towards the dock, I am increasingly certain that this is an attempt by Erving to undermine me. He's never looked so jovial about anything. I just need to figure out which angle he's playing.

"You don't seem excited about this," Quentin observes.

"We agreed not to socialize outside of work."

"Are you trying to pretend that either of us is here for a reason besides work?"

"I'm going to pretend that you didn't just attempt to loophole your way into getting in this boat with me."

"Look, you want to win. I want to spend at least half an hour of this evening not making smalltalk with my grandfather's many, many professional contacts. Do you know how many times you can repeat facts about yourself before they start to sound fake?" He makes a face, imitating his grandfather's boastful tone. "*Class five rapids.*"

I give him an unsympathetic shrug. "What's your point?"

"My point is we could use each other."

Use each other.

His choice of words buzzes under my skin in an annoying way. I adjust my simple necklace, my hair, the lime garnish on the rim of my drink. I survey the choice of canoes.

"I'll have you know I'm here to win. If you get in this boat, I expect a genuine effort at winning. And if you do happen to stay out of my way long enough for us to secure said win, I expect you to let me choose what we do with the prize money."

"I love it when you're bossy," he says. "Do you also need me to sign my life away or can you take my word for it?"

I refuse to return his smirk.

"Just get in the damn boat," I mutter.

He motions down the boardwalk. "After you."

We choose a bright, mint blue canoe close to the end of the dock. I settle into the front, and the little boat bobs precariously for a moment as Quentin positions himself behind me. We push off and cut a line through the gently rippling water. After a few sloshing strokes, I realize we're veering towards the bank. I sink my paddle more deeply into the water.

"What are you doing?" I call over my shoulder.

"What are *you* doing?" he counters.

Our trajectory is haphazard, and I'm worried we're going to crash into another boat. Eventually, the couple in our path gets the hang of it and sails away. We do not. I watch in frustration as other boats cruise easily across the lake.

"You're supposed to be good at this," I hiss.

"You're supposed to be trying to win," he argues.

"I *am* trying to win," I spit back irritably. "What exactly are you doing?"

This initial grace period, as the race coordinator explained, is to give everyone a chance to acclimate to the water. It'll be about ten minutes before they'll text us the parameters of the competition. There's no starting line or finish line, so it can't be a typical race. I'm trying to figure out the possible scenarios that we've gotten ourselves into but fall short. I check my smartwatch to ensure that no messages have come through. Ten minutes is a long time to be stuck in a canoe, drifting in choppy circles, with Quentin.

"Move your hand to the top of your paddle blade," he instructs. "Dig deep enough that you touch the water. We need to get up on a plane."

"I know how to do it," I argue.

"Well, the way you're doing it is going to make us lose."

I spin around to glare at him. "Why are you even here?"

"The same reason you're here, I think," he says. "We should probably re-evaluate our work-life balance."

My sour expression doesn't shift. This draws a laugh out of him.

"Why are you so mad?" he asks.

"Because Erving stuck you out here with me on purpose."

"And what purpose would that be?"

"To make me look bad."

Quentin barks out a laugh. "Tell me more about this secret evil plan. How does being out here with me make you look bad?"

God, where to begin.

"It makes me look like..." *I can't win on my own? I can't get a date?* I sigh, throwing a hand in the air. "It makes it look like we're... *friends.*"

"You didn't want to share a canoe with me because people might mistake us for *friends*?" He says it as if he's genuinely concerned about my lack of a social life.

"You know what I mean. People will talk."

"Talk about how we shared a canoe," he deadpans. "As coworkers. At a work event."

"You're a guy. You wouldn't understand."

"Explain it to me then," he challenges.

"If people think you're hooking up with me, it makes you seem desirable. If people think I'm hooking up with you, it makes me look like I have poor professional boundaries and am possibly trying to fuck my way to the top. Like the office floozy," I say in an irritated rush. "It makes me look like I can't succeed on my own merit."

I realize once I've let that last part slip that it's one of the things that bothers me most about Quentin – not only in the context of this boat race, but in the larger sense. They assigned him to my case. They stuck him in my boat. For all I know, they could just as easily hand him that partnership. And at the risk of sounding juvenile, it's not fucking fair.

Understanding seems to soften his features, and I wish I hadn't said it. I turn back towards the front of the boat with my face hot. Not in the least because I just used the word *floozy*.

"I'm sorry. None of those things are my intention," he says. "And nobody who has ever had a single conversation with you would think you're a floozy."

"Thanks," I offer, sounding more annoyed than I care to.

"You know if we win, that's all anybody will be talking about – our victory. Not speculating about if we're *friends*, or whatever."

"Sure," I say. "Whatever."

"Since we're already stuck out here together, let's imagine for a moment that I'm not your coworker," he says. "That there's no case. No partnership. No secret evil plan."

This is an incredibly dangerous path for my imagination to travel down. I try to keep a tight leash on my thoughts as I entertain it.

"Why would I be sitting here with you then?"

"Because you had a long week, and you came out here to have some fun and maybe win some money for a community organization that you're passionate about," he explains. "Same goes for me."

"Still not explaining why I'd hop into a boat with a stranger."

"Always with the stranger danger," he teases. "Okay, let's say we met at the bar, where we ordered at the same time – me, a Juan Collins, and you, a spicy ranch water – and the bartender revealed that he only had enough tequila for one drink."

"Wow, whoever was in charge of the bar in this story is terrible at their job."

He ignores this.

"And I graciously agreed to give you the last of the tequila, like a gentleman." He smiles as I snort. "And to repay me for my generosity, you offered me a spot in your boat."

"Mm," I say, nodding. "Are you sure I did it for that reason or because I heard rumors about your past experience with all those *class five rapids.*"

He ignores the jab. "Regardless, here we are. Now, what are you going to do about it?"

I suck in a breath, considering. My window of opportunity to get good enough at this to win is quickly closing.

"What were you telling me about how to hold the paddle, again?"

The corner of his mouth quirks, quietly pleased. He takes his own paddle in his hands, demonstrating the proper positioning. I attempt to mimic it, while trying to overlook the way that his muscles flex beneath the fitted fabric of his shirt.

"Like this?" I finally say.

He lowers his paddle across his lap before reaching for mine. When he leans forward, I can smell his woodsy, summertime smell.

"Like this," he says. His touch is tentative and warm as it moves across my wrists. "This hand goes here," he says, as he moves the fingers of my top hand until they curl around the grip of the paddle. "And this hand stays on the shaft. But, a bit lower. And... a little tighter."

He slides my bottom hand down until it rests directly above the blade. My face heats. I tell myself it's because it's a million swampy degrees out here and not because he's got his hands on mine while saying things like 'lower' and 'tighter' and 'shaft'.

He taps my pinky finger. "Sink your paddle up to here. If you're doing it right, your hand will be wet."

I bite my bottom lip, trying to keep my focus on the task at hand. Definitely not letting my mind wander to that place where Quentin is not my coworker and is saying words like 'wet'.

"Okay," I offer. "Anything else?"

"Once you've got the proper grip, it's really just the stroke. You want to make sure it's..." he trails off. "Why are you laughing?"

"You're purposely trying to make this sound dirty, and I need you to be serious."

Now it's his turn to laugh. "I am being serious. But we can talk dirty, if you want."

His eyes flash with mischief. This look twists effortlessly through my center. I will never admit how much I want him to talk dirty to me.

"Really close to pushing you out of the boat, asshole," I warn sweetly.

He arranges his smile into something slightly more serious. "When you *stroke* – that is the technical term for it, by the way, so please retrieve your mind from the gutter – lean as far forward as possible before you bury the blade, and then pull your body weight all the way back before you pull it out. Use your core – it's going to give more power than your arms. Also, try to keep the paddle perpendicular to the water. Everybody thinks they need to angle it away from the boat, like you see in movies, but you're wasting effort that way. You want it to go straight in. It's basic physics."

"Physics," I nod.

That's all this is. Science. Math. Coordinated movement. It's definitely not flirting.

I attempt all this, exactly as he explained, blocking out anything that could be misconstrued as innuendo. When I thrust myself back, I realize he was still leaning forward as part of the demonstration. My upper back lands hard against his chest. The boat rocks with the force of it, and suddenly everything feels a little too much like one of those dreams where I'm falling.

Oh my god are we falling?

An embarrassing yip escapes me. I nearly drop my paddle as I clamor for something to hold onto, which turns out to be... well, *him*. His hands seem to find my upper arms instinctively. I realize belatedly that I've got one hand clasped around his forearm, and another squeezing his knee.

I feel the huff of his laugh against the back of my neck. My grip softens, but he holds me for a moment more. The deep rumble of his voice tickles across my ear.

"You're going to have to try harder than that if you want to push me out of the boat, PBG."

His hands slip away from my arms, and I hear him pick up his paddle. My heart is doing something in my chest.

Skipping, my brain seems to supply. *Like the stereo in your first car when you hit a bump too hard while playing a favorite CD. Like grinning kids at the Girls Going Places headquarters playing double dutch in the middle of the courtyard.*

Like you like *him.*

Or at least, that I like the feeling I get when he teases those half-whispered words across my ear. The feeling travels down my neck, along my collarbone, following the deep V neckline of my romper. It suddenly seems so ridiculous that I chose this outfit – the kind that you have to take all the way off to access your bottom half.

Why am I thinking about access to my bottom half?

Our phones beep and buzz at the same time. He slides his from his pocket and I check my wrist, reading the rules quickly.

"It's a scavenger hunt," I say urgently, still skimming the message.

They've dumped a certain number of floating rubber duckies all around the lake. I've seen a couple up until this point, but I assumed they were some sort of cutesy decoration, because they were wearing little business suits. There is an inflatable pool floatie version lurking near the bar, and another near the place where the night's entertainment is set up. Now I wish I had paid more attention.

"The team with the most ducks wins," Quentin says, already scanning the lake. "You ready?"

I slide into action mode, everything before this gratefully forgotten. I don't care that I sound like I'm auditioning for a high-stakes-but-heartwarming kids' sports movie when I reply.

"Let's win this."

***

We spot the first rubber duckie about fifteen feet away and make a clumsy path towards it. The closer we get, the more our wake gently pushes it away. After a few failed attempts, we finally get close enough that I can scoop it out of the water and toss it into the bottom of the boat.

Quentin spots the next one, and we quickly strategize the coordinated motions it will take to turn in that direction. Eventually we make the save, narrowly missing another boat who was trying for the same one.

The growing collection in the belly of our canoe fills me with renewed energy. The clumsy paddling of the first few minutes gives way to a coordinated effort. I take Quentin's technical corrections in stride, and in exchange he lets me call the shots. If I argue that another duckie is more accessible than the one he points out, he yields with quick agreement. His focus is more on form, coaching from behind me with a steady, authoritative tone until our movements match. We're totally in sync. We're focused.

We're *effortless*.

Over the course of ten minutes, we zigzag across the lake, strategically scooping up every chance of winning we can find. Quentin has just pulled another duck out of the water when the fog horn echoes across the water.

The sound of applause quickly follows from the crowd on the boardwalk. A few cheers rise up from other canoes. We finally look at each other, faces flushed, chests heaving, and survey the collection of ducks between us. Our chase has taken us further than I anticipated. We both seem to realize there's a long, daunting stretch of lake between us and the dock. We let the boat bob in the current for a moment, drifting closer towards a set of actual real life ducks, who cruise past us at an enviable pace.

Quentin raises his hand in the air, offering me a high five.

"Not bad, PBG."

I can't contain my excitement, and I meet his high five with enthusiastic force. He smiles, victorious. I'm soaring. I'm exuberant. I feel so free.

Too free, actually.

A horrifying realization crashes over me. One of the cups of my adhesive bra has detached. That high five apparently used its last bit of sticking power. It has fallen down into the waistband of my romper.

"Oh fuck," I murmur.

"You okay?"

"Yeah, um." How to explain? "I'm experiencing a bit of a

wardrobe malfunction."

"Which means…?"

It means I cannot paddle up to a dock full of colleagues with a rogue boob.

"Just, um, give me a second?" I say, eyeing my chest and trying to figure out how to manage this delicately. Eventually I realize I can't. There's no way around this.

Quentin's mouth falls ajar as I dip a hand into my top.

"Don't look!" I shriek.

He dutifully shields his eyes as I cup a hand around my right breast and squeeze, hoping to re-adhere it. The faint sheen of sweat that previously made me feel accomplished and glowing is now working against me.

"Do you need…" I can almost hear him swallow. "Help?"

After a few more failed attempts at reattachment, I pluck the cup from my top and drop it into my lap. This is fine. I turn to face him. "How obvious is this?"

His gaze drops to my chest. I've given him permission to do so, and he takes full advantage, mapping the curves fast at first and then slowly. A blush warms my cheeks.

"Well?" I say.

He wets his lips, letting his gaze drop again to where I'm sure he can see the full, unobstructed teardrop outline and the obvious peak of my nipple through the soft fabric of my top.

"Somewhat. Noticeable."

I groan.

"Fuck okay. I'll deal with it when we get to shore." I eye the row of brightly colored canoes already meeting up at the dock. "You think we won, at least?"

"I mean this in an entirely professional and not personal way – but you're literally touching yourself in front of me, and you think I've got enough unoccupied brain power right now to know if we won?"

When I cut him a look, he shakes his head with a smile, dragging his attention back out to the water. "All right. Come on. Only one way to find out."

9.

We make the slow trek back towards the boardwalk, and we're one of the last boats to dock. An event coordinator meets us with a bucket labeled with our team number, and we load our rubber ducks into it before hauling ourselves out. They won't announce the winners for a while, in an effort to keep everyone milling around, talking and buying cocktails.

Down the boardwalk, I spot a wavy-haired guy I would love to never see again, wearing a big smile and a pair of shorts that are a touch too short. Unfortunately, he also spots me. This guy is bad news anytime, but especially in my current situation. He hits on me at these events *every, single, year.* He also prides himself on being my fiercest competition. (Did I mention he also suffers from an overinflated sense of self?) I can see him making excuses to the trio he's currently talking with, and my mind shifts into panic. I curse under my breath.

"You okay?" Quentin asks.

I fold my arms across my chest in a way that I hope looks casual and try to figure out which direction the restrooms are. "That guy in the coral shorts, your two o'clock? I cannot talk to him right now." Read also: ever.

Quentin takes quick stock of the situation and gives me a nod.

"Bathrooms are that way," he says. "I'll run interference and grab you a drink. Meet you on the lawn in ten?"

Against my better judgment, I say yes. We agree to meet at my picnic blanket before I make a beeline to the bathrooms. Once inside, I grab a handful of paper towels and attempt to dab the sweat from the sticky side of the cup.

Surely I can salvage this, I think. The longer I mess with it, the more I think perhaps I was wrong. As I'm attempting – unsuccessfully – to reattach it to my boob in a way that doesn't make me look slightly lopsided, a familiar face comes out of the nearest stall.

"Heidi Krupp," she grins.

"Mariah Wilson," I smile. For a moment, I attempt to stop prodding my breasts. "Wow. This isn't what it looks like."

She raises an eyebrow. "It looks like the Superbowl Halftime Show, circa 2004."

I laugh, tossing the useless cup to the edge of the sink in front of me. "Not my best fashion choice."

"I hoped I'd see you here," she says, washing her hands. "I saw the article. It was amazing, though I'd expect nothing less. Have those idiots at Freeman Maxwell figured out you're too good for them, yet?"

Mariah has never been discrete about her displeasure with what she feels is the outdated, corporate hierarchy at FML. She runs an employee-owned law firm in midtown. She's been after me since we worked together on a community outreach clinic for emancipated minors a few years back. It's become our running joke, how often I turn her down.

"Oh, you know me. I'm still fighting the good fight," I offer.

She smiles. "Well, when you're done playing their game, you know where to find me."

When she exits, I finally peel the other adhesive cup from my chest and toss them both in the trashcan by the door. I press my boobs together in the mirror and watch them bounce apart, trying not to be too hard on myself when they settle into their natural position. Honestly, I've got pretty great boobs. But they're also boobs I didn't plan to display to half the people I know – and my cute co-counsel.

Resigned to my fate and hoping the waning daylight works in my favor, I find my way to the small quilted blanket where I left my picnic basket and pop open a container of soft pretzels. They're homemade, of course, and they smell amazingly nostalgic, like hanging out at the food court in the mall as a pre-teen, when you've just spent the Christmas money your grandmother sent you on exactly two graphic tees from American Eagle and a bottle of lotion from Bath & Body Works, where you devoted half an hour to trying to decide between Cucumber Melon and Sweet Pea, as if it was the most important decision you'd make that year.

Yes, *those* kind of pretzels, but better.

I dig around, searching out the beer cheese. If I know Meg, I know there is beer cheese. I unload four containers of fancy crackers, crudite, and cut strawberries before locating it. I also find two sets of utensils, matching plastic plates, and restaurant-quality dinner napkins. My chest clenches, because my best friend is truly amazing, and I can only begin to deserve her on my very best of days. If I show my love by knowing I'd take a bullet for her before staggering over bleeding to apprehend the attacker, she shows hers by feeding me spectacular food that she knows I'll crave for the rest of my days, and I am here for it.

"This is quite the spread for a girl who showed up solo," Quentin says, passing me the promised drink.

The first thing I do when he hands me the plastic cup is lick the spicy seasoning off the rim. I do it on instinct. The action seems to register as a momentary flash in his eyes, entirely primal and masculine. It gives me that same surprising feeling in my chest.

Skipping. Like smooth stones across a lake. Like old records in Auntie Lena's shop. Like a class that you know will post all the notes online.

"My friend couldn't make it," I explain.

"I thought you didn't want people to think you had *friends*."

"She's not that kind of friend," I say. "And she had a wedding cake emergency."

"That sounds like something that only happens on Food Network."

I laugh, and he eases onto the other side of the blanket. I nudge the container of strawberries towards him.

"You want some?" I say. "I mean, we've got a few minutes before the winners are announced. It's probably best to stick together until then. I don't want you to be off hob-nobbing somewhere when I'm ready to accept the winnings."

"Hob-nobbing?" he laughs.

"Whatever you Maxwells do at these things," I say, waving a hand about vaguely. "I'm not taking the chance that they'll use your absence as a reason to disqualify us. Also, you're a very effective buffer."

He eyes the spread warily. "Does this count as 'sharing a meal'?"

I roll my eyes. "These are technically snacks, not a meal."

"Look at you, embracing the loopholes."

I let my smile simmer. We listen to the acoustic set as he nurses a beer. I can tell he's trying not to look at me as he says, "So did you get everything... situated?"

"You mean did I finally give up on the ill-advised adhesive bra? Yes, yes I did. Maybe if I act normal no one will notice."

I catch his gaze travel down the V of my top before sliding

back up.

"Maybe," he says, pressing his mouth into a very unconvincing line.

"I don't know that I can act normal if you sit here and keep checking me out."

"I'm not checking you out," he defends, tugging his gaze to the festivities again. "That was a professional courtesy."

I laugh, doing the same. I spot a few of my coworkers among the crowd, littered across their own respective picnic blankets and fold out chairs. They're interspersed with plenty of people I don't know, mostly twenty- and thirty-somethings who probably saw the event advertised online and are now spread across blankets, grinning and taking selfies. It's a particularly picturesque night for it, despite the lingering heat of the day. This is a part of the city that doesn't feel like a city: the sky feels bigger, the air smells grassier, the traffic fainter, in favor of nearby frog symphonies. The sun has sunk low, making a silhouette of the faraway tree line with its fading orange glow.

"So, that guy who seems annoyed I'm sitting here," he says. "Someone you used to date?"

I scoff. "I don't date. No, we just seem to run into each other a lot at these things."

"You don't date... like, ever?" he says.

"I'm busy, okay?" I defend. "Plus, I've seen your caseload. You're telling me you have time for a relationship right now?"

"For the right relationship? Sure. I'm a smart guy, I think I could figure it out."

"Well, *that* guy is a conversational leech who makes me feel drained every time he opens his mouth. So I'm going to go out on a limb here and say he's not 'the right relationship' for me. But hey, if you happen to get off on hearing someone tell you excruciatingly in-depth things about the stock market, he's your man."

"I think I'll pass," he grimaces.

"Right. I guess you prefer women who fall at your feet when you buy them a drink? I can't imagine how many of those there are."

"You jealous?" he smirks.

I pop a strawberry into my mouth. "Nope."

"Good," he says. "Because I prefer the smart ones who don't want to give me the time of day. Just so you know."

"That's a fatal flaw if I ever heard one."

"What can I say? I'm a hopeless romantic."

I smile. "Well, you certainly know your way around a shaft."

He laughs. "You think you're cute."

I tousle my hair, though all of the wave has probably fallen out of it by now. "I know I'm cute."

Quentin's eyes flicker like a late night fire, and I know he recognizes the borrowed line.

"What about you? What's the infamous Heidi Krupp looking for in a relationship? Assuming she ever finds the time to lift this dating ban."

"This sounds a lot like a personal question."

"Humor me."

I sigh. "The usual, I guess. Fun. Handsome. Loyal."

"You just described a Golden Retriever."

"Which I also don't have time for. But you make a solid point. Maybe if I get desperate enough for companionship, I'll just get a dog," I say. "Why do you care so much, anyway?"

He's wearing a look like he's about to say something incredibly charming, and despite my better judgment, I'd love to hear it. I catch myself leaning a little closer when a too-bright voice takes over the microphone.

"Good evening, everyone, and thank you for coming to Cocktails and Canoes, brought to you by Freeman Maxwell and Lewis! Before we announce the winners of tonight's race..."

"Ugh, they always do this," I tell Quentin under my breath. "They get you on the hook and leave you hanging *forever*. It's excruciating."

"Tell me about it," he says. There's something in his tone, but by the time I glance over he's looking ahead, tipping his beer to his lips.

"If we could have everyone who participated in the canoe race, please stand. Let's give these folks a round of applause!" the lady behind the microphone urges.

Quentin and I exchange a look before begrudgingly gathering ourselves up off the picnic blanket. On my feet, it's much more obvious how antsy I am. I'm shifting from foot to foot while the emcee announces the proceeds from ticket sales, the partnered organizations, and the sponsors. I hope that bouncing might somehow will them to announce the winners already. I don't realize I've got my fingers twisted into the ends of my hair until Quentin reaches over and takes my hand.

"Hold still," he says. "You're making me nervous."

He gives my hand a squeeze before letting it drop to my side. It's only a moment, and I'm left wondering why he did it – and if he'll do it again. I run my thumb between my fingers, one after another, realizing it's been a long time since I held hands with anyone. Like, a really long time. In hookups, you somehow seem to skip right over the hand holding phase. I'm halfway thinking about this, halfway listening as they announce third and second place. Neither of those are us. Which, I hope, can only mean the winners are...

"Boat seven, piloted by Quentin Maxwell and Heidi Krupp!"

I let out an involuntary squeal. This quickly leads to jumping up and down, which is probably ill-advised for a woman at a work function who is accidentally not wearing a bra. I don't care. I'm beaming as I meet Quentin's laughing expression.

"Holy shit!" I mouth to him.

"We did it!" he grins.

And then, almost as suddenly, my feet leave the ground, and I'm spinning. Literally spinning. Laughter bubbles out of me like a champagne bottle being corked.

The reality of what's happening catches up to me too late. I've thrown my arms around Quentin, and he picked me up, and he's spinning me around, and I'm laughing like I'm on a merry-go-round. By the time he sets me down I realize I've made a terrible mistake. In all this teasing and pretending, I forgot to hold onto the most important rule.

Never let your feet leave the ground.

10.

I'VE MADE PLENTY OF POOR DECISIONS in my thirty-two years on this earth.

I once sang – or attempted to sing – approximately half of "Gin and Juice" at my middle school talent show before being ushered off stage by a horrified teacher who promptly set up a meeting with the principal and my parents.

(No surprise, that completely blew up in my face, mainly because my parents got escorted off the school grounds for verbally assaulting each other during this meeting, which *kind* of overshadowed my performance.)

There was also that time I drank a five-shot espresso before participating in my first mock trial in law school, and by the time it was my turn to speak I had violent caffeine shakes, a completely full bladder, and a nervous leg jiggle.

(As soon as it was over and the instructor asked how I thought it went, I pulled a complete Forrest-Gump-at-the-White-House and said, "I gotta pee" straight into the tiny microphone, before jetting out of the room. It took me two semesters to live that down.)

I also once let a friend give me *kitchen bangs*, for god's sake. (Really, enough said.)

And yet, sharing my picnic blanket with Quentin Maxwell somehow tops them all.

Why? Why did I let my guard down, in front of half my coworkers and the one man whose current goal in life is to see me lose this promotion?

He could see it written all over my face the moment he set me down and pulled away from our spontaneous embrace. I watched his gaze decipher my features, registered the way his smile faltered, saw him easily translating my wide eyes as *holy fucking shit, what have I done*. We shuffled up to the makeshift stage like awkward, smiling strangers and posed for photographs with the giant cardboard check made out for ten thousand dollars.

I wore my cubic zirconia smile as I held the cardboard strategically across my bra-less chest and talked about the work that Girls Going Places does in the community. As I did this, I let myself feel high on ideas of what they could do with ten thousand dollars. Quentin and I shook hands. This felt simultaneously awkward and appropriate, serving as an unspoken agreement that we were abandoning any loopholes and returning to the original parameters of our deal, as written.

Shortly thereafter, we drifted our separate ways in the crowd of well-wishers. He got pulled into Erving's eager circle, and I slipped out sometime after the solo act had launched into the second half of her acoustic set, praying that no one noticed.

Even if they had, though, it's not like I've had enough time to hang around the coffee pot to catch wind of it. Whenever I make it to work the following week, the only thing anyone can talk about is the fact that everyone's favorite influencer is working a rebrand.

My suspicion is confirmed the moment Gigi Russo steps off

the elevator and struts through our office, trailing her attorney. The trendy free spirit has traded her flowy dresses, crop tops, and cut off denim for a business suit that looks straight out of the early nineties, complete with shoulder pads. She looks like she constructed this ensemble the way one might if she were going to a Halloween party as A Mature Adult Woman. Her hair is pulled back in a low bun, and her makeup is purposefully understated. When presented with documents to review, she puts on an oversized pair of wire frame glasses that remind me of an elderly librarian. I guess this is the look of *Gigi Russo, divorcee, social justice warrior.* I half-expect her to reach into her purse and pull out a Diet Coke with a straw, then pose for a selfie.

I am sitting across the conference room table from her, flanked by Quentin and our in-house stenographer. I know Gigi's attorney, Mike Murdock, from various encounters over the past few years. As expansive as family law can be, those of us running in these circles seem to overlap from time-to-time. I know that Mike's in his mid-sixties, lives in the suburbs with his wife Alisha, and that his oldest daughter is currently following in his footsteps and enrolled at Memphis Law. Jerica, I think her name is. I remember him saying she wanted to be a criminal attorney, that she was chasing the thrill of going to trial. At the time Mike had mentioned it to me, he'd laughed.

"In almost every way she's just like her mom, but that? That's the one thing I know she got from me. She's got the instinct to go in for the kill."

Like Gigi, Mike also loves a spectacle. He wears flashy cufflinks and a crooked smile. He thrives on showmanship. Seeing the two of them sitting shoulder-to-shoulder, I almost feel like I'm on the set of a TV legal drama, speaking to the casting director's interpretation of a plaintiff and her counsel.

I lead in with my well-rehearsed lines, as if on script.

"Ms. Russo, I am Heidi Krupp and this is Quentin Maxwell.

We are attorneys representing Mr. Glass. This is a deposition, in which I will ask you questions and you must answer them truthfully unless your attorney tells you clearly and directly not to answer. Although no judge is present, this is a formal legal proceeding just like testifying in court, and you are under the same legal obligation to tell the truth, the whole truth, and nothing but the truth. If you do not understand any of my questions, feel free to say so, and I will rephrase it. Before the deposition can be used in court, you will have the opportunity to read over it and correct any mistakes. Do you understand this?"

"I do."

"Do you feel physically and mentally able to participate in this conversation today?"

Gigi's mouth puckers into what I can only describe as a somber pout. She sweeps a non-existent lock of stray hair back into her bun.

"Well, as I'm sure you can understand, I've been under a lot of mental and emotional stress lately. This process so far has been..." she blinks, as if fighting back tears. "Well, honestly, it's de-humanizing, the way that everyone suddenly feels entitled to know intimate details about my personal life."

Details that she herself has shared with over a million followers, I think, *but hey, who's counting*. I keep my expression neutral, impassive.

"Ms. Russo, I'm hearing you say that you're unable to provide answers to these questions today due to your current mental state?"

Mike shifts in his seat, seemingly moving to make a note, but I notice that his elbow nudges hers ever-so-slightly.

"No," she says, lifting her chin defiantly, like a child who's just been told to be brave. "I am, despite everything, physically and mentally ready to do this."

"Thank you," I say, giving her my even, court-room smile.

"Can you state your full legal name for the record, please?"

"Virginia Marie Russo Glass," she replies. "But everyone knows me as Gigi Russo. I've never used the names Virginia or Glass socially or professionally."

"What do you do for income, Ms. Russo?"

"I'm an entrepreneur."

"What's your entrepreneurship, specifically?"

"I leverage my brand to make money from advertisers, mostly."

"So you influence people to buy products from other companies?" I clarify.

There's a flash of anger in her large eyes, and I can tell she wants to go in about this. Instead, she gives me another expression from what I'm learning is her pout repertoire: this one is 'annoyed'.

"I think that's an oversimplification, but sometimes, yes."

"What is your financial situation?"

"Well, unfortunately I've taken a sizable hit since I left Teddy. He's cut me off from almost everything I need to run my business."

"Such as?"

"Things that are critical to my brand. The studio." She huffs out a frustrated laugh. "Farkas."

You might think it odd, if you were new to this line of work, for a cat to come up in divorce proceedings. At this point in my career, it feels standard. I've negotiated the custody of dogs, reptiles, rodents, horses, livestock, and once, an African Grey Parrot that traveled everywhere on the client's shoulder. He'd taught the bird to reply with his name when asked who she wanted to live with. He was outraged when we declined to depose her.

"What's your relationship with Farkas?" I ask.

Gigi shows us the pensive pout.

"With all of Teddy's... abuse... I really started to feel like no one cared about me at all. Like I wasn't worth caring about. Farkas reminded me that I was. He was one of the only things that kept me sane during those hardest last few months. It's because of him I got the strength to leave. Not just for my sake, but for his as well. So I hope you understand why I cannot leave him there."

This testimony is surprisingly compelling. Quentin and I share a split-second glance before I continue.

"What role did you play in his care?"

"I was like a mother to him."

"Of course," I say. "Can you tell me what kind of food he eats?"

She blinks at me for a moment, and I catch that predatory flash in her eyes again. It's downright feline: eerily focused, ready to pounce without warning.

"Cat food," she says.

"How often does he eat?"

She's staring at me now as if this question is a personal attack. "Every day."

"Can you be more specific?"

"He eats whenever he wants. I leave the food bowl out."

I nod. "And what veterinarian do you use?"

She gives me a small smile, once again sweeping at hair that hasn't fallen loose from her bun.

"Only the best of the best, for my Farkie."

"Of course. And which vet is that, exactly?"

"The clinic is on Poplar. They have multiple doctors on staff. It varies."

It's a safe response. A clever response. Poplar Avenue runs the entire length of the city. The likelihood there's a vet's office somewhere on it – multiple vet offices – is highly probable.

"When's the last time you took him in? What was he there for?"

She blinks at me as her smile grows. It stretches into something that looks remarkably manic, with a deranged tilt to her head like it's about to twist off her neck. Eventually, she laughs. The sound is so surprisingly loud and off-putting that the entire room stops to look at her, including her attorney. The steady clicking noise coming from the stenographer's keyboard slows to an uncertain stop.

"I'm sorry, with the anxiety medication I'm on right now my memory really isn't so good."

"You testified earlier that you're in sufficient mental health for today's meeting. Would you like to clarify that statement?"

Mike shifts again, clearing his throat as he adjusts his tie. I wonder how many times they rehearsed these cues. Gigi transforms again into the picture of poise.

"No. No, I'm sorry," she says. "I'm perfectly able to answer your questions. I, um, think it was around Christmas. Last time he went in. Just for a check-up, you know. But I had Teddy take him. Well – actually, no – Teddy insisted that he would take him. Because he knew it upset me. He threatened to drop him off in a dumpster somewhere so that I'd never see him again. But I'm the one who made the appointment."

I can feel Quentin giving me a look, and I know without meeting it what it means: *move on from the damn cat.*

"What is your involvement in the business operations at Avid Records?"

"They were on the verge of collapse when I married Teddy. He won't tell you that, but their financial situation wasn't good. Their image was just... old. Outdated. I mean, who cares about a bunch of leathery, burnt out has-beens from before we were born? And that soundboard? It's so ancient they shouldn't even call it technology."

"So you changed the technology?"

She gives me a pitying pout, like I'm an actual idiot.

"No. I showed him how to make all that old stuff seem cool. I... basically became the Vice President of Marketing," she says, with a sweep of her hand. "Avid needed some rebranding, so I used my brand to build his up. Kitty Clayborn showing up to record "Firecracker"? That was all me. I met her on the promotional tour I did for the studio, during my stop at Coachella. Robbie Mack, collaborating with Teddy on the remix of "Hot Girl Summer", with that guitarist from Friday Morning? My idea. My connections. Every dime they've made over the past five years has come from the work I put in. Avid Records would be a middle-aged nobody if it wasn't for me."

I think about my meeting with Zelda, when we'd gone over the books. Both Zelda and the books were telling a very different story than Gigi was at the moment. I'd need time to sort out how much of this was legitimate, but for now I'm imagining what Zelda would say if she heard this self-aggrandizing speech. I worry, as I think about it, that I'm actually going to break character. I hide in my sip of water and give Quentin an imploring look, one that is intended to pass the baton. He comes to life without missing a beat.

"Ms. Russo, what is the nature of your relationship with Grayson Smith?" he asks.

I don't know what I expected, but this lead-in is surprisingly strong. I try not to feel too impressed. Anybody can come out swinging for the fences.

"Grayson is a very good friend," she says. "He's been so supportive of my healing journey. It's important to have people like that."

"When did your relationship with Mr. Smith begin?"

She does the unnecessary hair sweep before absently patting at her bun. "We met in the VIP lounge of the FedEx Open, last fall. Avid was a sponsor."

"In March of this year, did you tell Mr. Glass that you had

been engaging in a sexual relationship with Mr. Smith?"

Cue the defiant chin lift. "Yes."

"So you were having an affair with Mr. Smith?"

"No," she says. Her eyes roll to the ceiling, and she bites her lip. I can't tell if she's overcome with emotion, buying time to plot a believable follow-up response, or both. Finally, she gives us a small shrug. "I told Teddy that because I wanted him to leave me. I thought... well, he always said if I left him, he would find me. He told me there was nowhere I could go to get away from him. That I'd be nothing without him. So I figured, if he thought that I was sleeping with someone else, that he'd want out."

Fuck.

Quentin and I share a brief sideways glance, and in that split second, I can see the tension in his jaw. He rubs a hand across his face, as if to hide it.

"Ms. Russo," I say. "When you told Mr. Glass that you had contracted genital herpes from the affair with Mr. Smith, was this also a lie?"

"Yes," she says primly. "You can't cure genital herpes. I figured this way he wouldn't want to have sex with me. Ever again."

The truth writhes, shapeshifting and unwieldy, between us. Gigi's eyes have gone wide and glossy. Mike passes her a tissue from the box nearby before leaning back in his chair and leveling a stare across the table at me. One corner of his mouth lifts in an off-center smile, as if to say, 'Hey. You asked for it.'

I jot meaningless notes onto the page of prepared questions and attempt to regroup. As much as I say I'm not in the business of determining what's true, there's a gut-wrenching part of me that wants to know. That needs to know.

Is Teddy not who I think he is, or is Gigi a good actress?

Is she an abused woman, trying to get out of a bad situation, or is Mike manipulating this in search of another showy slam dunk?

Can all of those things be simultaneously true? And if they are, where do I go from here?

I find myself asking the same question Jeanine had posed in our brief conversation over chips and salsa: is there really any justice in this?

I take a steadying breath.

"Ms. Russo, I understand that you want out of this relationship as quickly and cleanly as possible," I say. "We've made an offer to settle this out of court. We did this in the spirit of preventing any further emotional or financial stress for the both of you. As you mentioned earlier, you don't feel that everyone is entitled to the details of your personal life, and reaching a settlement before going to trial would certainly limit your exposure. This could all be behind you. Have you given this offer consideration?"

I'm not sure what kind of pout this is. Predatory, perhaps. Like a jaguar licking its paws, satisfied with its catch, and yet unhurried as it plays with its food.

"Yes," she says. "I considered it."

She knows I want more than this. I let the silence stretch between us for almost a full minute, but she doesn't attempt to fill it. This is a standoff I will inevitably lose.

"And?" I finally prompt.

"And as much as it pains me to put my personal life out there, and to be persecuted in the court of public opinion, it would pain me more to know that the world gets to go on believing that Teddy Glass is a good person. And as much as you claim your offer is in my best interest, I know that you're only proposing it because it's in the best interest of *him*. So yes, I have considered your offer. But no, I will not accept it."

Now, she gives me a full smile, then looks to Mike for approval. He gives it to her in the form of twinkly-eyed nod. He's already gathering up his leather bound notebooks and sliding his fancy pens into the pocket of his pressed shirt.

"Heidi. Quentin. We'll be in touch?"

***

Quentin follows me into my office, closing the door behind us.

"What the hell was that?" he questions.

"A taste of what we'll see in court," I reply, settling into my desk chair.

"Did you know about this?"

"About what?"

He levels his stare at me, annoyed. "She alluded to some pretty serious abuse, Heidi. And you're acting like we just spent the past half hour talking about who gets the chaise longue."

"God I wish," I say. "That'd be so much easier. I can't imagine Teddy putting up much of a fight over a chaise longue."

"This isn't a joke," he says. "Do you know how this looks?"

I sober. This is a different Quentin than the one I'm used to. He's traded the charming smile for a hard set jaw. His gaze is hyper-focused. His energy, reckless. I have to reign this in.

"It was certainly more detailed than the information we've gotten up to this point," I offer, "but yes, I knew there were claims of abuse."

I see the muscles in Quentin's jaw flex again before he drags a hand along his face. He seems to be warring with what to do or say next. And he's pacing, like a lion in a cage.

"Do you... want off the case?" I ask.

The frustrated crease between his brows deepens. "What? No. Why would you say that?"

"You look like you're ready to punch something," I tell him. "And if you can't keep your cool, I need to know now. It's only going to get worse from here."

"Yes, I'm familiar with how these things go."

"Ah. Right. I guess you would be."

His irritation shifts to suspicion, as if attempting to decipher what exactly I mean by this. My eyebrows draw together. I can feel one quirking higher than the other in exasperation.

"Domestic violence," I say. When he blinks at me, I add, "Your work at the non-profit. C'mon, it's all public record. Don't act like you haven't Googled me."

He sinks into the armchair opposite my desk with a frustrated sigh. I wonder now if this is what Erving meant that first day, when he advised Quentin to put aside personal pursuits. I'd assumed maybe he'd been alluding to *me*, somehow, or to the fledgling relationship Quentin and I had flirted with. This makes more sense: a crusade for the common good. Some sort of savior complex.

"That's got nothing to do with this," he says.

"Good," I nod, "because I need to know that your focus is on our client – even if, somehow, the things that Gigi is saying about him are true. You've got to have your head in the game, or trust me, Mike Murdock will eat you alive in front of the jury. He'll enjoy it, too. He does it precisely, piece by piece, like he's Hannibal fucking Lector."

Quentin grimaces. "Thanks for that mental image."

"I'm just saying."

"You're saying you don't care if our client is the kind of person who takes pleasure in making someone else's life a living hell," he says. The casual accusation dripping from his tone slips under my skin, like the edge of a well-placed blade.

"I'm saying that I've heard couples accuse each other of much, much worse," I say sharply, "and I refuse to believe that any of that is my fault. Marriage isn't a fucking fairy tale. If you want to play the hero, go back to Texas."

As soon as the words leave my mouth, I want to forget them. I'm losing control of this situation. I'm letting my emotions get in the way. I expect a counter strike, but it doesn't come. Quentin's gaze is intensely focused on me now, something akin to shock, similar to when he gasped to the surface after I pushed him in the pool.

Now is not the time to be thinking about him in the pool.

I swallow past the tightness in my chest and summon a sense of measured calm.

"What I mean to say," I continue, "is that these things can bring out the worst in people. We're dealing with people's money, their insecurities, their broken hearts. Even the best-intentioned people can become unrecognizable in these situations. That's life. I'm not condoning it. But I also can't take responsibility for the fact that sometimes people screw each other over. That's not my job. All I can do is attempt to conduct this case with integrity. It's the only thing that's within my control. And if you let them get the better of your emotions, we're going to lose control of this case."

I'm worried that my voice is shaking. I know my eyes have started stinging, which probably means I look like I'm about to cry. The last thing I plan to do is cry in front of Quentin Maxwell.

"You're right," he says. "It's not your fault. I'm sorry."

He looks at me in a way that makes my heart hammer around in my ribcage. The danger of crying increases tenfold. I make it a point to look away, staring down at my notes, or really anywhere except at him. This is no place for heart-fluttering, fall-into-your-arms feelings because a guy let his gaze dance across my face like I'm some sort of mystifying, beautiful, broken ass puzzle he'd love to piece back together. I can hold my own pieces together. My will to hold everything together is like high-powered super glue. I could patent this shit.

"It's fine," I offer reflexively.

"It's not fine," he says. "That's why I apologized."

"Okay," I say briskly. "I accept your apology."

I busy myself with gathering notes for my next meeting. I hope it will hurry him out, but he lingers. He drags another beleaguered hand across his face.

"So, now that we have all this... new information, what are we going to do?"

As much as I'm ready to end this conversation, he has a point. I sink my head between my hands, threading my fingers into my hair to massage the tightness from my scalp. Eventually, I sigh, straightening up. As with most arduous journeys, the only way out is through.

"I think," I tell him, "that it's time to find the first Mrs. Glass."

11.

With my shoes slapping the pavement to the rhythm of 90s hip hop in my headphones, it's easier to let everything else fall away.

No mountain of work to be done on a dozen cases.

No pressing need to lock down my social media accounts or consider hiring someone to manage my online presence.

No precariously looming partnership decision.

On these early summer evenings, it feels like it's just me, the sinking sun, and the balmy breeze coming off the Mississippi. I jog the sidewalks of downtown to the paved paths of the manicured riverside parks. I pass the slow-moving barges and the long-armed laurel oaks, the men who toast me with their paper-bag-wrapped twenty ounce cans and the couples who cruise by with strollers, past the bramble of blackberry bushes clinging to a forgotten chain link fence near the bridge, before eventually looping back again. In these moments I feel strong and self-sufficient, moving forward with nothing more than pumping blood and thumping bass humming in my ears, propelling me through the world like I could forge a path anywhere, all on my own.

Of course, I'm also an avid consumer of murder podcasts and forensic investigation TV shows, with a higher than average distrust of most people, so I'm not actually running alone. I don't know the statistics about the likelihood of being assaulted when you're a jogger versus a non-jogger, but I do know that the stories that include elements like "woman" and "jogging" and "alone" hit way too close to home, so maybe this is how I ended up as a member of Best Workout, Bar None. I'm a few paces behind the folks training for a half-marathon, a few ahead of the ones who drank too much the night before, and about to lap the ones that consider this less of a jogging group and more of a walk-and-talk. I'll socialize later, when we're all sweat-drenched and endorphin-buzzed, soaking up the AC of our group's namesake dive bar and catching up on the week.

Is there really any other way to make friends as an adult, besides picking an arbitrary task, putting it on a twice-a-week schedule, and offering discounted drinks?

(Probably not.)

Lately more than ever, I'm grateful to be a part of this outdoor pack. I used to hit the fitness center in my apartment building most mornings, but I ran into Quentin around sunrise one day recently. There are only two treadmills in our small facility, so when he powered up the one beside me, my early morning escape quickly turned into an obsessive test of my peripheral vision. It's not that he did anything in particular to make things weird – he gave me a polite nod, plugged in his own headphones, and set his pace – but it was admittedly weird. I had sweat stains down the front of my tank top, which was clinging to me like I was aiming for runner-up in a wet T-shirt contest, and my cherry-red cheeks and limp ponytail felt glaringly obvious, my movements suddenly mechanical. Every few breaths I caught the faint high notes of his laundry detergent and the warm woodsy undertones of his skin, which flooded me with flirty thoughts of the night we met, juxtaposed with the stark contrast of our present relationship. It felt impossible to escape from thoughts about things like *Quentin* when Quentin was quite literally running alongside me.

When I tried to switch things up to avoid him, I stumbled upon him again one night after dinner. This time he was working with free weights, facing the wall of windows that gazes into the treetops of the city. The lean muscles of his arms flexed and extended, showing off subtle definition in places I'm not sure I have muscles. He was nowhere near the treadmills, but I slipped out before he could spot me. I can't decide if that evening run-in was proof that he's just a gym junkie or that he was trying to avoid me, too. In the end, I decided it would be easier to get outside more anyway. I spend nine-plus hours every weekday in relative proximity to him; I don't want to spend my free time devoting anymore brain cells to his existence.

Like I am right now.

I push myself harder, hoping a faster pace will help me outrun all of this. It does the trick. My lungs burn, my limbs throb, and my footfalls match the pace of the power playlist with such satisfying accuracy that I'm almost smiling. There's something triumphant about it, like I'm reenacting that scene from *Rocky*, complete with fist pumping and compelling music, and then I catch sight of myself.

Not my current, sweaty, jogging self, but my cross-armed, almost-green-eyed, professional-headshot-ready self, who is smiling into westbound interstate traffic like she wants to be the only thing you're thinking about as you leave our little corner of the state. That sing-songy tagline is plastered alongside my image in a clean, modern font.

The best part of breaking up is calling Heidi Krupp.

I slow to a stop, but my heart rate seems to speed up. I'm suddenly aware of every pint of blood in my body, pumping through my veins with the force of CPR chest compressions, as if my own organs are trying to resuscitate me. I have to remind myself to breathe. The logo and phone number for Freeman, Maxwell, and Lewis is perfectly positioned in the bottom corner of the full-size billboard.

When I first got the job, Meg used to cackle about the unfortunate acronym, and anytime I would have a bad day at work she found it particularly hilarious to reply "FML!" with a laugh-until-you-cry emoji. This is probably the first time in my tenure that I understand the irony. Here, with my hands on my knees, trying to steady my breath, looking at an advertisement for what is starting to feel like my alter ego, I cannot decide whether I want to laugh or cry.

"Fuck my life," I murmur.

I watch cars whir beneath the billboard in desperation, hoping it's one of those high-tech ones that cycles through multiple images, limiting my exposure as it cross-promotes NBA games, a local credit union, and the pandas at our award-winning zoo. Sandwiched between things like that, it would be likely that nobody would notice me. Nobody wants to think about divorce when they can think about pandas.

Unfortunately, it's not that kind of billboard. It's the old school kind, the kind that a team of people probably had to wear safety harnesses to plaster five stories up, static, there for all to see. I've never wished to see a road sign giving me questionable medical advice or warning me to get right with Jesus more in my life. Anything would be better than this.

Who would *do* something like this?

I think of Jeanine the journalist, but I know this isn't the magazine's doing. This was someone from my own firm – Quentin, maybe? I have to admit it could just as easily be the board. Or maybe someone closer, like Henry. Someone I trust. The sting of betrayal sears through me.

Josie claps me on the back as she speeds past.

"You good?" she says.

I give her the most half-hearted thumbs up of my life and call back, "Leg cramp."

She accepts this with a nod as she continues her trek, and I realize as I watch her ponytail swing behind her that at some point I'm going to have to make my way back. Hands on my hips, I pace the small stretch of clover off the edge of the sidewalk, torn between scaling the cityscape and ripping down the image with my bare hands or collapsing into the grass. It's really the rage that saves me. Its current comes quickly behind the hurt feelings, washing through me like welcome rain.

I turn on a beat that hits hard and fast. My lungs burn, my limbs throb, and half an hour later I collapse onto a cracked pleather stool under one of the propeller-style ceiling fans at Bar None. I chug two glasses of water before accepting my half-price beer. My fingers fidget with my phone, and I fight the urge to fling accusations around via text.

Throughout that first pint, I solidify the certainty that this needs to be a strategic investigation, one that will allow me to properly enact my vengeance. By the second drink – a hazy, raspberry lager – I catch myself briefly thinking about Callum, which I haven't done in ages. I wonder why I'm thinking about him now. Maybe this low-key fixation with Quentin and Callum is my body's way of reminding me that it's only thirty-two and does in fact still have needs. Or maybe this is just the comedown. I've cycled through plenty of primal emotions in the past half-hour: shock and shame, anger and desperation, with the result being that every cell in my body feels tight and coiled, itching for release.

I'm actually considering downloading one of those dating apps again when two of the interns, Yolanda and William, climb onto the stools beside me.

"Hey," Yolanda grins. "I thought that was you."

"A slightly different version of me than you usually see," I admit with a rueful smile, motioning to my drawstring shorts and damp tank top.

Yolanda laughs. "Best Workout, Bar None?"

"Yeah," I nod. For a moment that's all I think about saying, because a suspicious part of me wonders: were they in on it? I realize after an awkward beat that I'm being paranoid. They're interns; they don't have the signing power to rent ad space. I also know they don't have the combined disposable income to afford it as a joke. I've seen the way they argue over who's buying lunch and how to split delivery tabs down to the penny. I lower my hackles.

"You thinking of joining us?" I offer.

"No, but I've seen the t-shirts," she says. "You're a regular?"

"Sometimes. What about you guys? Come here often?"

Yolanda shrugs, and William looks evasive, and I realize that it's possible they're on a date. Yolanda is wearing a short, floral dress with sandals, looking much younger than she does on weekdays in her monochrome sheath dresses, and William has traded his shirt and tie for a polo and summery shorts. After a few beats, I see them realize that I'm realizing. William excuses himself to go talk to a potentially non-existent friend across the bar, and Yolanda scoots another stool closer. She waits to speak until he's out of earshot.

"Hey, so, we're just..."

I stop her before she can say 'friends'.

"I really don't need to know," I say.

"Understood," she smiles, seemingly satisfied with this response. "You don't ask about my love life, and I won't ask about yours. *Quid pro quo.*"

She pantomimes zipping her lips and tossing away the key.

I cough out a laugh. "That's very kind of you. Although

mine's pretty nonexistent at the moment, so, ya know."

She gives me an incredulous look before turning her attention to the water-stained drink menu. She's running her finger down the list like she's entirely preoccupied, but then I hear her say, "I see things, too, ya know."

My gaze drifts back to her, curious. "Yeah?"

"Yeah," she smiles, giving me a sideways glance and another little shrug. "But don't worry. I won't say anything."

I see her signal William before ordering them both the craft cocktail of the month (tequila and ginger beer, which is about as craft as you get at a dive bar) and handing over her card to start the tab.

"I'm sorry," I can't help saying, "you won't say anything about what, exactly?"

Her dark eyes slide over to mine. She gives me a nervous laugh, glancing both ways before offering in a low voice, "You and... *you know*."

I raise my eyebrows at her, because I clearly don't know.

She whispers now. "Quentin Maxwell."

I blink once. Twice. My face feels suddenly hot beneath the stretched tight feeling of dried sweat, and I wonder if it's redder now than it was when I ended my run and stepped in here.

"I, um..."

Yolanda gives me a wide-eyed, well-meaning smile. "Hey. Like you said. I really don't need to know."

"No," I insist, perhaps a bit too vehemently. "I'm not..." *With Quentin.* I can't even say it. A mirthless laugh escapes me. "Is that what people are saying?"

"People say a lot of things." She shrugs apologetically. "I'm not a gossip, it's just that cubicles don't leave much to the imagination. They're like the speedo of the professional realm. They give only the vaguest illusion of privacy."

I laugh in earnest now. I know how true it is. Most recently, half the time when I walk through the cube farm full of interns and paralegals, I hear murmurs about a "Dr. Pepper Thief". Apparently one of the associate's personal cans of soda have been disappearing from the break room fridge, and it was rumored he has offered a cash reward for the intern who rats out the culprit. Bets have been waged. An investigation was launched. You can't make this shit up.

"God. Yeah, I remember those days. You'd think they'd have something better to talk about, though."

"I wouldn't take it personally. He's all anyone's talked about. Showing up all mysteriously. Taking over Mr. Maxwell's office. And... well, you know. All the other stuff."

I smush my mouth into an expectant line that tells her I also don't know anything about any other stuff. If cubicles are the speedo, my office is one of those whole-body swim dresses from the nineteenth century that comes lined with full length pants.

"What other stuff?" I say.

She leans on her elbows, glancing over her shoulder again before replying. She's just loud enough to be heard over the laughter of a few guys from my group making their way through the door.

"God, okay. So, I don't know if any of this is true. I feel like an asshole even repeating it. But William's oldest brother or cousin or something went to high school with Quentin. Apparently he got kicked out for stealing a car?"

Everything about my face right now has to say, *I'm sorry, what?*

When she sees the way my eyes widen, she immediately backtracks.

"I mean, I don't think he was arrested or anything. Maybe it's one of those stories that got blown way out of proportion. I dunno. I just heard he was... you know, one of those out of control private school kids. Partied too much. Dropped out of college. Got completely cut off by his family. But obviously he went back.

I mean, law school and everything. And he seems fine now, right?"

"Yeah," I say. It comes out as an unconvincing croak. I take a big gulp of beer, hoping to wash it down. "I'm sure it's fine."

Of course, everything she's just told me sounds the very opposite of fine.

"And I mean, you know what they say," she says. "Everybody loves a comeback kid."

"Yeah," I murmur. "Unfortunately they do."

I would like the record to show that I have no interest in being a part of Quentin's comeback. Am I about to lose out on this partnership because he's trying to repair his reputation? Is he shady enough to be responsible for that stupid billboard? How have I been oblivious to the fact that all of this is happening in my own office?

She winces as if I've said all this out loud. "I'm sorry. I shouldn't have said anything."

"No, I appreciate you telling me," I say. "But if you could maybe do me a favor and discreetly spread the word that I'm not dating him...?"

The bartender deposits the cocktails in front of her, and she takes one in each hand, giving me another apologetic smile.

"I would, but the idea that you might have laid claim to him is seriously the only thing that's kept Aaron and Elizabeth from making it their summer's mission to bang him. And I... kind of need them to finish the research for that Herrington case?" she shrugs. "No offense."

I laugh out loud at this, lifting my glass in her direction. "None taken. I'd probably do the same."

"I'm learning from the best," she winks.

At this moment, Josie plops down on my other side, signaling for her discounted beer.

"Pickle juice," she tells me, never one to worry or notice that she's interrupting something. "It'll knock those leg cramps right out."

Somehow, this declaration summons Patrick, seemingly out of thin air. He can pick up a conversation about runners' ailments better than those creepy phone ads that strategically hound you about something you mentioned to a friend in a loud whisper exactly once. I can't begin to count how many hours of my life I've lost to his monologues about preventing shin splints.

"Don't listen to her," he says, edging his sweaty body between us. "Bananas. Potassium is totally where it's at."

I can't blame her: at this, Yolanda retreats towards the tables by the window, reconnecting with her not-date William. I stare into my half-empty pint glass for a while longer, listening to Josie and Patrick argue about the cure for my fabricated leg cramps. After a while, the circular argument about potassium versus sodium, calcium versus magnesium, does me in. I pay my tab and make the slow walk home, trying to ignore the simmering undercurrent in my veins that is desperate to know where this all went wrong and who, exactly, I can hold responsible.

12.

IT'S AFTER NINE O'CLOCK when I use my access card to swipe into the office. I know that nothing good can come from this, but it has consumed my thoughts to the point there didn't seem to be any other choice. It followed me into the shower. Hung around my shoulders as I tried to watch TV. Coiled in my ribcage when I considered heading to bed. During my walk over, the sky faded from faintly peachy pink to the color of overwashed denim, stretching over the city in a swath of soft, comfortable navy.

It feels weird to step off the elevator wearing high-waisted leggings and a DIY crop top, and even weirder to be walking through the office in lace-up shoes. Normally my heels click down the hallways, but tonight, my trek is smooth and silent. All around me, the glow of city light stretches beyond the walls of windows, but the fluorescent squares on the ceiling are dark.

I don't bother to click on the light in the file room as I tug the nearest cabinet open. I know this is where Bernadette keeps copies of recent invoices, and I'm desperate to find a signature. As much as I've spent the past few years begging us to go completely paperless, at this moment, I'm glad the Boomers on the board have held out. I flip eagerly through the file for this month, quickly passing over company car statements and utility bills. I get to the end of the manila file folder with nothing that links to billboard advertising. I double-check behind myself, ticking through each page again before sliding the drawer closed with a sigh.

I feel stupid, thinking I could sneak in like Nancy Drew and find the answer.

I'm about to retreat towards the elevators, but something about the darkened hall calls me. My eyes have adjusted, and the shadows of the space feel familiar. I wander past my office, beyond the sea of cubicles where the interns bandy about their speedo-style gossip, and into the corner office with the two-eighty view. Erving's office.

Quentin's office.

It looks mostly the same as it did before he showed up. The desk is still a smooth, L-shaped stretch of modern mahogany. The framed photos are still of Erving and his well-to-do connections, shaking hands at black tie functions and grinning on the greens of exclusive, manicured golf courses. His degrees still line the walls. His community accolades still adorn the shelves. It almost feels like Quentin was never here at all.

It's fortunate, given all this, that I didn't come in here to snoop.

I press the button to raise the automatic sun shades. There's a faint whir as the river, the bridge, and the interstate highway come into view. I stand so close to the floor-to-ceiling windows that my breath almost fogs the glass. For a moment, my own reflection is a ghostlike overlay across that ridiculous, smiling, uplit billboard ad. It looks a bit smaller from here than it did on my run, but I know it's still looming large enough to catch attention. I fold my arms protectively across my chest and watch the line of headlights travel beneath it.

I wonder what people think when they see it. Am I a jingle? A joke? A pretty girl begging for attention? Standing here, part of me still feels like the kid I once was: lost, angry, used. I spent years getting here, and all I ever wanted was to make sure I wasn't like those attorneys. The ones giving me Capri Suns, coaching my parents on how to best play me against the other, convincing me to go on the stand. The problem is that sometimes I feel like I never escaped them. Maybe all this time I fought to be here, what I was really fighting for was to work among them, the kind of people who would plaster me on a billboard without considering what it might mean. Not for them, but for me.

"Enjoying the view?" a voice says from behind me.

I start so hard that I smack my forehead against the window. The dull pain pools above my left eye as I spin around, holding one hand to my brow and jutting the other out to grab the nearest object. Within seconds I'm dazed and wielding a heavy, corporate award trophy. I aim the dull crystal point of it towards the shadow leaning against the doorframe. As I squint into the darkness, it smirks at me.

"Quentin?" I demand.

I hear him breathe out an amused sigh of a laugh.

"Don't sound so surprised. This is my office," he says. "Are you okay?"

I lower the crystal trophy, but I don't release it.

"I'm fine." I massage my forehead indignantly. "What the fuck are you doing here?"

"I was working in the archives," he says. "Glass v. Russo isn't my only case, you know."

I realize now that he's wearing tailored slacks and a button-down. At some point, he lost the jacket and tie, but his whole look is one that says he never went home, including the pieces of hair springing rogue across his forehead. His sleeves are rolled up his forearms, which are folded in casual amusement across his chest.

"What are *you* doing here?" he says.

I glance hopelessly to the billboard and then lift the trophy accusingly in his direction again.

"What do you know about this?"

"Err... it looks like something from the Chamber of Commerce, maybe? It's kind of hard to tell in the dark, when you're pointing it at me like a weapon."

"Not this," I say, waving the object for emphasis. "*This.*"

He cautiously eases up beside me, following the annoyed toss of my head as he peers at the landscape below. It takes him a moment to spot it, and when he does, his mouth falls slightly ajar.

"Whoa. Is that...?"

"Yeah," I sigh, lowering the makeshift weapon. "It's me."

"And you didn't...?"

"Didn't authorize this?" I blink at him in irritation. "No. Of course not."

"So who do you think did?"

"Well, if I'm ruling you out," I begin, giving him another assessing stare that tells him I have in fact *not* yet ruled him out, "then... I don't know."

He drags his gaze back out to the highway, studying the scene for longer than I want him to. Though I'm the one who showed it to him, I now wish I hadn't. Maybe he never would have noticed. Maybe he would have kept the shades down until I could have it removed. Now, he's going to have easy access to stare at it every single day. Not that there's any logical reason he would spend his time doing that.

"Why did you assume it was me?" he says.

Guilt swarms in my stomach, but I refuse to give him anything that resembles an apology. In the end, I simply clop the trophy onto the nearest shelf and prop myself against the edge of his desk.

"There was nothing in our contract prohibiting full-size billboard ads," I point out.

"No, not explicitly. But we agreed to conduct ourselves with integrity. And not to engage in acts of sabotage."

"You think this is sabotage?" I ask.

"Not inherently. I mean, honestly, it's probably pretty good publicity. Hell, I'd hire you." When I give him a look, he adds, "But it's also highly inappropriate, assuming you didn't know about it beforehand. You really didn't know?"

The expression he's wearing is bordering on sympathy. I brace my hands against the desktop on either side of me, hoping to fend off the way it makes me want to lunge at him. I would love nothing more than to smack that look of pity right off his face.

"If I find out you're involved in this..." I warn.

"Is that what you think? That I'd do something like this?"

He smirks, but there's a wounded sound in his voice. I almost backtrack, but the earlier conversation I had with Yolanda comes creeping up the back of my neck, telling me I'd be a fool to trust him.

"I don't know anything about you, really," I say dismissively. "You've only been here, what? Three or four weeks?"

He comes to sit on the top of the low bookshelf across from me, moving the picture frames aside as he mimics my posture.

"And here I thought our days back in the dorm had endeared you to me."

I shake my head with a small smile.

"Asshole," I murmur. "For all I know you're The Dr. Pepper Thief."

He chokes out a laugh. "The Dr. Pepper Thief? Really?"

"I don't hear you denying it."

His eyes dance across my face with playful intrigue. "What is it that you want to know, PBG?"

My heart dips. *Everything.* It is a response that seems to simmer in my veins. I drag my gaze out into the city lights, considering.

"Why do you want this partnership, Quentin? Why are you really here?"

I can feel more than see him tense. There's a shift in the air between us.

"Have you ever done the wrong thing for the right reasons?" he asks vaguely.

"Objection, your honor: non-responsive," I say. "I hate when you answer my questions with questions."

He gives me a look that points out that I am in fact also avoiding answering his questions. I roll my eyes.

"Yeah, I mean, of course I have," I offer. Not that I'm willing to broach any of those topics with him. "Do you think it was the wrong choice, coming back here?"

"No," he says. "If I hadn't come back, I wouldn't be sitting here with you, wearing... what are you wearing?"

He eyes my midriff in a smirky way that makes my skin come alive beneath the cut off concert tee.

"Fuck off," I murmur with a laugh. "I wasn't expecting to see you here, okay?"

"I'm glad you did. It's been the highlight of my whole day. You look like you came here to kick my ass, but, ya know, sexy."

I smile demurely. "Watch it, Maxwell. That almost sounded like a compliment."

"Almost? Damn, I'm losing my touch."

I catch sight of those dimples as he smiles. The honesty in his voice runs its invisible fingers down my arm. That coiled feeling twists itself more tightly through my center.

"Why'd you steal a car?" I say.

Somehow, he doesn't look surprised to hear this. He accepts this non-sequitur as if he'd been expecting it much sooner than today.

"There are many theories," he offers.

"Such as?"

He sucks in a breath. "Such as I was at a party and got rejected by a girl, so I stole her car to get back at her. I guess you'd call that angle 'vengeful'.

"Others speculated that I was drunk and entitled and joy-riding – one might say 'classically rebellious'.

"Or maybe I was trying to ruin my family's reputation – so, you know, 'spoiled'. Take your pick."

"That's quite the list," I say. I have to admit at various times, I've been ready to assume all of those things about him. "What's the truth?"

"The truth is my friend was drunk at a party, and she was trying to drive. I took her keys, drove her to my house so she could sleep it off on my couch without her parents knowing. She woke up before me, and I guess her boyfriend was blowing up her phone, so she panicked. She didn't want to admit to him that she'd been hanging out with me, and she didn't want to admit to her parents she'd been drunk. So she made her way home and claimed her car must've been stolen from her friend's house. The police located it in my driveway a few hours later."

His nonchalant expression sums it up. He's not trying to convince me, but somehow, he does.

"Did you tell them what happened?"

"I tried," he shrugs. "I realized pretty quickly the truth doesn't always matter. There's the truth, and then there's what people believe. That second thing is usually more important."

I blink at him, wondering if he's plucked this from my very soul.

"Why are you so quick to believe the worst about our client, then?" I question.

"Why are you so quick to believe the worst about me?" he

counters.

The answer hangs between us. Experience. Life. Bruises and armor and hard-won scars.

"I really wanted it to be you," I admit. "Behind the billboard, I mean."

"Yeah?" he smirks. "I'm flattered."

I give him a half-hearted laugh. "It's just that if it was you, then I could be pissed and hate you and know you only did it because of the partnership."

"Ah. I suppose then you'd know it wasn't potentially your bosses?" he guesses. "The people you've known for a lot longer. The people you trust."

I chew the inside of my lip, giving him a small nod.

"I mean, c'mon, admit it," I say. "There's at least some deep down part of you that would love to fuck me over."

He gives me an amused, searching stare. "I'd never fuck you over. Unless you wanted me to."

My heart does a little flip, like feeling brave on a trampoline. Everything about the way he says it sounds tempting, like maybe he meant to leave the last word off both of those statements.

"Yeah?" I tease. "What exactly would that entail?"

He runs his tongue between his lips. I see him notice that I notice.

"Things expressly prohibited by our agreement," he says. "Like what?"

I know I'm playing with fire. Maybe I'm in that kind of mood. I want to drop a lit match into the center of this and let it consume me. His gaze trails along my jaw, across my mouth, down the curve of my shoulder.

"Physical contact. Gratuitous compliments. Sabotage."

His eyes flash on that last word, and every syllable seems to sink into me. It takes an increasing amount of physical effort to hold myself in place.

What am I doing here, again?

I absently rub my brow, testing for tender spots, as if pressing on a bruise will distract me from the way my skin feels hungry and electric.

"Are you sure you're okay? You hit the window pretty hard."

"I'm fine," I say again, waving off his concern.

He slides off his perch, and suddenly he's within arm's reach, standing between my knees. I know we're too close, but I meet his gaze anyway.

"Your pupils are dilated."

"Of course they're dilated," I argue. "We're sitting here in the dark."

"I dunno," he says teasingly. "I might need to keep you for observation."

"That would probably be a breach of contract," I smirk.

He gingerly traces his fingers above my eyebrow. His touch is warm and tentative.

"Does that hurt?"

I swallow hard, hoping to quell the way my pulse is fluttering in my throat. "No."

His touch becomes a barely-there sweep along my jaw, a gentle lift of my chin.

"How many fingers am I holding up?"

I smile, only meaning to swat his hand from in front of me, but I end up catching it. His smile shifts, and his fingers tentatively thread through mine.

"Two?" I guess belatedly.

He rubs his thumb along the inside of my palm. "We should probably get you to a doctor. You're clearly not yourself."

"Yeah," I agree. "Probably."

I want to give in to this feeling. These eyes, as dark as the evening sky, searching mine with playful intensity. The insatiable late-night summer fire smell of him. This look like he could burn right through me. I realize we're still holding hands.

"In case there's any confusion," he says. "I'm not a doctor."

Instead of letting go, I tug him ever so slightly closer. Close enough that I can trace the buttons along his shirt with my free hand, so for some reason, I do. Down his solid chest. One after another. It's a nice shirt. And he's got a very nice body, one wrapped with lean muscles that harden beneath my touch. The lower I get, the shallower his breath becomes, and I can't help thinking about the way he looks shirtless. How his skin would feel against mine. What it would be like to trace that line of hair from his belly button, all the way down...

I guide his hand to my waist. His fingers spread wide instinctively, stretching across the strip of exposed skin along my ribcage.

"God, you're soft," he breathes.

"Observation or compliment?" I say.

"Sabotage," he murmurs.

I smile with a liquid ache spreading through me, and I can suddenly feel how it would be between us. Teasing and hot and sure.

I run my hands up his chest. I realize with sudden certainty that if I don't plan to kiss him, I should stop now. There's harmless flirting and then there's, well, *this*. Our hands on each other. Quentin standing between my thighs. The energy radiating off of him, seductive and playful and wanting. My lips feel ready to betray me, ripe and heavy in a way that feels urgent. Inevitable. Begging me to cross every boundary we ever agreed upon.

My heart hammers in my chest, reminding me that there is no turning back from here. If I linger for one more breath. If I tuck my fingers into the top of his beltline. If I lean in slightly, so close my nose brushes his. If I just... let things *happen*, for once.

And then – as if by divine intervention – something does

happen. It comes in the form of a loud, thunderous boom. It seems to vibrate through the building, and my breath catches in my chest. For a moment, I'm left blinking up at him. I seem to suddenly see myself: heart pounding, lips parted, a breath away from kissing Quentin Maxwell. And then, the resigned certainty that I'm *not* actually going to kiss Quentin Maxwell. Instead of matching my expression, his eyes spark with the ghost of a grin.

"Come with me," he says.

He tugs me off the desk in a smooth, unexpected pull and leads me by the hand, through the shadowy hallways. My unkissed lips feel tingly and confused.

"I don't actually need a doctor," I offer.

He shushes me, and for some reason, I stifle a laugh. He picks up the pace, and I follow him without knowing why we're running and ducking behind cubicles like assassins, as if anyone is here to catch us sneaking around.

"Where are we going? What is that noise?" I hiss, just above a whisper. (Hissper?) "Is this when you admit to me that you're The Dr. Pepper Thief?"

He lifts a finger to his lips when I let out a giggle.

A few maneuvers later, we find ourselves in a conference room on the south side of the building, just in time to see sparkling bursts of color light up the inky sky. I realize as I step up to the wall of windows that we're still holding hands. The lights of the minor league baseball stadium that's nestled in the middle of downtown have gone dark for this very occasion. The belated firework boom echoes on the other side of the windows. Up here, we're eye level with the sparks and embers. His hand slides out of mine easily.

"Front row seat?" he offers, swiveling a chair in my direction.

"Did you plan this?" I say suspiciously, sinking into it with a smile. He relaxes into one beside me.

"Oh yeah. I paid a fortune for that billboard in hopes that it would lure you to my office in the middle of the night, just in time for me to impress you with a private fireworks show."

"The long con, then," I say, nodding.

"Exactly," he smirks.

I smile, swiveling back and forth in my chair. I wonder if he realizes how close we were. I wonder if there's some part of him that's relieved, like some part of me is. I wonder if there's also a part that's unsettled, the way you feel when someone cuts a song to silence right in the middle of the chorus, but your lungs insist that you keep singing, if only to finish out the bar. I wonder if his heart is still fluttering in his throat.

If it was ever fluttering in his throat.

"You know I had my first kiss at a fireworks show?" I muse.

His gaze dips across my mouth. "Oh yeah? How was it?"

"Somewhat disappointing, on both counts," I chortle. "His name was Charlie, and he had nacho breath. And at some point before the grand finale, the fireworks trailer caught fire and they had to extinguish everything to prevent an explosion. Plus I had bangs, and it was humid out. Total disaster."

"What could possibly be disappointing about all that?" he laughs.

"I guess I imagined it would be more romantic."

"The boss babe of breaking up believes in romance?" he asks in mock horror. "Tell me more."

"Just because I don't have time for it doesn't mean I think it doesn't exist."

"Ah, yes. I'm sure you slide it right into your contacts."

"It hurts when you say things like that," I admit irritably. "Boundaries are pretty romantic in my book, thanks."

"Boundaries like yours seem to indicate the only way to your heart is to sneak in and steal it."

I shoot him a dirty look, while my heart thumps wildly in my chest, as if reacting to the prospect that it could be stolen. To the idea that maybe it might enjoy the thrill of being stolen.

"I guess I should be careful around you, then," I say. "Grand theft auto. Dr. Pepper. You're a regular Danny Ocean."

"I am *not* the Dr. Pepper Thief," he defends, thoroughly amused. "But I know who it is, if you really want to know."

"You know who it is because it's you."

"It's not me," he grins earnestly. "But if that's what you'd prefer to believe..."

"Who is it then?" I laugh.

"No. You've made up your mind."

"C'mon tell me. Now I need to know."

His gaze meets mine with such playful intensity that for a moment we're right back where we were on the edge of his desk. His mouth looks so damn kissable that I almost close my eyes and sway forward. At the last instant, his lips quirk up on one side.

"It's Ronnie," he whispers.

"What? No," I scoff. "Vegan, non-GMO, sugar-free Ronnie?? You're making this up to scandalize me."

He sits back in his chair with a smug grin, dragging his gaze back towards the windows.

"Trust me, Heidi. If I was trying to scandalize you, I've got much better ways to do it."

Holy hell.

The heat that spreads up my neck is immediate. Ideas of what exactly he might mean by that statement flick through my mind, and my pulse becomes a steady, impossible-to-ignore beat. In my chest. Between my thighs. Along the very edges of my being. I wet my lips, shifting in my seat, hoping to quell the way his words tighten through me.

"But that's not why we're here, right?" he says.

His voice is husky and warm and inviting. This is a challenge. An invitation. But also, a warning. This is everything I said I wasn't doing with him. I've clearly sustained a traumatic brain injury and am making questionable decisions, and somehow, he knows it.

I suck my lips between my teeth, giving him a resigned nod. "Right."

Sparkles of red, gold, and blue blossom in front of us, and suddenly the individual pops and booms become an overlapping roar. The grand finale is in full force, each burst more spectacular than the last, and I realize how long it's been since I stopped and watched fireworks. Surely I've done it since that disappointing first kiss? A few times in college, for sure, when Meg and I sat on the bluffs of the river for a big holiday spectacle, but even then there was a lot of tequila and at least one hangover-inducing diver bucket from Silky O'Sullivan's involved. But stone cold sober, in adulthood, with a guy who makes the energy in the room feel anticipatory, like standing at the edge of the world with a handful of lit firecrackers? This feeling is brand new.

The sky finally fades to dark. From here I can hear the boom of the announcer's voice, can almost imagine the crowd cheering.

Down the hall, the elevator dings. I hear the doors slide open, followed by voices and laughter. It takes a moment to register, like it's happening somewhere faraway, and then the lights flicker on in the hallway. The spell is broken. We blink at each other slowly, as if coming out of a trance. An unspoken understanding passes between us.

"I should go," I say softly.

I almost want him to argue with me, but he doesn't. He nods and extends his closed fist. I smirk before wrapping my fingers tight and bumping my knuckles half-heartedly against his, feeling at once satisfied and ridiculous. He lets his hand stretch wide in a mock explosion. I laugh as I gather myself up. I can feel him watching as I head for the door.

"You can still blame me for the billboard, and the minor concussion, and the Dr. Pepper, if you want," he says. "Most people would."

I turn back to see him silhouetted by the city light. Even in the dark he's handsome. All the way across the room, I can still feel the magnetic pull of him. I lean against the doorframe as if I can use it to anchor myself, only briefly, before giving him a small nod.

"Thanks. I'm not really like most people."

His gaze flickers.

"You're not like anyone I've ever met," he says. "Good night, PBG."

I keep my head down as I attempt to stroll casually towards the elevator, passing the curious stare of the overnight cleaning crew: a woman watering plants and a guy vacuuming the rugs. It's only once I'm in the reflective quiet of the elevator, staring at my blurry reflection in the doors, that I realize I'm still smiling.

13.

I SWEEP INTO HENRY'S OFFICE. "A billboard?"

"Isn't it great?"

This is the confirmation I was looking for, but it feels anything but victorious. My stomach twists.

"It would have been great if someone had checked in with me on this," I say. "I'm twelve feet tall."

"Fourteen, actually. I hope it's fourteen. We're paying for fourteen."

He acts like he's searching for the ad contract.

"This isn't about the extra two feet, Henry," I argue. "Is this really what you and the partners think of me? That I'm some sort of joke?"

"A joke?" he says, baffled. "This is some of the best publicity we've ever had. People love the tagline."

He's midway through the jingle when I interrupt.

"This is exploitation."

"This is a leg up," he says, more serious now. "Clients are our business, and since that article came out, clients want *you*. You can use this to your advantage during the partnership vote. Quentin might be Erving's grandson, but he's not doing anything for the reputation of the firm. Eventually, someone's going to dig up all the dirt on him, and I don't plan for us to fall into that hole."

"The car?" I guess, using that shred of gossip. "That's old news."

"The car, the drugs, that thing with the stepmothers," Henry says, waving his hand as if swiping away cobwebs. "Not to mention the other family issues."

This brings me up short. I want to stay out of it, write this off as more insidious gossip, but I hear myself asking, "What thing with the stepmothers?"

"I don't know all the details, but I know it's rumored he ran off three of them. Three! What kind of terror do you have to be to send three respectable women running for the hills?" he says vaguely. "But you and I both know, where there's smoke there's fire. Something is going to come up sooner or later."

"What are you suggesting I do about it, Henry? I'm not a trained circus animal. These are a lot of damn hoops to navigate."

"I want you two to work together, of course, but don't get *too* tangled up with him." He says this as if I am already in fact tangled up with him. He also seems to miss the way this makes me bristle. "When all this is over, I want you to walk away sparkling."

He starts typing as if we're done with this conversation. I roll my eyes in irritation, dragging myself out of the chair. For better or worse, since the ad went up, my calendar is beyond packed. He's lucky I have meetings to get to.

"Don't think I've forgiven you for this," I say.

"Sparkling," he calls after me. The musical tone of his voice trails me down the hall – part mocking, part warning, part... accusation.

I can feel the interns' collective eyes on me, peering above the cubicles as I leave Henry's office. When they see I've caught them staring, their heads duck back into the sea of desks like prairie dogs disappearing into their burrows at the first sign of a threat, which only serves to make me feel worse.

I lift my chin and strut, as confidently as I can, back to my own office. I've got too much damn work to do to justify worrying about any of this.

***

"Everyone thinks I'm sleeping with him," I tell Auntie Lena. "It's insulting."

We're sweating in the second-story stairwell of her three-story apartment/shop during the infamous Quarterly Window Display Update. I've got the lower half of a mannequin under one arm, and the upper body beneath the other. Occasionally, when I pivot to avoid an ill-placed cardboard box on the stairs, an errant white plastic hand smacks me on the backside.

We do this every year.

For whatever reason, Jack and Annie only come out of storage in July and hang around until December. The other half of the year it's Erin and Andy. This summer, though, she's had a grand new idea: block party. She says it with sparkling eyes and widespread fingers, like she's introducing a musical act. This is how it was determined that all of them need to come down.

I've avoided this requisite nightmare since I graduated law school and left Auntie Lena's payroll, but she's currently between employees, and she claimed she needed someone with experience for this. Experience being felt up by inanimate objects, apparently.

"Jack and Annie know you," she argued. "You're like family."

"I *am* family," I grumbled. "Unfortunately."

This is how I ended up trudging down the narrow stairs that have that musty attic smell, mingled with the smoky aroma of incense as we pass the landing for her apartment on the second floor. I readjust the mannequin halves less than gracefully, navigating around Auntie Lena's latest foster kitten, Pimento, before making the final descent.

"*Are* you sleeping with him?" she asks now, hauling a trio of hot pink lawn flamingos down behind me.

"No," I snap. "See, even you think it. Why?"

"Is it so ridiculous to think you'd be having sex? You're an attractive young woman who has never struck me as having antiquated ideas about physical intimacy. It makes sense."

"I work with him."

"So what? Half of everyone I know met their significant other at work. You spend a lot of time there. It only makes sense that it's where you might meet someone with similar interests."

I attempt, unsuccessfully, to blow a stray piece of hair off my face. I paw at my sweaty cheek. I wonder, beyond the prospect of partnership, if Quentin and I could really be classified as having similar interests. 'Helping people dissolve their marriages' can hardly be considered an 'interest'.

"Okay, but I'm a professional."

"Okay," she counters, "but that's not all you are. You're a person. People need more than work and money. They need companionship."

"Oh yeah? Where's your companionship?" I say.

She holds up the flamingos, as if for emphasis. "I've got plenty of companionship, thank you."

"I know you do," I offer, apologetic.

Auntie Lena dates. I know she dates.

Okay, I *think* she dates.

Regardless, I also know she's fine on her own.

She was married once, briefly, back when she was in her early twenties. She never talks about it, but my mom used to bring it up every now and then. He died in an accident, shortly after they were married. She got the shop that had been left to him by his late parents and sold the house they shared, eventually moving into the apartment upstairs.

After my mom married Eric, when she stopped going by Jenny and became Jen, she always lamented that Auntie Lena was living in the past, "with all that junk". Jenny was the woman who dragged me along with the two of them to estate sales, who rifled through bins at second-hand shops, who sang along in the car to Madonna's *Immaculate Collection*; she would have thought Nine Lives was a treasure trove. Jen wouldn't dream of doing any of those things.

Despite what my mom said, I always thought Auntie Lena was just carving out her future. Making lemonade, as they say. We all squeeze the lemons we're dealt.

"Tell me what you really want to say," she says, easing down the stairs behind me.

I chew the inside of my lip in frustration. I've been this way for weeks. I can't seem to get my thoughts in order, and my nerves feel like the end of a frayed wire, looking for its release point.

"Before I knew he was... well, *him*... I actually did kind of like him. Or at least, I thought I could."

She drops the flamingos into a pile with the other stuff we've hauled into the shop. A "hm" sound escapes her, and I can't tell if it's in response to making it to the bottom of the stairwell or a prompt for me to keep talking.

"So if he had another job or another name, you *could* still like him or you *would* still like him?" she asks. "Because those are different things."

"I dunno," I say.

Unfortunately, it's the truth. I don't know anything about how I feel when it comes to him, especially now that we got way too close after hours, not once but twice now.

"The reality, though, is that he doesn't have another job or another name," I conclude. "Hypotheticals are pointless."

"Maybe, but they're interesting," she smiles. "What's going on with work, anyway? One of the gossip accounts I follow is saying some pretty outrageous stuff about that big name client of yours."

Auntie Lena's guiltiest pleasure is celebrity gossip rags. I wonder if she's also seen the things they're saying about me. I heave another sigh, hugging Jack-the-mannequin's torso to mine for moral support.

"Yeah, that's a whole other issue."

The more depositions we collect, the more unclear this case becomes. Everyone has an opinion about Teddy and Gigi's relationship, and par for the course, they all vary wildly from each other. Her friends think he's a scumbag. His friends think she's a golddigger. The security team for their gated neighborhood thinks they're a typical married couple. Their housekeeper refuses to comment. Unfortunately, Teddy's first wife has also yet to respond to any of our attempts at contact. Quentin thinks that in itself may speak volumes. I remain unconvinced.

Auntie Lena takes Jack from me gingerly, as if I've drifted off somewhere and might look desperate enough to kidnap him. She plops his torso on the fake turf in the front window that reminds me of a mini golf course. Together, we survey the stacks of bright valencia tableware, clothing options mostly fun and floral, and a tangle of paper lanterns.

"I think if we just grab the yellow lawn furniture..." she considers.

I give her a resigned nod, and we make our third – or is it fourth? – trip back up the stuffy stairwell.

"Speaking of work," I say, "when are you going to hire more help?"

"I've interviewed a few people," she says, trailing behind me, "but none of them have been the right fit."

"All you need is someone to organize merchandise and run the cash register," I argue. "How particular do you really need to be?"

The help wanted sign has been stuck in the front window for almost three months. I've begged her to let me post it online, but she wants the whole thing to be "more organic". I've reminded her weekly that we're not talking about fruits and vegetables here.

"I spend a lot of time with these people," she defends. "I don't want them to be..."

Instead of finishing that sentence with actual words, she waves her hand vaguely.

"No, I actually have no idea what –" I pause, mimicking her hand gesture "– means. And apparently neither does anyone else. Why don't you scope out the local gym, hang near the stairmaster? Those folks may have the skillset you're looking for."

She laughs, squeezing my shoulder as we come to the landing at the second floor. "Okay okay. Hint taken. It's hot as hell up there. Let's take a break."

Much to Pimento's delight, we head into the air conditioning of the second floor apartment. He weaves a figure eight around her ankles, which she navigates without ever breaking stride as she heads for the kitchen. I plop down on the well-loved pink sofa, immediately throwing my feet up on the cluttered sunburst coffee table. She returns with a neon plastic pitcher of stevia-sweetened lemonade and a pair of highball glasses adorned with a lemon pattern, pouring us each a tall glass before settling into her retro green armchair.

"I'm serious about the job ad, though. Where have you posted it?"

"Around," she shrugs.

"Okay, as much as I love you, I am going on the record that I will *not* be doing this little exercise again in October."

"It'll be much cooler in October," she says.

"So not the point," I laugh.

I pause, taking a few long gulps of the refreshingly cold lemonade, but unfortunately the rest of our debate is lost to sudden chaos. When I move to set my glass down, I miss the edge of the coaster. The glass tips over with a clink, and the sticky liquid quickly begins to spread across the table. I begin grabbing magazines and junk mail instinctively, muttering curse words.

Auntie Lena laughs, waving a hand as she hurries for the kitchen.

"Nothing a towel won't fix," she calls.

Pimento hops up to inspect, unhelpfully dipping his paw into the puddle. He flings droplets of lemonade onto my face as he shakes it out. The corner of the magazine I'm holding drips onto an open letter. I snag it as well, and in my attempt to shake the moisture off, it falls open.

I don't mean to look at it, but the bold header catches my eye. It's from Delta Regional Medical Group. The list of labs and procedure codes is long, and I don't know what all of them mean, but I can clearly see they're extensive. And expensive. This wasn't from a run-of-the-mill appointment.

Auntie Lena rushes back in, scooping Pimento off the table as she tosses the towel onto the mess.

"Are you okay?" I ask.

"Oh, honey, don't worry about it," she says. "Most of this stuff needed to go anyway."

"No, I mean *this*," I say, holding the water-stained bill out to her.

Her expression goes temporarily shocked before she casually takes it, adding it to the mass of ruined coupon offers and car warranty reminders with a flutter of her hand, as if she could wave the thought away. She starts tittering about junk mail and insurance mistakes. My heart is thudding in my chest.

"Are you sick?"

"Do I look sick?" she laughs, patting her pixie cut. "No. I'm fine."

She cleans the table and dumps the soaked materials into the trash. When she returns, she's got a fresh glass for me. She sets it down and assumes her previous position in her favorite floral armchair, running a hand along Pimento's arched spine as if nothing happened.

"You're being weird," I say, narrowing my eyes at her.

"You're starting to sound like your mother," she teases.

"Objection, your honor: unfair opinion," I say, mock offended. "I don't mean it like that. That just looked like a lot of tests. You would tell me, right? If you were sick?"

"Maybe," she shrugs. "What? Stop looking at me like that."

"Like what?"

"Like I'm elderly. Like you're about to start driving me to my doctor's appointments, because I can't be trusted to safely operate a motor vehicle or make decisions about my own health."

"That is not how I'm looking at you," I argue. (Full disclosure: that's definitely how I'm looking at her.) "This is a look of concern. Loving concern."

"There is no need for concern. I just walked up a million flights of stairs, same as you," she says. "I don't want you to worry about me. I'm not even old enough to qualify for most of those fancy retirement resorts, you know. "

I want her to be honest with me. I want to dig the letter out of the trash and research all the codes. I want to find her doctor, demand a diagnosis, and find a treatment plan that will kick its ass, whatever *it* is. I give her another assessing stare and sink into one of the Heidi-sized divots on the pink couch.

"You can't control if I worry or not," I point out.

"Well, I'd still rather you wouldn't," she smirks. "I was just feeling a little run-down recently, and I wanted to make sure it wasn't something serious."

"And it wasn't?"

"It's probably just menopause," she says with a wave of her hand. I can tell this gesture is supposed to convince me.

"I like to think you'd tell me," I say. "I don't know why there would be a need for secrecy."

"Everyone is entitled to her secrets," she says demurely.

I eye her over the top of my fresh cup, semi-amused. "What else are you keeping from me?"

"Probably about as much as you're keeping me from," she smirks.

"You've been reading too many magazines," I say, rolling my eyes for emphasis. "I just hope you know I'm always in your corner. You know that right? No matter what."

She gives me a knowing smile. "C'mon. I'm in *your* corner. Don't forget you still have people rooting for you, babe."

I lift my cup to her in a sarcastic toast. "Go team." Then, "Just promise me you'll get some help in here soon? Otherwise I may be forced to hire someone myself and send them over. Don't put it past me. You know I will."

She grins. "Oh, I never had a doubt. So about this guy you're somehow still not sleeping with..."

14.

WHEN I RETREAT TO THE SOLACE OF MY BUILDING, all I can think is how much I need to cool off, and thankfully I've got the pool to myself. Nobody is ever up here this late. I prop my forearms on the edge and let the water cool my skin. I still feel hot, though, with that pent up energy that seems to vibrate just beneath the surface.

The truth is, I can't stop thinking about him. Part of me wishes I would have told him to fuck off the very moment he passed me that drink. Maybe if I had, I could've established him as an enemy proper. There would have been no confusion. No hand holding, no near-miss kiss, and definitely no full body contact. The only time I've gotten it right was when I pushed him into the pool, though there are still some other, very specific parts that would probably prefer that I push him straight into my bed. But the most unnerving thing about all of it was that feeling – however brief – of floating.

It's not unlike the feeling of being in this pool. Comfortable. Effortless. As if every molecule of my being is perfectly buoyant.

I let my forehead fall against my arms. Maybe those trolls on the internet are right. Maybe I do need to get laid. It's not like I *couldn't* get laid, if I wanted to. It's just that sex is such a give and take, and I'm not willing to let Quentin take anything from me. Not my heart. Not my job. Especially not my reputation.

I bet Quentin isn't worried about jeopardizing his reputation.

The more I think about it, the more agitated I feel. I swish my legs through the water, reveling in the simple easy feel of the current. My movements catch the flow from one of the pool jets. The steady stream of water massages my thighs. I run my hand in front of it, letting the soft pressure caress my fingers. It's got such a sensual feel to it, being here alone like this. The soft blue glow of the pool light. The inky sky stretched out above me. The sounds of the city surrounding me – the traffic and music and pedal pubs – though I can't see them, and they can't see me. I am suspended in my own private spa-like bubble.

And I sigh. Because, somehow, I'm still thinking about Quentin.

I realize he has edged into my thoughts again, the same way I realize that I've shifted until the gentle pressure of the water is now sometimes massaging a very *particular* spot. My eyes slide closed, and for a moment I can see him.

Can feel the tickle of his words across the back of my neck as he teased me in that canoe.

Can picture the flicker of his eyes as he leaned in close in the dark of his office, sweeping his fingers along my jaw.

Can imagine exactly what he would look like with his strong arms wrapped around me, with his hand over my hand, guiding it over my breasts, along my belly and down, and *down...* where the steady stream of water is currently meeting my need.

I let out a frustrated little laugh as heat laps up my neck. I push away from the edge, glancing around the empty pool deck as I tread water. Even here, alone in the dark, I can tell I'm blushing. Because what the hell am I doing?

Reasonably, the pool is "closed". Nobody would think to come up here at this hour, though I've lived here long enough to know that they only enforce hours of operation when there are noise complaints. So as long as I don't make any noise...

I drift back over, finding the edge of the pool with my forearms. I let the current innocently dance between the slow cycling of my legs beneath me. My movements create gentle ripples along the surface. The quiet wake caresses my shoulders, teasing at that invisible line that separates the parts of me that exist above the surface and the parts that are hidden below.

I close my eyes again, unable to turn off the way I'm suddenly sensitive to the feel of everything around me. The night air kissing my neck. The triangle top of my bikini cupping my breasts. The very strategically placed pool jet, teasing between my thighs.

Nobody will see me, I remind myself. I'm just enjoying a late night swim. Like, *really* enjoying it. And it won't take long, anyway. The throbbing heat that has pooled in my center is making that painfully clear. I release a frustrated sigh.

Oh, fuck it.

I reposition myself in a way that feels effortlessly good. Just like that, I feel my inhibitions slip, and with them goes my ability to hold back the flood of thoughts about Quentin. Not the ones where I want to professionally vanquish him. No, these are much darker and more delicious.

The ones where we lock my office door, and he wraps his arms around me from behind, kissing my neck as he undoes the buttons of my shirt.

The ones where he bends me over the desk and rubs his hard length up and down my slick center.

The ones that make me wonder what kind of dirty talk comes out of that beautiful mouth of his.

My body moves instinctively as all these thoughts turn hot and liquid. My fingers grip the edge of the pool as my hips shift in slow circles. I wonder as I stifle another sigh of pleasure if I'd let him fuck me in a pool. I can imagine the up close feel of him as he nibbles at my ear, can almost breathe in the intoxicating late-night smell of him, can hear his voice against the side of my neck.

"Come on, baby. Admit it. You're a horny girl who would beg me *to fuck you in this pool."*

Oh my god, yes, that shameless, aching part of me says. *A hundred times, yes.*

Fantasy Quentin unties my top and tugs off my bottoms. He drags his hands over the swell of my breasts, teasing my nipples into hard, sensitive peaks that he rolls between his thumb and forefinger, just to drive me crazy. And it does. In this impossible fantasy, I'm delirious with pleasure as he hooks one of his strong arms around me and knees my legs apart. He angles me just right against the jet, until I'm coursing with need and biting my lip to fight back a moan.

God, I'm so close.

From somewhere that sounds faraway, I hear the latch on the rooftop door click as it opens. My mind seems to register that it's the real rooftop door and not some imagined intrusion. By the time my eyes slide open, I see a shadowy figure letting the door close behind it.

Shapeless panic seizes me. I quickly snap my legs together, holding my breath and hoping to cling, unseen, to the side of the pool. Meanwhile, my heart is hammering in my chest, seemingly demanding to know – on behalf of my body – why I stopped about thirty seconds short of the much-needed edge.

I can't make out the figure, but it is definitely a person, and he's already at the stairs of the pool before he notices me.

"Oh," he stammers. "Hi. Sorry. I didn't realize anyone was –"

"Quentin?"

It comes out breathless. I blink at his shadowy outline, wondering in my stupor if I somehow conjured him out of thin air.

"Heidi?" he says, squinting. "Sorry, it's dark out here. I –"

"Didn't you read the sign?" I ask, keeping my voice just above a husky whisper. "The pool's closed."

The corner of his mouth edges up in a smile. "Then what are you doing up here?"

I know he means this innocently, but absolutely nothing about the heat in my body right now feels innocent. I'm grateful for the dark so he can't see the evidence burning across my face. I swallow thickly.

"Cooling off," I say.

There's a low, sensual quality to my voice that matches the way my entire body is still humming with electricity. It's the kind of energy that is still seeking pleasure, and if I'm not careful, I imagine it's going to reach for Quentin the way lightning seeks the ground.

"Mind if I join?" he asks.

"I was just leaving," I lie, already hauling myself up over the edge.

"Oh c'mon. Stay. We've still got at least four and a half minutes of smalltalk."

I ignore his teasing in favor of wrapping my towel snugly around me as if it can act as some sort of protective barrier, like a cotton blend chastity belt. "What could you possibly need to talk to me about?"

He peels off his shirt and drops it at the edge of the pool. He audibly sighs as he descends the stairs and wades into the water. It's a sound that gives me a flash of Fantasy Quentin.

"Damn, the water's perfect," he says, letting his gaze tip towards the sky as he runs both hands through his hair. "They don't lock it?"

"Not usually," I say. "But they will, if they get complaints."

"We'll have to be quiet, then."

He winks at me before he goes under. The words, the gesture – all of it – tug hard through my center, urging me to slip back into the pool so I can wrap myself around him. I'm fairly confident I could do it, too. He might have been respectful of our mutual boundaries thus far, but I have a pretty good feeling that if I wanted to seduce him, I could.

At what cost?

When he resurfaces, I'm still stranding here, clutching my towel around me.

"Have you solved the billboard mystery yet?" he asks.

"Yeah," I say. "Unfortunately I have."

"Unfortunate because I won't find you snooping around my office again, after hours?"

When he smirks, my stomach flips, and I wonder why I didn't kiss him that night, even though I know the answer to that a hundred times over. I perch on a lounge chair positioned at the edge of the pool.

"Unfortunate because it was exactly who I hoped it wasn't."

"That's tough, I'm sorry."

"That's business," I shrug.

His features shift with amusement. "That sounds a lot like an easy excuse for letting people act like assholes."

"Really. It's fine."

He wades deeper, treading water. "Why do you always do that?"

"Do what?"

"That thing, where you shrug everything off. Apologies. Support. Feelings."

I scoff, indignant. "I don't shrug off feelings. I have feelings. I'm not just a fucking billboard, I'm an actual person, you know."

I don't know why I feel this needs to be said.

"Yes, I *do* know. I'm just wondering why you're not more critical of the people who seemingly don't."

I am seized with the urge to jump into the pool and strangle him. Or seduce him. It's a fine line, mostly because I'm generally angry about how much I want him – and how much everyone *assumes* that I want him. The anger wins out.

"What do you want me to say, Quentin? That I'm hurt, and pissed off, and questioning every decision I've made for the past ten years?"

I mean it to sound sarcastic, but once again, as too often happens with him, it lands like something I didn't mean to admit out loud.

"That sounds closer to the truth."

"You're infuriating, you know that?"

"Because I'm right?"

"Because you're calling me out as if you have any right to. You're telling me you've never let anything slide? That you haven't made excuses to justify being here? You're playing their game, same as me."

"I know."

"Well, then you also know that we all have to pick our battles."

I realize he has drifted to the very edge of the pool, with his arms propped on the concrete in front of me. He's doing that searching stare, like he's looking for some hidden meaning in the contours of my face. His expression darkens, and he swims until there's a more respectable distance between us.

"You're right. We all do it," he says. "But don't you ever wonder if we're fighting for the right things?"

He sucks in a breath and dives under the surface again. His rippled image launches off the wall and glides across the length of the pool, towards the deeper end. By the time he makes the turn and resurfaces in the shallows, I've already gathered myself up and made it halfway to the exit door. I catch the dancing reflection of the blue glow behind me in the glass. Quentin props himself against the edge and drags a shadowy hand down his face, surrounded by glowing blue.

"Heidi. Come back," he calls after me quietly. "I didn't mean to–"

"Your five minutes is up."

I catch an unreadable expression clouding his features, and he doesn't offer to explain it. He just watches me go.

15.

Despite my continued distaste for the billboard, my calendar is packed with consultations for new clients. In all my years with Freeman, Maxwell, and Lewis, I've never been this busy, not even when I was an overworked intern volunteering for everything I could to make a good impression, which meant practically living at my desk. I've been enlisting the interns to do most of the legwork on this current caseload, but I have to admit it's *a lot*.

Of course, I'll never actually admit that to anyone but myself. And why should I? I always manage to get by, and I comfort myself with the knowledge that I'm in control here. If I reach the point where 'a lot' becomes 'too much', I can always pump the brakes. The fact that I've never actually done anything resembling that seems irrelevant, really.

Bernadette gives me a look when I say goodbye to my fifth client of the morning shortly after one o'clock, passing me another folder on my way past.

"I hope you weren't planning to eat lunch today," she says. "Your next appointment is already waiting for you in the conference room."

I glance at my smartwatch with a furrowed brow. Forget lunch, I'm wondering if I've even got time to pee at any point in the foreseeable future.

"Would you mind ordering me something?" I say. "I think I can squeeze it in after this, while I return a few calls."

"Optimistic, aren't we?" Bernadette teases.

I flip open the folder, scanning the intake form. It looks like a run-of-the-mill divorce consultation. She's claiming at fault. I could do this in my sleep. In fact, lately, I *have* been doing these in my sleep. Apparently when I finally crash into my oversized bed alone each night, discussions about financial assets and equitable division are all my subconscious can come up with. Unless you count the occasional appearance of a very shirtless dream-like version of Quentin Maxwell, which I do not.

"The benefit of doing these nonstop is that I'm getting good enough to shave precious seconds off my time," I smirk. "If I'm not done in twenty minutes, order me the cobb salad from the cafe downstairs?"

"You got it," she grins, simultaneously typing out an email and pressing one of the switchboard buttons on her phone, talking into her headset. "Freeman, Maxwell, and Lewis…" she chirps as I walk away.

I tuck the folder under my arm and navigate toward the conference room near the elevators. It's the one I shared with Quentin that night we watched the fireworks. Of course it is. As much as I've tried to forget about our little run-in, occasionally I catch a flash of that heart-flipping feeling that I got when he looked at me all searching and hungry. I can still hear the sexy tone of his voice, still feel my fingers tracing the buttons of his shirt.

"Things expressly prohibited by our agreement."

Warmth creeps up my neck as I think about it, partly because

I feel stupid for having done any of it in the first place, but also because I desperately want to do it again. Add that to the long list of things I'd fight someone before I admitted out loud. I find myself in the perpetual position of having to break the news to myself.

Sorry, Heidi. Never gonna happen.

Sure, it doesn't feel fair, but so what? Life's not fair. And Quentin? Quentin's definitely not fair.

I'm tucking the thought back into the recesses of my mind as I let myself through the door. Like all of our conference rooms, there's frosted glass along the bottom half, so I can't see my client until I'm already in the room. I'm already halfway through introductions when I register that she – Ms. Ashley Kate James, a brunette in tennis whites that I'd place in her late thirties – is sitting beside a very sulky looking elementary-aged child.

"Oh," I say, coming up short. "And who do we have here?"

"My daughter, Emma," Ms. James says, waving her hand as if the little girl's presence is inconsequential.

I glance at her again, taking note of the way her round cheeks are tinged pink. I'd almost think she'd spent too much time in the sun recently, except that this particular color looks a lot more like simmering resentment. Her big brown eyes stare at me somewhat defiantly before dropping to the table.

"How old are you, Emma?" I offer.

"Seven," she says without looking up.

Chills run up my arms. *Seven.* It echoes in my ears like a heartbeat.

"I had to let our nanny go recently, you know. I guess that's what I get for not listening to my mother when she told me the only thing they're good for is sleeping with your husband behind your back!" Ms. James titters out a laugh with a roll of her eyes. "Anyway, it's really put a twist in my schedule this summer. This whole thing has honestly been a nightmare, as I'm sure you understand. But Emma's fine. She won't be any trouble. Right, babe?"

Emma doesn't respond. I force myself to arrange my face into something resembling professionalism.

"This won't take long," I say amiably. "I can set her up in one of the chairs by reception."

"Oh no, it's fine. Really," Ms. James says. "She's heard it all before!"

"I'm sure she has," I say. My even smile adds, *And it's definitely not fine.*

"Well, I'm a modern woman. I'm not ashamed to admit it," she continues. "My husband left us. She deserves to know the truth."

The truth, I think bitterly.

I lean across the table, pressing a button on the conference phone positioned between us. Bernadette's voice fills the room a moment later.

"Yes, Ms. Krupp?"

"We've got a young guest who's going to hang out with you while we get through this paperwork," I say. "Can you send someone to escort her?"

"Yes, ma'am. Be right there."

I can sense that Ms. Ashley Kate James is not pleased with this. Her expression is wide-eyed and bordering on manic.

"This is really unnecessary," she tells me. That nervous laugh edges her voice.

A moment later there's a knock on the door. I expect an assistant. Instead, I see Quentin on the other side of the glass. I blink at him, wondering how or why he's standing here right now. I will him to go away. Instead, he opens the door.

"I'm here to escort Miss James to the front desk," he says. He's got the perfect executive assistant voice, all smooth and accommodating, like attending to my needs is his utmost priority.

Emma peers at me, interested. Until this moment, I don't think she expected that she was going to be able to leave the room.

"Be sure to ask for snacks," I tell her conspiratorially. "Ms. Bernadette has all the best snacks."

Emma gives me a sideways look that glimmers. It's not a grin, but it might be the closest I can get, given the circumstances. From a kid in her place – and I know far more than I'd like to admit about that place – it feels like a gold star.

"Anything else, Ms. Krupp?" Quentin says from the doorway.

I glance up, realizing he's studying me. I attempt to swallow whatever emotion has welled up in me in the few minutes I've been in here. If it were anyone else standing there, I wouldn't worry, but sometimes I get the feeling Quentin can see all my walls – maybe see *past* them – and it unnerves me.

"No," I say. "Thank you."

He nods once before ushering Emma into the hall and shutting the door behind them.

"So," I say, turning back to my stack of papers and attempting to get my bearings. "You're here to file for divorce?"

"Yes," she replies, still looking a little ruffled. "As I mentioned earlier, my husband left us –"

The words climb my throat, escaping before I can stop them.

"Left you," I amend.

For a moment, neither of us seems to believe I've said it. The screwed tight look of Ashley Kate's smile twists a little further.

"Excuse me?" she blinks.

"Your husband is still going to be a father after all this," I explain. "But he won't still be a husband. So I'd like for us to be clear: he's leaving your marriage, not your daughter. Unless he is in fact planning to terminate his parental rights?"

I check the papers in front of me as if scanning them for this detail. When I glance back up expectantly, she's still smiling, but she looks like her eyeballs are about to burst out of her head.

"What the hell is this?" she laughs, her voice high-pitched and grating. "*I'm* not the one who did anything wrong here. This is *his* fault. He's the one who couldn't keep his dick in his pants, and –"

"And right now you're putting it on your kid," I interject. "If we're going to work together, that's one of the things we'll need to agree on. It's a hard line for me. The kids stay out of it, as much as possible."

She bursts out laughing, and the sound scrapes across my already raw nerves. She's not that much older than me, but suddenly I feel decades older this woman, as if maybe I'm talking to a high school student instead of a tried-and-true adult.

"You're supposed to be the *best*, so I shouldn't have to explain this to you," she says, letting a mocking edge creep into her tone. "But I'm paying you to be my *divorce attorney*. I don't need your opinions about how I raise my kid."

I close the file and steeple my fingers under my chin. I've got a waiting list of more new clients than I could possibly take on. I know if I send her on her way that there will be more than enough people willing to take her place. But I also know that if she's looking for the kind of attorney who will help her use her kid as a bargaining chip, she'll find one. I wet my lips, gathering my patience. Not for her, but for Emma.

"Ms. James, I am good at what I do. You may be the one paying the attorney's fees, but I have an obligation as an officer of the court to act in the best interest of your daughter, and it's in your best interest to support that. This isn't just about ending your marriage; it's also about making sure that your daughter still wants to have a relationship with you when this is all over. I don't mean right now, when she's seven and relies on you for everything, but later, when she's grown and out of the house and doesn't have any obligation to speak to you, if she doesn't want to, ever again. And trust me, if you continue down this path you're on – blaming her, acting like you're sister wives who've been mutually wronged – she won't want to. That's not an opinion about your parenting. It's a fact."

She's staring at me like she wishes she had laser beams for eyes and could slice me in half. Instead, a frustrated tear rolls down one cheek. She swipes it away with an annoyed laugh. I'm holding my breath, ready to release it at any second, because I know I've got her. She's going to cave. She's going to agree. They always agree.

"God, I knew better than this," she says, gathering her purse and pushing back the chair so hard it smacks the glass wall behind her. The entire panel rattles. I know the moment she stands up, everyone outside is able to see her. See the angry tears on her face. See the way she's pointing at me. "What the hell did I expect? Some woman who's never been *married*, who doesn't even *have kids*, whose face is on a goddamn *billboard*."

She's cutting me down to size using society's rubric of womanhood: do I have a husband, have I reproduced, am I modest enough about my accomplishments? On all counts, that's clearly a no. It's easy by that metric to determine I'm not an adequate woman. I'm a self-centered witch. A well-dressed devil.

"Ms. James," I say evenly. My heart is thudding wildly in my throat, but I'm sure I can get this back on track. I always do. Any second now, she's going to sit back down. "Let's talk about what you really want out of this –"

She swings the door open with a wild fling of her arm.

"What I really want?" she screeches. "Fuck you! I want nothing more to do with you! Do I have some sort of sign on me that makes people think I'll stick around when they treat me like trash? Well I won't. And I'm not. Take a look at yourself, honey – you're the high dollar trash!"

The conference room door is one of those that can't be slammed. Its slow-close mechanism gives me plenty of time to watch Ms. Ashley Kate James stalk towards the lobby in that short skirt and snatch her kid off one of the chairs beside Bernadette's desk.

I see Bernadette wearing her headset, with her eyes wide and her mouth slightly ajar.

I see a couple of associates watching, dumbfounded, as their gazes follow the trajectory back to this conference room – directly to me – before quickly diverting.

Eventually, mercifully, the frosted door clicks closed. Then, and only then, do I allow my head to sink into my hands. I release a shaky breath, threading my hands into my hair. I realize it's not just my breath that's trembling: it's my hands, my arms, my bouncing knee. My thoughts are racing, and I can't seem to slow them down.

Your dad said he doesn't want you to live with him.

Your dad makes your mom cry, isn't that true?

Your dad makes you cry, too. That's not very nice, is it? Aren't you scared he'll hurt you, too?

Don't you want this to all be over?

Don't you want it to stop?

You just have to tell the judge the truth.

"What the fuck," I murmur. "What the fuck, what the fuck, what the –"

"Heidi?"

My attention snaps up to find Quentin standing in the door. He's doing that searching stare thing again, and this time I really can't. I close my eyes, pressing my fingers between my eyebrows as if there might be a reset button there, or at least some secret pressure point that's going to keep me from imploding. My entire body feels tense, like I'm about to scream until my lungs collapse.

"Quentin," I say. The sound is barely audible, even to my own ears. "Go away."

"You're not okay." He says it, and it's not a judgment, just an observation. One that seems, on some level, to quietly concern him.

"I'm fine."

He ignores this blatant lie. "Do you have any gym clothes here? In your office?"

My chest swells with a breath, and I blink up at him. "Yes. But what does that have to do with –"

"Grab them and meet me at the elevators," he says.

"No. I can't. I have…" I fumble for the right word. "Meetings." God, more meetings. "All afternoon."

"You're clear," he says. "I'll tell Bernadette something's come up. With the Glass case. The associates can cover."

I know when I look at him that he's lying about the case. Still, he holds my gaze like a lifeline.

"Trust me," he whispers.

It's such a big ask. Huge. Impossible. It fills up my chest until I'm sure that I'm actually going to scream. Instead, I swallow.

"Teddy needs us over at the studio," he says now, loud enough that the eavesdroppers – and I know without seeing them that there *are* eavesdroppers – can hear. "He said it's urgent. Can you make it work?"

I narrow my gaze at him. This feels like a trap. Somewhere in my brain, there are big red flashy signs telling me to turn around. DANGER: HIGH CLIFF. I should be mindful of the guardrails. Protective of them.

I make a mental map of all the motions I'll need to accomplish the thing he's asking: walking to my office, grabbing my black canvas bag of gym clothes, telling Bernadette where we're headed with a straight face, somehow managing to not cry. It feels like it'll take more resolve than I have at the present moment. It also feels like my only option.

I clear my throat, giving him a resolute nod.

"I'll get my things."

16.

WHEN I WAS SEVEN, I testified against my dad in court. I remember his posture more than anything. Slumped and defeated, like any moment he might crumple. He kept his face pressed into his hands the entire time, elbows propped on the table in front of him, so I couldn't see his expression. To this day I'd swear there were tears in his eyes, though I never actually looked at him.

"Focus on me," my mom's attorney had said. "Just like we talked about."

We'd gone through the directives a dozen times, and in the end, that's exactly what I did. I sold my dad out.

It's not that my dad had ever done anything wrong to me, but my mom and her counsel were incredibly convincing. Everything that my dad had perpetrated against my mom, they explained, he'd also done without regard for me. *To* me. They coached me say that I didn't feel safe with my dad.

But I did, I told them.

Didn't I?

They said I didn't know yet how untrustworthy he was being, that he was manipulating me so that he could keep more of his money. They told me that my dad didn't want me – or rather, they told me that my dad had said he didn't want me to live with him. To a seven-year-old, that sounds a lot like the same thing.

On the flip side, he was telling me that my mom was lying in order to hurt him. Saying anything she could to destroy his life. That he loved me to the moon and back. That I had to believe him.

How was I supposed to feel about all this? It was a tornado, silently ripping its way through me. They were each begging me to trust them. In the end, I didn't trust anyone, least of all myself.

I know there's a big trend now about reassuring your kids the divorce has nothing to do with them. As a present-day divorce attorney, I'm a huge proponent of that trend, but I can tell you that kids are still quietly used as bargaining chips in too many situations. People love to act like kids aren't people. They're great to brag about, or pose for family photos, or attempt to conform to your agenda. It's easy to get attached to that grand idea you had before they were ever born about how they were going to be with you: the activities they would participate in, the aspirational paths they'd pursue, the clothes they'd wear. And then we show up, and we're our own people, with our own feelings and ideas, and things get complicated. Sometimes it's subtle, and I can't prevent all of it, but on the legal side? In the ones I negotiate? I try to make sure kids aren't used as expendable trump cards. I never say things like, "We need you to speak up about this."

And, for better or worse, I never let kids stay in the room while we discuss the particulars.

What my dad had really said, I found out years later in court records, is that he thought it was best that I stayed with my mom.

I don't know if that's the same as saying "I don't want my kid", but that's how it was presented to me. And that hurt. It hurt down deep, in a way I still can't really explain. What was I left with after that? A mother who, according to my dad, was apparently so evil that she would willingly hurt the people she cared about – yet he wanted me to stay with her. At that moment it was him she was hurting. What if one day it was me?

Regardless, once they worked their magic, I didn't have as many issues saying everything they wanted me to.

I don't feel safe with my dad.

I don't want to live with my dad.

My dad makes my mom cry.

My dad makes me cry.

I'm scared my dad will hurt me.

I didn't look at the judge, but I knew he was there. The attorney stood nearby, gently coaxing me along. Everyone was murmuring about how brave I was. How mature. I remember afterwards, as a reward for my testimony, I got a Giga Pet. A fucking Giga Pet. As I descend the elevator with Quentin, I imagine the tiny screen filling up with little piles of digital poop.

I hide behind my sunglasses as we step onto the sidewalk. We walk without saying anything, and I follow without protest, though I have no idea where we're going. I know there's no Teddy emergency. I also know we aren't headed to our apartment building. Really though, I don't care. I'm happy to be anywhere except in that office. I keep picturing Bernadette's mouth in the shape of a perfect O, and Emma's bright red, summer sunburn cheeks as her mom grabbed her arm and dragged her away.

God, I'm sure my own face looks pretty mortified right about now. I feel hot all over, like I need to jump headfirst into the deep end of the pool without a single toe-dip teaser. This walk isn't helping, but I don't say anything. Maybe this is the fate of the Heidi who loses her edge and can't even keep a basic meeting under control: she's damned to wander the earth – or the sunny sidewalks of downtown – until her skin scorches off her bones.

About ten minutes later, Quentin holds open the door to an unimpressive little building that smells like sweaty socks. I wrinkle my nose, wondering if he actually expects me to go inside. The dim lighting and grimy windows make it look about as appealing as climbing into a basket of dirty laundry. He levels his gaze with mine, as if to say, *You've followed me this far*.

I roll my eyes behind my glasses, pushing them up into my hair as I step inside. Apparently I'm making all the worst decisions today.

The place is narrow, like most of the old buildings downtown, and somewhere deep in the shadowy spaces near the back I hear a gruff old man call out from a threadbare sofa pressed against the wall.

"Hey, pretty boy. It's early to be seeing you here."

"Hey, Frank," Quentin calls back. "Just stopping in with a friend. Good if we use the bags for a bit?"

"Go for it."

I'm standing amongst two rows of punching bags suspended from the ceiling and other types of free weights, mats, and equipment I wouldn't know what to do with if my life depended on it. Thankfully, we're the only people here at this point in the day, so there's no one – besides Frank – to witness what is bound to be my impending embarrassment. Quentin points me towards the seedy-looking ladies' room with an uneven W scrawled on the door in black paint.

"I'm going to get changed," he says. "Meet me out here in five."

"What are we –?"

"Go," he urges, giving me one of those ridiculous smirks.

I fold my arms across my chest. I don't want to do what he says, mostly because he looks like he thinks people will do anything he wants when he flashes those dimples at them. In the end, though, I don't want to stand out here with Frank eyeing me over his book of sudoku puzzles like he's never seen anyone in a power suit and heels before.

I duck into the changing room, which boasts one bathroom stall, one moldy shower with no curtain, and a row of pea green lockers, half of which stand ajar and may possibly be broken. I try not to touch any of the surfaces as I change into my running shoes, leggings, and a strappy longline sports bra, wondering why I don't have an actual tank top or t-shirt in this bag. Eventually, I give up feeling self-conscious, carefully stuff my things into one of the broken lockers, and step out into the dim lighting of the gym.

Quentin meets me, wearing a t-shirt with cut off sleeves and athletic shorts, and looking entirely different than he did in his suit and tie. The transformation makes me think of Clark Kent, or Peter Parker, or one of those comic book characters with an alter-ego. Attorney by day, sexy character out of Street Fighter by night.

Not that I think Quentin Maxwell is a superhero. Or a video game character. But there's no denying he's got sex appeal. And for some reason, he does appear to be attempting to rescue me.

"Okay, asshole," I sigh, too exhausted with the day to put much of the usual bite behind it. "What now?"

Long strips of what looks to be stretchy gauze are draped over his forearms. He motions me towards him, taking my hand without question. I watch as if it's someone else's hand he's holding, someone else's knuckles he's carefully wrapping. He winds the fabric around my wrist, across my palm, over that webby part between my thumb and forefinger, back and forth, making a pattern that seems as strategic as it is snug. Once he's satisfied with the first one, he switches to the second. He moves with practiced precision, and in a few minutes my hands hang at my sides, stiff and slightly heavy. When he leads me towards the nearest hanging bag, I feel I should be beyond asking questions, and yet, one still seems to roll out of my mouth.

"What?" I say defensively. "You expect me to hit this thing?"

He stands behind the bag to steady it, with his feet planted wide and his hands gripping either side. I can't help but think about the way his fingers spread across my ribcage when I was sitting on the edge of his desk.

He peers at me around the edge. "Yup."

"We really came all the way over here for this?" I say incredulously. "C'mon, Maxwell. This is a waste of time. I have work to do."

He reaches around the bulk of the bag to point to a spot almost even with his chest.

"Right here," he says. "Five with your right, five with your left. Show me what you've got."

I roll my eyes. *God, he's serious.*

I stare up at the ceiling for a moment and honestly think about leaving. Or punching him directly in the face. Instead, I square off in what is probably poor form and launch the first half-hearted punch. The chain stretching between the bag and the ceiling jangles weakly, like an impatient dog tugging at a leash.

"This is stupid," I grumble.

"Like you mean it," he says.

I roll my eyes again, feeling that tight feeling creep back up my throat. I roll my shoulders and stretch my neck, stalling for time. When I finally hit the bag once more, it connects solidly enough that I feel that dull, blunt pressure against my knuckles.

"Again," he instructs.

I heave my fist into that same spot on cue, landing it with a thud.

"Again."

This time, I put all of my weight into it. The energy reverberates up my forearm. I follow it up with a harder hit, allowing the force of it to knock the breath out of my lungs.

"Good," he says. "Like that. Keep going. Keep breathing."

I do the same thing with the left, five rounds. I switch off, right, left, left, right. I lose track of how many times I've made contact, until I'm wailing on this bag with everything I've got. I punch it, I knee it, I grunt and groan with every blow. At some point, I no longer give a fuck how ridiculous I probably look or how much noise I'm making. Quentin never changes his stance, never lets go. The chain rattles like it's attached to some wild creature that's fighting to break free.

I pant. I jab. I kick. I scream. I have no idea how much I need this until I'm already caught up in it, giving into this feeling that's been consuming me since Ms. Ashley Kate James sat down in my conference room – or is this feeling much bigger, much older, much deeper?

I swing again, and again. I feel the sweat beading on my skin. The ache in my muscles. The burning of my fists and knees and thighs and shins. I don't know how long this goes on, but I know my last few hits are weak and trembling.

When I collapse my hands to my hips, heaving with the force of my breath, Quentin releases the bag and steps up in front of me. In one easy movement, he reaches up and swipes his thumbs across my cheeks. It's only then that I realize I've been crying. He cradles my face in his hands as the tears continue to roll down to my chin. They're almost cool against the way my skin is embarrassed and hot. It's such a strangely intimate gesture, but I don't pull away. Some part of me feels that if he let go right now, I would crumple to the floor, which is a terrifying prospect, not in the least because these grungy mats look like the preferred place for staph infection to thrive.

So I don't fall apart. I also don't hold anything back.

I let the tears come honest and unbidden. I let his steady hands frame my face, let his dark eyes search mine, peering through my walls. I just stand here and let him see me. For a long beat, neither of us looks away.

***

I find myself sitting on a metal bench in front of the grimy windows of Frank's Gym, feeling like a husk of myself. Given the overflowing ashtray full of spent cigars, I figure this spot is where Frank comes to enjoy a smoke. It's got a nice afternoon view of the block and smells like today's thick, floral summer breeze and weeks' worth of burnt out vanilla tobacco. The latter is enough to make me consider moving, but I can't quite turn the inkling into action. Instead, I slouch my elbows against my knees, rubbing my hands over my face as if to make sure my eyes aren't still sneakily giving up tears. Thankfully, that threat has passed.

After a few moments, Quentin slides in beside me.

"I looked like a complete asshat," I say.

I wonder in which way I mean this: the situation with the client, or the uncontrollable sobbing while I wailed on a punching bag with my co-counsel.

At one point, before I fled the dirty sock smell to sit out here and catch my breath, Quentin pulled me into his arms and squeezed, but somehow it didn't feel like a hug. It was something unto itself, like he saw my walls crumbling and was trying to fortify me. Our height difference was just enough that his mouth pressed against my forehead, but it wasn't a kiss. It was… reassurance, maybe? He was only there for a breath, long enough to ensure I wasn't going to collapse without him, and then he let go.

"I think I need some air," I murmured. He nodded that he would meet me outside, and now here he is, sitting on this bench beside me like he never almost-hugged or almost-kissed me a few minutes earlier.

"You?" he scoffs now. "She's the one who showed up looking like she thought our office was the goddamn racquet club."

I rub my hands over my face again. "This has nothing to do with her clothes."

He gives me a knowing look, settling back with a sigh. "Her kid?"

I drag my gaze further down the sidewalk, where a girl plays a harmonica on a street corner by a pay-to-park lot, occasionally coaxing passersby into giving her tips via Venmo. It's a lonely, midnight train kind of sound that wrenches through my chest.

"She was just sitting there," I say, "and the more her mom talked, the easier I could see her whole damn childhood lining up. And something in me just…" I shake my head. I can't believe I'm telling him this. The truth of it burns across my face. "I saw her and suddenly I was seven years old."

This admission stretches between us. He doesn't attempt to fill the silence that follows. He doesn't seem bothered by it either. I can feel his gaze trace the line of my profile, out of my periphery.

"Your parents had a bad divorce," he guesses.

"My parents had *the* bad divorce. Seriously, I do this for a living and I've still never seen one quite like it. It dragged, and it was dirty. Both of them hatching petty, elaborate plots. Blaming the other for everything that ever went wrong: a dead car battery, a leaky dishwasher, the actual rain on my mom's wedding day, when she remarried. It's been almost twenty-five years, but you'd think it was yesterday, listening to the way they still snipe at each other. And I've always been right in the middle."

"I'm sorry. That's rough," he says.

I sigh. I sound like a petulant kid. "It's fine. I'm fine. I turned out fine. More than fine. But in the moment – all those years when you're trapped there... At some point, somebody has to be willing to *say* something, ya know?"

He gives me a slow nod. "Yeah, I do. And I think, today, that somebody was you. But for some reason, you don't seem happy about it."

I sink against the back of the bench and squint into the sunlight.

"I've been rejected by a client before, but it's never been so..."

"Loud? Personal? Public?"

"Yes. Thank you. I'd almost forgotten," I deadpan, cutting him a look. "God, I wonder how long until this makes it to the partners? The board?" I groan. "You're probably downright giddy about this, aren't you?"

"Seriously?" he laughs. "I want the partnership, sure, but I don't plan to win it on a technicality. Plus, if the board is worth half a shit, they'll admire your audacity."

I laugh in spite of myself. "My *audacity*?"

"I'm serious," he says. "You take bold risks. You stand up for people. You're not afraid to make a big embarrassing scene." He nudges me with his shoulder. "Anyone would be lucky to have you on their side, Heidi."

"Then why do I feel like I majorly fucked up?"

"As the Maxwell family's reigning fuckup, I can assure you that this is definitely not major," he says. "So you told someone that dragging her kid into the middle of a divorce was a dick move? Good! It's when you can sit there and not say anything that you should probably start to worry."

"Thanks," I say weakly. Then, "You don't seem like much of a fuckup."

"I know a few people who could make some pretty compelling arguments."

"You didn't steal that car," I point out.

"I didn't," he shrugs. "But honestly, that was just one thing in a long line of fuck-uppery."

"Is this some sort of character flaw I should know about?"

"I dunno. I like to think I outgrew it, maybe," he says, scrubbing a hand up the back of his hair. "When I was growing up, my older brother was the shining star, and I was... the other brother. The 'why can't you be more like your brother' brother. That label was so hard to peel off eventually I tried to own it. After the incident with the car, I kind of spiraled. I spent a few years playing the party boy. Failed royally at my first go-round at college. Spent way more time funneling cheap beer than going to class."

"Ended up half-naked in a dorm, eating microwave pizza snacks with a bangin' hot girl who was super out of your league?"

He has the decency to look mock-offended.

"I mean, she wasn't *that* out of my league," he laughs. "I may have been a fuckup, but I'll have you know I've always been charming as hell."

"Of course, how could I forget," I nod, giving him a playful roll of my eyes. "So what happened?"

"Eventually I ended up with no money, no plans – no girl – and a cracked rib from falling off the fraternity house's roof holding a half-empty bottle of Captain Morgan and wearing nothing but a Hawaiian lei."

"I love how many of these stories you're naked in."

"You would," he says, attempting to poke my side while I laugh, swatting him away. "The point is I knew I wasn't that guy, but I sure as shit wasted a lot of time trying to be. Sometimes it feels easier to live up to everyone's expectations than fight to prove them wrong. But I can assure you that *easier* doesn't necessarily feel *good*. Just because today wasn't easy, and just because you don't feel great about it right now, doesn't mean it was the wrong thing to do."

I let this sink in. For a second, I think I might start crying again out of sheer emotional exhaustion. To say that the afternoon has left me wrecked would be the understatement of the century. And yet, he's got a point.

"I have to go back to the office," I lament. "I've got so much work to do."

"You've got all night to catch up on work. Tomorrow, even. Do you really think *this*," he says, motioning me up and down, "is a productive state?"

I sigh, folding my arms across my torso. "No."

"We left the office because you looked like you needed to punch something. You've punched something. So – if you eliminate the possibility of going back to the office – what do you need right now? Like, really need?"

I close my eyes, trying to tap into this moment. I let the warm breeze tease my skin, let sweat prick the bridge of my nose.

"Food," I admit. "I totally missed lunch."

"Then let's get lunch," he says. When I hesitate, he adds, "It's only a violation of our agreement if we *share* a meal. Fortunately for you, I am not on a billboard and am nowhere near as high in demand as you, so I already had lunch. But I make pretty decent company."

My wary gaze slides over to him. I cannot say yes to this.

"What if someone sees us out together? You know the interns are already gossiping about us, right?"

"You know there's not an actual rule about us eating lunch together, right?"

When I give him a weak grimace of dissatisfaction, he gives me a look that can only be described as surreptitious.

"All right, all right," he sighs, peeling himself off the bench. "I might know a place."

17.

I follow Quentin all the way back to our apartment building, across the squeaky marble tile in the lobby, and onto the elevator with the accordion cage door. He presses the button for his floor, and I give him a look.

"I thought you were going to feed me lunch," I argue.

"Best sandwiches this side of the Mississippi," he says.

I cough out a disbelieving laugh, but I don't bother to select my floor. I follow him down the hallway of ten, which looks exactly like my hallway, all the way to the dark blue paint and gold number of his door, which looks exactly like my door, save for the digits.

I try not to think too much about this – me, following Quentin to his apartment. Everything that's happened since we left the office has felt like some inevitable kind of autopilot – if autopilot could make my pulse faintly flutter in my throat. Before I can rethink it, he lets us into the cool, clean space and tosses his keys on the table by the door.

I take in the details the way one gulps down a much-needed glass of water. He's got the requisite oversized TV. A well-loved couch that looks perfect for napping. A pull-up bar hanging over the doorframe to his bedroom. The layout is similar to mine, but the vibe is totally different. Where I've got potted plants, he's got a corner desk with a fancy ergonomic chair. Where I have my vintage Tiffany lamp, he's got crisp, functional lighting that looks like it came from Ikea. Just like his office attire, his apartment is filled with lots of blacks, grays, whites, and blues. And everything smells like him: like the embers of a bonfire, and late night summer breezes, and clean beachy clothes that have been left to dry over the edge of a balcony.

He reaches into the fridge and tosses me a Mexican lager. It's only three o'clock, but I crack it open anyway.

"This feels unprofessional," I say, tipping the bottle to my mouth. "Especially since I'm not even wearing a shirt."

He disappears into his bedroom, and returns with a t-shirt, which he tosses to me on his way past. When I catch it, I tell myself it's more to keep it from falling to the floor than anything. It's made of soft, blue, over-washed cotton, with a white water rafting logo splashed across the front, and it will absolutely swallow me.

That danger sign edges into my thoughts again. Now it's got flashing lights and a siren alert.

I should go.

Instead, I tug the garment over my head, knotting it at my hip. Instantly, I'm enveloped in the clean, warm smell of him.

As he props the door of the fridge open and gathers ingredients, I peer over his shoulder.

"You're one of those meal prep nutjobs, aren't you?" I say.

"Are you seriously judging my fridge right now?"

"I'm not judging. That's just a lot of chicken," I say, noting his stacks of glass takeout containers. "And... rice?"

"Couscous," he says.

"Fancy."

He slaps a puffy loaf of golden-crusted bread on a cutting board and grabs a knife from the butcher block, closing the door with his hip.

"It was on sale."

I settle onto one of the modern barstools. "I didn't take you for the kind of guy who appreciates a bargain."

"You mean you couldn't tell I buy this beer in bulk at Costco?" he grins. "Six figures worth of student loans will really change your outlook on life, I guess."

At first, I laugh like he's joking. Then I realize... he's not joking.

I know it's not really that unusual. I've got friends who would sell their left kidney to get out from under student debt. I was more fortunate than most; I scraped by, sure, but mostly on scholarships and grants. Still, I'm a few years away from calling it even. I think maybe I'm most surprised to realize that he's one of us. Are you really a millennial if you don't have a truckload of debt from getting a basic education?

I tip the bottle to my mouth. "I'm gonna be honest, I pegged you for a trust fund baby."

He registers my surprise with a shrug, like this happens all the time.

"Family fuckup, remember? I might be the only trust fund baby you know who worked his way through law school as a bartender, Ryde driver, late-night personal trainer, and line cook at a torta sandwich shop."

He ticks the items off on one hand before expertly slicing into a tomato.

"That's quite the resume," I say. "No exotic dancing? That's really the classic way to work oneself through college."

"Turns out I'm allergic to body glitter. Such a shame, too, considering my pelvic thrust is so on point," he jokes.

At least, I think he's joking. I'm too busy trying to avoid the way I'm imagining him as an exotic dancer to question it.

"So why come back? You made it in spite of your family. Seems like you wouldn't want to jump right back into bed with them."

"Interesting choice of words," he says.

"Sorry. Too personal?" I ask, wrinkling my nose.

"We can get personal," he says. "Getting cut off was maybe one of the best things that ever happened to me. Otherwise, what useless skills would I have to impress you with?"

He quickly constructs a sandwich that looks like it should be a taco, with a three-cheese blend, leftover carnitas, and some sort of greenish sauce he whisks in a small bowl. My mouth is literally watering by the time he slides the plate in front of me.

I gather up the sandwich with both hands. "Who says I'm impressed?"

He watches me with an expectantly cocky expression as I take the first messy bite. And *god*, it's good. I do my best to keep my eyes from lolling closed in ecstasy, but I can tell from the way he smirks that I failed. Spicy-delicious mystery sauce dribbles down my hand.

"Okay," I admit around another mouthful. "Maybe a little impressed."

Like the lady I am, I lick my fingers for emphasis. The shift in his features is visceral. His half smile has gone slightly serious. His eyes have gone hungry and hazy. I wonder if he registers the way his lips part slightly, how his beer hangs somewhere between holding and drinking. The entire effect is one that makes my heart speed up.

He punctuates our silence with a slow, belated swig. I can tell this gesture is meant to bring him back to baseline. He moves towards the living room, as if putting space between us might help, and he taps the icy cold of his bottle against the side of my neck on his way past. The sound I make falls somewhere between a laugh and a gasp. He fights a grin, entirely too pleased with himself.

"I'm going to expect a little more enthusiasm from your Yelp review," he says.

There is no limit to his ridiculousness, and some rogue part of me loves it. I'm not interested in investigating which part, exactly. It's easier to roll my eyes for the hundredth time this afternoon.

"Don't press your luck, Maxwell," I say.

While I eat, he sinks onto the couch with his laptop. I feel my mood lift as my plate clears, and I'm left wondering if *hangry* is an actual medical condition. I feel brand new as I rinse the dish and leave it in the sink. I have also regained enough of my senses to know that I should get out while I'm ahead.

I circle into the living room and perch awkwardly on the plush armrest of his couch.

"Thanks for lunch. And for the, um..."

Rescue workout?

Contraband hug?

This electric feeling thrumming beneath my skin?

"Beer," I say. "But I should probably..."

Go, my brain supplies. It's the logical thing to do. Even still, I can feel another word thrumming in my bones, see it like a flicker of light dancing behind his gaze.

Stay.

I almost think he's going to say it, but instead, his mouth curves in amusement.

"If you say 'go back to work', I'm going to be forced to hold you hostage," he says. His gaze goes gentle as I laugh. "You good?"

"You have sufficiently revived me," I confirm. "I think I just need a shower and a million hours of old school *Gossip Girl*, and I'll be good as new."

"*Gossip Girl*," he observes, smushing his mouth into an appraising line.

"Do not judge," I defend. "We all have our guilty pleasures."

He raises his hands in mock innocence. "No judgment here. I'm actually fascinated by this. Tell me, Heidi, what other guilty pleasures keep you up at night?"

I give him an amused roll of my eyes before gathering my things.

His smirk simmers, but to his credit, he still doesn't ask me to stay. "Text me when you make it home?"

"It's three floors."

"It's a common courtesy."

I laugh as I let myself out, but when I make it back downstairs to my apartment, I toy with the weight of the phone in my hand for a few moments. I type the short message with a lump in my throat.

H: *Home.*

I'm sliding my laptop out of my purse when his message dings.

Q: *Glad you made it. Now close your computer and get some rest.*

I huff out a self-conscious laugh, even though I know he can't see me. I type a quick response.

H: *Hey asshole, are you spying on me?*

My heart leaps as the three dots bounce at the bottom of our conversation.

Q: *It's almost like I know you or something.*

Q: *Enjoy your marathon, PBG. Xoxo.*

I bite into my smile, all giddy and glowing. I know those kisses and hugs aren't intended as an endearment, but they surprise me all the same. Quentin has clearly watched this show

– one of my comfort favorites – at least enough to be familiar with its classic sign off. This shouldn't give me such a thrill, but it swarms in my stomach like butterflies.

In the bathroom, I take off my shirt – *his* shirt – and climb into the shower, willing myself to let it go, as if I can wash the feeling off of me as easily as I wash away his scent. By the time I settle onto my couch with the episode menu loaded, I pick up my phone anyway, already typing a reply.

***

Somehow, we keep texting.

It's a long string that carries us through the next several days, until I find myself lying on my couch in the middle of the weekend, staring at case notes.

I massage my fingers into my scalp, beneath the floppy bun I've secured on top of my head, and roll my neck, hoping to release some of the tension that has knotted there. Beyond putting on leggings and heading out for coffee earlier this morning, I wonder when I last moved from this spot. I feel restless, like I should be doing something with my weekend other than sitting here and watching the strips of sunlight disappear from my ceiling, completely alone.

I slide my phone off the edge of the coffee table.

H: *What are you up to?*

Q: *Working the Glass case. You?*

H: *Lol. Same. We are pathetic workaholics.*

Q: *You're welcome to come up here, if you want to be pathetic workaholics together.*

I chew my lip, but I don't reply. I'm trying to puzzle through this like a flowchart, using my own boundaries and rules to determine if I'm actually able to say yes to this. I definitely want to say yes, but I can't help but question my motives for this. Question *his* motives.

His next text sweeps in like he's reading my mind.

Q: *This invitation is entirely professional, of course.*

H: *I could meet you at the office?*

Q: *No offense, but my couch is way comfier – and closer – than the conference room.*

H: *Hmm. Maybe. Are there sandwiches? I worked through lunch.*

Q: *Lol. Are you serious? It's the weekend.*

H: **shrug emoji**

Q: *Yes, there are sandwiches. Door's unlocked. Come on in.*

I tell myself this makes perfect sense, taking the elevator to the tenth floor and letting myself into Quentin's apartment. I've been so busy during business hours lately that there hasn't been a single sliver of my calendar where I can squeeze him in, and we desperately need to compare notes and start to finalize our strategy. Plus, we'll get more done this way, without the constant interruptions of the office. Also, the contents of his fridge are far superior to the questionable mismatch of items that can be found in the break room.

Quentin is wearing what I've dubbed as his off-duty outfit: dark gray athletic shorts and a v-neck t-shirt. I wonder if it smells like the one that is still hanging on a hook on the back of my bathroom door, which I secretly can't help but press my face into sometimes, like I can breathe in the contraband scent of him.

To my credit, I successfully manage to make it into his apartment without pressing my face against him. Everything feels easier from there.

We grab a couple of his Costco beers and eat award-worthy Cuban sandwiches that he throws together like it's nothing, before tucking ourselves into opposite sides of his couch. He eyes me over the top of his computer, where he's already typing, all business.

"So," he says. "Glass v. Russo?"

"That's why I'm here," I smirk.

He inclines his head. "All right. You're the boss, PBG. Tell me what you've got."

18.

The afternoon has turned to evening in that subtle way it does. One minute there's late afternoon sunlight streaming through the shades, and the next it's just the warm glow of the sleek lamps that illuminate Quentin's living room. Everything has become quietly easy and familiar. We've got a *Gossip Girl* rerun on his giant TV, volume low. He's got the kind of music Teddy would probably whole-heartedly approve of playing from a speaker. A few hours ago, I pilfered through the pantry and came up with an oversized bag of Goldfish crackers, which I thought only toddlers ate. I alternate between snacking on them and throwing one at him. There are at least three lost somewhere in the recesses of this comfy ass couch. We never grabbed anymore beers, but on some level I admit I feel a little drunk.

"Do you think this really happened, though?" he asks incredulously. "That she poured ridiculously expensive vodka all over his clothes and set them on fire in the bathtub?"

I stare at him over the top of the screen, which has the security guard's testimony pulled up on it, outlined plainly in black and white.

"I'm baffled as to why you seem to think this couldn't have happened."

"The part where she allegedly urinated on his records? Like, hiked up her dress and actually took a piss on them? And blamed it on the cat?"

I press my mouth into a line, bobbing my head from side to side in contemplation. "I'd buy it."

He laughs. "Come on. That girl? I absolutely don't buy it. Not unless she was planning to film it for her fans on the internet, which, last I checked, she didn't."

"You are highly underestimating the fact that, sometimes, bitches be cray. Like, in real life. No followers required."

He drags a hand over his face, hoping to hide his laugh. "You did not just say 'bitches be cray'. Who are you? What year is it? I thought you were a feminist."

"As a feminist, I have to acknowledge that doing fucked up shit is equal opportunity. Especially in a divorce. Jilted lovers know no gender."

"So you're saying you'd take a piss on someone's records? Set fire to their clothes in the bathtub?"

"Love rewires people's brains. Who knows what I'd be capable of?" I say. "You know I once heard someone admit to using the soon-to-be-ex's toothbrush to clean the rim of the toilet every morning for six months leading up to their separation? The *toilet*. I like to think they all start out as reasonable people, but somewhere along the line something snaps. In the end, I think we're all capable of being that person who sticks someone else's toothbrush in the toilet."

He's watching me now in a way that is entirely too amused.

"Wow," he says. "Just... wow."

"What?" I defend.

"Nothing. Just remind me to hide my toothbrush before you

use my bathroom."

I throw another cracker at him. He catches it against his chest, and instead of eating it, he flings it back at me. It hits me in the face. I snort out a laugh, snatching it from where it has landed against my boobs.

"And here I thought you admired my *audacity*," I say, launching it back at him.

He dodges it with a grin. "I did before I thought it might involve my mouth."

"You only *wish* I was involved with your mouth."

"That calls for speculation," he objects. "And speculating about what I would or would not do with my mouth seems very personal – not professional – in nature. But if we're speculating, how is it exactly that you think I wish to be involved with you, regarding my mouth?"

I level a coy look at him across the couch, flinging another cracker at him for good measure; this one he catches in his mouth. He crunches it in smug satisfaction.

"Badgering the witness," I object.

"Non-responsive," he retorts.

I smirk, and the best reply I can come up with is throwing crackers at him, one after the other, in rapid fire. He deflects, flinging them back as quickly as he can. I don't let up. He lunges across the couch, grabbing at my hands like he's attempting to stop the attack. I wrestle away like I'm desperate to continue the attack. Admittedly, neither of these actions probably has anything to do with the attack.

"Permission to treat as hostile?" he laughs, holding my arms.

I writhe and giggle.

In one moment we're pelting each other with fish-shaped snack crackers, and in the next we're simmering with the realization that Quentin is on top of me. He has settled between my legs, with his hips against mine and his hands pinning my wrists, so that he's hovering all strong and sexy right above me.

I meet his gaze with a slow smile. "Permission granted."

With my arms pinned above my head, I manage to throw the final cracker I'm holding with a flick of my wrist. It smacks him in the cheek. Quiet laughter erupts between us as it ricochets somewhere in the vicinity of my shoulder. His gaze follows it down, trailing along the spot just above my collarbone.

"This is definitely why we went to law school," he says. His voice has gone all smoky smooth. It makes me feel like liquid caramel: slow, sweet, melty.

"So we could fight to the death over partnership?" I tease.

"Nope," he says. "So I can do *this*."

In one teasing movement, he leans down, and I feel his breath against my neck.

Feel him nuzzle the collar of my shirt out of the way.

Feel him nibble at the exposed, sensitive stretch of skin.

Oh god.

The rush of heat is instant. That hungry, electric current buzzes through me in full force, and I feel myself shift into him. It's a gentle roll that starts with my hips, swells across my breasts, and tips my head back with the smallest sigh.

I've almost forgotten why he's doing this – god, does there even need to be a *why*? – when he emerges with the stray cracker victoriously between his teeth. He waggles his eyebrows at me and snaps it up with a slow smirk. When it's gone, he runs his tongue along his full bottom lip for emphasis. He meets my gaze with a teasing challenge.

"Objection," I murmur.

"On what grounds?" he asks innocently.

Coworkers.

Company policy.

Career suicide.

These responses swim through my periphery, but none of

them verbalize. Professionally, I know I shouldn't do this. Personally, though? My chest feels like it might cave in if he doesn't kiss me.

"I didn't want you to stop," I admit.

This response visibly affects him. I love that it affects him. His gaze dances down across my mouth, and it's such a short distance. We both seem to realize we're a breath away from breaking every rule. And I want to. My heart is pounding in my throat, between my legs where he's pressing against me.

His hands slide down my arms and thread into my hair, tipping my head back until my lips part. "Tell me when?"

He drags his nose down my neck. I feel his breath, the tentative brush of his lips, and everything in me comes alive in response. He strings kisses across the smooth, sensitive stretch of skin. A tiny little moan escapes me.

"Now?" he breathes.

I tip my head to give him more of me. "Not yet."

Just a little more, and I tell myself we'll stop.

He switches to the other side, angling my head with his hand. His tongue scrambles my thoughts. The gentle nip of his teeth sends sparks through my body. My nipples harden as he runs his tongue along my pulse point.

"What about now, Heidi?" The husky sound of my name on his lips is intoxicating. His mouth has worked its way up, and his teeth tug at my earlobe. "Have you had enough yet?"

The blush rises in my cheeks as a strangled moan escapes me. When he looks at me, his eyes have gone dark and feral, and I know he can see it as plainly as if it were written on my face: this absolute wanting, this primal *need*, pooling hot and liquid in my center. I'm almost embarrassed how turned on I am right now.

Because he hasn't even kissed me. He was just supposed to kiss me. Something playfully accidental, and mostly innocent, that we could laugh about later. Everything about that seems much safer than *this*, because now I want more of him. I want all of him.

He drags a thumb across my bottom lip.

"Sorry, I didn't quite get that," he murmurs.

I swell with a sigh, threading my hands up the sides of his neck and into his hair. It's thick between my fingers, and I grab fistfuls of it. I should stop. I tell myself I'm going to stop.

"Please don't stop," I breathe.

I pull his mouth down to meet mine. He kisses me, and suddenly, everything about this makes perfect sense. We are warm and hungry and sure. He tugs my bottom lip between his teeth, and his fingers thread into my hair, and I surrender to this impossible feeling. Another desperate sound escapes me.

"I expected a bit more enthusiasm," he teases.

I kiss him around my grin. "I didn't know you needed me to stroke your ego."

He breathes out a laugh, but I feel him growing harder against me, and I get the feeling there's another, very obvious part of him he wouldn't mind my stroking. My thigh has involuntarily hooked around his hip. His hand slides down it, palming my ass, pulling me closer with a ragged breath. I tease his tongue with another tiny groan.

He just feels so *good*.

Better than I imagined, in the brief, secret moments that I allowed myself to imagine him. Me. *Us.*

We fit together in an insatiable way, with him trailing kisses down my neck, kneading my ass, nipping at my shoulder, like he can't touch or taste enough of me. He smooths his widespread palm beneath the edge of my shirt, up the sensitive skin of my low belly, my ribcage, over the curve of my breasts. Why the hell am I wearing a sports bra right now? I consider taking it off. The way he's kissing me makes me consider taking everything off.

"Do you wanna talk about this?" he asks as he's peeling off my shirt.

I tug his shirt over his head, dropping it somewhere over the edge of the couch before pulling him back into a kiss.

"Is there anything I need to know about you?" I counter.

"Like what?"

"Condoms?"

"Yes."

"Fetishes?"

"You," he says, biting at my neck. "When you make that sound."

I exhale into a smile, only belatedly realizing the tiny little moans I'm making as he moves. I can't help it. He continues kissing down my chest, along the swell of my cleavage, licking and biting as much of me as he can reach. My skin feels tight, and I need more of him. More of this. It's going to take a contortionist act to get out of this bra.

Absently, I seem to realize someone's phone is vibrating against my hip. One message, followed quickly by a second. A third. I fish it out of the couch cushion and glance down to make sure it isn't an emergency – and I realize belatedly that if it is, it isn't mine. I don't mean to read the message, but the backlit words stare up at me.

"Like Melissa," I say flatly. "Who is texting, 'I really need you right now'."

This is joined by two other messages, which I don't read aloud, mainly because I've briefly lost the ability to form words: 'I know you said you couldn't keep doing this. I'm sorry.' and then simply, 'Please'.

His face shifts as his gaze registers them. "Okay. That's not what you think."

I wait for the explanation, but it doesn't come quickly enough. He seems dazed and confused. *Caught.*

"Care to elaborate?"

He swipes a hand through his hair as he straightens. "She's my, um... She's married to my dad."

This hits me like a physical blow, with a simultaneous shock and sting. Heat blooms across my face, but the rest of me goes cold. I conjure up the image of the thirty-something brunette who was eyeing him at the restaurant like she wanted to jump his bones. I tug myself out from under him, feeling especially exposed without a shirt. I search for it with my face hot.

"Wow," I say, the word tasting bitter. "I have to admit, I appreciate this plot twist less and less."

He doesn't respond, just sweeps another hand self-consciously through his hair. He looks... tortured. Not in a way I find very attractive. There's a palpable shift in the mood, and just like that, the moment has passed. Suddenly, we've gone from not being able to close enough space between us to feeling like we don't quite have enough distance. He's suddenly serious, looking for his shirt.

"What's going on there?" I prompt.

"Nothing."

The way he says it sounds more like *something*. A big something. He tugs himself up off the couch, adjusts himself in his shorts, seemingly starts looking for his shoes or keys.

"Hm. Yeah. I've heard that one before. As a divorce attorney, I'd expect you to be a little more original," I say. "I thought you were trying to avoid her?"

"I was. I am. I'm..." he sighs. "Fuck. I dunno. I'm sorry."

"Why would you be? Honestly, I'm the one who should be sorry."

Sorry for trusting him. For letting him see me cry. For practically begging him to kiss me.

"This is in direct violation of our agreement," I tell him. "*The partners won't keep secrets*, I think you said."

"This isn't my secret to tell," he says, exasperated.

"What the hell does that mean?"

"It means..." he drags a hand across his face, groaning in a way that sounds more like a growl, low and guttural. "You're right. You were right. We've got rules for a reason. Let's just call it a night."

He's in flip flops, palming his keys, his lips still swollen from making out with me.

"Can you, uh, lock up? When you leave?"

"You're gonna go see her?" I ask incredulously. "Just like that?"

I hate how jealous I sound when I say it.

"Yeah," he sighs. "I am."

I let out a humorless laugh. Of course he is. It's not like we have any obligations to each other, beyond getting through this case. Making out with him on his couch? Definitely not a social contract. Nothing more than a passing, physical need.

A mistake.

I snag my laptop off the coffee table and shove it into my purse. It annoys me how much of a hurry he seems to be in. Enough that he would leave me here, in his apartment. A woman he just felt up and abruptly abandoned – *for another woman*. I sensed it when we first met, and now it seems to ring true: this guy's got some fucking nerve.

I'm trying to locate my shoes. Meanwhile, he's opening the door behind me.

"Hey asshole," I call after him. "You might wanna pick up a new toothbrush on your way back."

He gives me one last glance, and I realize I haven't seen him look quite like this since the morning we declared ourselves adversaries. Tight jawed. Closed off. Resigned. After all this, I have to wonder if we're back there. If, even with guardrails, we were always doomed to be at odds.

Quentin's dark blue eyes hold mine for a moment. It's a hopeful moment, one in which I'm convinced he might say something that – *somehow* – that will negate everything that I'm feeling. Fix everything that just happened.

Eventually he nods. His hand slips away from the doorknob, leaving it awkwardly ajar as he disappears into the hall.

19.

"I HEAR WE'RE GOING TO TRIAL," Jeanine-the-journalist says over the hands-free speaker in my SUV.

I glance at Kamille in the passenger seat. We're on our way to Meg's, where periodically we work on "life skills" like baking (and eating) large amounts of cookies. Supposedly today we're going to make strudel, since Meg recently found out we've only ever eaten the toaster variety. She's on a mission to prove to us how life-changing fresh pastry can be. I could probably use a little life changing, right about now. Avoiding Quentin for the past couple of weeks has taken years off my life.

"Where'd you hear that?" I question.

"C'mon," Jeanine says. I can hear her grinning on the other end of the line. "I'd love exclusive media access. Interviews. Official comments. This will work out for both of us. It'll help you control the flow of information."

"Have you seen the internet lately? The dam has broken, assuming there ever was one. There's no controlling this."

With a trial date set, Gigi has upped her social media

campaign. The hashtag #FreeFarkas is the latest thorn in my side. If I know anything, I know Teddy will fight to the death over that damn cat. I've got my work cut out for me.

In the midst of this, we've spent countless hours digging through financials, collecting depositions, and trying to track down Teddy's first wife. I'm half convinced she doesn't exist. Maybe she moved to Mexico City and became an expat. Maybe she's living off the grid somewhere in Montana. She certainly isn't responding to any of our attempts at contact, and even Angela hasn't been able to sniff out a trail on where she might be. In the meantime, Teddy's losing business. A few bands have pulled out of upcoming recordings. One disappeared with an album halfway finished, which has Teddy's business attorneys working double-time, feeding us information that we're supposed to translate into damages. They're expecting more to follow.

"Which is why you need someone to tell the real story. Offer an official narrative," she insists. "Plus, I feel like we work pretty well together. Weren't you happy with the profile piece?"

"Given how little I gave you to work with, I was surprised," I admit, making her point. "I'll think about it, okay? But it's really up to Teddy's publicist."

"I'll send over the contract," she says. "Just in case."

I disconnect the call as we turn into Meg's neighborhood.

"You're basically famous," Kamille says.

"I'm not famous," I argue. "Plus, aren't the only famous people your generation knows about TikTok famous? Doing choreographed dances and whatnot? You know I don't dance."

"I mean, you're not, like, TikTok famous. You're more like... meme famous."

Apparently there's a hierarchy. Who knew?

"Am I at least as famous as those cats that jump over stacked toilet paper rolls?" I question.

She thinks for a moment. "I haven't seen that, but probably not."

At this, I can only laugh. I'd rather be a cat, right about now. Instead, I'm watching Meg demonstrate how to roll out puff pastry dough as if she actually expects us to be able to duplicate her efforts. Once we've thoroughly made a mess of our strudels, which look like pre-K art projects next to her blog-worthy ones, we stick everything in the oven and head out onto the back porch to watch Kamille chase around Meg's chiweenies with a tennis ball. The second I sink into the outdoor chair, I rub my eyes.

"You okay?" she asks knowingly.

"Long week," I offer.

As vague as I'm trying to be, I have to acknowledge that I told her about Quentin in a moment of weakness. One minute I'm grabbing my usual to-go coffee, and the next I'm muttering, "Oh, by the way, I made out with my co-counsel. But it's totally not a big deal. In case you were wondering."

I don't know why I told her. I mean, besides the fact that she's my best friend. But besties or not, it's not a given that you spill something like this. Honestly, I'd probably prefer no one knew. I'd prefer *I* didn't even know. But since I can't simply forget about it, I guess it makes sense to have someone to share the burden. Until she starts looking at me like this.

"Have you talked to him?"

"Beyond trial prep?" I ask. "No, not really."

She audibly sighs, so thoroughly disappointed I can feel it gnawing at my insides.

"What?" I defend. "There's nothing to say, Meg. We were never going to be anything."

"I mean, not with that attitude," she argues. "Didn't you *like* kissing him?"

That is a whole-hearted emphatic *yes*. I've never liked kissing anyone as much as him. That alone is thoroughly unsettling.

"Who doesn't like kissing?" I say. "Oh, but also – in case you forget – *he's probably banging his stepmother*."

She winces. "Okay. Fine. But I mean... are you sure?"

"Am I sure he's sleeping with her? I mean, I didn't follow him and peek through the bedroom window or anything, but all signs point to yes. You know me. I don't do –"

"Complicated," she nods. "I know. I just..."

"Just what?"

"I want you to be happy, Heidi."

"I will be," I say, steeling myself with certainty. "As soon as I earn this partnership, when we're sipping margaritas in Mexico –"

"I was thinking more like espresso in Paris."

"When we're sipping espresso in Paris," I amend. "Then, I promise, I'll be ridiculously fucking happy."

"And until then? After that?"

I swell with a breath. She gives me a wistful look. Eventually, I can only tug my gaze away. We both distract ourselves with Kamille clapping as the dogs semi-successfully execute retrieving the ball with their tiny mouths. One of them drops it. The other briefly tries to snatch it, but by then they're engaged in a galloping zoomies race, with the ball long forgotten. We all laugh, watching this scene that's so hilarious it should have circus music playing while it happens.

Meg doesn't say anything else, but the unanswered question crawls up the back of my neck like a whisper. Right now – in the middle of trying so hard to achieve everything and fiercely protect this life I have built – *am I happy?*

***

Quentin, Teddy, and I are sitting around the small round table in the kitchen at Avid Records, paperwork spread on the table between us. We're attempting, fruitlessly, to prepare Teddy for trial. He's half-listening in favor of strumming a guitar that probably costs more than my car. Periodically, he meanders to the cabinet and pours himself another two fingers of whiskey. We're not getting anywhere fast.

At one point, Farkas hacked up a slimy hairball, right in the middle of things, which was pretty impressive for a cat with hardly any fur. Since then, he's been curled up like a half-naked, yellow-eyed goblin in Quentin's lap. I'm doing my best to ignore both of them.

"Let's talk about your statement," I tell Teddy. "Since you haven't submitted one, we have drafted some options for you to consider."

"I wrote a statement," he says.

This is news.

"Great," I say. "Do you have a copy we can take a look at?"

He rummages around the kitchen for a while before yelling down the hall for Zelda. She appears like a disgruntled mother, who might be a billionaire if she had a dollar for every time someone asked her to find something around here.

"Where did you last have it?" she questions.

"It was right here, Zel. Did you throw it away?"

"Did it look like trash?" she reasons.

Finally, he plucks it from the top of the actual garbage can and slaps it on the table, victorious. Quentin and I peer at it simultaneously, and though it doesn't look like something I would normally touch, I'm still feeling petty and would prefer to pretend he isn't here. I snag the edge and slide it towards me, scanning the uneven handwriting.

"Teddy, this isn't a statement. It's a love letter. In... song format. Written on a used beverage napkin."

Zelda snorts before wandering out. "Like I said: trash."

"I don't know how many ways I can tell you this," he sighs, "but I don't want to testify against her. I don't know how it's come to this."

"Do you want to concede guilt and give her everything?" I question.

"I mean, no?" he sighs. When he sees the look I'm giving him, he adds with more certainty, "No."

"Then we've got more work to do."

"You don't know Gigi like I do," he says. "She gets like this. Sometimes she's sweet, silly, just happy to be anywhere, and other times she's... someone else entirely. But she doesn't mean it."

Quentin gives Teddy a sympathetic look. "Hey man. We get it," he says, playing Good Cop.

"See," Teddy says, pointing. "He gets it."

I struggle to keep my face impassive, while I'm internally seething about boys' clubs and wondering how the hell this has gotten so far away from me. I almost wish Zelda would come back, maybe take my side. Meanwhile, Farkas blinks at me, as if to say, *Three against one.*

"Of course I get it," Quentin continues. "I mean, we know how it goes. Sometimes these women get emotional. What can you do, right?"

"Dude," Teddy laughs, dragging a beleaguered hand through his hair. "You don't know the half of it."

"We've all been there. We've all made a few threats to keep them around. It's for their own good, right?"

"Yeah," Teddy says absently, tipping his glass to his mouth. "Wait," he chortles. "What?"

The same chain reaction is happening in my brain. I blink. Once. Twice. I'm watching Quentin in disbelief, but somehow, before I can think to intervene, he continues talking.

"C'mon," Quentin laughs. "Telling her you'd kill the cat if she left? Leaving her ass high and dry when she fucked around and got VD? Priceless. Nobody could blame you."

An unnerving grin is plastered across Teddy's face. I watch in horrified silence, and for a second, I think he's actually going to agree. Then he says, "Get the fuck out."

He offers it casually, the way someone might say 'the bathroom's that way'. You'd almost think he was kidding, except for the way he's holding his rocks glass like he might launch it at someone.

"Heyyyy." Quentin says it like a drunk frat boy, fending off a fight he started. "C'mon, man, we're just talking..."

"No," Teddy says. "*You're* just talking. I don't do business with guys like you. You think women are just around for your enjoyment or some shit? God, I've thought every one of them deserved more than me, but this dipshit?"

Suddenly, as if he preempted exactly how fucked up this is about to become, I realize Farkas has conveniently disappeared.

"Teddy," I begin. He's looking at me now, demanding backup.

"Heidi, you shouldn't be working with someone like this. *Dating* someone like this!" He grabs his head like it's about to explode. "God, I thought I was a moron. But this guy?!"

He motions to Quentin like he's the plague. Honestly, I'm inclined to agree with him.

"We're not –" I start.

"I think you misunderstood –" Quentin interjects.

"I think I understand just fine," Teddy nods. "And I think you should go."

Quentin is about to protest when I grab my things, snagging him by the sleeve as I head for the door.

"Yes," I say. "I think we should."

"Heidi," Teddy interjects. "Are you good?"

"Yes, Teddy. I'm great. Thank you. I'll call you tomorrow."

We trek down the wood-paneled hallways, across the plush carpet, and out into the warmth of early evening. The sky is streaked with pink and orange. This time of day, this entire corner of the city smells like gardenia and pit barbeque. My heels crunch across the loose gravel of the parking lot.

"What the hell was that?" I demand.

"I was trying to level with him," Quentin says. "Get him to tell us if anything Gigi said was true."

"Yeah? How's that working out for you?"

"Okay, obviously I didn't know he was going to blow up on me. And if he can't handle this, he can't handle Mike Murdock."

He's almost got a point, but I'm still furious.

"You agreed to do this with integrity!" I half-shout.

"Not everyone is who you think they are, Heidi. Some men are assholes with dark ass secrets."

"Like you?" I say.

He scoffs, but his jaw goes tight. He drags his gaze begrudgingly across the parking lot, leaving it lost somewhere in the distance.

"I can't do this with you if you're going to keep me in the dark," I say. "Tell me straight up. What's the deal with you? What am I in for?"

His silence stretches.

"You can't do this in court," I say.

"I won't do this in court," he argues. "What do you think, I'm an idiot?"

I let this hang unanswered between us.

"It doesn't really matter what I think, Quentin. What matters is the judge. The press. And let me tell you, if you pull some shit like that –"

"God, I'm *sorry*, Heidi. I took a chance, okay. I know that doesn't make any sense to you, but sometimes you have to try things even if you know they might not work out," he says. "I'm *sorry*."

It cuts deeper than I mean for it to. I'm barely breathing, as if being still will keep it from hurting. I tug my bag a little tighter under my arm and slide my sunglasses into place, moving for my car. I have to get out of here. I can't stand in this parking lot, trading blows with him.

"I really don't need your apologies, Quentin."

"I can fix this."

"No need. I'll fix it. You've done enough."

I slam the door of my car and put it in gear, leaving him standing, silhouetted on the sidewalk.

***

I'm developing a twitch in my right eyelid. I should probably file this under workers' compensation, citing the previous evening's events as the date of injury, but I don't. Realistically, I can't blame this on much more than my fitful lack of sleep and the fact that I haven't changed my contacts in over six months. Every time Meg and I incidentally discuss this, she goes on a rant about how she can't believe my corneas haven't peeled off yet.

"Are you really so busy being a total badass at your job that you can't focus one afternoon on the fact that you want to be able to *see*?" she regularly exclaims.

The answer is always: *yes, probably*. With a defensive, *I'll get to it*.

We have some version of this conversation when I swing by the cafe for my iced coffee, trying to pretend my eye isn't spasming like I'm deranged, before I ignore her amateur optometry advice and head over to Avid Records. When I get there, I don't find Teddy sleeping on the sofa in his office like I expect. He's also not in the kitchen. All I find is a half-empty pot of scorched coffee, that crumpled statement-slash-love-song beverage napkin, and Zelda, who looks over her yogurt cup at me like I should've known better than to show up here.

"He's already gone," she says, dropping her gaze back to the book she's reading and sucking her spoon.

"Gone?" I question. "Gone where?"

"Gone fishing."

She says it with such a flat tone that I can't tell if she's being sarcastic or not.

"Fishing," I repeat, seemingly weighing the validity of the word. "Okay. I can wait."

"You'll be waiting a while. I told you, he's gone fishing. As in, he took Farkas and headed out on one of his fishing trips. In Florida."

"Florida," I repeat. The declaration falls somewhere between shock and disbelief. I still can't tell if she's fucking with me, so I tack on a more direct line of questioning. "Florida?"

"Do they teach you that in law school, or is it some sort of nervous habit you picked up from a talking bird? Yes, Florida. Don't look so devastated. He'll probably wear himself out on sunshine, seasickness, and spiced rum in about a week or so."

"But we've got court on Monday."

"*You* have court on Monday," she corrects. "He's got a broken heart and a rundown fishing boat with her name on it."

I immediately pull up his contact card in my phone and hit the call button. It goes straight to voicemail. Though I know there's no use, I try two more times with the same result.

"I cannot believe this," I mutter.

Zelda has already returned to her book and breakfast, as if she's moved on to acceptance. But I can't accept this. I can see this case, the partnership, possibly my entire professional reputation slipping away from me. It's one thing to be involved in a messy, high profile case. It's another entirely to show up to court without the fucking client. As if this wasn't already a social media circus, I now officially feel like a clown. I sink into the chair across from her and try not to throw anything.

"We won't win this case without him," I rant. "Not showing up is like an automatic forfeit."

She turns the page without looking up, as if this isn't her

problem. "I'd say he's probably betting on it."

I blink at this, completely incensed. "Why would he hire a *divorce* attorney if he doesn't actually seem to want a *divorce*?!"

"Because *she* wants a divorce."

My mouth falls open slightly, but nothing comes out. I've officially been reduced to doing my best impersonation of a goldfish. Zelda must sense my brain imploding, because she finally sighs, looking up.

"Look, I know it seems silly to you. Hell, it actually seems downright ludicrous to me. But for some fucked up reason Teddy still wants to give her what she wants. He's wired that way. He thinks he's an unlovable castaway who has to try to win his way into people's hearts by giving, and giving, and giving some more. He forgets that some of us care about him anyway, even if all he ever gives us is a tension headache."

"You love him," I say. It's more an observation than a question, one that Zelda meets with a snort.

"Of course I love him," she says. "Just not in the romantic sense. Definitely not in the sappy-eyed way that pretty boy lawyer looks at you when you drag him in here every week."

"We're not involved," I say, eager to set this record straight.

"I didn't say you were," she says, casually dropping her gaze to her book. "The boat is at the marina on Santa Lucia Island. If you find him, maybe remind him that he loves this place more than her? He always says it gave him everything. I think he forgets that it never asked him for anything in return."

***

There are no direct or convenient flights to Santa Lucia Island. It's a little sliver of land that forms a barrier between the panhandle and the Gulf, positioned far enough from some of the more popular beaches to seem remote, but not so far that a drive is out of the question, which means that I quickly begin packing for a road trip.

This is really the only viable option. If I request that we postpone, Gigi's attorney will most certainly use this to their advantage. I can't risk it. The trip down the interstate and along the highways that hug the coast should only take about nine hours, and if I'm lucky I'll get there shortly after dinner, which will give me plenty of time to drag Teddy home in time for the trial.

While I'm simultaneously working with Bernadette to clear my schedule, I'm haphazardly shoving items into my suitcase. I change into a jersey knit dress that saves me from having to locate pants and fire off a quick email to Henry, assuring him I've got everything under control and alleging that this will help us eliminate distractions and get Teddy ready for trial, in a way that *almost* makes it seem that this whole thing was planned.

At least, I'm hoping that's how it seems.

Less than an hour later I'm loading my single bag into the backseat of my SUV in the parking garage, fully committed to the rescue mission. Whether it's a determination to rescue Teddy from himself or my career from embarrassment is anyone's guess.

"Got room for one more?" Quentin says from behind me. He hauls his duffel in with mine and closes the hatch. My heart thuds in my throat.

So yeah, okay, I didn't *tell* him about Teddy's absconding to Florida, but to be fair, it was *his* fault.

"What are you doing?" I ask.

"I was going to ask you the same thing. Since I think we agreed, *the partners will work all aspects of the case together.*"

"I think that ended when you went rogue and accused our client of being a lying sack of shit. To his face," I argue. "This will be easier if I just do it myself."

"This seems to be a theme with you. Which is ironic for a girl pursuing something called 'partnership'."

God I hate his analyses.

"I don't have time for this," I say, climbing into the driver's seat. Before I can buckle myself in, Quentin is tugging unsuccessfully at the handle of the passenger door. The safety locks have already activated, and I realize I could leave without him if I wanted. Toss his bag out into the parking lot and drive away. He levels a look at me through the window.

"Seriously, Heidi?" he says through the glass.

I crack the window enough that he can easily hear me.

"You're not supposed to be here," I say. "Who told you anyway?"

"Erving. I guess Henry told him, so he stopped by to tell me what a great idea it was for us to organize this little getaway."

"Us, or you?"

"Given that neither of us actually deserves any credit for this, I don't know how that matters. I played along and told him we were getting on the road soon. I went by your office and you weren't there. I did the math. I told you, I'm not backing out on the case."

"How do I know you even want to win? You're not taking any commission, and I feel like you're trying to sabotage this. Tell me what's in it for you."

The long-pressed line of his mouth holds steady. I can tell he's weighing how to respond – or perhaps, whether he's willing to respond at all. For a second, I actually think he's going to back away from the car without a word and let me leave. I put the car in gear, and he breaks with a sigh.

"Erving agreed to pay off all my student loans," he says. "If I came back, worked these cases, made an effort at taking his place. He knew I didn't want to come back, but he wanted a Maxwell to continue at the firm. He said we'd call it even."

I blink at him. I know vaguely how much money we're talking about, can almost feel the weight of it. I can also see the way that pink has crept across his cheeks, and I realize... he's embarrassed about this.

"Why didn't you tell me this before?"

"I've worked hard to get where I am. Half of everyone still thinks I'm a spoiled rich kid who pisses away opportunities just because he can. Do I really need everyone to know I'm here on a bribe?"

There's something raw and defeated in the hard line of his jaw, and he steps back from the car, far enough that I could back out of the space if I wanted. I know I'm losing valuable minutes sitting here, but I can't make myself move. I just keep looking at him, thinking that maybe if he wants this as much as I think he does – as much as *I* do – that it makes everything easier. Cleaner. On some level I always imagined this was about him, and me, or his feelings for me, but in the end it's always only been business.

It's sobering. It's comforting. The truth is that everybody wants something. And truthfully, I'm tired of doing everything on my own.

I unlock the doors with an audible click. I stare straight ahead as he climbs in beside me.

"No touching the radio. No superfluous stops. Don't ask to drive. And please don't make me regret this."

He extends his hand across the console to give me a fist bump. I tap my knuckles against his reluctantly. At the point of contact, he spreads his fingers in a slow motion explosion. Thankfully I'm spared the sound effects.

Still, I think about the fireworks. I think about lying under him on his couch, and the way my skin burned when he pressed his lips to mine. I think about the fact that this entire plan could go up in flames. I slide on my sunglasses and put the car in gear.

20.

THE THING ABOUT FLORIDA is that it's sticky, the way your skin feels in the summer when you try to dry your hair in the same bathroom where you just took a long shower. Which is to say: I don't want to be here. The balmy air seems to seep through the vents as we cross the state line on a two-lane highway around the sixth hour in my car, and I'm beyond ready to snap.

Up until this point, Quentin has been, for the most part, a model citizen, but it is at this moment that he begins tapping his window as if there's something of paramount importance that he needs me to see. In the split second glance I afford him, all I manage to see is more of the endless, pine-riddled nowhere that we've been speeding though for the past couple of hours.

"Pull over," he insists.

"No," I say automatically.

Another crooked mailbox whirrs by.

"Heidi," he says. "The sign said snow cones, fireworks, *and* lotto tickets. How can you say no to this?"

"What part of 'superfluous' did you not understand?"

"Boiled peanuts!" he exclaims now. "Alligator jerky!"

"Okay, not just 'no', but 'fuck no'."

"You're about to..." He heaves a sigh. "You passed it."

"I did you a favor."

"Who even are you?" he says. "Isn't there some little kid inside of you dying for a snow cone and a bottle rocket and the possibility of enough money to buy yourself everything you've ever dreamed of and more?"

"The little kid inside of me would probably laugh at all the little kids who think that's realistic," I offer.

"You could've at least let us stop for snacks. It's been *hours*. I think at this point you're withholding food and basic necessities as punishment."

"I don't let people eat in my car," I offer.

"Not even if one of those people secured us the last room on the entirety of Santa Lucia Island?"

I attempt to keep my eyes on the tailend of the car in front of us – which has annoyingly been driving exactly four miles under the speed limit for the past fifteen miles of an inexplicable no passing zone – and snag a peek at the phone in his hand. The image on the screen definitely has the vibe of a rental confirmation.

"It can't be the last one," I offer.

"I've been searching for hours. Trust me, it's the last one. Between the vacationers and the fishing junkies, we're lucky we aren't sleeping in the car. Normally I would never say this, but this place could use a couple of high rises."

I make a noise that falls somewhere between a sigh and a grunt. I can feel Quentin giving me a look.

"You know you could just say thank you," he says.

I silently acknowledge that yes, this is in fact a possibility. But by the time we're standing in the dingy little dive bar with garland string lights that have tiny red solo cups as lampshades, "thank you" is the furthest thing from my mind.

"This can't be the right place," I tell him.

"Can you just relax?" he says. "The GPS says we're here."

"Room's upstairs," the bartender finally says. "But I'm double booked. Triple booked, actually, if you count the pair of German tourists sitting in the corner. There's a pullout bed, though. They probably wouldn't mind if you wanna crash."

I give Quentin a look that tells him I will cut him if he agrees to this. The backseat of my car is sounding better and better.

"I don't know that we're feeling that adventurous," he offers. "You don't have anything else?"

"No, man. Sorry."

"Nothing? You're sure?" I interject. "A cot in the back room or...?"

"Ya know," he says, softening with sympathy. "I feel bad about this. I really do. Let me pour you and your lady a drink – on the house – and make a few calls."

From my creaky barstool, I scoff, and I'm about to announce that I am *not* his lady, when Quentin flashes one of his winning smiles.

"That'd be perfect, thanks."

A few moments later he ushers me away from the bar and parks me at a high top table on the weathered patio that overlooks a narrow, sandy beach and the docks of an old marina. The humid evening breeze comes in short sighs, like an old dog's breath, and I sweep my hair off the back of my neck in annoyance.

Quentin slides a sticky menu in front of me as if this will somehow make the situation better. I scan the list of items and try to ignore the infinite loop of Incubus playing on the speakers. I wonder which of these items is least likely to give us food poisoning. I rule out the oysters, the crab cakes, and the calamari before letting the laminated sheet fall to the scarred tabletop and dragging my gaze out across the boats bobbing along the decks at the marina.

We already checked before we landed here, and there's officially no sign of the *Virginia Marie*. It set sail at some point early this morning and has no expected time of return. Maybe it's for the best that we don't have anywhere to stay. I'm determined enough to camp out at this table until Teddy returns. With my outdated contact lenses, I can still see well enough to inspect the boats that are coming in. Or at least, well enough to know that none of them say *Virginia Marie*. It's more the length and shape of the words than anything. I'm squinting at one that might be called *You Shall Not Bass* when Quentin slides onto the stool across from me.

I stare at the items he's placed between us: two plastic cups, rimmed with salt and garnished with lime, and a red basket full of something that resembles egg rolls.

"What's this?"

"It's on the house."

"That… doesn't answer my question," I retort.

"Eat," he says. "Drink."

"Do we have a place to stay yet?"

"One thing at a time, PBG."

Against my better judgment, I snag a fried morsel from the basket and take a swig of my beverage. I have a feeling it's going to be a long night.

***

Three hours into said long night, my phone vibrates on the table. Against my better judgment, I answer it.

"Wait," Meg says. "Are you on *vacation??*"

"It's a work thing," I say, plugging one ear to hear myself over the sound of the Jimmy Buffet cover band.

"It doesn't *sound* like a work thing," she offers. "Is Quentin there?"

"What does that matter?"

She giggles. "Oh my god he's totally there. You're on vacation. With *Quentin*."

"Do not turn this into one of your harlequin romances," I say. "We're just... colleagues. Trying to save this case. The location is happenstance."

"Happenstance that landed you at the beach. With a hot guy who is totally into you," she says. "I'm so proud of you, Heidi!"

"Who said he's hot?" I argue. "You don't even know what he looks like."

"You wouldn't have accidentally made out with him on his couch if he wasn't hot," she reasons. "Also, I googled him. Is he tall? He looks tall."

From across the bar, I see Quentin grinning as he snags a couple of fresh drinks from the bartender. I have to admit, even across the crowded room, in this dingy, forgotten place, he's still hot. And reasonably tall.

"I dunno. I guess?" I say.

"C'mon, work with me here. Is he tall like you could perfectly rest your head on his shoulder? Or tall like he could probably kiss the crown of your head?"

Tall enough he can lean forward and kiss my forehead, I think. I'm not going to mention this. I'm especially not going to include that I know it from past experience.

"Honestly, I love you," I tell her now. "But I've gotta go."

"Go!" she says. "Have fun! And please please please consider making out with him again. Or maybe even –"

I can't stand to hear the rest of this, so I laugh.

"*Bye*," I insist.

I'm tapping the end button as Quentin appears beside me. His hand finds my lower back as a staggering group of middle-aged vacationers in floral shirts traipse past. He seems to realize, belatedly, that he's done it, and his touch slips away. I realize that I'm oddly sad when it does. Still, he stays close, ducking his mouth to my ear to be heard.

"Everything okay?" he asks.

"Yeah. Just my friends, checking in," I offer. "I don't exactly go out of town all that often. They were probably worried I'd been kidnapped or something."

"I appreciate that I've graduated from serial killer to kidnapper. This seems like a step in the right direction."

I smile in spite of myself. He catches me gazing out at the dark, quiet ocean.

"You okay?"

"This was a mistake," I say.

"No," he scoffs. "We'll find him. And we'll find somewhere to stay. Or we'll get so drunk that sleeping on the beach sounds like a great option."

"I mean, this whole case," I offer. "I wanted that partnership so bad."

"You don't anymore?"

"I do," I say. "It just feels... impossible. I mean, I'm in *Florida*. At *Barnacle Billy's*. With..."

He raises an expectant eyebrow at me, begging me to finish this sentence. Like any good attorney, I redirect.

"It's Friday night, and I have court on Monday, and I have *no* idea where my client is. I knew better. Everyone told me not to get in the middle of this, and here I am. I mean, what the hell am I doing? I'm over thirty, and I'm probably going to lose my dream job, and I'm absolutely undateable."

He scoffs. "You're not undateable."

I give him an unamused look. "Come on. I'm 'the best part of breaking up', remember? Guys don't want to date me."

"Sure they do."

"Name one."

The way he looks at me tugs at something deep and low in my belly.

"Just because we agreed to set some professional boundaries doesn't mean I ever stopped being attracted to you." He says it like it's obvious, but it's somehow news to me. I feel the blush rise in my cheeks, but I blame it on the tequila.

"Whatever," I murmur.

"I'm serious. There hasn't been a single moment since the day I met you that I haven't thought you were a fucking... forest fire."

I squint at him. "You're comparing me to a natural disaster?"

"No, I'm saying..." he laughs, dragging a hand across his face. "What am I saying? You're intimidating. All consuming. Devastatingly beautiful. We agreed I'd conduct myself like I never noticed, but I always notice. There isn't a single day I haven't wanted to be irrationally close to you. Haven't imagined what it would be like to..."

"Feel me up on your couch and leave me for your stepmother?" I finish.

He gives me a wistful smirk.

"To hold you. To wake up next to you. Make you breakfast. And yeah, maybe feel you up on my couch. You know you make this sound?"

"What sound?" I blink.

"This soft, sexy, completely maddening sound, every time I kiss you. I'm pretty sure I'll never get that sound out of my head. It's like once you know it exists, you can't understand how you ever lived without it."

My gaze slides up to his, heavy and searching. "Why are you saying this?"

"We're going for broke here, right? Isn't that what this trip is?" he half-smiles.

"Tell me what's going on with your..." – I choose my words carefully – "family situation."

He takes a breath, and I feel that he's about to spill it.

Whatever *it* is. This could make or break us. This could be everything.

It's at this moment that Billy Barnacle himself approaches our table, and it's increasingly apparent this man has no concept of timing. He gives us an oversized grin and an overloud, "H! Q! I've got great news! I found you a place!"

***

Quentin and I make the short walk from Barnacle Billy's to the house located five doors down without speaking. The gentle rush of low tide and the sound of our shoes crunching across the loose gravel of the road's shoulder suck up the conversation – if that's even what that was back there. The wheels of my suitcase rattle along beside me in the bike lane. After a few long minutes, we're being greeted by a tall, auburn-haired woman who looks shockingly like Susan Sarandon.

(I cannot promise this is not the result of old contacts and copious amounts of discount tequila. But seriously, if I could still have boobs like *that* when I am almost eighty? Sign me up.)

"I rent the room out. To fishermen, mostly," she explains. "Gone all day, just need a place to rest their rods for the night. You two do much fishing?"

"We're here for –"

"Antiquing," I interrupt with a smile. I can't take a chance and have him telling everyone – especially some potentially gossipy old lady we don't know – that we're here searching for Teddy Glass. He's not Johnny Depp famous, but he's not exactly a nobody either.

"Oh, well there's plenty of that!" she says. "I can tell you about all the best spots first thing in the morning. But I'm sure you're ready to get to bed now. Billy told me what a day you've had. Such a sweet man but no head for hospitality, let me tell you."

"Bed sounds great," Quentin says. "We appreciate your help, Norma. Really."

As she leads us down the hot pink hallway, I know in my very soul of souls that there is only going to be one bed in this room. That's how it always goes, right? The couple who hates each other is forced to share a double bed – or worse – a twin.

God, please don't let it be a twin.

I am already considering how much I'm not above making him sleep on the floor when Norma leads us into the small room and clicks on the yellow-orange bulb of the table lamp. The entire room is overwhelmingly navy blue, with a heavy-handed nautical theme, like something an eight-year-old might request if he got really into mermaids or *Moby Dick.* The furniture is bright white. The throw pillows have little anchors embroidered on them. There's a woven rug covering the tile floor that looks like it was made out of weathered rope from a pirate ship.

"I'm sorry to say I only have bunk beds. I'm sure you were hoping for something a bit more *intimate.*"

"We'll make it work," Quentin says. His hand finds my low back again. Just briefly – so briefly, that I wonder again if I imagined it.

"Bunk beds are perfect," I tell her.

"Do you need any help getting your things inside?"

"We've got everything we need," he assures her.

"Okay. Well, I'm right down the hall, so just yell if you need anything," she smiles.

When she's gone, I click the door closed behind her and sigh.

"Could you have made that any weirder?" I whisper.

"What?"

"She thinks we're together."

"I mean, we are here *together.*"

"You know what I mean," I grimace.

I begin trying to make sense of the items I threw in my bag this morning, wondering if I've got anything in here resembling pajamas. I wasn't planning to be within a few hundred miles of

Quentin – much less sharing a room with him – when I packed.

Across the small space, he takes off his shirt with a groan. The muscles of his back flex, and the sound that escapes him makes me feel suddenly aware of my breasts, my hips, the fact that his half-clothed body is barely an arm's distance away. He unbuttons his jeans, hooking his fingers into the waistband. Alarm bells go off in my brain.

"What are you doing?" I say.

"Changing for bed..."

"Right here?" I half-whisper. "This isn't a strip club. You know there's a bathroom down the hall."

One of his dimples winks at me as he smirks. "Why? Are you worried you might be unable to resist me?"

I roll my eyes, but my heart skips. Standing here – this close to him – I feel utterly defenseless, which in turn means that I become very, very defensive.

"I can't say that I find dirty lying cheats particularly irresistible," I shoot back with a sarcastic smile.

That dimple disappears, and he accepts the jab with a tight nod.

"If you want us to be all incognito, then our best bet is to let her think we're a couple," he says. "Which she won't, if we sneak off to the bathroom every time we need to change clothes."

A few moments later he unceremoniously slides the denim down his hips, revealing dark blue boxers. I know they don't actually *reveal* anything – at least not anything more than I've seen of him at the pool – but I can't help but feel my entire body heat. I try to ignore the shadowy contours of his chest, that trail of dark hair beneath his belly button, the subtle V-shaped set of muscles above his hips, leading down... and down...

"Why are you always trying to convince me to fake date you?" I ask. "Don't you have enough women in your life?"

With another smooth movement, he hauls himself into the

top bunk, dramatically draping an arm across his eyes.

"I don't have *any* women in my life," he says. "Probably because I'm such a dirty lying cheat. But I won't ogle you, if that's what you're worried about. I guess if you don't believe me you could always whip up a contact real quick."

"Fuck off," I mutter.

"Gladly," he says. "Just turn the lights off, when you're done trying to defame me?"

I click the switch, enveloping us in darkness.

"I'm not trying to *defame you*," I argue, snatching a pair of shorts out of my bag. I shimmy into them before peeling off my dress. "I'm making a judgment based on the information that has been presented to me. Isn't that what we do? If you wanted me to come to a different conclusion, maybe you should've offered up a little more evidence."

The room goes quiet except for the whir of the window unit AC. Even in the shadows, I turn my back to the beds to slide out of my bra and slip into a tank top before crawling into the detergent-and-sunscreen scented sheets of the bottom bunk. I hear the springs above me shift as Quentin turns over. I wonder if his mattress feels as much like thin, springy cardboard as mine does, but I'm not about to ask. I close my eyes and will my brain to succumb to exhaustion, the way my road-weary muscles already have.

I'm somewhere between running through case notes, cursing Quentin's very soul, and trying to meditate on the faint sound of ocean waves from outside when I hear him say, "My dad abuses women."

I open my eyes and blink at the bottom of the mattress above me. For a second, I'm sure I imagined this.

"What?" I ask quietly.

"My dad," he repeats, "is a controlling asshole who abuses women. He doesn't do it in the way you can see, but he's brutal, all the same."

I'm staring at the bed above me, mouth open, at a loss of what to say.

"Quentin... I..."

"It started with my mom," he continues. "She left, but she didn't take us with her. It was the only way my dad would let her leave without a fight. She didn't have the money for one anyway, and she thought he was a good dad. I guess he was fine. He didn't hit us or anything. We always had more than we needed. He said he loved us. But he is a disaster at relationships. Every time one imploded he always seemed to find a new one, and the cycle started over. Six months of bliss, a wedding, and then... a tectonic shift. We did our best to keep our heads down and ride it out. Like a goddamn earthquake or something.

"Eventually, I started trying to scare off the women he dated. I threw tantrums into my teens. I started outrageous arguments at the dinner table. When I got older, I targeted them with pranks and insults until I hoped they'd leave. That's really how I got my start as the family fuckup. Scaring off potential stepmothers. They probably assumed I was just like him.

"I always wanted to be *better*. Stronger, I guess. At first I figured I knew how to handle his shit better than them. But ultimately, I wanted to help people fight back. I did, for a while. I worked my ass off in Texas, trying to prove that I wasn't like him, that I was so much better than he would ever give me credit for. And I really felt like I was past so much of it, but I came back home, and there it was. A new woman. A new cycle. And I felt..."

He sighs.

"Melissa knew about my work in Austin, and she asked me to help her. That's what she was doing that night at Maestoso – asking for my help. I didn't know for sure why she was pursuing me at first, but I had a good idea, and I avoided her. I explained to her that I'm not a social worker or psychologist; I'm just an attorney. My grandfather told me to stay out of it, and I did my best. But I'm definitely not hooking up with her." There's a pause, and I can hear him sigh. "I want to check all the right boxes and do all the right things. And as stupid as it probably sounds, I want my family to realize they were wrong about me. To really *value* me. I want it all, even though I know that none of these things can coexist. Sometimes I'm not sure we can outrun ourselves. Lather, rinse, repeat."

For a few moments, I'm quiet, barely breathing.

"Anyway," he says. "I wanted you to know."

There's another long pause. So long I'm sure he might be asleep. And in it I'm fighting with myself. Maybe he's right. Maybe we can't outrun ourselves. Because I'm paralyzed with fear. I'm scared that Quentin Maxwell is my single biggest weakness. Scared that he has the power to ruin my career. Scared he'll break my heart. That he'll take *everything*. And the thing about me is that I don't know that I'm willing to risk *anything*, let alone everything.

"Thanks," I finally say. "For telling me."

It's a cheap line, and I know it. I hear the springs creak above me. I hear his breathing steady. Eventually, we both succumb to the quiet.

21.

"HOW'D YOU SLEEP?"

I turn from the kitchen table with a start. I've been staring out the window towards the docks of the marina, squinting into the early morning clouds and wondering if Teddy has managed to make it back to port yet, for so long that I seemed to forget where I was. The details of the bright yellow kitchen come back to me. Norma moves toward the turquoise cabinets and pulls out a pair of coffee mugs.

"Good," I tell her.

It's a lie. It turns out I can't sleep around Quentin. I spent half the night listening to his breathing, and the other half turning over everything he said. I crawled out of bed around sunrise and decided to set up at the kitchen table with my laptop and get a little work done. I guess at some point I spaced out.

"Good," Norma says. Her smile is a small, amused quirk of her lips, like she's got a secret tucked between them. "Coffee?"

"That'd be great, thanks," I offer.

In the brief quiet, my thoughts spin in circles. I just can't figure out *why* Quentin said anything of the things he did. It's one thing to trust someone with his secrets. It feels like another entirely to trust *me* – the person who is competing with him for a promotion – with secrets that I could use to quite literally guarantee he won't get the promotion. He might as well have handed me a live grenade: the kind an enemy would probably use against him.

But are we enemies anymore? Were we ever, really? Every time I try to tally up the points and see which column he lands in, I feel like I lose track. Normally in situations like this, I would take a deep breath and go with my gut. I don't know what my gut is telling me in this situation. My stomach flips every time I think about the way he looked at me across the table at Barnacle Billy's, with that flicker of flame in his eyes and the ocean breeze in his hair.

There isn't a single day I haven't wanted to be irrationally close to you. Haven't imagined what it would be like to...

I rub my eyes and consider showering soon, or taking another jog down to the marina and inspecting the rows of boats myself. Maybe we could charter one to track Teddy down, and then we could board his vessel and take him by force. Which I guess would mean I'd basically need to locate a bounty hunter. Or Captain Jack Sparrow.

"You'll be excited to hear I've already taken the liberty of writing down the locations of all the good look-sees around here," Norma says, rescuing me from this hopeless spiral.

"Look-sees?" I ask.

"Antique stores. Flea markets. Quirky little year-round yard sales. The kind of places where you have to take your time to look and see if there's anything worth buying. Isn't that what you said you were here for?"

I catch up in starts and stops.

"Oh. Yes," I stammer. I tack on a smile for good measure.

"Yeah, of course. All that sounds great. That's why we're here, like you said. To look and see!"

She gives me an uncertain sideways glance before turning to fill our mugs. I wasn't one-hundred percent certain I was being a scattered mess, but that look solidified it. I'm losing my edge.

"I haven't checked The Pole this morning, but you'll also want to do that," she adds. "You can't miss it. It's at the corner, by the bank. Any of the pop-up sales are going to be posted there."

When she comes around to set a mug beside my computer, her eyes light up when she sees my screen.

"Oooh, is that the #Glasslighting girl?" she says. "I've been following this!"

At some point before I zoned out, I pulled up Gigi's Instagram, and the aesthetically coordinated grid is front and center. I've been stalking it for the latest updates, poring over details to see if anything new sticks out.

"Oh," I stammer. "I... Maybe? I dunno. I wandered here for... fashion tips."

"Oh," Norma chirps, deflating slightly. "Well, normally I wouldn't circle around the carcass of someone's relationship like a vulture, but she's divorcing some music guru, and the whole thing just sidetracked the recording of an album I've been waiting for."

Somewhere, a chain reaction in my head makes my brain want to explode. I reach for my coffee in an effort to buy time to respond and end up scorching my tongue. Norma looks immediately stricken.

"Oh honey, let me get you some water," she says. "And let me know if you see anything on there about them settling this whole thing soon, or none of us may live to see that reunion album. It's The Blinding Lytes. You know them, right? Even people your age usually know their song "Come Cruise Along", from the eighties. I actually kissed the guitarist once, way before they were famous.

I'm such a sucker for a good power ballad.

"Anyway, the label pulled the studio deal and the band is digging in their heels – Johnny always was too damn stubborn – and it delayed the whole tour. Such a mess. I was trying to figure out if they're ever going to reschedule for Jacksonville, and that's how I got sucked in. There's this ugly cat. He's so unfortunate looking that he's actually kind of cute – a lot like my second husband. And the record guy is scruffy and handsome, much like the man who was almost my third husband. And this girl may or may not be one of the greatest actors of her generation. She's either been through hell or is completely working this guy over, possibly both. It all sounds too crazy to be true."

I gulp down the glass of water she brings me in hopes that I can get away with simply nodding and raising my eyebrows in a way that whole-heartedly agrees: *Yes. This is totally crazy.*

When she wanders back towards the stove, telling me something about that list of shops, I'm only halfway listening. I close the lid of my laptop. My chair makes a scuffing sound across the tile as I scoot away from the table.

"I think I'm going to shower really quick," I say around my semi-scorched tongue. "While the coffee cools down. I just need to, um. I'll be right –"

I'm watching Norma as she watches me in my attempt to skirt out of the room. This is how I miss that Quentin is coming through the doorway. This is also how Norma definitely doesn't miss the subsequent collision, when I ram right into Quentin's chest. We both make an embarrassing sort of 'oof' sound. Our eyes meet, dazed.

"Hey. You okay?" he asks. His hands find my upper arms. It's an innocent enough touch. Warm. Steadying. The way I jerk away from it, though, is definitely *not* what someone who is here on a romantic weekend getaway would do.

I try to make it better by patting his chest. Spoiler alert: it doesn't make it better, it only makes the whole thing more awkward. I can feel two sets of eyes boring into me.

"I'm great," I say. "Just gonna…"

I point in the direction of the bedroom, and I'm about to scurry off, but then I remember that I don't trust Quentin not to say something idiotic, like telling her why we're really here. After the thing with Teddy that landed us in Florida, I'm taking zero chances. I snag him by the arm and give him a toss of my head, indicating we've got serious business to discuss, in private.

"Sorry," I tell Norma. "We'll just be a minute."

"Oh honey, don't apologize on my account. I wouldn't be able to keep my hands off him either," she smirks. "Take all the time you need."

Quentin is still giving me that dazed and confused look when I usher him into the bedroom and close the door behind me.

"Is everything…?" he begins.

"She knows. Not about us. About Teddy and Gigi."

"What? How? I mean, I know this case is big, but we're five hundred miles from home."

"She listens to The Blinding Lytes," I say, throwing a hand in the air as if this fact is completely ridiculous and made up.

Quentin accepts this with a knowing nod. "Yeah, they postponed the reunion album."

"How could you possibly know that?"

"It's big news," he says. "I added it to the case notes last week."

I bristle. Is he trying to act like I don't know as much about this case – *my* case – as he does? We've got tomes of case notes at this point. It's hard to keep up.

"Well, none of our notes mean anything if we can't find Teddy and get him back to Memphis before Monday morning."

"We'll find him," he says. "But in the meantime, we probably need to keep our host from figuring out that we're…"

"Not in here banging each other's brains out?" I finish. There it is again – that flash in his eyes, like the flick of a lighter. I hold my bottom lip between my teeth, clutching my clothes. "Sorry, that was…"

Accidental?

Off color?

Entirely stupid?

"I know this is all a little weird." His gaze seems to land on the fact there's a picture above the chest of drawers of a little boy in a sailor outfit riding a giant whale through outer space. "*Very* weird. But I promise you I won't do anything to screw this up. I'm all in, Heidi. I want this to work. It *has* to work."

I still. This feels like such a non sequitur and yet… isn't it what I was worried about when I shoved him in here? Isn't it why I feel like I can't relax? Everything is out of control. First Quentin, then Teddy, now this situation with Norma. I'm going through the motions, hoping to strongarm everything into being totally normal, in hopes that I can regain my sense of control. Maybe that's the only way *I* know how to handle things. Lather, rinse, repeat.

"You won't talk to her about the case?" I ask in a voice so soft I'm not sure it's mine.

"What case?" he says. He drops his hands on my shoulders, and the weight of his warmth is reassuring. "Don't worry. Norma and I have plenty to talk about. And I hope you brought comfortable shoes, because I have a feeling we've got a lot of antiquing to do."

***

I meet Quentin outside half an hour later, where he's standing on Norma's sandy front lawn, studying his phone. I take a deep breath, willing myself to shove past the signals in my brain that note how good he looks in his gray shorts and dark blue V-neck. I know before he turns around that it's the kind of blue that makes his eyes look that much more like the ocean at dusk – dark and deep and wondrous.

He's the reason we're on this rescue mission, I remind myself. *Despite whatever he said last night, I have to stay* focused.

"You look like you're about to star in a Michael Bay movie," he says.

I grimace at him before glancing down at my basic sundress, through the lenses of my favorite sunnies. "Like the electronics are going to turn against us, and everything is going to start blowing up in dramatic, up-close slo mo?"

"Like you're wearing heels as if they aren't highly impractical footwear to run around in all day."

"These aren't heels," I argue. "They're wedges. Believe it or not, they check all the boxes for comfort. Plus they make my legs look extra long. Better to round-house-kick you with, if you get out of line."

He doesn't argue this. His gaze seems to trail up the length of my legs before he can catch it. He scrubs a hand up the back of his hair, looking away. "Let's check the docks first?"

We head in the direction of the marina. I know before we get there that there is going to be no sign of the *Virginia Marie*. Just like last night. And at the first light of dawn, when I jogged over.

"You know you don't actually have to go antiquing with me," I offer. "You can go hang on the beach, or whatever. I've got plenty of work I can do. I'm sure I could con Billy Barnacle out of the wifi password."

"*The partners will work all aspects of the case together.* That includes going undercover," he says. "Today, your only job is making people believe you're actually here on vacation. Which begins with *enjoying yourself.*"

He says that last bit as if it's completely beyond my skill set.

"Fine," I say. Please let the record show I am accepting this challenge begrudgingly. I will not miss an opportunity to prove him wrong. "Where to first?"

He passes me his phone, with all of the coordinates already mapped out. "You pick."

I scan the list. The Treasure Trove. Island Thrift. Shelluva Deal.

"Oooh, this one. Mary's Place."

I can tell that he's surprised. Of all the catchy names, it does seem the least appealing, but it's the instincts from my childhood, tingling like spidey senses. The cutesy names are sometimes marketing schemes. Mary's Place? It's organic. It's the kind of thing that named itself in conversations, when locals said things like, 'I got it over at Mary's place.'" I can hear my mom and Auntie Lena in the front seat of our old Toyota, scanning the newspaper and arguing over which ones to hit first. Somewhere like Mary's Place is a great start, because you never know what you'll find. It's easy. It's unpretentious. It's eclectic.

"Trust me," I add, as if we've hashed all this out loud.

There's a glimmer in his eyes, and he nods, looking away. "I do."

***

The sun burns off the morning's thin layer of clouds, and we walk half a mile down the main stretch of road that runs the length of the island. A few times I think he might say something, but Quentin is uncharacteristically quiet this morning. My head is too much of a swirly mess, so we move along in companionable silence, watching the cars cruise past on the main road and the seagulls waddle along near the dunes that separate us from stretches of beach. The navigation on my smartwatch buzzes, and we veer off into an old neighborhood with weathered shiplap houses painted in bright colors.

Mary's Place is exactly that. It seems she's converted the first floor and carport to shop space, and she lives up top. All the first level doors and windows are thrown open, inviting the salty breeze and a trio of beach cats to roam in and out as they please.

It reminds me of Auntie Lena's place so much my chest clenches, and I love it immediately.

Don't get me wrong – on the surface, they look next to nothing alike. Auntie Lena's shop is that clean kind of retro, like maybe you're stepping onto the set of *Grease* or went cruising around '40s Las Vegas. While my aunt's shop smells like lemon and old paperbacks, this place has an aroma of sage and storm clouds, and it feels like you've stumbled into the cottage of a coastal forest witch. But they're kindred spirits, I can tell.

I quickly get caught up picking through boxes and spinning racks of jewelry near the front window, and Quentin's hand sweeps across my low back as he edges past, slowly disappearing into another room. I find myself glancing over my shoulder briefly, wondering where he's gone, and why his touch always seems to linger longer than he does.

I distract myself with beaded bracelets, shiny necklaces, and dangly earrings. Eventually I find myself sorting through an entire box of rings, like coins in a treasure chest. I'm trying on a mood ring with an oversized square stone when a woman who looks like Esmerelda from my childhood obsession with *The Hunchback of Notre Dame* sweeps through a beaded curtain made of seashells. It swishes and clacks behind her. Her dark hair is streaked with silver, but her eyes are curious and vibrant.

"Hey there," she says. "Looking for anything in particular?"

"Just browsing," I offer with a smile. "I love your place."

"Glad to hear it," she grins. "A few things you should know. Large items can be shipped for a small fee. Everything in that corner is 50% off. The cats aren't for sale. And there's a very handsome gentleman browsing in the next room, about your age, I think. You could probably leave with him, too, if you wanted. He seems to have his eye on you." She winks. "Let me know if you need anything."

I'm left biting into my smile when she disappears, ignoring

the way her teasing made my stomach flip and flutter.

As it always does when I'm in a place like this, time seems to warp and bend. I sniff a dozen different varieties of incense. I contemplate carved driftwood keepsakes. I imagine I'm the kind of woman who wears sparkly pashminas instead of pantsuits on weekdays.

I'm trying on a straw cowboy hat adorned with a jaunty peacock feather when I hear him chuckle behind me. The way he's smiling when I turn around makes me uncharacteristically self-conscious. I prop a hand on my hip.

"What?" I defend.

"You look right at home."

It's an observation that makes me feel disarmed. Normally this feeling comes with the sudden urge to wield sarcasm like my favorite weapon, but I soften with a smirk.

"Thrift stores happen to be my natural habitat," I admit. "My aunt owns one back home."

"Nine Lives," he nods.

I narrow my gaze. "Have you been stalking me again?"

"That retro sign they have out front is in the upper corner of the only framed photo in your entire office," he says. "Context clues."

"Hm. You're more investigative than I gave you credit for."

"All this time you've kept me around for my good looks?" he teases.

I'm removing the jaunty headpiece and tousling my hair when he says, "Keep the hat. It's yours. I already paid for it."

I bristle with a laugh. "What? Why? I can buy my own hats, you know."

"Don't worry. It's entirely selfish," he says. "I like the way you smile when you wear it."

It's entirely unintentional that when he says this, a small, strange little smile plays across my lips. His gaze travels along the curve of my mouth and up again.

"Yup," he smirks. "Just like that."

He tips the brim of my hat, and before I can react, he's already halfway out the door. I trail after him, slipping back into my sunglasses as we breeze outside.

"I see you found something you liked," Mary-Esmerelda calls from her spot on the front porch swing. She winks at me in a way that makes my heart flip. It's so knowing. What does she know? I don't have a chance to ask. She is returning to her book and bidding us goodbye. "Make sure you check The Pole when you go through town. It's by the bank. You can't miss it."

I thank her with a wave and jog to catch up to Quentin, who is halfway down the sandy stone path that connects to the street. When I fall into step beside him, I inspect the small canvas shopping bag he's carrying. I reach for it curiously.

"What did you get?"

He hesitates, holding it out of my grasp. "Why do I feel like you're about to judge me?"

"*The partners won't keep secrets*," I say.

His mouth edges up at the corner as he passes me the bag. Fluttery anticipation spreads through me as I carefully sort through his purchases. They include:

An actual fountain pen.

Stunning vintage cufflinks in a combination of mother of pearl and gold, with a maritime compass design inlaid into them.

And... a chipped Ninja Turtles coffee mug. The green cartoon character smiles up at me with an orange bandana tied around his face.

"One of these things is not like the others," I observe. "Is this... Rafael?"

"Michaelangelo," he replies, retrieving the items from me protectively. "Rafael is the red one."

"Ah," I say. "My apologies, I'm not exactly up on Ninja Turtles fashion."

"I actually used to have this great costume, when I was a kid. My mom made them for us one Halloween, back before she left. She made the shells out of cardboard and pillows. They had straps like a backpack."

"Resourceful," I smile.

"Yeah. Anyway, my brother always got to be Michaelangelo, and I got stuck with Donatello."

"I'm assuming from the look on your face that nobody wants to be Donatello."

"Well, I'm sure somebody does. But I didn't," he smiles.

"Well, I'll totally let you be Michaelangelo," I say.

"Yeah? Which one are you gonna be?"

"I dunno. That big rat?"

He bursts into laughter. "Splinter?"

"He seems wise," I defend. "And like he knows how to use the fact that people underestimate his abilities to his advantage."

"Nobody in their right mind would ever underestimate you."

"Thanks," I offer wistfully. "So, are you gonna call me sensei?"

"Absolutely not."

We're grinning as we continue to the next pin on our map. It's easier, with this stretch of road ahead and this bag of thrift store finds between us, to forget why we're here.

"About last night" lodges itself in my throat, itching to tumble out so many times, but I can't form the words. It's easier to listen to the steady crunch of our shoes along the bike lane, watch the sweep of seabirds across the sky, and pretend I'm on vacation.

22.

The Pole turns out to be exactly that – an electrical pole at the lazy little intersection by the bank, the bottom of which is so covered with old rusted staples and nails that there's no exposed wood anywhere within arms reach. It is littered with flyers advertising yard sales and local auctions, but also repair services available for hire, a free hot tub, and a notice that someone is looking for a missing rooster.

Some neighborhoods have apps; Santa Lucia has The Pole.

"There is a five hundred dollar reward for this rooster," I tell Quentin with a laugh.

"Oliver, 6 months old," he reads. "Very friendly and petable. Petable?"

"I mean obviously we just need to start trying to pet every rooster we see today," I reason. "That way we'll know if it's Oliver."

He laughs, scanning the other weather-crinkled flyers and poster boards and pointing out a wanted poster for a local racoon. A grainy security camera image has been printed to help with proper identification.

"Do you think he's the one who snatched Oliver?" he asks.

"Damn, I hope not. Maybe they're secretly best friends. Maybe they ran away together."

"The rooster and the raccoon?"

"It's an enemies to lovers story," I offer.

Quentin laughs incredulously. "Is that a real thing?"

"It's totally a thing."

We hit two of the advertised yard sales – one where I snag a secondhand deck of playing cards with artsy koi fish printed on the backs – before making our way to The Treasure Trove, which boasts shelves upon shelves of highly breakable tchotchkes. It makes me nervous just to browse the narrow aisles of crystal dolphins, elaborately handmade art that may or may not double as smoking devices, and precariously stacked frames made of sea glass. At one point Quentin's hand finds my arm, and he leans in close.

"Can we please get out of here before one of these shelves spontaneously combusts and we have to max out our credit cards?" he says against my ear.

"Don't trust your Class Five Rapids reflexes?" I tease.

"I trust myself less in this store than I trust myself around you. And that's saying something."

My heart skips. I turn, but he is already edging his way back down the aisle. I watch him head outside through an overloaded shelf of sea life snowglobes.

We don't break or buy anything, but we do rent some beachy vintage bikes from the rack out front. A guy sitting in a lawn chair under a beach umbrella gives us the rundown of all the return locations, one being Barnacle Billy's, which means I'm sold. We load our purchases thus far into the little baskets attached to the handlebars and cruise to the marina – where there's still no sign of Teddy or the *Virginia Marie*.

Eventually we cruise down to the pier, stopping for ice cream so we can listen to a trio of street musicians play a mini concert that we saw advertised on The Pole. I dance to covers I haven't heard since high school until ice cream melts down my hand, and I lick vanilla off my wrist, earning one of those distracted, two-beat stares from Quentin. We pack up our things and head to our last stop as the afternoon clouds are rolling in.

Shelluva Deal is one of those tacky stores that lurks on every coastline, peddling neon pool noodles, borderline inappropriate shot glasses, and airbrushed t-shirts. It's nostalgic and terrible all at once. We dodge a group of teens carrying skim boards as we park our bikes and head inside.

"Should we get matching nose rings?" Quentin says. "Tribal henna tattoos?"

He spins the display of bracelets by the register. They're the kind made of thin twine that remind me of middle school friendship bracelets. They promise things like Love and Happiness and Calm. I snag one and grab his hand, sliding it around his wrist and pulling the strings until they tighten.

"For luck," I offer, pointing to the sign.

He slides a matching one off the rack and adds it to my wrist, working the ties until it's snug against my pulse point. The trio of stones are smooth and green.

"They match your eyes. And your hat," he says, tipping my feather. "You feelin' lucky, PBG?"

I give him a coy smile, laughing in spite of myself, until I realize the pimply kid is watching us from behind the register.

"Do you, like, wanna pay for those or whatever?" he asks, half looking at us and half checking his phone. I wonder why he thinks he's standing at a cash register if not to accept forms of payment from customers who are also standing at a cash register.

I slide some money across the counter and we slip back out

into the humid, suddenly gray afternoon. I squint at the sky.

"Is it supposed to rain?"

"It's Florida," Quentin offers. "These things blow through quick."

Turns out, it does blow through quick. Unfortunately, we're about a hundred yards from Barnacle Billy's when the sky opens up. The rain pelts us with big, warm drops that makes splotches across the fabric of my sundress. We leave our bikes against the building and jog up the steps, shaking ourselves out and laughing as we step in through the propped open door, with a sign that says 'No Shirt, No Shoes, No Problem'.

"H! Q!" Barnacle Billy announces from behind the bar. "You two crazy lovebirds. You're early for the wet t-shirt contest."

"That's too bad. I was a shoe-in for first," Quentin says, peeling his shirt away from his torso with a grin. "Just a couple of drinks then?"

"You got it!"

We settle in at a table beside the wall of unshuttered windows, where a sheet of rain pours off the roof and onto the patio. We've caught the place between lunch and dinner, and the crowd is sparse, only a few gray-bearded men and sun-weathered women wearing bright beach cover-ups, smoking at the bar. We order a couple of sandwiches and settle in.

"You're a bad influence on me," I say, sucking the lime of my drink. "You know I think this is the first Saturday I haven't worked since... ever?"

He smiles. "Yeah? How does it feel?"

I think for a moment before admitting, "Good."

We both laugh at the surprise in my voice.

"Good," he nods.

The feeling expands in my chest, and I bite into my smile. It simmers into something vulnerable and forlorn. I gaze out through the sheets of rain pouring off the roof.

"We aren't going to find him are we?" I say softly.

Quentin holds my gaze like he wants to be optimistic, but he gives me a small shrug. "I dunno, honestly."

I let this possibility settle into my stomach. It's one part desperation, two parts resignation.

"You know what hurts the most?" I say. "That, after all this – after *everything* – I'm going to have to show up to court alone. It's a gut punch."

"You won't be alone."

I find his gaze, and he holds it. Two beats. Three. There isn't enough room in my chest for this feeling. The certainty that even if we can't find our client, Quentin will be there.

That he's been there this whole time.

That he's *right here.*

It tingles down my neck, along my shoulders, between my ribs. I snag my bottom lip between my teeth, giving him a nod. He returns the gesture before dropping his attention to the sticky menu.

"You know what I worry about?" he admits. "If this all blows up, they'll know it was my fault."

"It's not your fault," I scoff. "And I would round-house kick anyone who dares to say that."

His smile comes slow, and I can tell he's surprised. Hell, even I'm surprised. A surge of protectiveness is thrumming through me. For *Quentin.* I usually reserve that for... well, people who aren't him.

"Thank you, sensei," he says.

We finish our sandwiches with the storm still simmering, and I break out the playing cards I picked up at the yard sale. To Quentin's apparent surprise, I shuffle the deck with a flourish.

"The game," I say, "is five card stud."

His eyes flicker with a smile. "Oh, PBG. You sure you wanna do this?"

"Why, are you scared I'm gonna take you for everything you're worth?" I tease.

My skin tingles again when he looks at me like that. Down my arms. Along my inner thighs. This time, his eyes are playfully predatory. Alight with a challenge. He tips the last of his margarita to his mouth and orders another. Then he smirks, entirely unafraid.

"Deal me in."

***

The rain clears, but we hold down our spot for a while, ordering drinks and making wild bets against each other. At one point, Quentin entertains the bar set with his hidden talent, guessing each of their preferred beverages with such astonishing accuracy that the regulars start buying our drinks and sending them over. We're more than a few rounds in when I hear him suck in a sharp breath.

"Jackpot," he says.

I check my cards. "Um, no. What?"

I glance up to realize that he's not even looking at his cards – he's eyeing his phone. The way he's eyeing his phone reminds me of that night on his couch. Of Melissa's messages. Even though he assured me there's nothing going on there, I can't help but remember that sour sting.

"Do you want to take a break?" I say.

"No. Sorry. It's, um, Angela."

My brain stutters, and I lower my cards to the table. "Angela? Like... *my* Angela?"

"The P.I.?" he clarifies.

"Yeah. I didn't know you were working with her," I say.

"I didn't know she was yours exclusively," he smirks. "She's a total badass. Much more efficient than Lyle. Or Tim. I don't know why anyone hires Tim. He's about as stealthy as a buffalo."

"Yeah, I know," I chortle. "I'm just... surprised that you know."

"I guess I know more than you give me credit for," he says. "Fortunately for you, I'm willing to share."

He turns the screen of his phone to me, and I see the message from Angela. *Kimberly Winewright, formerly Glass. Iowa City, Iowa. 319-555-2989.*

Holy shit.

My eyes meet his with wide intensity. "Is that…"

"The former Mrs. Glass," he confirms.

"Jackpot," I breathe.

A few minutes later, we're sitting in the warm sand, crowded around Quentin's phone. The sun is setting across the water. The few beachgoers that emerged after the pop-up storm are now packing up their chairs and umbrellas and sand castle molds. I tug my knees up to my chest as we wait to see if the call will connect.

"Hello?" a woman answers. Her voice is commanding but cheerful. I swell with hope.

"Ms. Winewright?" Quentin says.

"Dr. Winewright," she corrects amiably. "That's me."

"Dr. Winewright," he amends, "I'm Quentin Maxwell from Freeman Maxwell Lewis. My partner and I have a few questions for you about Teddy Glass –"

"I'm sorry, I don't talk to the press –"

"We're not the press," I break in. "We're his attorneys."

There's a pause on the line, and I stare at the call timer on the screen, waiting for the notification that she has disconnected the call. The seconds keep climbing. She doesn't hang up.

"You're Heidi?" she says.

"Heidi Krupp," I confirm. "Mr. Maxwell is my co-counsel. We're –"

"Teddy mentioned you, when I talked to him a few months ago. Said you weren't like the other attorneys he met with. That you cared."

I push past the way that does something to my chest. Seriously, what is with today? I'm scheduling an EKG the moment I get home.

"That's me," I offer. "We're committed to helping Teddy resolve his divorce, and we have a few questions for you if you have time."

"What questions?"

"You were married to Teddy?"

"Yeah," she laughs. "About a million years ago."

"What can you tell us about him?"

I hear her soften. "Teddy? He's... um, *Teddy*. Genuine. Funny. Way too into music. He's honestly one of the best men I ever knew."

"That's good to hear," I say. "Why'd you split up?"

She sighs. "We were young."

"Care to elaborate?" Quentin says.

"I got accepted to a grad program in California. It was a dream come true for me. When I applied, I thought it was impossible I'd ever get in. So when the letter came, there was no way I could say no. But Avid was always Teddy's first love. I used to joke that I was his mistress, because he was very much married to his work. It was mutual, in the end. He wasn't going to leave. I wasn't going to stay."

"How did he take it?"

"He was heartbroken, but he understood. He even helped me pay my first semester's tuition," she says. "We filed no contest and went our separate ways. But I'd like to think we remained friends."

"Did you ever know Teddy to have a temper?"

She laughs. "Have you met Teddy? No. Teddy is the sweetest man I've ever known. He'd give anyone the shirt off his back if they needed it, even if he didn't have another. He loved helping people – helping them make great records, sure, but it went beyond that.

"When we were married, I once woke up to this random kid sleeping on our couch because Teddy found out he didn't have anywhere to stay. He let him do odd jobs around the studio for a week before he sent him on his way with a little extra cash.

"Look, I don't know exactly what happened with him and Gigi, but I'm glad he's getting away from her. Nobody deserves that kind of abuse, least of all him."

Quentin and I share a confused glance.

"Abuse?" I prompt.

"He would never call it that," she says. "But Gigi was ruthlessly manipulative. She threatened to leave him often, if he didn't do what she said. She knew which things he cared about, and she used them against him to get what she wanted."

"How do you know this?"

"She told me, once. Teddy and I were supposed to have dinner the last time I was in town. I encouraged him to invite Gigi. He told me she'd never agree, said she felt threatened by me – the ex wife, hot shot professor, whatever. I laughed because I thought he had to be kidding. I'm remarried myself. I've got two kids. When I reached out to personally invite her, she was vicious. Told me she would burn down his studio and kill his cat if he ever contacted me again."

Quentin and I exchange a look.

"I didn't hear from him after that, and my number was blocked when I tried to reach out. My degrees aren't in psychology, but I've read enough true crime to recognize sociopathic tendencies when I see them. Eventually I called Zel and asked her to beg him to get help, to leave her, that whatever was going on there wasn't love."

"What did Zelda say?"

"I doubt she ever gave him the message. She said I was preaching to the choir."

I swallow hard. Quentin drags a hand down his face, covering his mouth.

"Kimberly, I know this is a long shot, but is there any way you'd be willing to testify about this conversation in court?"

"Yeah, of course. If you think it would help."

"Could you make it by... Monday?" I hold my breath.

"Monday," she laughs. "*This* Monday? Are you serious?"

"I know it's a huge ask. But it might be our only chance."

There's another long pause on the line. I watch low tide gently sweep along the shore before pulling back out.

"I'll see if I can get a flight in tomorrow," she says. "If I can't..."

"If you can't, you can't. If you can, let us know. We'll book your hotel," I tell her. "Thanks for taking our call, either way."

When the call ends, I fall back in the sand with a thud, letting the cotton candy sky swallow my gaze as I run my hands through my hair. My mind is racing with all the work I need to do to prepare for this, and all the documents I'll need to submit. Quentin seems to be two steps ahead.

"There's wi-fi at Norma's," he says. "If we hole up in the bedroom, she won't ask questions. We can work this out."

"You sure?"

"I'll make scandalous sounds, if you think it'll help."

"Do you usually audibly moan over legal documents?" I tease.

"This time?" he grins. "Yeah, I really just might."

I laugh. He offers me his hands, and I let him tug me up to my feet. I realize we're still holding hands as we start walking towards the brightly colored house down the beach.

23.

WE MISS DINNER. By the time we emerge from our frantic attempts to square everything away, it's almost midnight. Norma has long since gone to bed. We grab snacks from the fridge that she left labeled with a yellow post-it – *in case you're hungry* – and head out by her pool. It's a modest, kidney-shaped refuge tucked in the middle of the patio. The sky blue of the pool light glows, and we don't bother to turn on the outdoor sconces. We settle into the dark as easily as if we've done it a dozen times. I sit on the edge, letting my legs swish through the water. Quentin wastes no time diving in. When he surfaces, he sweeps his hair back with both hands, turning his gaze up toward the stars. He releases one of those weight-of-the-world sighs. I love how he always seems more at ease near water.

"You're not getting in?" he asks.

"I didn't bring a suit."

His laugh is quiet. "Seriously? Who doesn't bring a bathing suit to the beach?"

"Someone who came here for work and thought she'd be at

least halfway back home by now."

He beckons, all sexy and shirtless. "Just get in."

"In what? My underwear?"

"If you want," he says. "Either way, you know I owe you one."

"One what?"

I realize too late that he has drifted closer. It happens in slow motion: he hooks a strong arm around my waist and tugs me into the pool. I'm engulfed for a few moments in lukewarm, glowing blue. My dress clings to me as I push to the surface. For some reason I'm laughing.

"Now we're even," he says.

I wipe saltwater from my eyes. I know we're trying to be quiet, but I splash him anyway.

"You are *so* going to regret that," I vow.

He's laughing and splashing defensively as I wrap my arms roughly around his shoulders, fully intent on dunking him. Unfortunately, he's strong, so I don't successfully dunk him. I end up wrapped around his back like a spider monkey, with his hands gripping my forearms in a way that says *if I go under, I'm taking you with me*. I stifle another laugh as we struggle against each other. Eventually, we reach an unspoken stalemate. Our trashing slows. Our subdued laughter simmers.

It's then, once the water has gone quiet, that I realize exactly how close we've gotten. He seems to realize it, too. For a few moments all you can hear is our uneven breaths and the gentle rush of ocean waves. This is the moment I think about the guardrails. The contract definitely outlines that I should pull away. And yet, haven't we sped so far past that point, so many times before? Somehow, we're still here. We haven't driven over a cliff yet.

I soften against him, resting my chin on his shoulder.

"Thank you for today," I say softly. "I didn't realize how much I needed it. Sometimes I get so busy fighting everyone's battles that I forget how to just... have fun."

"You're surprisingly good at having fun, for someone so out of practice," he teases. "Maybe you should do it more often."

"Maybe," I say, and to my surprise I mean it. I'm feeling suddenly wistful. I let my gaze wander into the dark abyss of sky and ocean and stars, settling a little further into his warmth. "Do you ever wish we weren't us?"

I feel him shift, smoothing his hands along the hug of my forearms against his chest. "I dunno. I kind of like us."

"I mean, do you ever wish we weren't here undercover. Wish we were just..." I release a small sigh. "Here on vacation?"

He makes a humming sound. We're moving slowly through the water now.

"You mean like how we met yesterday at Barnacle Billy's, because he triple booked a room, and we ended up sharing bunk beds at Norma's?"

A slow smile blossoms across my face. "Exactly like that. Except you left out the part where I thought you were obnoxious."

"For guessing your favorite drink, like a possible serial killer?"

"And for being so damn good looking."

He huffs out a laugh. "Fortunately, as fate would have it, this is when I – the good-looking potential serial killer, sleeping in the bed above you – bought you dinner, because I realized I love the way you look when you think I'm obnoxious. And then I invited you antiquing. And I spent the whole day wondering how I walked into that dingy bar and found the most heart-stoppingly beautiful woman I've ever met."

My breath catches, and he must feel it. He loosens his hold and lets me slide off his back. I can tell he's attempting to put appropriate distance between us, but I snag his hand before he can get too far away. I tug him towards me until we're face to face.

"I thought you said I was a forest fire," I argue softly, wrapping my arms around his neck. "And that you wanted to make me breakfast."

He seems to register the teasing in my eyes, and the way his gaze dips to my mouth makes my heart skip. His throat works as he swallows.

"To be fair, there are a lot of other things I want to do before that."

"Like what?"

When he pulls me closer, I instinctively wrap my legs around him. I feel weightless in his arms. My breasts crowd against his chest as he eases my back against the cool tile edge of the pool.

"That depends. Am I still your coworker?" he asks. "Or am I here on vacation?"

I consider this – along with the water clinging to his eyelashes, the magnetic way he's studying me, the kissable curve of his mouth, hovering close to mine. Bravery laces my veins.

"Which one wants to fuck me?" I say.

A blush burns across my cheeks, and I can't believe I've said it. From the momentary flash in his eyes, he can't either, but he doesn't miss a beat. He smooths one of his hands up my neck, angling my mouth like he's going to kiss me.

He doesn't.

He drags his thumb across my bottom lip. Along my jaw. Over the spot where my neck meets my shoulder. His dark, smoky voice warms through me like embers.

"There isn't any version of me that doesn't want every single thing about you," he says.

He trails a finger straight down from my shoulder, tracing the lines my bikini has left these past few weeks of pool time. His touch slides over my collarbone. Along the curve of my breast. Stopping only to trace along the low neckline of my dress. Tingles spread beneath my skin, teasing my nipples to attention.

"I want to know how you look wearing nothing but these tan lines. Are they just here?" He cups his hand around the fullness of my breast before letting the other trail up my thigh. He smooths a long line up to my hip, slipping easily under the floating fabric of my skirt, spreading his hand wide to map my curves. "Or maybe, here?"

He caresses my backside, slipping a finger beneath the edge of my underwear and humming in appreciation. I can feel his hard length pressing against me.

"Because I've spent a lot of time thinking about bending you over my desk, spanking this gorgeous ass of yours, and I think they've gotta be here."

My eyes have gone wide with need, and I can't drink enough of him in. *This* Quentin, with his lusty, late-night mouth, that looks ready to devour me.

"Would you like that, Heidi?" he asks, his voice deep and rough.

My lips part, ripe and heavy. "Yes," I breathe.

His mouth hovers only a couple of inches from mine, and I feel desperate for him to lean in. Still, he doesn't.

"Aren't you going to kiss me?" I ask.

"Not yet," he says. "I want to tease you, the way you've been teasing me."

He slips a finger under the strap of my dress, gently allowing it to fall over my shoulder. After a moment he does the other one, tugging the wet fabric down to expose my breasts. I ache with anticipation. He runs his fingers down the tan line strap of my bikini, tracing the triangle outline where sunkissed skin meets light. He makes lazy circles around one perky pink tip before testing its sensitivity with a gentle flick. A whimper escapes me.

Oh god.

He kisses my neck, breathing across my ear. "Do you want me to stop?"

I thread my fingers into his wet hair, holding him close.

"Fuck no," I breathe.

He kisses down the plane of my throat, across the firm swell of my breasts, sending a liquid ache through me as he trades his tongue for his fingers. He sucks one of the sensitive peaks into his mouth, taunting me until I moan. I pray the sound is lost to the wind and the waves, but honestly, I don't care. I want him like this, with his tongue and teeth worshiping my body in a way that makes me ache to have him inside me.

"What about now?" he teases.

He bites at my nipple, caressing it with his teeth. Heat rises in my cheeks as my need for him becomes obvious.

"Please don't stop."

"Such a horny girl," he breathes. "How'd you know I want to hear you beg?"

He kisses his way to the other side, gently rolling the abandoned nipple between his fingers as he teases the other with his mouth. Pulsing heat pools between my legs. I grind against him.

"Ohmigod ...fuck... *you*..." I breathe.

"Fuck me?" He brushes his nose against mine, tipping my head back. "Oh baby, I've got so many more things to do before I fuck you."

I snag his bottom lip with my teeth, drawing his mouth against mine with the teasing invitation of my tongue, kissing him hard. He meets me with a strangled sound, angling my head so he can take more of me.

"Is that what you want? You want me to fuck you?"

"I want you so fucking much." It feels almost as good to say it out loud as it does to have his hands all over me. He massages the ache between my thighs over the top of my underwear. I kiss him again.

He lifts me onto the side of the pool with torrents of water cascading down my body. His hand slides up my bare thighs, where my dress clings up around my hips, and he kisses the inside of my knee, higher. I can't tell if it's the night air or his mouth sending chills across my skin.

"You'd let me take you right here, wouldn't you?" he says. "Make you come out here where anybody could see us?"

Another burning ache twists through me. This man has no idea how badly I want him to make me come. When I feel him smile against my skin, I wonder if I said it out loud. He pushes my legs further apart with the press of his mouth on one thigh, then the other. I melt back onto the smooth tile and realize he's right. I really would let him do this here. I'd let him do this anywhere.

For a second I think he's going to do it – tug my clothes off and fuck me under the night sky – but instead he pulls himself out of the water with a flex of muscle. He hovers above me, stealing slow, sensual kisses. His need for me is obvious, straining against his wet trunks. We both seem to realize belatedly that I'm trembling. I can't tell if it's the fact that I'm soaked or the sheer insanity of this moment.

"Sorry. I haven't done this in a while," I admit between fervent kisses.

"Don't be sorry," he says. "I haven't either."

"Perfect."

"If I take you inside, can you be quiet?" he asks.

"Probably not," I breathe.

"Good."

He drags himself away and wraps us in the single towel he brought outside. Once it's around my shoulders, he tugs my dress the rest of the way off, kissing me once before snagging my hand. Wordlessly, we creep into the dark house and sneak into our room. The chill of the air conditioning sends goosebumps over my skin. I feel like I'm holding my breath until the bedroom door clicks shut behind us. He turns on the small lamp, bathing us in warm light.

"I want to be able to see you," he whispers. "Is that okay?"

"Yeah," I smirk. "I want to see you too."

As I let the towel slide to the floor, I catch his gaze roving down my body. His hands find my waist, mapping my outline as he kisses my wrists, my neck, claiming my mouth again. I work his wet trunks off as he tugs my panties down over my hips. He slides his fingers along my slick, swollen center. I try my best not to moan, kissing him harder as I wrap my hand around the thick length of him, and now it's his turn to fight a moan. I rub the tip of him against me, up and down, until his knees almost buckle.

He grabs my wrists, guiding my hands above my head as he backs me against the wall. "You're trying to skip ahead."

"But it's the best part," I pout.

"We'll see." His voice spreads through me like liquid honey – warm and slow and sweet.

He kisses down my neck again, tugs a nipple between his teeth, lets his fingers play along my wet crease. My fingers thread into his hair, and I grind against his hand. I've gone delirious with pleasure, and I don't exactly know when I started, but I'm stroking his hard length again, rubbing my thumb over the swollen tip, coaxing him against me. He pulls away, grabbing my wrists with a sultry smile.

"You are such a greedy girl," he says. "Didn't I tell you to wait?"

"I don't want to wait," I say teasingly. "And I'm pretty good at getting what I want."

In a smooth motion he bends me over the dresser, twisting a hand into my damp hair. When he gently tugs, I can see our reflection in the mirror. My lips are parted, my pupils dilated, and he's standing behind me with the muscles of his chest taut and his hands smoothing across my ass. I arch my back, wondering how far I have to shift before I can feel him against me.

"What am I going to do with you?" he says.

He caresses the outline of my tan with his open palm, then he slaps my ass. *Hard. A* blush rises in my face like flames. The rush of pleasure is immediate. I bite my lip against the moan.

"You like that?" he says, swiping a matching sting across the other cheek. "I can stop any time you want."

I have never felt this fucking dirty, and I love it. Guys usually let me call the shots. They certainly don't undress me in public and bend me over dressers and spank me for being horny, which in turn makes me very, *very* horny.

"Please don't stop," I say again. It could be my new mantra. I want everything this man can give me.

He sinks low behind me, kissing up my inner thighs, nudging my legs further apart. His tongue plays at my swollen center, alternating with his hand and his mouth.

"God you taste so good," he says against me. "Do you have any idea how good you taste?"

He slides wet fingers up my body, hooking them into my mouth. I moan, sucking them instinctively.

"Answer the question, baby."

"I can't... think... when you," I murmur.

He slips a finger inside me, moving slowly, licking gently. It's all a tease. He's found just the right spot, but his rhythm is too slow. Tantalizingly slow. I've already forgotten what the question was.

My legs are trembling with the absolute pleasure of it, but I realize belatedly that he's not trying to make me come. I lift myself off the dresser with a low growl, pushing him back against the floor. He looks like he's about to protest, and then I straddle his face. I have a moment of hesitation as I prop my hands against the bed behind him.

"Too much?" I say.

He grins, sliding his hands up my thighs and tugging me down to meet his eager mouth. "You could never be too much."

I smile, because I love the sound of this. I move against his tongue, rolling my hips in tiny little circles. He groans encouragingly, until I am nothing but heat and pleasure and wanting. I'm so very close. My breaths are coming short and fast. Every flick of his tongue coaxes me closer to the edge, leaving every nerve in my body begging for release. I'm *right, there.*

Suddenly, he lifts me off of him.

"No, no, no," I breathe. "Wait, I was –"

He tosses me onto the bottom bunk, and I sink back as he hooks my legs over his shoulders and buries his face against me. He's returned to his original rhythm, tantalizingly slow. I whimper, bucking my hips against his mouth. I can feel him smile as he trails a hand up my body.

"You were what?" he says, licking me again. He pinches the hard peak of my nipple, sending a shock of pleasure through me.

"I was..." I pant. "Going to..."

He gives my breast a gentle slap before switching to the other side. The sting is subtle, bringing the blood to the surface. He teases the sensitive skin beneath his fingers while his tongue works against my clit. I've been reduced to nothing but need. I am coiled so tightly with it, all I can do is clutch his hair as I whimper. I realize there are actually tears rolling down my face, because this feels...

So.

Fucking.

Good.

Every nerve in my body is vibrating, and I'm close to outright begging, when he hooks two fingers inside of me, rubbing gently.

"Were you going to come?" he teases. I whimper again, because I can't take much more of this. He tugs the hard peak of my nipple with his other hand. Aching desire has pooled in my center, and he's found the exact spot to make me crazy. "You greedy, horny girl. You're so wet. You need it so bad, don't you?"

Yes, yes, yes.

I'm vaguely aware of him repositioning himself, rubbing his hard tip against me again. Up and down. I spread my legs wider, arching to meet him, begging him in. I feel him hesitate.

"Please," I beg. "I have an IUD. I just need…"

"You're sure?"

"Yes," I breathe. I don't get the second yes out. I suck in a sharp breath as he slides into me. He thrusts once, twice, kneading his thumb against my swollen center. The feel of him in me is too much. The force of my orgasm rocks through me, tightening around him again, and again, as he buries himself all the way inside me.

24.

WE MAKE LOVE IN A WAY I NEVER HAVE. Slow, sensual, like he's moving inside my very soul. He hooks my thigh around his hip, tugging me under him, against him. His thrusts are deliberate and careful, and he watches, gauging my every reaction.

"You're still coming aren't you?" he breathes.

I manage a strangled nod. Every time I think I've stopped, he angles just right, and I'm pulsing with pleasure again. And again. Until I can see the war waging on his face. All of his muscles go tight as I pull him out of me, letting him finish across my belly in deliciously sticky lines. I run my fingers through it as he kisses me, reveling in the slick feel of him across my skin. I have never felt so good.

Everything feels good. The way he collapses beside me in the too-small bed. The way I curl against him, tugging at his bottom lip with pleasure-drunk kisses. He drags a hand up to frame my face, tracing the lines where my tears have dried.

"Are you okay?" he asks softly.

"I've never been more okay than this," I say.

"Let me get you a towel," he says.

I snag my arms around his neck. "No. Stay."

His gaze dances across my features. He smooths another stray lock of hair away from my face. So far tonight I've been caught in a rainstorm, dunked in a pool, and fucked within an inch of my life. I'm sure I probably look horrendous, and I don't care. I smile when I catch him staring.

"Do you wanna talk about this?" he asks.

"Tomorrow," I say. "Tonight, we're on vacation. Okay?"

He smirks. "More than okay."

In the next instant he sits up, careful not to knock his head against the top bunk. He tugs me to my feet and hoists me up, with my legs wrapped around his middle and my arms around his neck. I feel melty and weightless as he carries me towards the door.

I giggle in spite of myself. "Where are we going?"

Though the hallway is pitch dark, it feels scandalous to have him carry me – naked – out of our room. Three feet later, he ducks into the bathroom and nudges the door closed with his foot.

"Shower." He lowers me to my feet, removing his hands from my body only so he can reach into the tile stall and start the water. "I'm going to clean you up. Then I'm going to get you all dirty again."

I bite my bottom lip, holding onto my smile. "I love this side of you."

"Good," he says, with a fiery gleam in his eyes. "Because it's all yours. Anytime you want it."

My heart thuds in my chest. Steam quickly begins to fill up the small space. I watch him test the temperature with his wrist, making minor adjustments.

"Anytime?" I ask.

It's foreign, how uncharacteristically husky and hopeful my

voice sounds. I recognize it for what it is. I'm vulnerable. And not just because I'm standing in front of him, completely naked.

"Add it to the contract," he says. His eyes are playful, but his voice is dark and sincere. He snags my hands and tugs me into the shower with him, kissing me deeply. "I'm all yours."

***

I wake up with daylight, and the room is a navy blue blur. I sit up so quickly that I smack my head on the top bunk. I hold my head and groan as I blink at the fuzzy shapes around me.

I've gone blind for my transgressions, I think. *This is like a fucking Greek tragedy.*

I realize, belatedly, that I haven't actually gone blind. My outdated contacts have officially rolled into the back of my eyes. Or fallen out. I groan again.

I gather clothes off the floor that I hope are mine and tug my way into them. Cautiously, I feel my way down the hallway towards the smell of coffee and bacon, which I hope will lead me towards the kitchen. It's no surprise that Quentin sees me before I see him.

"'Morning. You... need some help?" he says. I can hear the smile in his voice, but I definitely can't make it out. It gets a little clearer as he moves closer. "I know round three was probably ill-advised, but I didn't expect you to wake up literally unable to walk straight."

I want to laugh, but I bite into my smile and shake my head.

It wasn't a sexy dream. I actually slept with Quentin. Thrice. It pains me to think about how many people would be thrilled to learn this secret. I allow him to pull me into the warm, clean smell of his embrace, and I momentarily melt against his chest.

"It's my contacts," I explain. "They've officially tapped out."

"Ah," he says. "You don't have extras?"

"That was my last pair."

"I can drive you to... an obgyn?"

"What? Why would you do that?"

"Aren't they the ones who check your eyes? Ob… Op… something? I don't know, I don't wear glasses."

"*Optometrists?*" I say, stretching out the word to include every syllable. A laugh bursts out of me. "It's Sunday. On an island. There's no way they're open. And regardless, we don't have time. We still have to find Teddy. And we have to drive home. And… oh god."

Everything I have to do today comes at me in a rush. I lean against the counter like I'm going to be sick. Quentin eases me onto a barstool.

"They sell glasses at Treasure Trove, right? Beside the register."

"Those are reading glasses, Quentin. Those aren't Heidi-hasn't-updated-her-prescription-in-over-a-year glasses."

"How blind are you right now?"

"Um, like twenty-five percent?" I guess. Okay, maybe thirty-five. "I definitely can't drive."

He slides a cup of coffee in front of me. That, at least, I can see.

"I can drive," he says easily.

"My car? Ha. No."

"Seriously?" he laughs. "What choice do you have right now? Consider me your seeing eye dog."

"Dogs do not drive cars," I grumble, scorching my tongue for the second time this weekend. I wonder why Norma's coffee pot is turned to boil.

He kneads my shoulders. They're unnecessarily tense. He presses his thumb into the spot where I apparently hold my entire to-do list. My head lolls back against his chest, and a moan of a sigh escapes me. He drops his mouth to my ear, so that his words tingle down my neck.

"Dogs also don't argue before breakfast."

I tip my head back far enough that I can gaze up at him. In my current state, he doesn't have his usual clean edges, but he's handsome all the same. I try to think of something to say. It seems like I should have a lot to say, especially after last night, and maybe I do, but they're not any of the things I expected.

My go-to lines are useless here. *Last night was fun. I just want to keep things casual. I'm swamped with work right now; maybe we can catch up next week?*

No. Last night was *hot*. I want to crawl back in bed with him and not emerge for weeks. I want to sink my teeth into his shoulder and claim him as mine. I couldn't stay away from him for an entire week if I tried. And best of all, he knows I'm swamped with work, but so is he. Even better, he's part of the excavation team, helping me tunnel my way out.

I'm trying to figure out how to formulate any of this into something coherent when Norma enters the kitchen. I tip myself upright like a teenager who's been caught ogling her crush. I fuss with my hair, wondering if this thing between us looks as obvious as it feels.

"You two are up early," she says. I hear but cannot see that secret tucked into her smile. "Especially for a couple of kids who stayed up all night."

I can feel the innocent, smirky, sideways look Quentin is giving me, and I pretend to be suddenly engrossed with the contents of my mug. I take another scalding sip.

"We've got to get on the road soon," he tells her. "It's a long drive back."

"Well I hope Santa Lucia was worth your while."

"Thanks for your hospitality, Norma. And I hope you get that Blinding Lytes reunion album very, *very* soon."

I eye him when she leaves the room. "Was that really necessary?"

He grins at me. "What? I meant it."

***

We make our way to the marina, and though I can't see well enough to make out any of the boat names, I can hear Quentin cough out a chuckle beside me.

"I'll be damned," he muses. "Our wayward sailor has returned to port."

As relieved as I am to hear this, I'm clutching Quentin for dear life as we step onto the boat. I can feel the current gently rocking beneath our feet.

"Of all the fishing boats…" Teddy says. "What the hell are you two doing here?"

"Looking for you," Quentin replies. "Listen, man, I'm sorry."

"Teddy, we need to talk," I begin.

At the same time, he announces, "I've done some thinking."

We all go quiet. Teddy's blurry figure shifts in front of me, holding what I'm fairly sure is Farkas, wearing a little red life vest. I squint as if this will help bring anything into focus.

"You first," he says.

I can't tell exactly who he's pointing to, but Quentin sighs.

"It was a stupid tactic, Teddy," he offers. "Gigi said a lot of things that made me question if I wanted to work with you on this case. I've known men who threaten and belittle their partners, and I know they're more likely to talk if they think you're one of them. I'm sorry. I'm not one of them, and I don't think you are either."

"Is this true?" Teddy asks. I assume, this time, that his attention is directed at me.

"Yes. All of it," I say. "Tell us straight up, Teddy. What happened between you and Gigi?"

I hear him swell with a breath. I hear him let out a long, slow sigh. He invites us to sit down. He offers us whiskey. Then, with the sun warming our faces, he says, "How long have you got?"

***

Quentin is behind the wheel of my car as we cross the state line into Alabama. My self-preservation instincts won out, and I allowed him to drive. After some debate, I even let him adjust the seat so that his long arms and legs weren't scrunched up around the steering wheel. I retained control of the stereo, at least, so there's that. We've been listening to a new episode of my favorite true crime podcast for the past hour. Actually, we've been halfway listening to it, halfway arguing about if this is the reason for my latent paranoia. Eventually the episode ends, and I switch over to the latest Steve Aoiki pop remix I'm obsessed with. Quentin does not yet have any idea how many times I'm likely to replay this before we make it home. I do him a favor and turn this one to a conversational volume.

"So," I say. "About what you told me the other night." We stay steady in our lane, but I can sense the way his knuckles tighten on the wheel, can hear the uncertain pause in his breath. "I may know someone who can help your, um... Help Melissa."

He processes this for a long beat. "Yeah?"

"There's a licensed family counselor I used to refer clients to – until the board basically gave me a cease and desist for driving away potential business. She's good. The best, in my opinion. She doesn't sugarcoat things, but she's compassionate. She'll be able to lay out all the options. Sometimes that's all people need. Options. Opportunity."

"That sounds great. But... unless she's giving out services for free, I'm not sure how much it will help," he says. "Financial freedom was one of the first things to go, but Melissa's weird about taking money from anyone. I guess I get it. Money from a Maxwell usually has strings."

I note the loaded quality of his tone.

"My friend's well-connected. Even if she can't help, she'll know someone who can."

He nods. "Are you sure you want to get involved in this? If

the wrong person finds out..."

"No one is going to find out," I say.

My words hang between us, gently shapeshifting in meaning. Nobody is going to find out about Melissa. And maybe, nobody is going to find out about us. We've proven we can trust each other. We can keep each other's secrets. As we close the distance between us and home, I'm laced with newfound certainty.

"Thank you, sensei."

I incline my head to him graciously. "Cowabunga, dude."

When the song ends, I hit repeat. He doesn't protest. It's a few more minutes before he says, "So. About *last* night."

Now it's my turn to hold my breath.

"It wasn't my intention to... complicate things," he says. "Between us."

I chew my bottom lip and pretend to suddenly be engrossed with the passing scenery. My heart dips and sways in my chest. The truth is that last night didn't feel complicated. My feelings about Quentin have never been clearer.

I love the way that I feel when I'm with him. Challenged, but not defensive. In control, but vulnerable. Happy. Safe.

I love the way I fell asleep with his arms around me, with his heart beating steady against mine.

I love the way that I woke up with the scent of him on my skin, the subtle ache of him in my body.

"What happens after the partnership vote?" I ask.

"It's going to be you," he says. "It was always going to be you."

"And if it isn't?"

He threads his fingers into mine. "For me, it's you."

I roll my eyes, but I can't fight my growing smile. "You don't seem too upset for a guy who's talking about losing out on hundreds of thousands of dollars."

He huffs out a laugh. "Does this guy have you?"

I chew my lip. "Yes."

"Then he's way too busy counting his lucky stars to be upset," he teases. "But there are a few things he needs to know."

"Such as?"

"Tell me your terms and conditions."

"Who says I have terms and conditions?"

"Um. I know you."

I give him a coy smile. I consider my usual parameters, and none of them feel necessary. Quentin is so different. Or maybe it's that he makes me feel different.

"Only one," I say finally. "Don't break my heart."

There's a beat of surprise. I can feel it simmering between us, the realization that I've just admitted that:

a.	I – Heidi Krupp, the best part of breaking up – have a heart;

b.	It's fragile enough to be broken; and

c.	Quentin undeniably has it.

He stretches my hand across the console and kisses my wrist just above the twine wish bracelet.

"Deal."

I settle into the comfort of the passenger seat with my bare feet propped on the dashboard and our fingers still intertwined. Behind my sunglasses, I close my eyes, smiling as sunlight and shadows shift across my vision, like a kaleidoscope of warm, red-orange color, mapping the way home.

2 5.

Quentin never makes it to his place. We get off the elevator at my floor, and he walks me to my door under the guise of making sure I don't accidentally attempt to enter the wrong apartment. The moment we're inside, we drop our bags by the door and tug each other closer.

"Are you happy now that you've seen me home safely?" I say, looping my arms around his neck.

He meets my lips with a subtle groan. "Very happy."

The moment I'm kissing him, I wonder how I just spent eight hours *not* kissing him. He teases my tongue with his, letting his hands spread wide across my hips so he can pull them against his. I can already tell this is going to get away from us.

"You promised we'd do more trial prep," I pout.

Reasonably, we don't need more trial prep. We went over the details of our defense for the entire two-hour stretch from Birmingham to Tupelo. We talked through tactics and played devil's advocate, each attempting to tear down the other's arguments and poke holes in the case. We've inspected this from every angle. It feels solid.

Still, the stakes are high. I know the courtroom will be full of cameras tomorrow. Every detail will be scrutinized, from the words I use to the outfit I choose to wear. Part of me is ready to head into battle. Another part of me, one I never would have let Quentin see before this weekend, is nervous.

"This *is* trial prep," he defends, threading his fingers into my hair and running his thumb along my jaw. "I need you relaxed tomorrow. Feeling your absolute best. With all your needs properly met."

I smile against his lips. "Aw. So you're going to procure me a set of fresh contacts and order us DoorDash? You're so thoughtful."

"Yes," he says, "but first I'm going to pour you a glass of wine and draw you a bath."

He scoops me up, and I giggle in spite of myself.

"I've never been drawn a bath before. It makes me feel like I'm in one of those Victorian novels."

"And you like this feeling?"

"Very much," I murmur, kissing him again. "As long as you don't, like, have me committed to the sanatorium for being a strong, independent woman."

"Hmm. Tempting," he teases.

I laugh again, playfully elbowing him as he sets me on the sink in my bathroom. I watch in mute awe as he follows through on his promise. He grabs me a glass of wine as the tub fills. He passes me a fluffy towel from the linen closet and asks if I want bath salt or bubbles (both, obviously). When I start to shimmy out of my shorts, he stops me.

"If you want food or contacts or any of these other things to happen, I need you to keep your clothes on until I'm out of the room."

I bite my bottom lip, reveling in the absolute power I feel

when he looks at me like this. I toy with the hem of my shirt, edging it up above my belly button.

"You're just going to leave me in here all alone?" I watch his lids grow heavy, following the dip of his gaze to where my fingers trace the crease above my hip. "Naked?"

He wets his lips, eyes meeting mine with playful intensity. "I'm going to order the shrimp scampi from Maestoso, because I know it's your favorite. I also know they don't deliver on Sundays, and it'll take about thirty-minutes to grab an order for pickup, and if I don't feed you before eight o'clock you'll get hangry."

He drags his thumb across my bottom lip, and for a second I feel like it's the only thing holding me up. I want to melt at his feet.

"While I'm doing that," he continues, "I want you naked in this tub. And I want to know you can't keep your hands off yourself when you're in here thinking about all the ways you want me to make you come. Can you do that for me?"

The blush rises in my cheeks, and heat gathers between my thighs. I want this fire to consume me. I snag the front of his shirt, tugging him close enough to steal a kiss.

"Is that a yes?"

"Yes," I smirk.

Before he leaves, he clicks off the light, leaving me with the flicker of the vanilla candle on my vanity. It's just as well: though I've somewhat adjusted to my current level of vision impairment, candlelight is easier on these tired eyes. He connects to the bluetooth speaker and hits play on that pop remix I made him listen to no less than ten times on our drive home. When I cut my gaze at him, he winks.

"Relax," he insists. "I'll be back."

***

As much as I'm out of practice at relaxing, I vow to give it a try. I slip into the bubbles up to my collarbones, taking a long sip of wine and closing my eyes. The loop of my thoughts immediately cues up the slideshow of our weekend.

How angry I was when I pulled out of the parking garage.

How hopeless I felt each time I realized there was nothing but vacant ocean where Teddy's boat should be.

How my mind raced to absorb the details he gave us this morning, and how I spent half the drive home struggling to organize them into something coherent.

And then of course, Quentin.

I sink a little deeper with a sigh. When I run my hands through the silky water, it's impossible not to think about being in that midnight pool with him. I draw lines through the suds, tracing the exposed tops of my knees, the half-submerged outline of my breasts. I only mean to lean into the sensual feel of it, to revel in the way the deep tone of his instructions made my skin tingle, teasing myself just enough to feel sexy, but I should've learned by now that thoughts about Quentin are a slippery slope. Slippery enough that my hands slip lower, that my movements get sweet and syrupy. By the time I hear the door, I'm outright aching with need.

When he appears in the bathroom, I don't know how to pretend I'm not on the very edge, so I don't try. Even in the flickering shadows, he seems to register the color in my cheeks, the sensual part of my lips, the breathless rise and fall of my chest.

"Oh, you perfect, greedy girl." He drops to his knees beside the tub, sweeping a hand through my hair, kissing me deeply. "Did you come already?"

"Not yet," I breathe. "I was waiting for you."

The bath sloshes as I attempt to draw my knees together. He nudges them back open.

"Don't stop." His hand dips beneath the water, sliding down my inner thigh. He kisses my knee. "Seeing you horny like this is my new favorite fucking thing. You need it so bad, don't you, baby?"

"Fuck," I breathe. "You make me feel so dirty."

"I love you dirty," he says. His fingers thread between mine, circling my swollen center. "God, you kill me when you make that fucking sound."

Another moan escapes me, and I realize I've been doing it ever since he put his hands on me. I can't help it. I open up to give him more of me, pressing his fingers into the perfect spot, rubbing at the hot liquid ache between my thighs. He gingerly flicks a finger across one nipple. Up and down, innocently, like he's testing a goddamn light switch. It scrambles my thoughts.

"I can't... think when you..."

"Then don't," he says.

I let go, becoming only pleasure. This time he doesn't tease and wander. He's learned exactly how to touch me, and he coaxes me to my absolute breaking point. My breath comes in tiny, desperate pants. The waves of release rock through me as our intertwined hands press against my sex. It only makes me want him inside me.

"What else do you need?" he says.

I drag his face towards mine, punctuating my response with rough, desperate kisses. "You. Naked. In my bed. Now."

We don't make it to my bed. I push him back onto the tile, letting water cascade off of me as I free him from his pants. The element of surprise works in my favor. I take him inside me with a gasping moan. He's so hard, and I'm so sore, and it feels so good.

"Fuck," he breathes, grabbing my hips to slow my movements. "You are so... goddamn... fuck."

I don't slow down. I love the desperate set of his jaw, that subtle little growl he gives me when I take control, the way he kisses me when he's close to coming completely apart. Another wave of pleasure is already building with every roll of my hips, and he just *feels, so, good*. The closer I get, the harder he becomes.

My breaths come shallow and fast, matching his, and I realize now that all the time I've spent believing things like this never happen, it's because I also believed 'things like this' took the kind of painstaking choreography they describe in magazines. This isn't a coordinated production. There's no great mystery. It's so hopelessly simple.

When he goes, every cell in my body can't help but follow.

***

I feel around, locating the pair of glasses I keep in the drawer of my bedside table. When I slide them on, Quentin comes into perfect focus. I can see his dark eyes, dancing across my face.

"What?" I ask.

"You look so hot right now," he grins. "Like you're going to send me to detention for not returning a library book."

I laugh, snaking my arms around his neck. "Is that another fantasy of yours? Hot librarian?"

"If you're the librarian," he says, kissing me. "But first, fed librarian."

We miraculously make it out of my bedroom and position ourselves on the floor between my couch and my coffee table. My mouth waters as he portions our takeout shrimp scampi into bowls for reheating.

"Well, hopefully by tomorrow I'm looking less like a hot librarian and more like a serious attorney who completely crushes this case. You know those three desperate messages I left for my optometrist on our drive home? The on-call doctor has emailed to explain that it's been so long since my last visit that I'm basically considered a new patient. So if I plan to be able to read any of the court documents, these are my only option."

I snag a stray noodle from the container and slurp it into my mouth. "Oh my god, this is divine."

"You couldn't wait ten more seconds?" he laughs.

"It was alone. I was rescuing it."

"Always so impatient," he says with mock disapproval.

I give him a smug grin as he passes me my reheated bowl. I'm careful not to get any garlic-butter-sauce on my spare copy of our notes and briefings as I slide them between us. He eyes them as he settles in beside me.

"You are obsessed," he says. "You thought you were just going to sneak this in? That I wasn't going to notice a giant stack of legal documents, staring up at us while we try to enjoy our dinner?"

"C'mon. I can't remember the last time I had dinner without legal documents in front of me. They're the perfect pairing. Like popcorn and movies. A podcast and a long plane ride. Don't act like you've never done this."

He chortles. "Guilty on all counts. Should we find something to watch?"

I'm two steps ahead, already turning on the TV and going through the autopilot motions of locating one of my standby shows. I don't select it. Instead, I find myself hesitating on the menu, suddenly studying his profile. The tousled mess of his hair. His smooth brow. The perfect slope of his nose.

"Sure," I say, passing him the remote. "It's your turn to pick."

He scrolls for a few moments before settling on a nature documentary. A soothing soundtrack softly sweeps through the room, followed by stunning images of our planet's oceans. Quentin is already half-eating, half-perusing the papers I laid out. My heart feels so full there's barely any room in my chest when I inhale. I twist pasta onto my fork and reach for an interrogatory, letting myself swell with the hope that we could really do this.

That somehow, like Jeanine said in my interview, I can turn this into a win-win.

That I really can have it all.

Win, win, win.

"All right, PBG," he prompts. "Hit me with your opening statement."

26.

If you told me six months ago that the biggest case of my life would be a media circus that would devolve into a never-ending fight to the death over who gets custody of a scraggly, yellow-eyed werewolf cat, I probably would have laughed in your face.

And, well, *here we are.*

I should have known something was wrong when we had to wade through a gaggle of protestors to get into the courthouse on Monday morning. I clutched my cold brew in close to my chest, ducking through the small but enthusiastic group. I've been shouted down on the sidewalk before, but never by a bunch of twenty-somethings holding signs with a cat's alienesque face on them. When we finally make it to the metal detectors, I can still hear chanting.

Stop Glasslighting. Free Farkas. Stop Glasslighting. Free Farkas. Stop Glasslighting. Free Farkas.

"That was... different," Quentin notes. "Do they realize this is a divorce trial? For humans?"

"Apparently not."

The whole thing gives me the eerie sense of old photos I've seen from the Manson trial, and the devoted followers who camped outside, awaiting his release. Gigi might not be a full-blown cult leader, but she definitely has her own brand of devoted followers. It's a strange sort of power that seems to crackle in the air. As we settle into the courtroom, I attempt to shake the feeling of uneasiness.

A few minutes later, Teddy shows up in a pair of jeans, a sport coat over a band T-shirt, and beat up Vans. But hey, he showed up. And he showered, as far as I can tell. His hair is extra glossy and smells faintly of pears. He sweeps a hand through it with a sigh as he settles in between me and Quentin. Mike Murdock is already grinning at us from across the aisle, adjusting his tailored suit. Gigi is sitting beside him, prim and proper in her damn 1980s power suit. I see her smirk when she glances over at Teddy.

His clothes are the least of my worries.

Mike is suspiciously agreeable for the first half of the day. We easily settle determinations on the house (they'll sell and split the profits), the cars (each walks away with one), and the boat.

Okay, maybe the boat wasn't easy. As Mike points out, it *does* quite literally have her name on it. But in the end, he chuckles at our pointing out that Teddy owned it long before he met Gigi – and that, to our knowledge, she's never set foot on it – so we all move on.

It's all going so smoothly that by lunch, I wonder why the hell we didn't do this in mediation.

But every now and then I become aware of the faint murmur of people behind us. The quiet sounds of shuffling. The intermittent click of cameras. The courtroom is only half full, but it feels like a lot of media for a run-of-the-mill divorce trial. The protestors sit in the back with their signs, which the judge allowed as long as they promised to behave themselves. So far so good.

After lunch, we launch into arguments about Avid. These

begin and seem to have no sign of ending. We provide testimony from bands who have produced albums there in the past few years, all of whom signed under oath that Gigi did not factor into their decision to record there. We cite revenues prior to Teddy's courtship with Gigi and compare it to present day. It's surprisingly steady. If anything, business expenses increased upon Gigi's arrival, and profits went down. Flights, hotels, and VIP tickets to all those festivals – which she listed as 'scouting trips' – weren't cheap. If anything, she owes him.

But, Mike argues, the divorce will separate Gigi from her means of employment and thus significantly reduce her future earning potential. It's because of this that they're pursuing her stake in Avid, in the form of a large financial sum – so large that it would require Teddy to sell Avid in order to pay up. And I can only imagine this will also turn into a sizable request for alimony, once we get to that stage of the trial.

We trade blows.

Close to the end of the day, when I can see the judge getting antsy like she's ready to call a recess, Mike Murdock suddenly transforms into the respectful, reasonable attorney again, conceding that Avid is Teddy's. It feels like a win. I can tell from the way the whites of Mike's teeth flash when he looks at us across the aisle that it isn't. This was always his plan. They just wanted us to waste our time on this. They also wanted us to show our cards, warm up to our tactics. And they wanted Gigi to stand outside the courtroom and take somber selfies with the protestors. It'll be all over social media before dinner.

I see Paolo and Jeanine on our way out.

"She's good," Jeanine says.

Yeah, I don't say out loud. *That's what I'm worried about.*

I also worry, even though we've put the former Mrs. Glass up in a nearby hotel, that she will have to fly back to Iowa before we get to character references. Classes at the university where she teaches start soon. She's a good sport, but she's not willing to sacrifice everything for this case. She has a life – unlike me, apparently. All I seem to be able to do is obsess over the details. What is their next play? What are we missing? It feels like we're walking into a trap.

And then, of course, we do.

On day two, Gigi produces tears as Mike makes the case for why she deserves ownership of Farkas. This is the first time he brings up spousal abuse. He puts Gigi on the stand, and she is a star. She paints a picture of a woman who was scared into silence, who was smiling on the outside to hide the horrible pain she carried on the inside. I can hear sniffling from behind me, no doubt the result of tears of solidarity being cried by some in attendance. At one point a woman is sobbing so loudly that the judge has her escorted out. Teddy stares at his hands, and testimony regarding the cat – and his character – drags on.

By day three, I imagine pitching one of those ridiculous movie scenarios where we haul Farkas into the courtroom, place him somewhere that is equidistant from Gigi and Teddy, and see which one he runs to. You know, like late-nineties *Air Bud?*

(Obviously I can't do that. At this point, would I if I could? Probably, yes.)

"You're not going to let them take him away, are you?" Teddy asks, worried. "He's all I've got."

I refrain from pointing out that he now has the studio, half the house, and a car, because on some level, I get it. While the law may see Farkas as personal property, I have to acknowledge that loving a pet is not the same as the studio, or a house, or a car. Farkas is Teddy's best bud. As much as I don't care for the little goblin-looking alien, it will gut me if he actually goes to Gigi.

"I know," I say, firmly but gently. "We're doing our best. And we've made good progress. It's not over. You know if you would consider testifying –"

"No," he says. "Like I told you in Santa Lucia, I won't talk about it in court. And like you agreed, you'll find another way."

The truth wriggles a little further out of reach. I swell with a breath, wondering if we can save this sinking ship without *his* piece of the truth.

Each day we arrive, there are more protestors. More people filling the courtroom. You'd think they have jobs to go to. Lives to live. Or that eventually they would get bored listening to two grown adults pay people to argue for them. But no, the duration of this trial only seems to fuel their indignation. And their interest. A couple of podcasters have made this the highlight of their week. The whole thing is bizarre enough that we're starting to pop up on morning radio shows.

Dane & Zed in the Morning: *Currently in bizarre news, a Tennessee divorce trial between social media influencer Gigi Russo and recording studio mogul Teddy Glass has turned into a fight to the death over custody of their cat. Now, this isn't any ordinary cat. It's known as a lykoi cat. Have you seen pictures? Pull up a picture.*

Zed: *Dude, that is one ugly cat.*

Dane: *Ugly enough to win the hearts of millions, apparently. Social media hashtag #FreeFarkas is now trending on three platforms. A group of protestors is camping outside the courthouse in downtown Memphis.*

Zed: *Who do they want him to stay with?*

Dane: *I think they're Team Gigi. But we want to hear from you. If you're following this case, give us a shout. Or go online to cast your vote. Who should get custody of this cat?*

Zed: *Maybe no one should. Maybe he should be emancipated. Can cats be emancipated?*

Dane: *I'm so glad you asked, Zed. And fortunately we've got our favorite guest attorney on the line to help us understand exactly what's going on here...*

By midweek, I finally have to lock down my socials and stop reading the news. This doesn't stop Meg and Auntie Lena from prying when we hit the pool with Kamille. They're sitting under an umbrella, drinking lemonade and using foldable paper fans to stave off the heat.

"C'mon. Give us *something*," Meg says. "You can't expect us to have to wait for information like everyone else."

"You know I cannot comment on an active case," I remind them. "And we're here to support Kamille."

August crept up on us the way that the end of summer always does, just when you're sure its merciless heat will stretch on in a shapeless, hazy-humid kind of eternity. This means the moment we've been training for all summer is finally upon us. This weekend, Kamille will board a charter bus that will take this region's best and brightest to the state-run music camp for all the top performers in her age group. She's been practicing her violin nonstop, and I know she'll shine at the end-of-camp concert, where I will be sitting front and center with her family. And ideally, when they finish up their show and spend that last glorious day at the water park, she won't be hanging out in the kiddie pool.

Quentin settles beside me on the edge of the pool with his suit pants rolled up to the knee, swishing his feet through the water. We were only released from today's session half an hour earlier; I went to pick up Kamille, and he ran by the office to grab some files for another case. He's got an entire evening of work ahead of him, but when he heard we were hitting the pool, he said he had a few minutes to join.

I'm aware of the way he leaves a respectful amount of space between us. When I thank him for coming, he winks at me. My heart does a shameless flip in my chest. Auntie Lena and Meg do their best to behave when I introduce him.

"How was Florida?" Meg asks him over the rim of her glass. "I hear it's awfully *hot* this time of year."

I cut her a look, and she gives me an innocent smile. Auntie

Lena's eyes are alight with mischief, like she's grabbing the popcorn and settling in to watch a rom-com.

"Florida was... successful," Quentin offers. "We got lucky."

There isn't a hint of innuendo in his tone, but I feel myself suppressing a self-satisfied smirk. He's still wearing the twine wish bracelet with the green stones. *For luck*, he told me, when I saw it tucked beneath the tailored edge of his shirtsleeves on Monday morning. As far as I know, it hasn't left his wrist since I secured it there in that tacky beachfront shop. That also makes my heart do impossibly brave somersaulting tricks.

"So about this cat..." Auntie Lena begins.

I interrupt her with a disapproving smile. "You're as bad as the media."

So far this week, they've speculated heavily about my choice to suddenly start wearing glasses (to appear smarter, obviously), my power heels (this ain't a fashion runway, sweetheart), and whether or not I'm sleeping with – drumroll please – *Teddy*. Yup, you read that right. Everyone wants to know if I'm hooking up with my client, who is in fact not yet divorced and is also roughly twenty-five years my senior. Nobody on the outside is concerned about Quentin.

Except of course to post online about the fact that he's hot.

A couple of podcasters from North Carolina think we planted him on the case as a distraction, and their followers on the internet took up the torch of speculation. I teased him about this last night while I roamed his apartment with a glass of wine, wearing nothing but one of his t-shirts as he made us chicken tacos for dinner. As I admired his culinary acumen, I took back everything negative I ever thought about us living in the same building, because with suspicion and smartphones lurking around every corner, it's amazing that nobody would question why we are both entering this building every night and leaving it every morning. Bernadette did me a huge favor with that one, and she doesn't even know it.

I shield my eyes from the sun, squinting to where Kamille is emerging from the changing rooms, confident but not smiling. She walks into the water, adjusts the straps of her no-nonsense one-piece, and gives me a determined nod. Auntie Lena and Meg cheer from the sidelines. Quentin enthusiastically joins them.

"All right, Kami!" I say. "Show us what you've got!"

I don't know why I'm nervous. She swells with a breath. It's a false start, and she sucks in another. She deflates. She hesitates. I almost think she is going to back out when she dives under.

My heart is in my throat as the surface of the pool begins sloshing wildly with her movements. It's a little hard to make sense of it at first, but within a few seconds I confirm: she's swimming.

She's actually swimming.

There are no uncertain starts and stops like we've been seeing the past few weeks. She makes slow, steady progress across the length of the pool, with her arms and legs moving in tandem. I expect her to cling to the far edge when she reaches it, to stop and catch her breath and maybe give us a grin, but she doesn't. She immediately launches herself off the wall and heads back across. I feel a cheer escape me, though I know she can't hear it. By the time she makes it back to the stairs where she started, we are celebrating like the Grizzlies just won the NBA championship.

I launch myself into the water with a squeal, meeting her with a double high five and a huge, sunscreen-scented hug.

"Didn't I tell you you could do it!" I laugh.

"Yeah," she says sheepishly, smiling as she rolls her eyes.

"You have officially reached dolphin status," Quentin tells her. "Those water slides are *yours.*"

She wades towards him, grinning now.

"Thanks. You're coming for pizza with us?" she asks.

He's already pulling himself to his feet and shaking loose his pant legs. "I'd love to, but unfortunately I've got a lot of work to do tonight. Rain check?"

She scrunches her nose at him. "It's not raining."

"Another time," he laughs. "Have fun at camp." To me he says, "I'll see you?"

"I'll see you," I nod, giving him a small, secret smile.

When he's gone, I catch Auntie Lena and Meg staring at me.

"What?" I say defensively.

"So, at first you were fake dating, and now you're fake *not* dating?" Auntie Lena says. "It's so hard to keep up."

"We were never… fake… not…" I groan. "You know what I mean."

Meg tosses back her head with a devious laugh. "Oh honey. I hope you're more convincing than that in court tomorrow."

I splash them both, and they shriek indignantly. Still, I'm smiling. We're all damp and laughing when we pack up to go for pizza, and I can't help hoping that all my hard work is paying off. That everything is really truly coming together.

***

Whatever you prefer to call it, fake not-dating works for us. It *really* works. Quentin makes dinner, while I read case notes. We dive into another nature documentary and make plans to white water raft in New Zealand and explore volcanoes in Iceland. I get him hooked on one of my reality TV dramas, and he endears himself to me by learning how to quickly differentiate – and properly take sides – between all the characters. We make love in the middle of the night, somewhere between falling asleep and waking up, as if suspended in a delicious, pleasure-drenched dream.

Meanwhile, just like a soap opera, our daytime saga continues. Gigi has moved on from the pout to the deep frown. She cries as if on command. She makes claims that there are no police or medical records of Teddy's abuse because she couldn't seek help out of fear. Teddy remains quiet. It's damning. We're trudging closer to the end of their witness list, and I'm itching to put Kimberly on the stand as soon as possible, but dread has crept into my bones.

What if we can't win this?

When I crawl into bed with Quentin's table lamp still on and a stack of notes across his knees, the possibility seems to be gnawing at him as well. He rubs his eyes and sets the papers aside, sighing as he wraps me in his arms and tucks me against his chest. His fingers make lazy lines through my hair. I nuzzle against the warmth of his skin.

"You ready for tomorrow?" I say.

"We're ready," he counters. When he says it, his words vibrate through his chest, against my ear.

"I'm ready for it to all be over," I admit.

"So impatient," he teases. I trace the line of hair down his chest, along his belly, until he's threading his fingers through mine.

We talk through the details again, as we have so many times before. The words are starting to lose meaning. The facts are beginning to blur.

"You know what I don't understand," he says. "Whatever happened to Grayson Smith?"

The implication of this seeps into my consciousness slowly. I sit up, suddenly struck by the strange realization that this could mean something. What exactly I don't know but... something. We exchange a confused, curious, hopeful look.

"That," I say, "is an excellent question."

"Well," he says, with a spark in his eyes. "Maybe we should find out."

27.

LATE SUMMER AIR whips through my hair as we cruise the paths of a private golf course. Quentin had to name drop Erving just to get us a tee time, which happens to be conveniently located one spot ahead of Grayson Smith's standing daily round.

"Do I have to pretend to golf?" I ask.

"Yes," Quentin says.

"I'm going to be bad at this," I argue, adjusting the collar of the polo shirt I begrudgingly bought for this occasion. "You know how much I hate being bad at things?"

"I'm counting on you being bad at this," he says.

He gets to the tee box and puts a club in my hands, wrapping his arms around me from behind.

"What are you doing?"

"Stalling for time," he says against my neck.

Eventually, after a few embarrassingly awful practice swings on my part and three balls that I send skittering in haphazard directions, another cart rolls up behind us. The tanned, lean guy and his caddy climb out. The latter is already selecting a club.

The former approaches us with an apologetic tip of his head.

"Mind if we play through?" he asks.

Quentin slips away from me, grinning and extending his hand. "Grayson Smith. You're just the man we were hoping to see."

***

"Look, this is bad publicity for me," Grayson says, readjusting his white golf hat nervously. "My manager said they'd pull me from the tour if this keeps up. None of this has been worth the trouble. Lesson learned: don't get involved with a woman who tells you she's in the middle of a divorce."

"I thought you weren't involved with her?" Quentin says.

"I mean, not *involved* involved. I guess I could have been. She made the rounds for a while, made it known she was available, even managed to hook up with a few guys I know. Let's just say that one of them is rumored to have the kind of thing Ajax can't wash off, if you know what I mean. And I don't like to share. Only child syndrome, I guess."

Quentin and I exchange a glance.

"So what was in it for you?" I finally ask. It's always right there. Everyone has a motive. A polished guy like Grayson Smith can pretend otherwise, but the guilty glint in his green eyes is telling a different story.

"Look," he sighs. "She told me that she could work out some new sponsorships for me through her online following. She said this would be huge, that she would get tons of money from the divorce, and that this could work out for both of us. All I had to do was come along for the ride."

"And you didn't think this request was... unusual?" Quentin asks.

He laughs. "Have you ever been around this game before? Everybody in this business wants something from me. Money. Sex. Publicity. And honestly, she wasn't a bad time. Fun to hang with. Plenty of hot friends. A bit of a handful when she starts drinking. But yeah, she promised a lot of things. She was playing me. I'd bet that she's probably playing you, too."

"And you're no longer willing to testify about this?" I ask.

"I told you. My hands are tied. They will pull me from this tour if I say another word."

"We could always subpoena you," I offer.

He heaves a sigh. "You don't even need me. Just ask her guy."

"What guy?" Quentin says.

"Gigi had a driver. He took her everywhere. He knew her comings and goings, but he also heard everything. He's the only one you need."

"They didn't have a driver on the books," I argue.

"She met him through rideshare one night, and they set up an arrangement. She kept him on call and paid him cash. He worked with her for a couple of years I think, but recently they had a big falling out."

Grayson pauses to step up to the tee. Without any fanfare, he takes an expert swing. The thwack of clean contact sends the ball soaring through the air. We all pause to watch it land smoothly on the fairway. Grayson passes his club back to the stocky, curly-haired caddy and hops into the waiting cart.

"Trust me," he tells us. "He'll talk."

***

To say that this is the strangest set of witnesses I've ever called in a family law case is the understatement of the century. We've got the ex-wife. Farkas's veterinarian. The pet sitter. Their neighborhood's security detail. The cleaning staff. Zelda. And a seemingly random Ryde driver.

The judge glances at our list and gives us an exasperated look. "Is all of this really necessary?"

"Yes, your honor. Unfortunately it is."

It starts strong. Kimberly describes Teddy as a sweet and

gentle husband, even during their divorce, and a lifelong friend. She reveals what she knows about Gigi's temper and her tendency for threats. The vet verifies the exceptional level of care that Teddy has provided for Farkas and corroborates that they've never met Gigi. The pet sitter similarly says all of his dealings were with Teddy, and that Teddy called at least once a day to check on Farkas for the two weeks they were vacationing in Europe.

Mike Murdock objects, and I know before he speaks where this is going: the question has never been if Teddy coordinated Farkas's care. We move on.

Meanwhile Teddy silently drums his fingers on the table like he's trying to keep time to an imaginary bass line, refusing to look up from the smooth surface of the wood.

The security detail gets a little more traction. They were called to the Glass residence three times over the course of the past couple of years. One was due to the fire that Gigi started in an attempt to burn Teddy's clothes and a few of his records.

"They smelled like urine."

"Whose urine did you think this was?"

"Objection, your honor: calls for speculation."

I redirect. "What happened after you saw the clothes?"

"Mr. Glass was yelling. He was saying, 'Why would you piss on my records?' At this point, I even asked her, 'You pissed on his records?' She said, 'It wasn't me.' I said, 'Well, who was it then? Did he piss on his own records?'"

At this, a few members of the court laugh. The judge taps her gavel before motioning for the security guard to continue.

"Did she respond to this question?" I prompt.

"Yeah, she laughed and said, 'Maybe it was the fucking cat.'"

"What happened the other times you were called to the residence?"

"Another time Mr. Glass had a pretty nasty knot on his

forehead. He claimed he ran into the door. Mrs. Glass – I mean, Ms. Russo – was tearing the house apart at the time. We asked Mr. Glass if he was in danger, and he said no. We asked if we should call the police, and he said no. We told them to keep it down and left."

"The last time that you were called?"

"Mr. Glass had locked himself in a car in his driveway. We were called because neighbors reported yelling. When we arrived Ms. Russo was attempting to smash in the vehicle's windows with a baseball bat. Mr. Glass was sitting in the front seat, and he was holding the cat. I remember because at first it didn't look like a regular cat; it looked kind of... diseased. And Mr. Glass was crying, begging her to stop."

"No further questions," I say.

When I move to return to our table, I catch Gigi pouting at me, and this one is very clearly 'pissed'. I guess when I out her for pissing on her husband's records, I get the pissed pout. Meanwhile, Teddy has a hand threaded into his hair and is staring at the table. He taps his foot to a steady, silent beat, and I pat his arm encouragingly.

Mike Murdock stands with a flourish. "Did you file any reports about these visits? Any security logs?" he asks the witness.

"No," the security guard says.

"Why not? Isn't it part of your job to keep records?"

"Mr. Glass... asked us not to."

"And you just complied, out of the goodness of your heart?"

"He, um." The guard's gaze drops. "He paid us not to report it."

"So he bribed you?"

"I dunno. Yeah. I guess."

"No further questions."

***

"What the hell are we going to do?" I whisper to Quentin as

we hover near the water fountain during recess. "That was the best shot we had."

"We've got the Ryde driver."

"Quentin. What are we doing? We're going to call a surprise witness and roll the dice? What if Grayson was wrong? Better yet, what if he lied? This could all be part of Mike Murdock's plan. Send us after Grayson, feed us a fake witness, and unleash his wrath, like a damn Trojan horse."

"What other choice do we have right now?" he says. "Go big or go home."

This is how I end up making what will either be the best or worst decision of my entire career.

The Ryde driver's name is Andre. He's a self-described entrepreneur in his mid-thirties. He smells like patchouli and looks like he was once an extra in Jersey Shore. Against my better judgment, I put him on the stand.

"Are you aware of Ms. Russo having an affair?" I ask.

"Which one?" he laughs. "Yeah, she had a lot of guys. She usually had me drop them off before her."

"How do you know they weren't just friends?"

"Do you make out with your friends in the backseat?" he counters.

"Did Ms. Russo ever say anything to you about her marriage?"

"Only that she was planning to end it and that she expected a large sum of money."

"Did she say why she wanted to end it?"

"She said it had served its purpose. She was really interested in dating one of the golf pros. She was convinced she could turn the relationship into a reality show. She was talking to some low-level producer about it."

"Objection, your honor. Relevance?" Mike says.

"Sustained."

"Gigi told me she would ruin me if I told anyone what I knew.

Look, you don't have to believe me. I've got recordings. I started recording her once she started threatening me." He slides his phone out of his pocket. "I can play them if you –"

Suddenly, everyone is murmuring at once. The noise swells like cicadas in the summer, reaching the point of a deafening chatter in seconds and dying just as quickly as the judge bangs her gavel.

"Counsel, please approach the bench," she demands.

Mike is already grinning his fluorescent grin, attempting to smooth this over. I notice, though, that for the first time, Gigi looks panicked. Everything else we've presented thus far is hearsay. He said, she said. This is proof.

"Did you know about these recordings?" the judge asks me.

"No," I say. "But I think we need to –"

"This is inappropriate," Mike argues. "How do we know that these are real? And if my client didn't know she was being recorded –"

"Let's take this to my chambers. We'll listen there. No reason to turn this courtroom into any more of a circus than it already is."

We agree. We gather ourselves and our clients and move to the chambers. Behind us, the protestors have gone quiet, and in that moment, as I catch their wide, hopeful eyes watching us go, I feel a pang of remorse.

I want to win this case. I want to be right about the situation between Teddy and Gigi. But I don't want to think that all of these women – many of whom had suffered and survived absolutely unacceptable treatment by those who claimed to love them, who have been brave enough to share their stories, who use their experience to educate and support others – are about to realize they put their faith in the wrong person. That someone would actually be horrible enough to use them in this way. That someone would actually *lie* about this. It's a slap in the face to every person who has ever come forward with their story and had its validity questioned. And it's this heavy feeling that settles into my stomach as we position ourselves in the upright chairs in the small room. Maybe it's Gigi's as well, because I realize now that tears are settling into the lines of her deep frown.

Andre puts his phone on speaker, and the judge gives him the go ahead. It takes everything in me not to reach for Quentin's hand and squeeze it hard. The room goes so quiet that I'm convinced we're all holding our breath. He hits play.

I don't even have to hear the final ruling. I know the outcome the moment I hear her voice on those tapes. In the end, Teddy didn't have to tell the court that Gigi emotionally, physically, and psychologically abused him for the majority of their marriage, because – over the course of thirty-six hours of recordings – she does, in perfect, damning detail.

28.

QUENTIN SLIDES HIS HAND over the curve of my hip, spreading his fingers across the soft, smooth fabric. His mouth finds my ear, and I can hear him smile.

"How am I supposed to keep my hands off of you for the next four hours?" he says. "You're killing me in this dress."

We're alone in the elevator, heading up to Victor Freeman's penthouse apartment along the bluffs of the river for our victory dinner. Of course, they aren't calling it that. It's technically a retirement party for Erving Maxwell. But everything about the energy around the firm the past few days has felt victorious.

I hook my arms around his neck and watch the numbers climb. We've got at least ten floors before we have to pull apart. I steal slow, sensual kisses. I can't get enough of how he tastes like us, as if he spent the past hour tangled up with me in bed. It's subtle but it's there, the same way I know if I took his shirt off you'd see the imprint of my fingernails in the muscles of his back. We've left the evidence all over each other.

"Maybe later I'll let you take it off of me," I murmur.

His fingers trace up the strip of skin exposed by the thigh-high slit in my dress. "You know that's all I'm going to be thinking about for the rest of the night?"

"Good," I smirk.

We part just in time for the doors to open. The apartment is sprawling and modern, with a long line of windows boasting a view of the river, and a set of open doors leading to the balcony. It's crowded with smiling people in evening wear. Each of us grabs a glass of champagne from a passing tray and heads our separate ways into the crowd. Just before I lose sight of Quentin, he gives me one of those signature, heart-flipping winks.

Just like the crowd, I buzz with anticipatory energy. I set my sights on some board members I know and smile, accepting congratulations from colleagues as I weave my way towards them. All anyone can talk about is the case, the article, the billboard. The fact that Quentin and I are an absolute dream team. It feels like almost forty-five minutes have passed by the time I finally hit my mark.

"I'm so relieved to know that the firm is going to be in such good hands after Erving's departure," Victor's wife Dania says. "And it's exciting to have another Maxwell at the helm."

"We'll see," I smile. "The board still has to vote."

"Oh no. That happened weeks ago," she says, giving me a confused look. "It was unanimous. Quentin's taking over as senior partner."

The noise of the party is suddenly too loud. Clinking glassware, idle chatter, the mood music dancing through the speakers – it all creates a horrifying cacophony that rings in my ears like the aftermath of an explosion.

"Heidi," Dania says. "Are you okay?"

I recover my smile. "Yes. Yeah, I'm fine. If you'll excuse me?"

I wander through the crowd in search of Quentin. All night I've felt as though I could feel his presence, near in a way that only I would notice, but now he's nowhere to be found. My heart has dropped into my stomach, heavy like a stone. When I finally spot him, he smiles, oblivious. He motions to the man he's in the middle of a conversation with and begins introductions.

"Heidi, this is –"

"Can we talk?" I interrupt. "Alone."

Both men look at me with a beat of surprise. Quentin nods, gently touching my arm and excusing us. I guide him to a quiet corner at the edge of the balcony. The lights of the bridge reflect off the river that stretches beneath us. I suck in a lungful of the warm air.

"Are you the new partner?" I ask.

He blinks like I've slapped him. He measures his words.

"Why are you asking me this?"

"Are you?" I repeat.

His throat works as he swallows. Eventually he nods. All the blood seems to drain from my body.

"What the *fuck*, Quentin?"

"The decision isn't final," he says quickly. "I've asked them to reconsider –"

"How long have you known?"

"A little while."

"After Florida?"

He drops his gaze. "Before."

"*Before* Florida?" I say. I can hear the betrayal in my voice, and I hate it. My vision blurs, but I can't look away from him. I swallow past the lump rising in my throat. "Has anything you've told me been true?"

"I haven't accepted the position. I'm trying to leverage this in your favor – in both our favors. I didn't lie –"

"Omissions are lies, Quentin," I say. "*The partners won't keep secrets*, remember?"

"I told you, they're going to reconsider –"

"Do you hear yourself right now?" I say. "It's been weeks. If they were going to do it, they would have done it. You don't have any leverage."

"Then I'll quit," he says.

I scoff. "So I can have your leftover pity job? No thanks. What the fuck are you even saying?"

"I'm saying this isn't over."

"No, it's definitely over. You used me. You made me think I still had a shot and distracted me with sex so you could keep me out of the way," I say, laughing at my own stupidity. "Everyone was right. It was a mistake, getting involved with you."

I see the hurt flash across his face like I've stabbed him in the gut. I want to bury the blade and twist it. I want him to hurt as much as I'm currently hurting.

"Stop," he says. "You don't mean that."

I laugh. "You have no idea how much I really, *really* do."

I turn and escape back into the apartment. My stride is angry enough that it draws attention. Those who don't notice my furious trajectory for the elevator can't miss the way Quentin sprints after me. When he reaches for my arm, I fling myself free.

"Don't touch me."

"Heidi, please," he says, his voice low and urgent. "I can explain."

"You can explain? The same way you explained about your stepmother? Was any of that true, or are you sleeping with her, too?"

I realize from the way his face twists that I've said this too loud. We have an audience. My face burns, and I set my jaw in a hard line. I watch the numbers of the elevator creep higher, but too slowly for my taste. I begin searching for the stairs.

"Can we talk about this somewhere else?" he pleads.

"No," I say.

"What's going on here?" Erving says. He has appeared beside

us, drawn like a moth to the flame.

"As if you don't know," I say bitterly.

"You're causing a scene." He tells us this as if we don't already know.

"You'd prefer we do this quietly?" I ask. "The same way you quietly voted your grandson into your position? The same way you quietly gave him hundreds of thousands of dollars in exchange for keeping quiet about the fact that your son is an abusive sack of shit?"

Erving stammers, and there's genuine anger in his eyes. I realize I'm telling everyone their secrets. I don't care. I just don't care anymore. I want to drop a match in the middle of this and watch it burn.

"Did you have something to do with Melissa leaving?" Erving asks Quentin now. When Quentin doesn't reply, Erving sighs. "Didn't I tell you to stay out of this? It was a simple request! I don't need you meddling in everyone's personal matters."

"Personal matters," I snort. "Is that what we're calling it? You do realize that if she went to the police, some of the things he did could be considered a crime?"

"Do not think you can lecture me about the law," Erving says, pointing a finger at me.

Quentin steps between us with rigid posture. "Hey. This isn't her fault. She didn't do anything –"

"You care more about protecting your girlfriend than you care about doing the right damn thing!" Erving bellows.

I blink irritably at Quentin, wondering if my face could get any hotter. "You told him I was your girlfriend?"

"No, I didn't –"

I jab the 'down' button again, willing the elevator to hurry the fuck up.

Henry edges into the mix now. "What's all this? This is supposed to be a party."

"Did you know, too?" I demand.

"Know what?" Henry says. As I glare at him, realization begins to dawn. His smile droops. He suddenly looks like an irritable child.

"I asked you not to get tangled up with this Maxwell kid, didn't I?" he redirects. "This is what he does!"

"Oh fuck off," I murmur. "*You* put him on this case with me. I didn't want him on this case, if you recall. I practically begged you. And now you're going to blame me for –"

"You're right," Quentin says bitterly. I can't tell who he's saying it to – Erving or Henry or me. "It's like you said in the beginning. I'm a fuckup, remember? This is what I do."

Erving and Quentin are engaged in a head-on argument now, and I see his dad attempting to edge into the conversation. The entire room is devolving into gossip and chaos. Finally, I give up waiting. I escape through the emergency exit, which sends an alarm wailing through the stairwell. Henry follows me. Between holding my skirt to avoid tripping and trying to block out the noise of the door alarm, I barely register any of his long string of commentary.

At some point, in the midst of Henry detailing his grand plan for me to issue an apology and request a meeting with the board, I start laughing.

"What's funny?" he demands.

"This. The whole thing. I'm such an idiot," I tell him. "They were never going to give me that partnership, were they?"

I know Henry's courtroom face when I see it, the one he slips into when he's about to craft a well-disguised half-truth. "We were working on –"

"No, Henry. Just stop. I shouldn't have to beg for a promotion that I've earned. And I won't. I'm done. With all of it."

"Don't say things you'll regret."

"I'm not," I say. "You'll have my resignation on Monday. I'll give the standard thirty days so I can transfer my cases."

As we reach the ground floor, I realize that he's too winded to trail after me any further. He heaves a red-faced sigh as his hands find his knees.

"Heidi," he calls. "I'm going to pretend this conversation didn't happen. Give you some time to reconsider."

"Good night, Henry."

I head home, stopping at the corner market to grab a bottle of wine and wondering if it's enough to fill the gaping hole in my chest. I uncap it before I even make it to my building.

Only one way to find out, I think.

***

I wake up to someone banging on my door. My head is pounding as I squint into the daylight. I fell asleep on my couch. I can feel the imprint of a throw pillow on the right side of my face. I snag my phone off the coffee table to check the time: it's after nine a.m. I also have thirty-seven missed calls. My stomach twists.

Fuck.

I stumble towards my door and find Meg standing on the other side. "Thank god you're alive," she says.

"I'm alive," I offer. "What's the emergency?"

"Kamille's grandmother called. They were expecting you to ride with them today, but you didn't show up. They had to leave, or they were going to be late. She had my number from back when you dropped your phone in the pool."

Everything catches up to me in a rush. Saturday. Nashville. Kamille's concert. A wave of nausea hits me, and I prop myself against the doorframe, certain I'm going to be sick.

"Oh my god," I say. I repeat it a few more times, for good measure. I'm already stumbling back into my apartment, searching for my keys.

"Heidi, what are you doing?"

"I'm leaving right now. I can still make it."

I say it out loud, but I know it isn't realistic. Even if I hopped in the car wearing this stupid dress and last night's make-up, with mascara tear stains no doubt streaked across my face, it's impossible. Nashville is three hours away. The concert starts at eleven. It'll be over before I can get there.

Those details feel highly irrelevant at this moment, because this is a defeat I cannot accept. I have to try.

"Hey, slow down," Meg says. "It's not that big of a d –"

"It's a huge deal!" I half-yell. I'm digging clothes out of my dresser drawer the way a burglar searches for hidden jewels. I just need an outfit, any outfit, but I can't think. I realize when Meg grabs me by the shoulder and spins me around that I'm crying again.

"Heidi. Honey. What's *wrong*? What *happened*?"

I wipe my swollen face, sucking in short breaths. I don't have time to explain, nor am I sure that I want to. Everything that has happened is my own damn fault.

I'm the one who stupidly believed I was going to get that promotion.

I'm the one who trusted Quentin. I'm the one who broke all the rules. I'm the one who let him in, and I'm the one who put myself in a position to get hurt.

I'm also the one who overslept, the one who is going to break a promise to a kid that I am supposed to be a role model for.

"Five minutes," I say. "I just need five minutes. Can you drive me? Please say you'll drive me."

She is obviously confused, and concerned, but she concedes. "Yeah, okay. Five minutes."

I hide behind my sunglasses in the car, wondering if I've got enough makeup in the bag I grabbed to make myself presentable before we get to the liberal arts campus where they're hosting the music camp.

"So, Paris?" I say to Meg, once we're on the interstate.

"Paris?" she questions.

"Our vacation," I say. "How's the second week of September?"

"September is fine, but… where is this coming from? Did you get the partnership?"

I suck my lips between my teeth, staring out the window at the passing strip malls, wondering how to explain. Or if I even want to explain.

"I resigned."

"I'm sorry, *what*?" she says. Her mouth is hanging open. I realize if she wasn't driving, she would be gaping at me like I have a hole in my head.

"Everything will be wrapped up by mid-September," I say. "I was thinking two weeks – fourteen days – if you can get the time off?"

"Heidi. What the hell is going on?"

I can hear the shock in her voice. The nervous undertones. She's still blinking in absolute disbelief, like I've just told her I have a terminal illness.

"It's over," I say. "It ran its course. I'll find something else."

"And… you and Quentin?"

"Over," I say simply.

I can feel my heart hardening. My walls rebuilding, more impenetrable than before. Even here, sitting in the car with my best friend, I can't let myself go down this road of thinking about Quentin. He was a mistake. A stupid mistake.

"Babe, please tell me what happened." The softness in her voice kills me. I will *not* let her feel sorry for me. Poor pitiful Heidi, who let herself be blinded enough not to see the sucker punch coming.

"I don't want to talk about it," I say. "Right now, all I want to do is make it to that concert. Apologize to Kamille. And talk about Paris."

"Heidi, I –"

"*Please*, Meg."

The desperation makes my voice come out quiet. I'm worried if I say anything else that I'll start crying again, and my eyes are already swollen beyond belief. Meg's brow is furrowed with concern, but eventually she just nods.

"Okay," she says reluctantly. "Let's talk about Paris."

***

By the time we navigate traffic and the winding streets of the college campus, we miss the whole concert. We find our way into the dining hall during the white table cloth lunch reception, and I can tell from the way she won't make eye contact with me that Kamille is crushed. *I* crushed her. We all make smalltalk, while Kamille mothers her younger siblings, and we exchange half-hearted hugs before we leave. I find myself leaning against the car in the parking lot, staring into the manicured gardens at the edge of the music building and trying not to cry. The threat of it stings like saltwater in my nose.

Her grandmother, Audrey, finds me a few moments later.

"I'm glad you made it," she says, squeezing my arm. "Are you okay?"

"I am so sorry," I say. "If you want to request someone else in the program, I understand. I can recommend someone. Jamie is really reliable. Or, I think Caroline plays an instrument. It would probably be a better fit."

Tears are slipping from beneath the rim of my sunglasses, tickling my chin. I wipe them roughly. Audrey shakes her head and gives me a hard look.

"Stop that talk," she says. "I don't want anyone else. You know why I've always liked you? Because you're someone who doesn't quit. And I know you're not going to quit on my granddaughter."

"You trusted me with your kid, and I let her down."

"There are plenty of people in Kamille's life who have let her down," she says. "The difference between you and all those other people is that you keep showing up. *You keep showing up.* She doesn't need you to be perfect. She needs to see what it means to apologize when you mess up. She needs to know that one mistake doesn't automatically ruin everything. She just needs you to be human."

Audrey pulls me into a hug. Her skin feels soft and doughy, her hair smells like lavender soap. It's so comforting that I cling to her longer than I mean to, wondering if I could just stay wrapped in this feeling forever so I don't have to face the fact that everything is falling apart. She rubs my back with finality.

"Go home," she tells me. "Get some rest. Kamille will forgive you. But in the meantime, you need to figure out how to forgive yourself."

29.

I TAKE ANOTHER STACK OF BINDERS and add them to the precarious tower forming at the edge of Yolanda's desk. I've been systematically combing through my active cases, with the help of the interns, in an attempt to wrap up loose ends. The ones that can't be neatly tied up are being transferred between three of our other associates. They're grateful, but everyone seems confused by my departure, though few are bold enough to broach the topic.

"Why do you keep bringing me these things like you're really leaving?" Yolanda asks, still typing.

I give her an even smile. "Because I am really leaving."

"What happened?" she asks quietly. Her eyes flit side to side to make sure that no one is eavesdropping, but I know that the cubicle farm gossip mill has been a'churning since my resignation was announced. They have no doubt been speculating on the answer to this very question. I'm both curious and horrified to know what they've come up with.

"At some point in your career, you'll be forced to make hard decisions," I offer. "This was mine."

"I meant at the party," she says, as if it was obvious. Her dark eyes search the shifting landscape of my face for clues. I attempt to arrange my expression into the same neutral mask I've been wearing for the past two weeks.

"Erving retired," I shrug.

"I heard there was... *some drama*," she says knowingly.

"Maybe. I left early," I say noncommittally. Then, "What are people saying?"

She can barely hide her smile. "They're saying that Quentin and Erving got into a fist fight, and that Quentin filed charges, and that's why he's packing up his office."

"That is... unlikely," I say. Then, "What do you mean he's packing up his office?"

She shrugs. "He's been offloading cases, same as you."

"Why?"

"I was hoping maybe you knew. But Aaron and Elizabeth have a few theories. They said that they caught Quentin texting some mystery woman last week. Somebody with the code name 'Bagel Girl', or 'Pizza Girl', or something, if you can believe it."

My stomach twists. I give her a practiced smile. "No, I cannot believe it. What kind of ridiculous code name is that?"

"I once found out I was in a guy's phone as 'Freckle Tits'. It happens," she says. "Anyway, that's not important. They're convinced that something major happened between them. Elizabeth caught a glimpse of a bunch of one-sided text messages, sent unanswered to this Bagel Girl person. And then Aaron said he ran into Quentin at the corner market, and he had that look like someone who had just been dumped. All shadowy eyed, with a vacant stare. He definitely tried to swoop in and invite him for a drink, but Quentin dashed Aaron's hopes of an end-of-summer fling by saying no."

"Interesting," I say, in a tone that I hope insinuates this is not interesting to me at all.

Still, I can't help but wonder how many messages would be sitting in my inbox if I hadn't blocked him. I also wonder what they would say. What could he possibly have to say? Even if he is in fact leaving Freeman Maxwell, it all feels too little too late.

"Interesting enough," Yolanda shrugs. "Elizabeth has theorized it's a Romeo and Juliet sort of thing, like Quentin and this Pizza Girl got caught up in some sort of family feud and it ripped them apart. Alternately, Aaron thinks that Quentin is secretly trying to sort out his feelings for him. And William thinks that we all owe him twenty bucks, because he called it months ago."

"Called what, exactly?"

"That Quentin was handed this job on a silver platter, and he was going to manage to fuck it all up somehow. Rich people, right?"

I nod weakly. "Yeah. Right."

I head back to my desk and grab the last of the binders: Glass v. Russo.

Everyone thinks that the work on a divorce case ends after the judge makes the final decree, but that's hardly true. There's a mountain of paperwork to be filed, and that's assuming that nobody appeals. Given the way that Gigi's followers have all vilified her for using them – and rightfully so – her follower counts have plummeted, and I can't see her rallying without a posse. In two more weeks, this whole thing should be final. Unfortunately, I still need some of Teddy's signatures before then.

I find him in the recording booth at Avid. I slip in while he and Zelda are quietly hovering over the Frankenstein's monster of a soundboard. They're both wearing giant, oversized headphones, speaking in that seemingly nonverbal way people do when they've been working together for as long as they have.

Farkas is perched on the back of Teddy's chair.

Ungrateful little gremlin, I think fondly, as I meet his yellow stare.

He gives me a slow blink when I take a seat on the rolling stool near the back. Through the window I can see into the live room, which looks more like a living room from the seventies than a professional workspace. It's all wood paneling and strategically placed rugs. The band is playing with the well-oiled coordination of a group that's been doing this together for decades. When the music ends, they all grin.

Teddy presses a button, and a red light comes on. "Rock and roll. Let's run it back?" Before he can follow through, he spots me with a grin. He nudges Zelda with his elbow and then holds up a few fingers to the window. "Actually, let's take five," he amends.

We head down the carpeted hallway towards the small kitchen. Teddy slides into his usual chair at the formica table, and I remove the stack of documents from my purse, placing them between us.

"The band sounds great," I offer. "Anyone I know?"

"The Blinding Lytes," he says. "You maybe know their big hit from the eighties, 'Come Cruise Along'?"

For the millionth time this week, I think of Florida. Snapshots of that secret weekend are always playing in my head, like a bad breakup song on repeat.

"I may have heard of it," I say.

"Recorded here in eighty-eight, when I was just a skinny kid making store runs and begging John Qualls to teach me everything he knew about sound," he smiles. "So, what have you got for me today?"

"A few things from the realty company in charge of the house sale. I need your signature here and here. Initials here, here, and here."

He begins scribbling across the papers as indicated.

"I heard you're leaving Freeman Maxwell," he says.

"You heard correctly."

"I guess my case wasn't the big win you hoped for?" My eyes slide up to his, trying to gauge what he means by this. "People talk. I know you were up for a big promotion, if everything went well."

"It wasn't really about your case," I tell him. "They knew who they wanted, and in the end it wasn't me."

Teddy makes a humming noise before flipping the page, following my finger to the next dotted line.

"Where's Quentin been lately?"

"No clue," I say. "Texas, maybe."

Teddy gives me a long, assessing look. I flip a few more pages, and he slowly adds his uneven signature. "You're not together anymore?"

"I don't usually discuss my relationship status with clients, Mr. Glass."

"C'mon. After everything we've been through?" He gives me a twinkly eyed grin that makes him look like a carefree teenager. I give him a chastising smile. "You know, I get that I don't have the best track record with relationships or anything, but I thought you two had something special."

Yeah, I thought so too, I think woefully. The signature combination of shame and regret swims in my stomach.

"We were just doing our job," I offer.

"Maybe. But there was a vibe. Really," he insists, when he catches the incredulous look on my face. "I've been in this business a long time, and part of that is being able to look at something in the beginning stages and really see it – not for what it is – but for what it *could* be. It's this feeling that kind of vibrates in your bones, you know? A sixth sense. It's like hearing a band play for the first time. I can always tell if they're going to make it. If they mesh. If they've *got it*. And you two definitely had it."

I give him a narrowed stare. "Have you been drinking whiskey for breakfast again?"

His boyish face stretches into a grin, and he signs the last page with a flourish, passing my pen back to me.

"Look. For the past six months you've been telling it to me like it is. I appreciate that. In a world full of bullshitters, it's an admirable quality. It's why I hired you. Consider this me returning the favor. Call him. Despite what that billboard says, your life is about a whole helluva lot more than breaking up."

"I probably won't," I admit. "But thanks."

***

I sweep through the aisles of Nine Lives, where I've been summoned to check out a set of barware that Auntie Lena is sure I can't live without. Of course, this is her new favorite way to lure me into the shop. First it was an art deco wall clock. Then it was a pair of boots that she swore would be great for fall. I can't help but suspect that, ever since the breakup – if that's what you'd even call the end of fake not-dating one's coworker – that this is Auntie Lena's way of making sure I'm not sitting home alone. Meg has adopted a similar tactic, suddenly needing emergency taste-testers for coffee cakes and breakfast pastry recipes she's hoping to sneak onto the cafe's menu for autumn. As much as I want to call them on their thinly veiled tactics, it also makes me feel like the human equivalent of the baked brie Meg served last time I was at her house: tough on the outside, all warm and gooey underneath. All I can do is greet them with grateful hugs that I hope say everything I can't.

Thank you for being here.

Thank you for not making me talk about it.

Thank you for not telling me I made a huge mistake.

As the weeks march on, the more I begin to wonder exactly what kind of mistake I made.

Was it all those things that dawned on me the night of the

party? That I shouldn't have put my heart on the line? That I shouldn't have trusted Quentin?

Or was my biggest mistake the sheer stubborn way I tend to dig my heels in? The way I refused to hear his side. The way I pretended none of it hurt. That I'm invincible. That I don't miss him.

Maybe that's what hurts the most, how much I miss him.

Auntie Lena is busy talking with a few customers from out of town, but Melissa sees me from her spot behind the counter. Once she started seeing the family counselor I recommended, she also decided she needed a job, and as luck would have it, Auntie Lena still desperately needed the help. What started as a situation of convenience turned out to be the perfect fit. They both read the same celebrity gossip rags. They both love to rearrange items to achieve some sort of perfect visual balance that no one but them can envision. They both adore adopting alley cats.

Now, Melissa snags a box of barware from behind the counter and begins unwrapping it for me. The pieces are pretty – cornsilk-colored wine goblets in pristine condition – and while I like them, I certainly don't love them. That's always been my threshold for taking anything home: *can I live without it?* In the case of these goblets, unfortunately, that's a definite yes.

"No problem," she says. "I'm sure we can find just the place for them."

She gathers the glasses with a small smile and begins strategizing where to place them on the shelves. I grab the extras and follow her into the part of the store that's set up like a small kitchen. Turns out, she used to do merchandising work for a high end retailer and is a master at placing items to sell. She's also done amazing things with the window display. The family of mannequins currently occupying the space have never looked happier.

"He's still asking about you, you know," she says.

I know without the use of a name which *he* she's referring to. I pass her another glass from the box.

"He'll move on, eventually," I say. "They always do."

"Maybe," she says, giving me a wistful smile. "But do you really want him to?"

***

I slide the framed photo off my desk and tuck it into my bag. The only thing left is my bird of paradise plant, which was a birthday gift from the team a few years ago. I figure I'll grab it on my way out, but for now, all I can do is admire the view from the office that will no longer be mine.

A couple of weeks earlier, when Mariah Wilson answered the phone, she laughed and said, "I've been wondering when you'd call. What's the occasion?"

"Officially tired of playing their game," I admitted. "Does your offer still stand?"

Fortunately for me, it did. I'm moving into shared office space in the employee-owned firm right after Meg and I return from Paris. It's going to be different. No partnership to aspire to. No high rise office with a riverfront view. But there's an opportunity there to do more than deal in family law, to dig deeper and branch out, especially without the opinions of the board hanging over me. This new firm has a lot of nonprofit affiliations and community accounts. I could explore new avenues. I could do some real good.

Still, my leaving feels bittersweet.

"You have to admit you'll miss the view," a voice says from the doorway.

I turn to find Erving Maxwell leaning against the frame. He nods to the scene behind me. The clouds across the river are stretched thin, the thick trees on the opposite banks are a vibrant line of green against blue. It's a pretty day that's hinting of a late summer storm that most would welcome at this point in the season. The air outside is thick and humid, like the city itself is holding its breath, waiting for the moment it can finally let go.

"Is there something you want?" I ask.

He adjusts his tie. "I want to say I'm sorry."

This is the very last thing I expect him to say, so for a few moments, I'm speechless. What is it with these Maxwell men? It takes a long beat to collect myself.

"That's really not necessary," I say.

"No, it is," he replies. "You're a talented attorney, Heidi. Possibly one of the best we've had. You're compassionate and concise. You work hard. What happened – what I did – wasn't fair to you."

Anger flares in me. This conversation only serves to stoke the embers of a fire I've done my best to let die.

"Then why did you do it?" I demand.

"It was never about you," he says, shaking his head. "When you get my age, you think a lot more about what you'll leave behind. I wanted Quentin to be it. He's got quick wit, and he's not afraid to work hard for what he wants; he always reminded me a lot of myself, when I was younger. And unlike the rest of them, he never takes the easy route. If any of my sons had been cut off the way he was, they would have sunk straight to the bottom, but he didn't. He thrived. He turned it into the fuel that rocketed him straight to the top.

"So no, I don't think it's a secret I wanted him to continue the work I started. But I realize now that maybe what I've left behind isn't the legacy I imagined. People think of me as another old man stuck in the past, whose antiquated ideas forced you out. Maybe I am. And maybe I did. In the end, none of us got what we wanted."

"Quentin's your replacement," I counter. "You got exactly what you wanted."

Erving gives me a rueful smile. "I guess you two haven't talked. Like I said, for better or worse, Quentin never takes the easy route."

I'm dying to know what this means, but I won't reduce myself enough to ask.

"If you're trying to offer me the job because he's stepped down, you're more of an asshole than I thought."

"No. I know better than that," he says. "I came to wish you luck. You've got a lot of fight, Heidi. Don't ever let an old man like me take it away from you."

I find myself hugging the oversized potted plant against me. I swallow hard.

"I won't."

Erving nods once. He's about to leave, but before he can turn, he reconsiders. "He really did try to fix it, before it was too late. But if you know him at all, I think you know that already."

He pats the door frame with finality. When he disappears, I'm left with another hole in my chest, and I wonder this time how I'm going to fill it. I gather my nerve and the rest of my things, giving the city one final look from this vantage point. I suck in a breath and for the last time, I head for the door.

***

I pull into a street-side parking spot in front of the dark windows of a narrow shop in the arts district. It's in a colorful, quiet edge of the city, tucked between a brewery and an oyster bar. This is Meg's favorite part of town. When we climb out of the car, she's already following our usual trajectory towards the co-op at the end of the street, which we always hit for the latest seasonal produce. When she realizes I'm not beside her, she stops short. Reluctantly, she doubles back to where I'm standing in front of the empty storefront.

"What's up?" she says.

"I figured we'd check this place out," I say.

She gives the dark windows a once over, then does the same with me.

"It looks… closed. Whatever it is. Nothing's here."

I pull a set of keys from my pocket the way a magician produces doves from a hat. Meg watches in confusion as I unlock the door and hold it open for her. She reluctantly steps inside.

The space was recently vacated by an Italian pasta shop that literally never had any customers. Every time we used to walk by, we would speculate if it was a front for the Memphis mafia. They advertised homemade pasta in the front window and yet, the one time we went in, they didn't actually have any pasta. They looked genuinely confused when we asked.

Regardless, it's now empty. It's only been closed for a few weeks, but it has developed the faint musty smell of old buildings that have been shuttered too long. Dust motes glitter in the strips of sunlight coming in the front windows. There's one lonely table in the back that didn't get swept up in the auction, probably because it has a bum leg. Meg walks over and smooths a gentle hand over its surface, the way one might pet a stray three-legged dog.

"Are you going to tell me what we're doing here?" she says, somewhat bemused.

I toss the keys in her direction with an underhand pitch. She catches them uncertainly.

"It's yours," I say. "Your bakeshop."

Her eyes have gone wide, but she shakes her head like this is some sort of practical joke. "I don't understand."

"All the money I was planning to put in when I made partner – I don't really need it anymore. And I wanted to do something with it that would… *matter*. I'm investing in your business, Meg. No more fighting with your owner over the menu. We've got a twelve month lease. We've got enough money to build out the kitchen and get things going. This place can be anything you want it to be. ”

"Heidi. No. You can't just *buy* me a bakeshop!"

"Well I did," I say. "I mean, sort of. We're *renting* it, technically."

"Okay, but I can't just accept it!"

"You can," I laugh. "If anyone can, you can. I'm all in. I believe in you."

When she laughs, I can hear her throat constricting with the threat of tears. She gives me a warning look.

"I appreciate this, babe. Really, I do. But this is a huge risk."

Once, I might have agreed with her. I might have believed, on some level, that it was too big of a risk. Relationships are messy. Partnerships are often precarious at best. But is there anything more important than this? The dreams we dream. The chances we take. The people we love.

I wrap Meg in a hug. "There's nothing I'd rather invest in than this."

30.

THE EARLY EVENING BREEZE teases at the hem of my dress as I make my way to the market near my apartment to buy myself flowers. I'm supposed to be meeting Meg for cocktails at a new place on the corner, so I got dressed early and found myself here, running my fingers across the delicate softness of mid-season peonies. My smartwatch buzzes, and when I move to silence it, I am met with a reservation reminder.

The High Limit. Rooftop dining. Two guests. 7:30pm.

My heart twists. I clear the notification with a grimace.

Of all the things our technology knows about us, shouldn't my devices have enough sense to pick up on the fact that Quentin and I are no longer speaking and therefore have no need to meet for dinner? It can advertise me a pair of shoes I daydreamed about exactly once, show me fifty versions of a sports bra I once gave a ten second glance, but it can't figure out that we abruptly stopped exchanging texts and calls and spending time in each other's immediate proximity? It really can't come to the logical conclusion that there's no way in hell I'm going to make this date?

I wonder, though, if maybe it also knows how many times I've imagined opening my door to find him standing there. I know every detail of this scene by heart. The way he would tug me against him. The way his mouth would catch mine. The way I would simply ignite under his touch.

Maybe it also knows how many times I considered the absolute pleasure of him. The easy give and take. How he mapped the location of every secret desire with his hands, and teeth, and tongue, and how I can't forget the insatiable feel of him. The fact that – even knowing what I know now – I don't know if I could stop myself from falling in love with him. I don't know if I would want to.

I buy the flowers, walk to the bar, and order a cocktail. Shortly after seven, Meg texts.

M: *So sorry, babe. I think Jojo ate baker's chocolate. We're on our way to the emergency vet.*

H: *Omg. What can I do? Should I meet you?*

M: *No, we've got it under control! Enjoy your Saturday night. I'll keep you updated.*

I swirl the last few sips of my drink in the glass and deflate. Going home to sit alone feels utterly depressing. Though I've spent plenty of weekends during my adult life alone, lately they've felt... lonelier. I pay my tab and wander out onto the sidewalk.

The High Limit is located at the top of a historic hotel, which I have to pass to get home. It's old-fashioned and romantic, with a big fountain in the lobby and ducks – actual ducks – in the lobby bar. I think about taking a longer route, maybe veering onto another street, but eventually I find myself standing right in front of its revolving gold doors, with the cool air conditioning sweeping past me every time someone walks in or out. I go inside and make my way onto the elevator, hitting the button for the top floor.

I doubt he ever canceled the reservation. I'll just go up for one drink, I tell myself. Or maybe I'll have a beautiful dinner alone. There's nothing wrong with being alone. Read also: Independent. Self-sufficient. Fully confident that I can eat a meal without anyone sitting across from me.

The hostess smiles when I step off the elevator. "Good evening. Do you have a reservation?"

"Yes," I tell her. "I believe it's under Maxwell."

"Ah yes. Table for two. Right this way," she tells me.

I want to correct her, explain that it will only be me, and I plan to address this as soon as I'm seated. But the moment we make our way into the dining room, I realize I don't have any breath left to speak the words. The air has been knocked out of my chest, because Quentin is sitting at the table. When we approach, he stands so abruptly that the strategically placed glassware on the white tablecloth rattles.

"Um, hi. Hey," he stammers. "I didn't think you would..."

The unfinished words hang between us. Remember? Show up? Ever speak to him again?

I swallow thickly. "Yeah. It's good to see you."

He looks familiar and surprising all at once. His hair is a little longer, framing his face in unruly waves. His tan is a bit darker. His cheekbones are a bit more defined, as if maybe his face is a bit thinner. He dressed up for this. He's wearing dark pants and a gray sport coat with the sleeves pushed up. The cuffs of his light blue button down are folded back at the cuff, giving the whole thing a sexy-casual vibe. They make his eyes look especially deep-ocean dark as they dance across my face.

"Sit," he insists. "I mean, um... please, have a seat."

I sit, if only so that he'll stop doing this gentleman bit with the standing. The hostess drifts away, and we both preoccupy ourselves with studying the menus so that we don't have to make eye contact. The server comes by, and Quentin orders a bottle of wine. Part of me wants to criticize his presumption, but mostly I'm grateful. It makes this feel somewhat normal, as if sitting across the table from one's ex-coworker – ex-whatever-we-were – can feel normal. I realize I'm twisting my hands into the ends of my hair, and I lower them into my lap. My heart flails in my throat. I feel ridiculous.

"I don't really know what I'm doing here," I admit.

"Me either," he says.

"We have that in common, at least."

His mouth quirks at the corner.

"You know, when I first made this reservation, I had this crazy feeling we were, I dunno, soulmates or something," he says sheepishly. "So even when you told me you weren't available until now, I thought... that's okay, I'll wait. But I feel like I have to tell you that I'm not the same guy I was three months ago."

I allow myself to be quietly intrigued by this. "How so?"

"For starters, that guy had a lot to prove. He thought he was here to prove to himself that he could be worthy of his family's approval. He wanted to show them that he could be successful – that he was better than any of them ever gave him credit for – and he was willing to do whatever it took to prove it, even if it cost him. And it did. Cost him."

"I see," I say, though I don't really. I can't understand the point of all this. The server returns and pours us each a glass of red wine, leaving the bottle on the table between us. "And what about now? You don't want their approval?"

"Now I know that I never really needed it. I get to define what success looks like for me. I get to decide whose opinions matter. And theirs don't. They really don't. I'm not that kid anymore."

"Sounds like quite the revelation," I say.

"You can thank my therapist," he smirks. "Unfortunately, the realization came a bit later than it should have."

He lifts his glass to mine, and I tap the rim to his with a gentle clink. I take a long, slow sip, distracting myself with the way the wine is dark and decadent, just the way I like it, and I wonder if he knew this when he ordered it. I can't decide if I think this is a clever trick or if it's just so very Quentin to know all those little things about me.

He watches me enjoying it for a moment, before swelling with a breath. "There's something else."

I wet my lips. "Okay."

"Over the course of this summer, I fell in love with someone. Someone I work with. She's smart, and determined, and beautiful. I've never known anyone like her."

My heart aches in my chest: from excitement, from longing, from being so recently broken. I do my best to keep my face impassive.

"She sounds way too good for you."

"She is," he says. "Things kind of fell apart. I let my family – *let myself* – get in the way. And she…"

"Felt like you were a professional and emotional liability and decided she was better off alone?"

He gives me another wistful smirk. "Yeah. That about sums it up."

"So here you are," I offer.

"Here I am," he nods.

"That was a hell of an opening statement."

"This is a really important case."

I can't take the way he's looking at me, so I glance across the intimate, candlelit tables of the restaurant. The light of dusk teases through the windows, soft and romantic. Couples lean in close, sharing comfortable conversation. If anyone noticed us, perhaps they would assume the same. That we're here as a couple. That we're comfortably intimate. I finger one of the peonies that I bought myself on the way here, now perched on the edge of the table.

"I heard you moved back to Texas," I say.

"I thought about it."

"What stopped you?"

"My heart wasn't in it," he shrugs. "I took a position as the in-house counsel for a non-profit here. They do the same kind of thing I did back in Austin. It was a better fit."

"And you still..." I swallow again. "Love her? This woman you worked with?"

"I feel like I was made to love her."

My heart skips like a secondhand record, but those walls that I've carefully rebuilt over the past couple of weeks hold steady. The old guard slides back into place, offering up those tried and true excuses.

"That wasn't love," I tell him. "That was bad decisions and too much tequila."

It's a lie. My face warms with the shame of it. Why does it feel so much easier than the truth?

"What makes you so sure?" he says.

I laugh in spite of myself.

"Because I also had a hell of a summer, Quentin. A crazy, stupid, impossible kind of summer. The kind that changes everything. I broke all my own rules, and in return, the world broke my whole fucking heart."

"But you're here. That has to mean something. You seem to forget that I was there with you. I know I wasn't the only one. You fell for me, too," he says. "Why are you here, Heidi?"

I cough out a laugh, because this is becoming increasingly ridiculous. My heart twists in my chest. Emotion stings in my throat.

Why am I here?

"Because today my phone reminded me that once – before any of this happened – I met a guy at a bar and I felt... like everything was possible. And maybe I wanted to feel like that again. Possible. Like all the odds are stacked in my favor. Like I could really have it all. The whole stupid package. Win-win-win." I take a breath, hoping to blink back the tears brimming in my eyes. "Or maybe I was just hungry."

He watches me for a beat, and he looks so hopeful it hurts. "Then let's order some food."

I close my eyes, hoping to hold back the impending flood of emotions. "Quentin..."

"You don't have to say that you love me. You don't ever have to forgive me," he says. "Please, just have dinner with me. Let me show you this is possible."

It's not that simple. Is it?

I shake my head. "I'm sorry."

I'm not sure what exactly I'm apologizing for. The only thing I know for sure is that I cannot cry in the middle of this restaurant. I push back my chair. I'm already walking towards the exit when I hear him leaving cash on the table, telling the hostess we have an emergency, and rushing onto the elevator behind me.

"Heidi, I'm sorry. I should have told you about the partnership. I should have –"

"I don't think I can do this, Quentin," I say, pressing the 'close door' button in rapid succession. "And I don't even know why you want me to. I've already proven I'm not great at this. Did you forget how I blew up on you in front of your entire family, and blocked your number, and didn't even give you a chance to present your side of things? I'm not girlfriend material. Maybe we should just call this what it is."

The door slides closed, shutting out the soft sounds of the restaurant. I realize maybe this is already over. My arms are folded tightly across my chest. My bottom lip is held firmly between my teeth.

"I know what this is. And I think you do too," he says. "Can't we talk about this?"

"What do you want me to say?" I demand. "That I think about you every single second of every single day? That I wake up and wonder why you're not beside me? That I miss your stupid nature documentaries and the way you smell and the way it feels when you call me cutesy nicknames?" I grab his forearm, holding his hand up in front of us. "That the fact that you're still wearing this bracelet makes my heart feel like it's too big for my chest? *Why* are you still wearing this?"

His gaze searches mine, and it tugs hard through me, holding me in place.

"For luck," he says. "And because I can't stop thinking about you either. Don't you get it? I never want to. I want to think about the way you laugh when you argue with me. And the way it feels to be on your team, just you and me against everything. I want to think about making love to you until we can barely breathe. And I want to remember the way it feels to wake up with my arms around you and the sunrise on your skin, feeling like the luckiest man in the whole fucking world. Even when it hurts, if all I can have of you is this, I don't want to let it go."

The exhaustion of holding back these feelings for the past few weeks hits me in a rush. Then, just as suddenly, my walls threaten to crumble. There's nothing left to hold me back from him – no partnership, no contract, no pretending that staying away from him will keep me from getting hurt – especially not when staying away from him has hurt most of all.

"Fuck," I swear. I think maybe I mean to say something else. Something along the lines of, *That was some speech*. Or maybe, *Hey asshole, I love you*. It never gets a chance to verbalize.

All at once, I'm kissing him.

His lips meet mine with a surprised groan. I'm quickly enveloped in his insatiable late summer smell as he weaves his fingers into my hair, hooking his thumb under my jaw. His other hand fumbles behind us, hitting the emergency stop button of the elevator. It jolts us to an immediate halt. The alarm buzzes, buying us time.

"Did this just become a hostage situation?" I say. "Are you trying to kidnap me?"

He punctuates the moment with hungry kisses. "If it means you'll stay."

I clutch the front of his shirt in both hands. "You know you stole my fucking heart, you jerk."

That's what he turned out to be. Not a serial killer, or a kidnapper, but a thief.

His dark eyes search mine. "Do you want it back?"

"No."

The alarm continues to buzz, but we're oblivious. I melt against him, reveling in the warm teasing of his tongue, the gentle tug of his teeth against my bottom lip. He slides a hand up my thigh, hooking it around his hip as he presses my back against the plush paisley fabric of the elevator wall.

"I missed you," he breathes.

I frame his face with my hands, tugging him closer. "I'm right here."

A voice comes over the speaker, startling us apart. Suddenly, I have a panicked moment of wondering if there's a security camera in here. A quick survey reassures me that at first glance, there isn't.

"Hello," the voice says. "You okay in there?"

Quentin clears his throat. "Yeah, we're good."

"We got an alert," the crackly voice continues. "Did you hit the emergency stop button?"

Quentin tips my chin up, kissing me again.

"Yeah, sorry. Accident."

"No problem. Happens all the time," the voice says. "Give me a second and I'll get you moving."

The crackle cuts to silence. We're still holding each other

close, seemingly wondering what happens next. I mean, we can't make out in this elevator forever. At some point the doors will open, and decisions will have to be made. Quentin's gaze is lusty and hopeful as it maps the contours of my face.

"Do you want to go back upstairs?" he asks. "Have dinner with me?"

"No," I say. There's a flash of disappointment in his eyes, and I brush my nose against his. "I don't just want to have dinner with you. I want to have everything with you. If that's okay."

I realize belatedly that the alarm has stopped and the elevator is moving again. This moment is on a timer. Like a little kid without a chaperone, I hit the button for every floor. The likelihood that anyone will be waiting on most of them is slim to none.

"That's... Yeah. That's more than okay," he smiles, kissing me again.

I snake my arms inside his jacket, brushing a thick packet in his inner pocket. I pluck the papers out with a slow smile.

"Did you bring legal documents to our date or are you just happy to see me?"

He scrubs a hand sheepishly through his hair. "So, um, I may have drafted a new relationship agreement? On the off chance you showed up."

The elevator doors slide open on a random floor, and we both glance to make sure it's empty before continuing.

"You're serious," I say, thumbing through the pages.

There's so much in here that I want to read. At first glance, it's part explanation, part apology, and full of promises. So many promises. If they're anything like Quentin's other work, I know that they're all written in that concise, clever way of his, and thorough to a fault.

"There's just a lot I needed to say," he says. "And I know there's probably a lot we need to figure out."

My chest swells with emotion at the sight of him, standing in front of me, absolutely, unapologetically in love. I bite my bottom lip, re-folding the papers and tucking them back into his jacket pocket. He furrows his brow, peering at me nervously.

"Is that a no? Because we can make revisions. We can –"

I interrupt him with a kiss. "No."

"No?"

I laugh in spite of myself. "No contracts."

He gives me an incredulous look. I think about explaining to him about my own revelations from this summer. Like how I figured out that no amount of written guidelines can guarantee I won't get hurt. Or how I finally had to admit to myself that saying I was better off on my own could get very, very lonely. But most of all, I figured out those cliche sayings you come across in self-help books and post-breakup corners of Instagram carry some truth. Real strength is knowing that you're strong enough to be vulnerable. To take chances. To let people in.

Maybe, to my surprise, when Quentin broke my heart, he didn't actually break me. My world didn't actually fall apart. I didn't lose everything. I found out how resilient I am. I remembered how strong my support system is. I realized I'm no longer that kid who's terrified of losing herself in a breakup. Because I didn't lose myself. Maybe – cliche of all cliches – I actually *found* myself.

Yeah. Put that on a billboard.

I peel myself away from him and adjust my dress in time for the doors to open on the ground floor. I thread my fingers through his.

"Really," I say. "I trust you."

He follows me out onto the busy sidewalk. Early evening wraps around us, and the last of the warm breezes of summer kiss our skin. Though everything is winding down – my job at FML, this part of my story, the season itself – somehow it doesn't feel like the end.

"You know if we're going to reconcile properly, I have to feed you first," he says.

"I might know a place," I muse. "Intimate. Exclusive. Best sandwiches this side of the Mississippi. But we might be overdressed."

His eyes spark with a smile. He pulls me into a warm, searching kiss that promises everything and more. "We can fix that."

"Lead the way."

31.

My heels click across the black and white tile of the entryway as I sweep into Maestoso, bringing with me a whoosh of brisk spring air as the ornate doors close behind me. I push my sunglasses into my hair and flash the host a smile, never slowing down.

"I'm meeting someone," I tell him.

I weave past the crowd of suits holding down the bar for happy hour and make my way to the balcony stairs, which are closed for a private party. I let myself in through the rope and wonder if I'm underdressed. I just came from work, which these past few months have meant fewer power suits and more dark jeans and blazers, as if my wardrobe has shifted right along with the rest of my life. When I make it to the large space at the top of the stairs, the crowd bursts into an off-key chorus of "happy birthday", accompanied by Kamille on the violin.

I scrunch my nose as I laugh, coming to an uncertain stop as I blush. I didn't expect to see an entire room full of people, all smiling at me, nor did I expect to be serenaded with strings. Kamille's playing is so confident and beautiful that it seems to pull the cacophony of voices together into something delicately poetic. It's one of those moments that expands in my chest like there's no room for air, and I love it. I take a little bow when the song has ended, accepting a glass of champagne from Auntie Lena as she pulls me into a hug, and everyone applauds.

"I thought this was supposed to be small," I argue. "There are dozens of people here."

"I can't help it that so many people know how special you are," she says, brushing a lock of hair over my shoulder in that easy way she does, like she's arranging the little details of my appearance the same way she reorganizes shelves. "Happy birthday, Dee."

Kamille approaches me now, already a half a head taller than she was six months ago. I greet her with enthusiastic praise.

"Is this your first paid gig?" I tease.

"I did it *pro bono*," she says with a smirky, nonchalant shrug. I laugh, knowing how just a few weeks ago we discussed the Latin meaning of that phrase over pizza at our favorite weekly place.

"Well, the public is certainly better for it," I smile.

I spot the towering birthday cake that is far too ornate for my simply turning thirty-three and know Meg can't be far, probably wearing a retro dress and looking like an entrepreneurial bakeshop pin-up girl. My sweet tooth immediately aches, and I hope it's the amazing strawberry lemon shortcake recipe that she's been selling out of everyday for the past three weeks. I may have even grabbed a slice for breakfast a time or two, when I stopped in for my usual cold brew.

I greet a couple of old colleagues from Freeman Maxwell, a few friends from my volunteer work, and some of my post-run pint pals. But I break into an outright grin when I spot a pair of beat up Vans and a sport coat leaning against the balcony railing.

"Teddy Glass," I say. "What are you doing here?"

"Crashing your party," he laughs.

"You're kidding."

"Nope. I was hanging at the bar, and I asked the server who the private shindig was for. It felt like too much of a coincidence for me not to come up and say hey."

"I'm glad you did. How've you been? I saw the article."

It had run a couple of weeks earlier in *The Memphian*, and Jeanine had really outdone herself. It was a story about Avid, or maybe about Teddy, though the two of them are kind of one in the same, aren't they? It was the ultimate tale of a comeback kid, complete with rock stars, and personal obstacles, and a very smug-looking Farkas, perched on Teddy's shoulder like some sort of pirate's parrot.

"Yeah, it was a great piece. Business is booming. I really couldn't have done it without you two."

I give him a wistful smile and nod. "I'm glad everything worked out."

"Me too," he says. "Hey, I'll have to tell Zel I saw you. She's going to be jealous."

"I don't know that I was ever her favorite," I laugh.

"Aw, that's just Zel," he says. "Tough on the outside. Big ol' gummy bear underneath. How's your new gig going?"

"It's great." I give him a genuine smile, not in the least because I can't remember the last time I worked through lunch. "I'm working with a lot of local organizations, combining a lot of my previous experience with stuff I'm passionate about. I love it."

"I'm glad to hear it. If anyone deserves it, I know it's you," he nods. "Hey, if you don't mind my asking, who's the woman with the dark hair over there?"

I follow where he points with his martini glass to where Auntie Lena is laughing. I give him a measured look. "That's my aunt, Helena."

"She single?"

I burst into laughter, and he flashes me a grin. "You putting yourself back out there, Teddy? Bold move."

"Hey, we all lose a hand now and again," he says. "But you've gotta play to win."

"She's single," I smirk. "But she doesn't put up with bullshit. And her radar is pretty good. You've gotta go in honest."

"Honest as an attorney," he says. He gives me a wink and weaves his way into the crowd.

I take a moment to lean my forearms on the railing, overlooking the dinner crowd and the handful of couples dancing to those old Fred Astaire and Ginger Rogers tunes. It's just then that a guy steps up beside me, smiling with a sure sense of recognition.

"Hey," he says smoothly, passing me a fizzy cocktail. "I didn't expect to see you here."

I blink into a set of hopeful dark blue eyes, and I wonder if maybe the champagne and unexpected crowd have already gone to my head, as if perhaps I dreamed up this heart-stoppingly wonderful man.

"You look amazing," he continues. "How've you been? How's everything?"

My gaze drops to the spot where exactly two of his fingers are touching my elbow. They slip away, and I'm left contemplating the weight of the highball glass in my hand. It's rimmed with spicy seasoning, garnished with a lime, and is undoubtedly one of my favorite cocktails. I give him an amused, assessing stare.

"Everything's amazing," I say. "I can't believe you did all this. How do we share a bed and I didn't realize you've invited forty people to my birthday dinner?"

Quentin meets my smile with a kiss. "Forty-five. And I had help."

"This is suspiciously elaborate." I loop an arm around his

neck, giving him a coy smile. "You're not planning to propose are you?"

"Me? No," he scoffs. "I already know you're going to spend the rest of your life with me."

I laugh. "Confident, aren't we?"

"You know I've always been a hopeful romantic, PBG. But if you need diamonds, just say the word."

I brush my nose against his. "You'd buy me diamonds?"

"I would scour every estate sale from here to the East Coast in search of the perfect vintage ring," he says. "I would get on a plane right now and head to Vegas and find the first Elvis impersonator I could to do the honors."

"You realize we live in Memphis, right? You don't have to go to Vegas just to find an Elvis impersonator."

"Whatever you want."

I kiss him, slow and soft. "I just want you."

"Always?"

"Always."

Acknowledgements

Behind every late-night writer, I imagine there's a partner who encourages her with a kiss before he heads to bed with the dogs. Or at least, there is in my case.

This book wouldn't exist if not for all the times my husband Spencer has said, "Stay up and write."

It might still be sitting unedited in my archives if not for the honest criticism and encouragement of my beta readers: Brittany, Josie, and Amanda.

It also may not have been published without all the readers who have enthusiastically supported my previous work. Julie, you're still holding the OG spot at the top of that list, I hope you know.

To everyone who has taken the time to hang out with Heidi and Quentin, share this story with others, or send me your kind words – you have my sincerest thanks.

About the Author

Heather McPeake is a full-time corporate professional, part-time yoga instructor, and lifelong late-night writer. She lives in Memphis, TN with her husband and their houseful of pets.

For updates, follow her on Instagram: @heathermcwrites

www.ingramcontent.com/pod-product-compliance
Lightning Source LLC
Chambersburg PA
CBHW011847300726
48970CB00009B/2687